"Emily Hamilton's *The Stars Too Fondly* begins as a quippy heist with an endearing cast, then evolves into a space comedy that has as many thoughtful explorations of the inner workings of dark matter as the—equally complicated—relationships that make up a found family. This highly self-aware novel prioritizes care and connection, without sacrificing any of the fun of space (mis)adventure. Because sometimes saving the world starts with saving each other. I cannot wait to see readers who love Tamsyn Muir's Gideon and Harrow go absolutely feral for Cleo and Billie."
— MICAIAH JOHNSON, AUTHOR OF *THE SPACE BETWEEN WORLDS*

"Heart-pounding, heartwarming, and flat-out fantastic, this book is as brilliant and beautiful as the stars! I laughed, I cried, I cheered—I absolutely loved it! A new favorite!"
—SARAH BETH DURST, AWARD-WINNING AUTHOR OF *THE BONE MAKER*

"A perfect hope-punk science fantasy that reminds me of *Doctor Who* in all the best ways. *The Stars Too Fondly* is magnificent in its spaceship-stealing adventure and twisty plot. Where Emily Hamilton excels is the bonds between friends and loved ones that stretch between light-years and dimensions with the comfort of a weighted blanket. It is an achingly beautiful and hilariously funny debut."
—K. B. WAGERS, AUTHOR OF *A PALE LIGHT IN THE BLACK*

"*The Stars Too Fondly* is a romantic, joyful, and often poignant sci-fi romp that scratched an itch I didn't know I had. An utter delight." —HANNAH FERGESEN, AUTHOR OF *THE INFINITE MILES*

"*The Stars Too Fondly* is a sparkling debut filled with found family, queer joy, and a delightful romance that made me swoon. It hooked me from the start, and I couldn't put it down as I rooted for Cleo to find her way home—both literally and figuratively. I adored every word, and I can't wait to see what Emily Hamilton writes next!"   —JESSIE MIHALIK, AUTHOR OF *HUNT THE STARS*

"The vacuum of space is anything but dark when your found family is with you. This cozy space opera is delightful and full of heart."   —AL HESS, AUTHOR OF
WORLD RUNNING DOWN AND *KEY LIME SKY*

"The fate of the world rests in the hands of a ragtag group of queers stuck on a spaceship bound for Proxima Centauri B. Even though they live in the future, their concerns are all too familiar: astrology, quoting Mary Oliver, watching *The Watermelon Woman*, and processing their feelings. Emily Hamilton's debut is as addictive as it is funny and as interstellar as it is human."   —AMELIA POSSANZA, AUTHOR OF
LESBIAN LOVE STORY

"Funny and charming, *The Stars Too Fondly* perfectly balances Starfleet 'can-do' attitude, punk swagger, and cozy rom-com vibes. Emily Hamilton's debut is a wildly original tale that feels cozy and epic at the same time. My Trekkie heart adored it."
                        —MIKE CHEN, *NEW YORK TIMES* BESTSELLING
AUTHOR OF *A QUANTUM LOVE STORY*

THE STARS TOO FONDLY. Copyright © 2024 by Emily Hamilton. All rights reserved. Printed in the United States of America. No part of this book may be used or reproduced in any manner whatsoever without written permission except in the case of brief quotations embodied in critical articles and reviews. For information, address HarperCollins Publishers, 195 Broadway, New York, NY 10007.

HarperCollins books may be purchased for educational, business, or sales promotional use. For information, please email the Special Markets Department at SPsales@harpercollins.com.

Harper Voyager and design are trademarks of HarperCollins Publishers LLC.

FIRST EDITION

Designed by Alison Bloomer

Library of Congress Cataloging-in-Publication Data has been applied for.

ISBN 978-0-06-332081-9

24 25 26 27 28 LBC 5 4 3 2 1

THE STARS TOO FONDLY

TOO FONDLY

To Rachel, my light in the darkness

How soon unaccountable I became tired and sick,
Till rising and gliding out I wander'd off by myself,
In the mystical moist night-air, and from time to time,
Look'd up in perfect silence at the stars.
—WALT WHITMAN,
"When I Heard the Learn'd Astronomer"

You came, and I was mad for you,
And you cooled my mind that burned with longing.
—SAPPHO

Though my soul may set in darkness,
it will rise in perfect light;
I have loved the stars too fondly to be fearful of the night.
—SARAH WILLIAMS,
"The Old Astronomer to His Pupil"

THE STARS TOO FONDLY

CHAPTER 1

ARCHIVED: SMS Conversation — Kaleisha Reid, Ros Wheeler, and Abraham Yang, July 10, 2061

ROS WHEELER
Alright, who's gonna be on Cleo duty tomorrow

ABRAHAM YANG
What do you mean???

KALEISHA REID
Ros believes that our very best friend Cleo is in danger of, among other things, blacking out when she sees a spaceship in person for the first time and doing something stupid and killing us all

ABRAHAM YANG
No way!! Cleo is extremely smart and not at all stupid, Ros

ROS WHEELER
You know I know that
But you ALSO know that Cleo can be a bit ah
Impulsive?
Incautious??
Prone to ignoring things like hazard signs when there's a cool new gadget she wants to touch???

KALEISHA REID
She doesn't need us to babysit her, Rozzy
By which I mean, I am not going to babysit her
And neither will you
We have a plan! We love the plan. We're gonna follow
    the plan

ABRAHAM YANG
Seconded!!

ROS WHEELER
Fine yes alright
I reserve the right to be an anxious wreck about it

KALEISHA REID
I will give you a shoulder rub when it's all over

ABRAHAM YANG
Me too!! Prepare your shoulders

ROS WHEELER
Ugh

※

TWENTY-SEVEN YEARS OF OBSESSIVE amateur research had not prepared Cleo McQueary for how simple it was to break into the
Erebus Industries compound. She'd seen the exclusive news
reports, the official behind-the-scenes TikToks, the infamous
photos of impassive security officers restraining bereaved family
members at the compound gate—Cleo knew that this place had
been crawling with guards and dripping with unbreakable security
measures, once. But now, the only thing protecting each spiraling
level of the circular compound was a dusty steel door, locked by a
decades-old retinal scanner and a series of cascade ciphers. Cleo
could have cracked them all in her sleep, which was a shame—
she liked a challenge.

"Well," she said, punching the last sequence into the last keypad and thinking that the rare excuse to wear fingerless gloves with her most practical pair of coveralls almost made up for the disappointment, "there's no turning back now."

"Corny," Kaleisha whispered behind her, also looking incredibly heist-chic in her black dress and leather jacket, locs tied back in a ponytail and killer green eyeliner standing out against her dark skin. Cleo stuck her tongue out. Thanks to Erebus Industries' bankruptcy, they were the first people to walk through these long-abandoned doors in a decade; a little melodrama was absolutely warranted.

Abe fidgeted with the straps of the backpack he'd meticulously packed with things they might need (Band-Aids) and things they definitely wouldn't (Kaleisha's tarot cards). He was Chinese American, tall enough to rest his chin on the top of Cleo's head, and bouncing on the balls of his feet so rapidly that his floppy black hair was getting in his eyes.

"Actually," he whispered a little too loudly, "I think this would be the perfect time to turn back, if we wanted to."

"Yeah, isn't this the part where Cleo says, *That was easy . . . Too easy?*" Ros said. They tucked a long ginger curl behind the ear that wasn't adjacent to their undercut, a smile masking the on-edge jitters that Cleo knew they were hiding. "And then a bunch of robot ninjas jump out to foil our plan?"

Cleo winked at Ros as the last gate—blazoned, as all the others had been, with the grayscale sunrise of the Erebus Industries logo—slid open with a metallic clunk. "Don't worry. Fighting robot ninjas is the first thing they teach you in engineering school."

Kaleisha smacked Abe lightly on the ass to shove him toward the gateway. "You're not getting soft on us, are you, Yang?"

"I've always been soft, and you love it."

"I do."

Behind their backs, Ros made a gagging sound. Cleo mimed a dry heave back. "Can we focus on how I just hacked the last gate open, you nasties?" she whined as Abe kissed the top of Kaleisha's head. "It was very impressive, probably."

"Extremely impressive." Abe cut Cleo off with an easy ruffle of her curly brown bob. "I'm going through first, though."

"Very sexy of you," Kaleisha said, and she took Ros's hand, who took Cleo's hand, and tugged them all after Abe and into the wide-open launch complex at the center of the Erebus space center.

And there it was, looming over them like a skyscraper, steepled black against the starry sky: *Providence I.* The other three stopped just inside the wall to stare up at the thing, so Cleo stopped too, and did the same.

Oh, it was beautiful. Probably the most beautiful thing people had ever built, Cleo thought, just as she had when she'd first seen it on TV all those years ago. Everything about the spaceship was darkly glittering ceramic quartz and gracefully curving lines; it was sheer artistry, the way the wide, winged base swooped upward into the delicately pointed nose. It was right in front of her, just like she'd always impossibly dreamed, and it stirred something she hadn't realized she'd forgotten— not just a feeling of wonder, though of course she was in awe of it. There was something rising in her throat that she hadn't quite felt since she was a kid, watching the lead-up to the launch on TV. Hope, maybe. Faith in humanity, even.

"Alright, gang, Operation Space Heist is a go," Kaleisha said, knocking them all out of their reveries. "Let's roll."

Cleo blinked away the tears that were threatening at the corners of her eyes and quickly stopped fingering the logo on the arm of the old, thrifted NASA jacket she'd stolen from her dad when she went to college. "Who's corny now?" Kaleisha lovingly flipped her off.

They all speed-walked toward the ship, very aware of how exposed they were, trying not to crunch their feet on the twenty years of accumulated trash and leaves that drifted across the tarmac. Abe's head swiveled like an owl's, but no floodlights flickered on, no speakers screeched at them from the nearby mission control tower, and no beefy guards emerged from the darkness. If this had been a government site, the security might have been a little tighter. But all-but-defunct private companies didn't spend precious dollars on their long-abandoned mission centers. Cleo almost told Abe to chill, but she knew her friend— he had an impeccable mental map of their surroundings, thanks to all his research, and he would never chill while there was even the slightest possibility that they were in danger.

Plus, the place *was* kind of spooky. Full of history and grief and the shadows thrown down by the clouds as they crossed the moon.

"Lots of ghost energy," Cleo whispered to Ros.

Ros snorted, which belied the fact that they were looking even paler than usual. Cleo knew Ros well enough to recognize the telltale sign that they were internally flipping out: sarcasm. "Space ghosts?"

"Space ghosts."

When they reached the base of the *Providence*, Kaleisha stood aside and waved Cleo toward the entrance to the external elevator tower that still stood clamped to the side of the ship. Another outdated keypad, more old-ass software. Cleo cracked her knuckles and dove into the code. She'd broken more complex encryptions in high school. She deciphered the initialization vector in seconds.

"I want to say I'm surprised that they haven't forked out the cash to update the security system at all in twenty years," she muttered, just as the door slid open with a clunk. Kaleisha brushed past her and through it, leading Abe and Ros along with her. "But I'm also not surprised at all."

Abe laughed. "They couldn't have possibly accounted for you, Hack-ie Robinson."

Cleo grinned back and bounded into the elevator. "What have I told you about leaving the nicknames to me?"

"Hack Skellington," he said. Kaleisha pushed the lone button on the wall panel, and the elevator doors grumbled shut.

"Keep going," Ros said as the elevator lurched upward, clattering loudly. "You can do worse."

"Hold on, hold on—Hack Kerou-hack."

"Aw, babe." Kaleisha reached up to ruffle Abe's hair. "That was your worst yet."

Cleo wanted to keep the bit going, but then the bit didn't matter because they were flying stories and stories into the air, and Cleo got distracted by the surface of the *Providence* whizzing past them almost close enough to touch. She pressed her nose to the elevator window, watching wide-eyed as they ascended past the rockets, the wings, the name of the ship in silver letters taller than Abe twice over—then the hatch that led to the flight deck. And the elevator was stopping, and the door was opening, and they had arrived.

✳

ONCE UPON A TIME, there was a spaceship that never took off. It was supposed to, of course, full of people and bound for another world. It was going to be the first mission of its kind, the first with the goal of putting a population on an exoplanet—Proxima Centauri B, specifically, an Earth-sized number orbiting in the habitable zone of the red dwarf star Proxima Centauri. It was going to be the ship that launched humanity into a new age. That's why they called it Providence.

A generation of children grew up watching this ship on television. These kids watched documentaries about astronaut training every Saturday morning, traded details about the 203 people on the crew like baseball cards, and hung on every word the captain and the chief engineer said in the Erebus-branded educational videos they watched in school.

They were all raised on the same delirious idea: that Providence I would change everything; that even if they weren't on it, they would be on another ship like it someday. They could dream as no one else had ever been able to dream: of distant worlds, of impossible creatures, of uncovering the secrets of the universe.

And then, on the day of the launch—marked by celebrations and breathless news reports and the entire world watching the same broadcast for the first time in living memory—something went wrong. To this day, nobody on Earth knows exactly what happened. Oh, there are theories, each one stupider than the last. But the only thing anyone knows for sure is what they could all see with their own eyes: that the dark matter engine was engaged, and there was a blinding flash of light, and then every passenger on the ship was—is—gone.

Not dead. Not vaporized. Just gone, as if they had never been there. And a generation of children, ready to punch a hole in that exhilarating unknown, got to watch on live TV as the unknown punched back.

In the aftermath, there was chaos. Grief and confusion and anger, of course, but also existential fear. Fear of what could happen if Erebus tried again, and fear of what would happen if they didn't. What happened? Was it even possible to know? Was staying on a dying planet officially a better option than throwing more sacrificial lambs into the universe's gaping maw?

The only surviving member of the crew, Chief Engineer Kristoff Halvorsen, might have had answers, or at least acted as a guiding light. But he retreated from the public eye immediately after his failed countdown was seen by every eye on Earth, and then disappeared on the first anniversary of Launch Day.

So the Providence I *mission was canceled, obviously. And future missions around the world were shuttered, their resources redirected toward figuring out what the hell just happened. The human race told itself it was taking time to grieve. But as months stretched into years with no answers forthcoming, the remaining scientists started quitting their jobs out of frustration and disappointment and barely repressed trauma. The hallways and computers and unused common rooms of* Providence I *started gathering dust, and it became clear that no one was left who wanted to try again. No one wanted to find out the hard way what had happened. No one wanted to go to another world. So instead of using it, Erebus Industries just left the* Providence *where it was, as a monument to whatever the hell that was. And maybe, sort of, as a warning.*

That generation of children became a generation of adults, full of the bitter nostalgia that comes with knowing what could have been. And they never got over that loss, that wistful grief, that desperate sense of if only. The irony is that those kids, the ones who spent their formative years soaking up information about relativity and flight control algorithms and dark energy scalar fields, grew up to be the most STEM-obsessed adults in a century. Turns out that growing up with a space captain and an engineer as your heroes tends to make people want to go to tech school. And as the years stretched into decades, those young people were often the only ones still arguing for a renewed space program.

Many of them thought, privately, that another mission would be worth the risks. Some of them argued, loudly, that they were owed another shot at the stars.

And four of them decided, idiotically, that if no one else was going to solve the mystery of Launch Day, they were going to do it themselves.

✳

THE LIGHTS FLICKERED ON with a sizzle and a groan as the four of them climbed through the hatch, and they could see the flight deck in all its glory: brightly colored buttons and dusty screens covering every inch of the piloting console and the steel-gray walls, two enormous chairs outfitted with harnesses and countless toggles, and a window stretching most of the way around the semicircular room, through which they could see the night sky and the empty, rolling plains surrounding the complex.

They all stood and looked for a moment, mouths hanging open. And then Cleo couldn't take it anymore.

"Dibs on the captain's chair!" she called—but Kaleisha flung a hand out to catch her in the chest before she could go anywhere.

"Hold up," she said. "We have a plan, remember?"

"Search the ship for clues, record everything, and don't touch anything that might get us zapped out of existence," Abe recited, his voice muffled by the window he was pressing his face against.

"I *am* a fan of existing," Ros said. "Not being a pile of dark matter dust is my ideal scenario, medically speaking."

"Listen to the good doctor, Cleo," Kaleisha said as Abe took out his phone and started shooting a panorama of the flight deck. "You can sit in the chair later, as long as Ros determines it's not covered in instant death goo or whatever."

"Promise?"

"Promise."

Abe finished his panorama and moved around the room, snapping pictures of everything from the chairs to the tape over one of the switches. Ros went over to the door opposite the hatch and bent down to look at the small, silver button next to it.

"I think we can safely assume," Cleo said, with only a trace of sarcasm in her voice, "that the button opens the door, and doesn't start up the dark matter engine that's gonna kill us all."

Ros wrinkled their nose at Cleo and pushed the button. The door slid open with a whoosh and a ding, revealing another elevator. Ros stuck their head in and peered around.

"Alright," Kaleisha said. "Where do we want to go first?"

"Med bay?" Ros said, their words echoing around the elevator.

"The crew's quarters?" Abe offered.

"Engine bay, engine bay, *engine bay—*"

"I agree with Cleo," Kaleisha said, stowing Abe's phone back in his backpack as Cleo stopped chanting to pump her fist in victory. "The only thing we can be relatively sure of is that the crew's disappearance is linked to the dark matter engine, so we should look there first."

"Thank you!" Cleo nudged past Ros into the elevator and held her finger over the bottommost button, marked *E*. "Come on, slowpokes, I wanna see the greatest engineering achievement in all of human history. And you know I'm gonna need some alone time with her."

*

IT STARTED AS A JOKE, initially. It was the twentieth anniversary of Launch Day, and it had been McQueary's idea to turn the president's cookie-cutter address into a drinking game.

"The crew of Providence I *were the best of us," the president*

said. Drink. "We must ensure that their sacrifice will never be in
vain," he said. Drink. "In their honor, we are reviving our off-world
colonization efforts," he didn't say. Drink.

By the end of the night they'd all had too many of Reid's notori-
ously lethal dark 'n' stormies. They were young and exhausted and
far too smart for their own good, and, in that moment, it was the
funniest idea McQueary had ever thought of.

"What if we broke into Providence I?" she said, and they all
laughed their drunk asses off.

But that hypothetical hung in the air, electrifying, and became a
conversation that kept them all up into the early morning. It stopped
being funny and started being a familiar kind of exhilarating, the
idea that they could steal into the most infamous crypt in the world,
and—what? See how the engine worked? Find out where the passengers had gone? They didn't know, but that night the four of them
felt more driven, more inspired, more alive than they'd felt since
they were kids, watching the broadcasts. They were goners.

From there, it became a project, a word problem to be worked
out together on Saturday nights, sitting on the floor of their living
room surrounded by empty pizza boxes and notepads full of equations and crackpot theories. They were all perfectly matched, all
with something to contribute: Ros Wheeler, the medical resident,
with their ideas about what dark energy might have done to all
those human bodies. Kaleisha Reid, the brilliant botanist, with
an eye for details and a fascination with all forms of life. Abraham
Yang, the history of science PhD, with an encyclopedic virtual
archive of information on the Providence mission that he'd been
building for his postdoc research, and a heart too big for his own
good.

Then there was Cleo McQueary. The one who had spent her
childhood stealing her mom's tablet to watch Providence news past
her bedtime and filling up graph paper notebooks with mission

trivia and dark matter facts. The one with a PhD in computer engineering, who could do anything if it involved machines or computers, and who was the only reason the rest of them could even consider the possibility of getting anywhere near the ship.

And don't forget the most important part: These people were more than friends, they were family. In high school, McQueary, Yang, and Wheeler had discovered that Reid's house, full of plants and fluffy blankets and the smell of her father's famous chocolate hazelnut cookies, felt like a home in a way that the houses they'd been raised in never had. Together they'd gotten through hurricanes, through grad school applications, through the months of oblivious angst that preceded Reid and Yang getting together their sophomore year of undergrad. If anyone was ever fully and utterly prepared to leap into the void together, it was these four.

The Space Heist, *as Yang took to writing across the tops of the pages of his yellow legal pads,* stayed an "if" scenario, technically speaking. Until one night, McQueary said "when." When we do it. When we break into Providence I. *And they all went quiet, waiting to see if anyone else would correct her. And when no one did, they carried on.*

✳

ARCHIVED: Briefing on Exoplanet Proxima Centauri B for the Crew of *Providence I*, February 1, 2040

Proxima Centauri B is a 1.27 Earth mass rocky planet orbiting in the habitable zone of the M-type red dwarf star Proxima Centauri, and your future home. You have all made the tremendously brave decision to join the first outer-system colonial expedition in human history. Rest assured that we at Erebus Industries do

not take the enormity of your dedication to the future
survival of the human race lightly, and we thank you,
on behalf of ourselves and the rest of the world.

Proxima B is, despite its perfectly breathable
atmosphere, a hostile environment in many ways.
The planet is tidally locked in its orbit around the
host star, resulting in a surface that is scorched by
perpetual daylight on one side and intractably cold
and dark on the other. The result is a 30-km-wide
habitable zone at the planet's terminator line, or
twilight zone, where you will live in perpetual sunset
at temperatures of about -30°C, due to the relatively
low heat output of the host star.

As you will remember from the Starshot probe
expeditions of twenty years ago, the surface of the
terminator zone is covered in water ice, leading
us to believe that liquid water could be present
at the edges of the zone or in the measurably
warmer underground tunnels detected by the probes'
seismological pulsors. Note that, as living flora and
fauna—lichen-like organisms as well as signs of small
vertebrates—were discovered on the surface, colonists
should be prepared for more life to be present in
these underground caves.

We know this doesn't paint the most welcoming
picture of Proxima B. However, we trust that, as
you acclimate, you will find comfort and even beauty
in your new home. In that vein, a final observation.
Proxima Centauri is a highly active flare star, meaning
Proxima B is consistently buffeted by solar winds; we
also know that Proxima B's super-Earth level mass and
powerful magnetic field keep its robust atmosphere in
fighting shape. All this to say: The skies of Proxima B
will be near-constantly alight with auroras in every
color of the rainbow. We can only hope that you send
us postcards.

✴

NO AUTOMATIC LIGHTS CAME on when they entered the engine bay; the elevator door closed and left them in almost total darkness. Abe took a flashlight out of his backpack and shone it around. From what Cleo could see, the space was positively cavernous— the ceiling stretched at least forty feet above their heads, and rows and rows of server stacks and other hulking, shadowy machines she couldn't even begin to comprehend towered over them, dusty and dead like everything else on the ship.

"Guys," she whispered, since a reverent whisper seemed the right way to go, "I think I'm in heaven."

"Awfully dark for heaven," Ros whispered back, though they sounded just as astounded as Cleo was.

And then Abe swung the flashlight beam down another aisle and there—*there* was the dark matter engine. Cleo was sure her brain would explode.

They had never shown the engine itself on TV, see, because it was top fucking secret, because no one outside the research team could be trusted with that kind of technology, or maybe so Erebus could keep it all to themselves. Captain Wilhelmina Lucas, in all her months of glitzy press conferences and slick appearances in documentary footage, had only ever dropped a few crumbs about the newly discovered type of physiochemical reaction. Despite Cleo's lifelong obsession with Captain Lucas, her very shiny blond ponytail and the old-fashioned tape recorder into which she was always muttering her certainly genius notes-to-self, Cleo remembered her own childish exasperation at the cageyness surrounding the revolutionary technology, one that would apparently eliminate the need for fuel as we knew it. *All very proprietary, of course, you understand.* And twenty-seven-year-old Cleo understood the secrecy, on a cerebral level, but the piece of seven-year-old Cleo that still lived inside her was screaming out in smug euphoria—*I'm looking at it, you jerks, and there's nothing you can do about it*—because there it was, massive and shining even under the dust of two decades, a patchwork ring of fiberglass and metal standing on its edge, reaching almost to the ceiling. As Cleo drew closer, her eyes drinking in every detail Abe's annoyingly small spotlight managed to catch, she almost would have believed that the engine was prehistoric, eternal, some kind of portal to another dimension that the ancients had built and worshipped.

Kaleisha crept up next to her and squeezed her hand. "It's really something," she said softly. Cleo nodded. "You think you can figure out how it disappeared everyone?"

"No idea," she breathed. Then louder: "I've gotta touch it."

"Whoa, hey," Ros called out from behind her, "let's maybe consider the benefits of *not* doing that—"

"This thing is our biggest clue, right?" Cleo marched over toward its base, glancing back at Ros's concerned face. "I'm gonna have to get a little bit up in its business to deduce anything."

Ros met Cleo's eyes and must have seen all the endless determination in them, because they nodded, though their concerned frown didn't go away. Cleo heard them brushing off Kaleisha's and Abe's soothing murmurs as she turned back to the engine.

The ring was almost twice as thick as Cleo was tall, and up close she could see that it was built from several giant fiberglass tubes, held together with countless crisscrossing wires and overlapping panels of titanium alloy. The tubes made her think of particle accelerators—surely they were dark energy conduits, or pathways for ions or Weakly Interacting Massive Particles, the hypothetical stuff that made up dark matter. If she could just see where they intersected, if she could just figure out what kind of reaction was meant to happen—

So she reached out with one hand and touched the smooth surface of one of the tubes, couldn't be any harm in that—

And then the air itself *vibrated* in a concussive blast that blew her backward.

And there was a deafening rumble, a mechanical whine that quickly rose in pitch, and Cleo had only a second to raise herself onto her elbows and see that the others had also been knocked to the ground, dazedly struggling to push themselves up, before—

Flash, the dark matter engine ignited with swirling, dazzling light, streams of sparking particles flowing through the glass tubes and around the ring. And Cleo, shielding her eyes, saw that there was also something happening in the center of the ring, in the empty space. Something was forming there, a spiraling vortex that her eyes were seeing but her brain wasn't quite understanding, because it looked like golden light but it wasn't. It was *darker* than light—

"Cleo!" Kaleisha screamed over the noise. "The rockets are starting!"

That's what it took for Cleo to realize that, duh, the floor beneath them was shuddering. So she scrambled to her feet, pulled Ros up by their hand, and followed Kaleisha when she gestured at them all to *run*.

Abe had dropped the flashlight somewhere, but it didn't matter. The engine flooded the room with that impossible, black-gold glow. Tiny blue lights were flickering to life on the server stacks around and above them, and they could easily see their way through the aisles to the elevator, which dinged open for them far too pleasantly when Ros jammed the button. They piled in, Cleo twisting around to get one last glimpse of the engine—

And *shit*, she was looking at a dark matter reaction, wasn't she, in the vortex, that was what it looked like—

And then the door closed, and Kaleisha whirled on her. "What did you do?"

"Nothing, you saw me, I just touched the glass!"

Kaleisha scraped a hand over her hair. "The rockets. They're—we're going to take off, Cleo, we have to stop it, or get out of here—"

"I know, I know, but—but if we're lifting off there'll be no way to stop without crashing everything down—"

"You're the computer girl, figure it out!"

Cleo's throat caught, whatever she would have said killed by the frantic dread on Kaleisha's face. She must have seen the hurt on Cleo's, though, because she grabbed her by the shoulders and looked into her eyes.

"I'm sorry," she said. "I'm sorry, but Cleo—"

And then the door dinged open again onto the flight deck, and they all tumbled out. The rumbling of the rockets was quieter here, farther away, but still growing louder. Abe fruitlessly tried to open the exit hatch as Kaleisha dragged Cleo over to the captain's chair, and Cleo gave herself a fraction of a second to appreciate the irony before she started pressing screens. They all lit up at her touch, luckily, and only some of them gave readouts that were completely incomprehensible to her.

"Abe," she called out, "on the wall, there might be something like a kill switch, see if you can find it." Cleo heard Abe follow her instructions as she pounded every button in the neighborhood of a screen that read *THRUSTERS* above some terrifyingly large numbers. "Ros, see if you can find anything that looks like it'll access the ship's main computer. Kal?"

"Yeah," Kaleisha said, sinking into the copilot's seat next to Cleo like she was born to do it.

"See if there's still a radio connection to—I don't know, the base, some unsuspecting trucker, *anything*."

Kaleisha clamped the seat's enormous headphones over her ears, grimaced, pressed a few buttons. "I just hear buzzing."

"Great. Cool. Fantastic." Cleo tried to breathe, tried to focus on reading all the screens in front of her at once, tried to remember which buttons she hadn't tried—

"Cleo," Abe said, "I can't find any—"

"The computer, Cleo, I don't know if I can—"

Cleo turned to see Ros fiddling with an orange panel on the wall that was steadfastly resisting all their efforts. "Ros, no, that's the black box, it's not going to listen to—"

And then the world *lurched*, and Cleo knew they were lifting off. She turned and made horrified eye contact with Kaleisha as the console and both of their seats started automatically shifting into horizontal positions, heard Abe and Ros cry out as they were knocked off their feet—

"Abe, Ros, lie down flat on the floor!" Cleo shouted over the sound of the rockets, hoping they could hear her, praying she wasn't about to watch her friends die from the g-force. "Whatever you do, keep your backs straight!"

They nodded and scrambled to the floor. Cleo kept slamming up against the unresponsive ship, looking for something that would take her into the main operating system instead of just giving her individual programs, trying to ignore the roaring and the sight of the stars sliding past the window faster and faster—

And then she had a thought, and it was maybe the stupidest thought she'd ever had, but hey, this was a goddamn spaceship—

"*Computer!*" she yelled.

And then a woman appeared in front of her, a tall white woman with a tight blond ponytail and a face that Cleo would have recognized even if her eyes weren't watering and her brain wasn't being pressure-cooked into soup, wearing a black sweater and black jeans and standing calmly in front of the window with her arms crossed.

"*Captain Lucas?*" Cleo choked out.

And then the woman *flickered*, like an image on a busted television. She seemed less bothered by this than by the sight of Cleo's face melting backward into her seat.

"*What?*" Captain Lucas asked, her voice somehow audible over everything. "What did you idiots do?"

leo blinked. Breathed hard. "Are you the computer?"

The hologram hesitated, her eyebrows knitting together like she had to think about it. "Apparently."

"Well, can you *stop the ship*?" Cleo shouted over the noise, gripping the sides of her seat as the pressure built against her fragile, squishy body.

The hologram's head froze for a few frames, like a badly buffered video. "No, I can't," she said, looking around like the four of them and their situation was a puzzle she was trying to put together. "Please stop asking stupid questions."

"*Excuse* me—"

"Wait!" Kaleisha cried. Cleo turned her head with some difficulty to face her friend, who was looking at the hologram with wide eyes. "Why do you look like Captain Lucas?"

"Now, that's a better question." The hologram ran a hand over her mouth, in a gesture that made Cleo astral-project back to being seven and watching the woman's TED Talk fifteen times in a row. "I'm . . . I'm"—her head twitched again—"I am a perfect replica of Captain Lucas's consciousness, programmed to act as the interface for the *Providence* operating system." She looked down at her own hands, then back up at Kaleisha. "For simplicity's sake, you can just call me Captain Lucas."

"Are you still technically the captain if you're just a replica?" Cleo asked through gritted teeth.

Lucas raised an eyebrow. "Since you don't look particularly equipped to take up the mantle, I'm going to go with *yes*. So as long as we're speaking *technically*, you're in my chair."

Cleo couldn't believe that she was about to spend her last moments being insulted by a dead woman in a computer, but before she could say anything to that effect, Kaleisha yelled at Lucas for her. "Okay, so, if you're the captain and the computer, are you going to do anything?"

"I told you, I can't stop the ship. At this point in the trajectory, with the *Providence*"—Lucas's irises went blurry, like they were flicking back and forth inhumanly fast—"hmm, about sixty-four kilometers in the air, there's not much I can do without, you know, letting you all plunge to your fiery deaths." Her eyes landed on Abe and Ros, who were still pressed against the floor like swatted flies. "I can probably bring out the extra chairs for your companions. If that would help."

"*Yes!*" Cleo and Kaleisha shouted in unison.

Lucas waved a hand dispassionately, and out of the corner of her eye Cleo saw a panel in the floor slide open. Two more big, padded chairs rose out of it, and Ros and Abe reached for them, dragging themselves into the seats. Cleo sensed rather than heard it as they exhaled in relief.

She refocused on the hologram, who was now frowning at her. For reasons she couldn't quite place, the intense scrutiny filled Cleo with rage, or maybe panic. "Okay, you want a useful question?" she shouted, over the roaring of the engine and the blood in her ears. "Riddle me this, *Captain*—"

"You could thank me," Lucas cut in, "for saving your friends. Or at least their spines."

"Are you serious right now?"

"It would be the polite thing to do."

"*Tell me*," Cleo bellowed, "what is going to happen to us!"

Lucas heaved out a beleaguered sigh. "In the short term? You're on track to achieve escape velocity with, I'm thinking, minimal-to-survivable damage to your circulatory and nervous systems—"

"Damage to our *what now*?" Ros yelled, and Cleo was sure she heard Abe whimper behind her.

"It's not my fault you decided to launch yourselves into the stratosphere without taking any safety precautions," Lucas said. "Long term, once you leave the Oort Cloud the dark matter engine will kick you into near-lightspeed, and you should arrive at Proxima Centauri B in precisely seven years, three months, and twenty-four days." She plucked at her own sweater, then at her jeans. "Do you think I chose this outfit because it's easy to animate?"

Cleo's chest tightened and the edges of her vision started to go gray, whether from the mortal terror or the g-force, she couldn't tell. "Christ on a cracker."

"This isn't happening," Kaleisha babbled, more to herself than anything. "This wasn't the plan, we can't go to another planet—"

"Yeah, well, I'm not too happy about being a computer," Lucas grumbled, "but we'll all just have to muddle through."

Cleo squeezed her eyes shut and stretched out her hand. Despite everything, through everything, Kaleisha took it. Cleo could suddenly think of nothing but Kaleisha's dad, of Kaleisha's house that stood up on that hill against the levees, clean and warm inside even when the streets were flooded and the sky was grimy.

"I know this isn't ideal."

Cleo squinted through her twitching eyelashes. Captain Lucas was staring at her.

"You obviously didn't sign up for this," she continued. "So. Sorry."

Cleo blinked. Lucas looked regretful, she looked angry, she looked—she looked lost, maybe, standing there with the sky behind her growing darker, clearer, more speckled with the shining watercolor spray of stars. Behind the ship, the atmosphere would be gritty and glowing with the flames of a forest burning somewhere. Cleo wrenched her head around to lock eyes with Kaleisha, ready for the desperate fear on her face. But she only looked as grimly certain as Cleo felt, as they'd maybe always been.

"This is happening," Kaleisha said, squeezing her hand.

Cleo squeezed back. "This is happening," she echoed, right before she passed out.

✳

HERE'S WHAT EVERYONE ON Earth knows about the late Captain Lucas. They're all woefully misinformed, of course, but that's not entirely their fault.

Any massive public undertaking that involves a lot of money from taxpayers and venture capitalists needs a human face. For the Providence I *project, that face was Captain Wilhelmina Lucas. She was a wunderkind physicist, a veteran of the Erecura Deep mission to Europa, and even at the tender age of thirty she was the obvious choice to lead the most carefully selected and painstakingly trained crew in history. It didn't hurt that she looked good in a suit and could be blindingly charming when she needed to be, or that she had a hilarious and equally exceptional younger* brother who was coming along on the mission, or that her fiancé had died three years previously and the whole world had decided that made her a better person for some reason.

It wouldn't be an exaggeration to say that Captain Lucas was a major reason the world fell so hard for the Providence mission. It was going to be a big goddamn deal no matter what, obviously. But Lucas gave them a hero to revere, an avatar of all their last, best hopes for the survival of the species, and a friend to make them feel like they understood what was happening in those deepest, darkest halls of impossible science and corporate secrets.

They didn't understand. Not by a long shot. But the important thing was that they thought they did.

When Captain Lucas disappeared with the other 202 crew members on Launch Day, she was mourned just a little bit more than the rest, because humans have no sense of proportion when processing large-scale tragedy. Wings of universities were named after her. She got a statue in front of the Air and Space Museum. And for years afterward, people like Cleo McQueary, even if they didn't consciously realize it, applied to tech schools so they could one day be just like her.

Here's what only four people on Earth (if rapidly tearing through the thermosphere even counts) know about the late Captain Lucas:

In the weeks leading up to the launch, she spent what precious spare time she had uploading every gigabyte of her brain processes into Providence's operating system. Which was an odd thing to do, considering that Lucas thought she was about to spend the next seven years, three months, and twenty-four days on that ship. There was no reason to make a copy of herself.

Unless she thought something else.

✳

ARCHIVED: Medical Report — Veronica Ruiz, MD, to Chief Engineer Kristoff Halvorsen, PhD, September 26, 2040

> **ASSISTANT ENGINEER BEN ANDRIANAKIS:** Displays fever symptoms, circulation issues in extremities, and possible absence seizures.
>
> **ENGINEER LYDIA GOLDSMITH:** Displays weight loss, hyperactivity, and a compulsive need to exercise.
>
> **ENGINEER TIMOTHY LU:** Displays confusion, cognitive delays, delusions, and possible hallucinations he has taken to calling "visions" of future events.
>
> **DEPUTY CHIEF ENGINEER DELLY JEFFERSON:** Displays muscle spasms, fatigue, and periods of increased metabolism and bodily strength.
>
> **RECOMMENDATION:** Suspend patients from work on the *Providence* engineering team to allow for further medical supervision. If possible, suspend all work on the engine until more research can be conducted into its effect on the human body.

✳

WHEN CLEO CAME TO, she couldn't feel anything. It wasn't that her nerve endings had gone numb—she could still wiggle her fingers, and she had a shredding headache—but she wasn't touching anything. No floor under her feet, no pillow under her head, no chair under—

Her eyes flew open. She was still on the flight deck, floating weightlessly a few feet over the captain's chair she'd been sitting in, her hair swirling in a dark, curly halo around her head. Through the window she could see a curving, fuzzy blue strip of the Earth's horizon, and above it, nothing but black.

"Guys," she said aloud, something hot and intoxicating bubbling in her stomach, "you gotta see this."

No one answered. Cleo twisted her neck to the right and saw Kaleisha, still unconscious and hovering above the pilot console. Shit. She knew that Abe and Ros must be behind her, but however she paddled her limbs or contorted her back, she couldn't spin herself around to look at them. Cleo's heart started galloping against her ribs. Ros should have been the one to wake up first. They would know exactly how worried to be about, like, swelling? In everyone's brain membranes, or something?

Okay. Small problems first. Then the big problem.

Wishing for the millionth time in her life that she'd gotten proper zero-gravity training like the astronauts on TV, Cleo folded her knees into her chest so she could untie one of her sneakers. Once she had it off and in her hand, she wound up, said a little prayer that it wouldn't hit any important buttons, and threw the shoe at the window.

It worked just like Cleo had known it would—*thank you, Isaac Newton, you brilliant gay bastard*—and she drifted slowly backward in the opposite direction of the sneaker, laughing in relief. It was a lot lazier of a pace than she would have liked, but after a few moments she passed Abe's gangly, suspended form, then Ros's ample one, just before she bounced back-first against the rear wall. They were both still unconscious, like Kaleisha, but the three of them looked like all the important parts of their bodies were still in the right place, so Cleo's heart stopped palpitating.

"Hey, Computer?" she called out.

A *pop*, and there was Captain Lucas, arms crossed, mouth set in an unamused line. She looked at the sneaker floating by the window, then at Cleo drifting away from the wall, half shoeless, and drew a few conclusions.

"You proud of yourself?" she said, deadpan.

Cleo wrinkled her nose at the hologram. "Yeah, quite a bit, actually."

Lucas's frown deepened. "What do you want?"

"Are you gonna be like this every time we call you?" Cleo asked, trying to project competence despite the fact that she was slowly rotating sideways relative to the hologram. "Because I know that you're going through a lot right now, waking up as a computer and all, but I'm not sure I want to deal with your attitude for seven years or whatever."

Lucas glowered at her. "Then stop calling me 'Computer.'"

"What, you don't like that? What if I did it in my Scotty voice? I can do the accent and everything—"

"I have a name, dipshit."

Cleo went quiet, partly because internationally renowned astronaut and genius Wilhelmina Lucas had just called her a dipshit. But also because, she thought a bit abashedly, twenty-seven years of watching *Star Trek* should have prepared her for the possibility that this hologram would have feelings. Even if this hologram was also kind of an ass.

"Okay, sorry," she said in what she hoped was an honestly apologetic tone, "but do I have to do the formal thing and yell 'Captain Lucas' every time? Can I call you Billie? I feel like I read somewhere that—"

"My friends call me Billie." The hologram blinked at her. If Cleo hadn't known any better she would have said that the mildly aggravated slouch on Lucas's face had softened, but then the impression was gone. "Sure. Whatever."

"I'm Cleo McQueary."

"I'm calling you McQueary."

"Suit yourself. So, Billie," Cleo said, blowing a curl out of her face and trying to ignore the fact that she was now fully upside down, "you may have noticed that my friends and I are in a bit of a situation here."

"Yes."

"Is there anything you can do to *help* us?"

"I'm having trouble—" The upper half of Billie's body waved like an image on an old television. "It's taking some time to re-orient myself to my *own* situation. This may shock you, but a life-time of memories and a couple hundred gigabytes of extraneous data is a lot to sort through. You'll have to be more specific."

Cleo sighed. "The ship has an artificial gravity drive, right?"

"No, we were all going to spend seven years losing bone mass and bouncing off of each other like M&M's. *Of course* there's a gravity drive."

"Why haven't you engaged it, like, yesterday?"

"I didn't want you all to fall and injure yourselves," Billie said gruffly, which almost made Cleo soften a little toward her, at least until she kept talking. "If you had strapped yourselves into your seats, like, I don't know, people with *brains*—"

"Hey now—"

"—then we wouldn't be having this conversation, and I'm sure we'd both be a lot happier for it."

Cleo pinched the bridge of her nose, trying not to think about how much more her head would hurt when she landed on it. "You know what, just do it. Ros is a doctor. We'll be fine."

Billie looked skeptically at Ros, who had a small solar system of drool globules orbiting their head, and sighed.

"Okay."

And before Cleo could so much as put her arms out to break her fall, Billie had flicked her head and the floor had come up and whacked Cleo in the face. *Ow.* Cleo may have been pretty solidly built for someone so short, but that was still going to hurt in the morning. She heard the others hit the floor too—heard Abe yelp as he landed on his chair and rolled off, actually—and then she heard Ros's groan and Kaleisha's whispered "Jesus fuck," and she couldn't even be mad, because she knew they were all safe.

Rolling onto her back, Cleo saw Billie walk with silent footsteps to stand over Ros, who was pushing themself up to a sitting position.

"Are you Ros the doctor?"

"Yes?" Ros said, rubbing their head.

"You should examine your accomplices for head injuries and g-force shock. Meet me in the med bay and I'll, um. Try and answer any questions you might have."

And with a tiny sigh, Billie *popped* away again. Ros turned to stare at Cleo, their eyebrows crawling up toward their red hair, and Cleo couldn't find it in herself to do anything but shrug back at them.

✳

ARCHIVED: *Providence* Intracrew Messaging Service Conversation — Capt. Wilhelmina Lucas and Mission Specialist Elijah Lucas, April 24, 2041

ELIJAH LUCAS
Hey Bilbo

WILHELMINA LUCAS
I told you never to call me that at work, dumbass

ELIJAH LUCAS
What is "at work," really?
Can a digital message ever truly inhabit the
    imagined, though indisputably physical, community
    we call "the workplace"?

WILHELMINA LUCAS
You're texting me on our work comms. Stick that up
    your indisputably physical ass

ELIJAH LUCAS
Now you're thinkin like a philosophy major!

WILHELMINA LUCAS
God, I hope not. What do you want?

ELIJAH LUCAS
Alright alright
So you didn't hear this from me, but a few of the
    other mission specs I hang with have been rumbling
    about some ALLEGED health issues among the
    engineering team
And I was wondering if you knew anything about why
    those four got put on leave

WILHELMINA LUCAS
Sorry, Eli, but that's classified.

ELIJAH LUCAS
Yeah but is it Baby Brother Classified

WILHELMINA LUCAS
I haven't even seen the report to the board. That's
    how classified.

ELIJAH LUCAS
Ah
Kris handled?

WILHELMINA LUCAS
Yeah.

ELIJAH LUCAS
Fascinating
So, hypothetically speaking, if those techs got sick
    because of a problem with the engine or, like, some
    heretofore undiscovered dark matter disease, said
    problem would have been quietly fixed by now, right

WILHELMINA LUCAS
[. . .]
[. . .]

ELIJAH LUCAS
Ignore me
My lunch buddies are very conspiracy-minded
Of course it would be fixed
They wouldn't send us off on a seven-year deep-space
   mission with a faulty ship, obviously

WILHELMINA LUCAS
Yeah
Obviously

ELIJAH LUCAS
And you'd tell me if there was a problem that you
   knew of

WILHELMINA LUCAS
Of course
Always

※

CLEO SAW ROS'S KNEES literally go weak when the elevator deposited them in the glittering med bay. Rows of plush beds filled the room, all of them with screens and panels and other digital doodads built into the headboard, and the soothingly green walls were lined with cabinets and diagnostic machines. Ros ran over to one of the hospital beds and immediately started pressing buttons to see what they did.

"Oh man," Cleo said to Kaleisha, who had stopped next to her, "I knew they'd love this."

"Yeah." Kaleisha's voice went rough and quiet the way it did only when she was angry. "Glad you two are having such a blast."

Cleo turned to her friend to see her face drawn tight. "Are you okay, Kal?"

"I'm stuck on a one-way flight to another godforsaken solar system, Cleo. In what universe would I be okay?"

"I'm sorry, did I miss something? Has something gone down since you were holding my hand, all, like, *we'll get through this together, Cleo*?"

Kaleisha blinked slowly. "Now, I know you didn't interpret that as an acknowledgment that I'm cool with dying in deep space so you can have the interplanetary adventure you've always wanted, Cleo. I know you're not that selfish."

Cleo's lungs seemed to suddenly clench around nothing. "Did I do something? Something that made you think I'm deliberately, callously dooming you to a gnarly space death?"

Kaleisha flexed her fingers and breathed deeply. "All I meant is that this is happening, and we will get through it together, because we have no choice. But in between touching all the deadly machines you can reach and chatting it up with your childhood hero and, apparently, assuming we're all content to fly to Proxima Centauri B on a lark, have you been able to spare a single, measly thought about how, exactly, we're going to get through it?"

"Uh." Cleo ran a hand agitatedly through her hair. "I know we'll figure it out?"

"*See?*" Kaleisha said, her voice growing louder than she usually allowed it to. "You can't even pretend that you've taken the rest of us into consideration."

"Jesus, Kal, we've been awake for all of fifteen minutes, I don't see why you're already jumping down my throat—"

"Because I know it hasn't occurred to you for even a second to wipe the stardust out of your eyes and *think*!" Abe came up behind Kaleisha to put a calming hand on her waist, but she shook him off. "We have lives, Cleo, despite your best attempts to escape yours at every opportunity. My *Annals of Botany* article is supposed to publish in a few weeks. I told my dad I would call him in the morning. Abe's already planning his family's mid-autumn festival party, Ros was supposed to go to Alabama for their grandma's ninetieth next month, and now we're going to spend seven *years*—"

"Hey. Hey." Cleo tried to ignore the queasy swoop of her stomach that accompanied any mention of her friends' sickeningly healthy relationships with their families. "We'll find a way to radio your dad. And shit, Kal, would it really be so bad to see another planet? Maybe we could even find out what happened to the crew along the way, and show everyone that the space program is worth another shot."

Cleo had been sure that would help, but Kaleisha's glare just grew darker. "Great," she said. "You can get on that. Meanwhile, I'm going to ask Ros if there are any goddamn HRT meds for me on this ship, because I guess I'm the only one here thinking pragmatically."

Kaleisha stomped off toward Ros. Abe followed close behind her, but threw Cleo a look over his shoulder that was half *You should apologize, bud*, and half *You should* really *apologize, dumb-dumb.*

Cleo mentally kicked herself in the shins as Ros squeezed Kaleisha's hand and immediately started searching the shelves for hormone pills. Of course this situation sucked in so, so many ways. Of course she should have thought of Kaleisha's hormone pills, and their families, and their lives.

But the way the Earth had looked as they soared above and away from it—God, it was like all the longing she'd ever done was pressing back into her at once.

"Hey, Cleo," Ros called over their shoulder, standing on their tiptoes to rifle through a cabinet. "How did you summon that Captain Lucas hologram? 'Computer'?"

Pop.

"What did I *just* tell you?"

Ros, Abe, and Kaleisha whirled around to see Billie leaning against the elevator door, glaring at them.

"Dude, slow your roll, I haven't gotten a chance to debrief them yet," Cleo said. Billie's eyes narrowed when they met hers, and Cleo got the very skin-crawly feeling that Billie could tell she was upset, even though that was silly, because Cleo was an absolute legend at hiding it when she was upset. She distracted herself by gesturing dramatically between her friends and Billie. "Guys," she said, "this is Billie. I've been informed that calling her 'Computer' is not very polite. Also, it's taking her a little while to figure out her computer brain, so be gentle."

Billie's eyes un-narrowed, which Cleo took as a win.

"Billie," she continued, "these are my friends and, uh, partners in space crime, I guess. Abe Yang, who's a historian, Ros Wheeler, who's a doctor, as you know, and Kaleisha Reid, who's a botanist and the most badass person I know." Kaleisha rolled her eyes, and Cleo's eyelid twitched involuntarily.

Billie nodded at the others, eyes still on Cleo. "And how about you, McQueary?" she said. "What are you?"

"I have a PhD in computer engineering. And also sneaker physics, obviously."

Billie's eyes crinkled again, but in a smiley way, almost, right before Abe stepped forward and poked at Billie's arm. His finger slid right through, and Billie fizzed into static again. She yelped.

"Oh no! Sorry! I just, there was nothing in any of my research about the ship having a holographic operating system—"

"Do that again, Yang, and we'll both find out if I have the power to sic all the ship's chairs and forks on you, *Beauty and the Beast*–style."

Ros laughed in a breathy, bewildered way, looking shocked that it had even occurred to someone to be rude to Abe. "Easy, tiger. Was the real Captain Lucas this much of a grump?"

"The *real*—" Billie's head twitched, and she clenched her jaw. "I don't know. Why don't you ask her?"

Out of habit, Cleo glanced out of the corner of her eye at Kaleisha, who was frowning uneasily at Billie. It hadn't occurred to Cleo—though it should have—that the hologram probably hadn't come online since before Launch Day. Billie would have no way of knowing what had happened.

"Billie," Cleo said, trying to keep her voice neutral, "do you know what year it is?"

"I—" Billie sucked in a breath, and her eyes started buzzing back and forth again. "I don't—"

"It's 2061," Kaleisha said gently.

Billie blinked, and her eyes went still. "What."

"One sec." Abe pulled out his phone to tap through what Cleo knew was the massive drive of files for his postdoc project, "Ain't No Sunshine When She's Gone: Understanding the *Providence* Disaster." "Let's start, um—here."

He held the phone out to Billie so she could watch as the headlines scrolled by. All of them had been burned into Cleo's brain long ago.

DISASTER: "PROVIDENCE" CREW VANISHES

EREBUS CEO: NO RESULTS IN HUNT FOR LOST CREW

TEN YEARS ON, STILL NO ANSWERS FOR FAMILIES OF
   "PROVIDENCE" VICTIMS

Billie read with her lips just parted, her breath growing quicker and tighter by the second.

"I'm so sorry, Billie." Abe reached out a hand like he was going to pat her shoulder, then thought better of it. "It must be awful to find out this way."

Billie looked up from Abe's phone, and Cleo thought her eyes might have been watery. Except Billie was a hologram, and that would be silly. "They're just—gone? No one's ever found them, or at least figured out . . ."

She choked on the end of her sentence, looking hollowed out. She'd had—or Lucas had, anyway, though the distinction didn't seem important—a brother on the ship, Cleo remembered with a sinking feeling. Elijah.

"What, ah—" Billie took off her glasses and pinched the bridge of her nose, hard, her fingers trembling. "What is Erebus doing to find out what happened to them?"

"Nothing." Abe stowed his phone and eyed Billie cautiously. "They tried for a few years and then gave up."

"They *what*?" Billie let her hand fall and glared at Abe. Her eyes were definitely wet, and Cleo wondered distantly why Lucas would have programmed her hologram to cry. "Kris would never let them just abandon everyone."

"Kristoff Halvorsen, you mean? The chief engineer? He also went missing a year later, unfortunately." Abe frowned slightly. "Took his own life, is what they ended up deciding."

"What? No—that can't—*fuck*."

Cleo almost didn't want to disturb Billie further, but she had to know, had to ask—

"Do you know why it might have happened?"

Billie blinked, her bloodshot eyes starting to vibrate again, searching for something. "No, I don't—there's too much, I can't—"

"Are you sure? Could it be in a memory you're still down-loading?" While Billie's irises flickered, Cleo sucked in a breath and held it till it hurt. The best chance of her lifetime to under-stand what happened on the *Providence* was standing in front of her; Billie had to know. She had to.

Billie's eyes came to a stop. "I seriously doubt that I would have forgotten something like that." She straightened up, apparently deciding that the time for telegraphing even the tiniest bit of despair was over, and scanned the group imperiously. "But here's something I know for sure: You idiots knew what could happen, and you still started up the engine."

There she went again, making it impossible to like her. Cleo opened her mouth to rage at Billie, or maybe to start crying, but Ros cut her off, trying to head off an argument as subtly as an eighteen-wheeler skidding into a U-turn. "Oh, Billie, what do you know, I almost forgot why I called you! Did your medical team stock estrogen? Spironolactone?"

Billie jerked a thumb at a cabinet to the right of the machine.

"We absolutely did not think that *this* would happen," Cleo said as Ros clattered past. "We had a plan. It was a great plan. Kaleisha's whole thing is plans."

"Don't patronize me right now, Cleo—"

"Well, *clearly,*" Billie interjected, "the plan was bullshit."

Kaleisha redirected her affront at Billie. "Hey!"

"You should have at least been self-aware enough to realize that you don't know jack about the *Providence.* But you're post-docs or whatever, so I guess that was too much to ask."

"And where did self-awareness come in," Cleo shot back, "when your engineers inexplicably decided to design the dark matter engine to turn on at the touch of a hand?"

Billie's brow furrowed. "What are you talking about, Mc-Queary?"

"A brush. A caress. A gentle graze of lovers' fingers." Cleo stood aside, not breaking her eye contact with Billie, to let Ros noisily bustle past her so they could noisily hand Kaleisha the pills they'd found. "I wasn't anywhere near a switch or a big red button or anything else one would conventionally take to mean *press here to launch yourself into space.* I put my hand on one of those particle tubes and the thing started up all by itself."

"That's impossible."

"No, Billie, we all saw it happen," Kaleisha piped up, crossing her arms. "Why would it do that?"

"I don't know."

"You don't know that either, huh?" Cleo said with a humorless laugh loud enough to carry over the sound of Ros noisily putting a blood pressure cuff on Abe's arm. "What's the point of having the brain of the lady who was in charge of this whole operation if you don't remember anything useful?"

"You tell me," Billie said through clenched teeth. "You're the computer wizard—what's my purpose? My program directive? Is this a Three Laws of Robotics situation or do I get a little more leeway than that?"

"I don't know, man!" Cleo threw her hands up in exasperation and tried to ignore whatever was twitching across Billie's face, because it was something less than angry and maybe a little sad and she did *not* have the time or energy to parse it even if she wanted to. "I would be more inclined to help you figure it out if you weren't such an asshole—"

Kaleisha cleared her throat loudly, and Cleo realized that she had somehow gotten all up in Billie's space without noticing. She felt her face get hot, and tried to ignore that too.

Kaleisha swallowed her pills dry and looked at them both like she was already bored of their bickering. "Not to break up whatever *this* is, but we have a few more pressing questions on our hands right now."

Cleo ran a hand through her hair and tried to let some of the tension seep out of her shoulders. "You're right, Kal. What are you thinking?"

"I, for one, would like to know how we're expected to live on this ship. Billie, can you take us to the food stores so we can check that they're still okay?"

Billie blinked and, miraculously, didn't argue. "Sure."

"Great." Kaleisha flicked a loc out of her face and fixed Cleo with a glare. "After that, Billie, you should teach Cleo about how the ship works. She's our best shot at keeping this thing running." Cleo smiled a tiny smile, and Kaleisha pursed her lips in return. "Ros and Abe can go check the quarters for other supplies, possibly clues, and I will try my best to radio Earth."

Abe took Kaleisha's hand. "Sounds good, babe."

"Do you want my help with the radio?" Cleo blurted, knowing as soon as she said it that she was pushing her luck.

"No, I think you should focus on the ship with Billie." Kaleisha's expression would have been unreadable if Cleo didn't know her so well.

"Kal, please—"

Kaleisha was already walking toward the elevator. "No time, babe. I need brain food if I'm gonna come up with a plan to get us home."

✳

THERE WAS ONE PERSON who might have known why the dark matter engine did what it did, and it wasn't Wilhelmina Lucas. The original, not the hologram. But also not the—whatever. You get it.

Remember, Lucas was only one half of the dream team leading the Providence mission. She was the captain and media darling, but she didn't build the ship or its engine. Wasn't down in the engineering trenches, so to speak.

No, the man leading that charge was Lucas's co-commander, the chief engineer. He was the soft-spoken visionary to Lucas's intrepid explorer, the leader of the underground lab where scientists learned more about dark matter and dark energy than anyone could have previously imagined. The man did more to advance human knowledge than possibly anyone who had ever come before him, and he never even seemed to care about getting the credit for it. His TV appearances were largely limited to guest spots on PBS shows for children, and he was happy to let Lucas do the schmoozing at all those black-tie fundraisers. He told her what to say about how the engine worked, and she said it. He just wanted to focus on his work, and science, and progress.

Their partnership was perfect like that—both bringing skills to the table that, together, made them an unstoppable juggernaut of genius and charisma. They had started out as colleagues, thrust together by Erebus Industries' need for both the energy of a hot up-and-comer and the gravitas of a veteran physicist. But they quickly became friends, odd couple though they were, each finding that they enjoyed the other's company through the years of all-night work, endless training, and coauthored papers even more than they respected their drive and expertise.

He may have shirked the spotlight, relatively speaking, but McQueary and her friends would still recognize him on sight. They'd seen his recurring educational segment, Quantum Chatter with Dr. Dark Matter; they'd seen the press conference where he'd announced, tears gleaming in his brilliant blue eyes, that the dark matter engine was fully operational. They'd also watched as he counted down on Launch Day; they'd been unable to look away as he watched his life's work obliterated in a flash of light with cameras from every major news network on Earth trained on his face. They'd also seen the news when, a year later to the day, he disappeared from his home as if he had never been there and was officially declared dead.

They knew his name: Kristoff Halvorsen. They couldn't have known that his friends called him Kris. Lucas, specifically, had called him Kris.

CHAPTER 3

Billie brandished an arm half-heartedly at the plexiglass cube in front of them. "Bon appétit."

Cleo cocked her head; there was nothing inside the cube but a syringe suspended from the top by two perpendicular tracks, like a claw machine. Ros squinted at it, mouth hanging open a little. "Please don't tell me we're getting our food injected intravenously."

"No, man, these are the coolest," Abe said, cutting off whatever Billie had just opened her mouth angrily to say. "It's a 3D food printer. No one wanted to spend seven years eating astronaut ice cream, so they built these to squirt out any food they wanted."

"'Squirt out'?" Ros repeated, biting their lip. "That doesn't sound particularly—"

"All the ingredients are stored in shelf-stable powder form," Billie said coldly, "then rehydrated and *extruded* molecule by molecule."

"Okay, but 'extruded' sounds worse. You *do* understand how that sounds worse?"

"Billie," Abe interjected, "how do I make a cheeseburger?"

Billie ground her teeth at him. "Push the button and ask."

Abe pressed the green button on the side of the cube. "Burger, medium rare. Hot."

Cleo snorted, and out of the corner of her eye she could have sworn she saw Billie look down at her feet, like she was trying not to laugh. But Cleo was quickly distracted from that development by the sight of a burger being built inside the printer chamber, line by line.

"Oh shit," she said, smacking Abe on the arm as the needle created a perfect squiggle of ketchup.

"Oh *shit*," Abe said, and smacked her cheerfully right back.

Once they'd all loaded their arms with food—hot, fried things and discontinued candy and fruits that had gone functionally extinct sometime in the last two decades—the others scurried across the ballroom of a mess hall to pick a table. Despite its size, the room was almost cozy, full of wood-paneled walls, virtual fireplaces that crackled gently, and long tables and benches for communal eating. Cleo hung back to walk slowly next to Billie. She took a deep breath.

"Hey," she said, hoping she wasn't about to start another argument, "are you, like, okay?"

Billie looked down at her, eyebrows raised skeptically. "In what sense?"

It occurred to Cleo that she didn't know how to tactfully ask whether Billie was just angry due to the probable deaths of her brother and all their crewmates and the failure of the *Providence* mission and her apparently unexpected transformation into a computer, or if she was simply a jackass by nature.

"I mean," she said slowly, "do you have, like, hologram food you could eat?"

Billie blinked at her. "What possible purpose could that serve, McQueary?"

Cleo shrugged, which almost dislodged an impeccably formed

banana from her arms. "I just thought—you probably remember food, right? And maybe there's something you'd like to be eating right now, and—I don't know. I just thought it would be nice if you could eat with us."

Something sad, almost soft, flitted across Billie's face, but it was gone before Cleo could fully interpret it. "I've only been"— Billie scowled, searching for a word—"*awake* for a few hours. I'm not desperate for a hot dog just yet."

Cleo squinted at her. She didn't quite believe Billie, not least because of the way she was stealing hungry glances at the snacks in Cleo's arms. But she let the subject go as they arrived at the table where the others were sitting, their faces already stuffed and greasy.

"How does a *printer* make pastry this flaky?" Kaleisha asked, staring wonderingly at the perfectly fried Jamaican beef patty in her hands. Abe, who had somehow already finished his burger and was now scarfing down red bean–filled mooncakes, nodded emphatically. "And how is the Scotch bonnet still so spicy after spending twenty years as a weird powder, hmm?"

"Billie," Ros said, managing to look anxious around a mouthful of hush puppy, "where are we right now? Like, in the solar system?"

"Um—" Billie frowned at the chair Cleo had just pulled out for her. "I can't sit in that, McQueary. I can't touch anything that's not built into the ship."

"Oh, sorry." Cleo abandoned the chair and sat down on the floor, taking a first, life-affirming bite of her steaming chocolate-chip pancakes. Billie's right eyebrow twitched, but then she sat cross-legged next to Cleo and turned back to Ros.

"We should be passing Jupiter any moment, Wheeler."

"Seriously? Is—is there a way to see the planet? Y'know, as we pass by?"

"Sure." Billie waved a hand toward the nearest wall, and the wall disappeared.

"Shit on a *stick*, Billie—"

Cleo's voice was lost in the awestruck cries of the others as they all dropped their food and leapt to their feet. The wall wasn't gone, Cleo realized, just projecting the view outside onto its slightly curved surface with perfect clarity. She drew closer, winding her way between the tables and drinking in the view of the stars shining steadily against the pitch dark of space. Had she ever seen true black before, undiluted by the world? Had she ever seen the stars as they honestly were, without air pollution and light pollution and thousands of old, dead satellites in the way? Cleo didn't think so, now that she was looking at them, now that she was *seeing*, now—

Now that she was seeing *Jupiter* in the distance, sliding across their range of vision all too fast and far enough away that she could have blocked it out with the pad of her thumb, but still, wondrously there. The sun side of it swirled hazy and bright against the night side, and Cleo could just pick out a few moons, glittering tiny and precious around the planet, if she squinted.

"You don't have to—"

Cleo turned just in time to see Billie lift and spread her arms. The image on the wall zoomed in, and suddenly Jupiter was as tall as the ceiling and Cleo could see every cloud swirling its way across the red-striped surface.

"Never gets old." Billie was at Cleo's side now, and her reverential whisper was the kindest she had sounded yet.

"You were on the Erecura Deep mission to Europa, right?"

"Ah." Billie blinked hard, blinked again. "I guess I was."

Cleo waited, but Billie didn't elaborate. "Well, I could get used to this."

"You shouldn't have to." Billie cleared her throat then, snapping the other three out of their reveries. "Anyway. We have about three hours before we exit the Oort Cloud and make the jump to sub-lightspeed, after which you're all going to quickly become very useless, so I suggest you get moving if you want to send any messages or do your little gumshoe act."

"Christ." Kaleisha glared angrily at Jupiter. "What happens when we jump to sub-lightspeed?"

"Well, first your bodies will need time to . . . adjust."

"That pause was so pregnant it's probably four centimeters dilated," Ros said. "So what, pray tell, do you mean by that?"

"Ever been motion sick, Wheeler? It's like that, but all the way down to your soul. I'm remembering it now. Not fun." Ros and Kaleisha shared a very apprehensive look, but Billie didn't seem to notice. "Following your recoveries, we'll hopefully have at least a response from NASA, and we can begin strategizing in earnest."

The idea of a message from NASA sent a little thrill up Cleo's spine, despite everything. She still couldn't help feeling excited about getting her hands greasy in the *Providence*, rather than being scared. The unfortunate fact remained that spending years on a spaceship with her best friends sounded like her ideal scenario.

Before the guilt and confusion over all of that could overwhelm her, Cleo shot some finger guns at Billie. "I believe we have a date," she said, immediately putting her guns down at the look on Billie's face. "I hope you remember how the ship works. I don't know how many more surprises I can take. Kal—"

"I'm headed to the flight deck," Kaliesha said, maybe reading Cleo's mind and maybe cutting her off before she could do any more damage to their friendship. "See if I can get a message back to Earth." She turned to Abe and Ros. "You guys go check out the crew's living quarters."

Abe held out a hand to Ros, who grimaced and high-fived it weakly. "Go team!"

"Good luck with that, you two," Billie deadpanned. "Let me know if you find anything that a megacorporation and a yearslong investigation couldn't—"

"Alright, Oscar the Grouch." Cleo forgot herself and reached out to grab Billie's arm. Billie buzzed, and she spun around with an affronted noise, just in time to miss Abe sticking his tongue out at her behind her back. "Come give me the all-access tour of your trash can and leave my friends alone."

✳

ARCHIVED: "Progress Report" — Dr. Kristoff Halvorsen to the Crew and Board of the *Providence I* Mission, June 2, 2041

My esteemed colleagues,

I am pleased to report that the engine has completed final testing and is now fully operational and ready for launch on July 1. This is, of course, thanks to my brilliant and unflagging engineering team, who have been working around the clock for years to pull off what is arguably the greatest technical accomplishment in human history. I don't need to tell you all how crucial our achievements here are going to be to the continued survival—and prosperity—of our species. Here's to even more to come.

With gratitude,
Dr. Kris Halvorsen

ARCHIVED: "Re: Progress Report" — Capt. Wilhelmina Lucas to Dr. Kristoff Halvorsen, June 2, 2041

Kris, call me. I have a couple questions.

✳

IF, TWENTY-FOUR HOURS AGO, Cleo had been asked to guess what the personal lab of Captain Wilhelmina Lucas, PhD, looked like, she probably would have imagined sleek surfaces and immaculately indexed bookshelves. She was thrown, therefore, to discover that the space looked like a college town flea market the week after the seniors from the queer dorm cleaned out their rooms. The lab took up nearly an entire level of the ship, and every inch of it was cluttered and colorful and full of outlandish things. Bookcases covered every wall; cabinets and workstations of all kinds turned the lab floor into a maze of tables and stools and machines. Cleo saw a chemistry set, a carpenter's bench, an easel, what looked for all the world like a tiny urn on its own tiny shelf, a desk practically sagging under a mountain of circuit boards, a rusting cast-iron skillet that her hands itched to take a steel-wool scrub to—and that was just in the immediate vicinity of the elevator.

"Damn, Billie," she said, picking up a circuit board the size of her face. "I've been told my bedroom is, to quote Kaleisha, 'a danger to all who dare enter,' but this is next level."

"Don't touch that," Billie snapped, even though she had her back to Cleo and was marching deeper into the maze. "If you make a mess, you'll have to put everything back, and I'll have to suffer through watching you put it back wrong."

"I hate to break it to you, but this is, uh. Already a mess."

Billie turned to glare at Cleo, but didn't stop walking. "I don't expect you to understand, but everything in here does have a place."

"Mm-hmm." Cleo's eyes landed on a pile of old, coffee-stained books. "And why does *The Mushroom Hunter's Guide to New England*, third edition, have a place in your space lab, exactly?"

"I get bored. Easily." Billie was already half obscured by

stacks of boxes, and Cleo scurried between a sewing machine and a bin of tarnished handsaws to catch up. "Space gets very boring."

"Rousing words, Captain."

Billie huffed out a humorless laugh. "What makes you think I have any interest in rousing you?"

"I don't know," Cleo muttered, kicking a tennis ball out of her way and under a table, "maybe the fact that I grew up watching you be all cool and reassuring on TV?"

Billie stopped dead, and Cleo had to whirl her arms to avoid tripping through her. Billie turned to face her, suddenly closer than Cleo ever expected her to be. She craned her neck up to meet Billie's eyes, which were green and blazing behind her glasses in a way that made it hard to believe she was just code and light, rather than flesh and blood and simmering feeling.

"Let's get one thing straight right now," Billie growled, her voice an angry register deeper. "I am not the woman you grew up idolizing."

Cleo swallowed. "Yeah, okay, because you're a hologram, I've picked up on—"

"No." Billie flexed her fingers, inhaling deeply through her nose. "Because that woman never existed. She was a fiction, invented for the donors and the cameras. She's about as real as I am."

And Billie turned on her heel and stalked away. Cleo stood frozen for a moment, then gave her head a little shake and began picking her way determinedly after Billie again.

"So you *are* just an asshole," Cleo called, trying not to let any hurt into her voice. "You just used to be pretty good at hiding it."

Billie didn't answer. So, without giving herself time to second-guess it, Cleo picked up the nearest Allen wrench she could lay her hands on and threw it.

Of course, it sailed right through Billie, who flickered, flinched, and then growled in frustration.

"What is your *problem*, McQueary?"

"*My* problem?" Cleo rounded a hulking old television to look Billie in the eye again. "My problem is that I'm finally, *finally* on a spaceship, just like I've always wanted to be, except I don't understand how it works or how me and my friends are going to survive for the next seven years, and the only person who can help me is the giant shit stain of an operating system!"

"Sounds like you've got it made, actually," Billie snarled. "I'll just go back into the computer, and then you'll have everything you ever wanted."

Cleo stared. The detail in the projection really was immaculate—she could see Billie's pupils dilating, the loose hairs flying free from her ponytail, the muscle twitching in her jaw. "But I don't want you to go away. I want to work with you."

Billie's frown deepened. "Well, you can't always get what you want."

"But—"

"You don't want to work with me, McQueary," Billie said, stepping even closer in a way that made Cleo very aware of her heartbeat in her ears. "What would you say is the appeal, hmm? That the first crew I ever led, which included my little brother, are all dead and gone now? That my life's work, apparently, is a failure on a historic scale? That I'm a *fucking computer* now, with no obvious purpose and questionable recall abilities? Or is it that I have had about two hours and sixteen minutes to process not only these new developments, but the fact that I'm going to have to spend the rest of my goddamn life on this goddamn ship, which will consist of—if I'm lucky—getting you and your friends to Proxima Centauri B in one piece before I have to watch you freeze and starve to death?"

Cleo blinked. "Do you, uh . . . Do you need more time to process, is that—"

Billie pinched the bridge of her nose again. "No, McQueary. I need to teach you how this ship works so you don't die in some horrible dark matter explosion."

"Hey." Cleo surprised herself by reaching out and floating her hand through the space just above Billie's holographic arm, so it was almost a reassuring pat. "I can't do much about the, um, everything else. But I promise I have no plans to freeze or starve or get dark matter exploded to death."

Billie frowned down at Cleo's hand. "You're being nice to me again."

"Yup."

"Because you think I'm going to be your cool space mentor or whatever."

"Uh, no, because you're sad and you need someone to be nice to you. And that 'I am not the woman you grew up idolizing' thing was, like, three whole minutes ago. We're reluctant allies and equals now, try to keep up."

When Billie looked back up at Cleo, she was still frowning. But this time, she didn't look combative so much as she looked like Cleo was a Rubik's Cube she was finding mildly difficult to solve. It made Cleo's skin vibrate. She dropped her arm.

"I don't know about *equals*," Billie said slowly. "I'm still the captain, technically."

"You're as much the captain as I am the chief engineer, Billie. Things have *changed*."

"They sure have."

And with a tiny smile, Billie turned on her heel and kept walking deeper into the lab. Cleo stayed frozen where she was for a second, partly because her heart was pounding like crazy, and partly because it was only just starting to dawn on her exactly what caliber of emotional whiplash she was going to be dealing with here. She watched Billie disappear behind a giant centrifuge. Then she heard her call out, her voice echoing around her cathedral of a lab.

"Come on, McQueary. You'll never make chief engineer if you keep slacking off like this."

✳

TEMPTING AS IT IS to watch McQueary and the hologram bicker, the other three are off elsewhere, doing more important things. Reid is on the flight deck, fiddling with the computer until she figures out how to fire off a radio message. Alone, she calls out into the darkness:

"If anyone's listening, we're on Providence I. If anyone's listening, we're about to jump to near-lightspeed, and we can't turn back. If anyone's listening, tell my dad I love him."

Meanwhile, Yang and Wheeler are searching the quarters. For some reason, they think they'll find some sort of hint as to where everyone disappeared to, which is stupid. But there is plenty else to find in there, if they can manage to recognize it.

The crew of Providence I was unusual in a lot of ways, see, the most relevant to our purposes being that only fifty of them were, technically, crew. The other 153 passengers were civilians—"mission specialists," in Erebus parlance—highly vetted, highly trained, and highly competent civilians whose sole purpose on the ship was to survive the voyage, then figure out how to make farms and babies and civilizations on Proxima B.

As such, the passengers were allowed to bring a lot of personal effects. Most of them were young prodigies, precocious twenty- and thirty-somethings with aspirations too grand for a single, failing planet. Our intrepid investigators could guess what skills they were expected to bring to Society 2.0 based on their belongings: a cello here, a draft of a novel there, a well-loved book of handwritten recipes somewhere else.

Yang, who can presumably list off the names of each specialist from memory, gets wet around the eyes. "This is the worst, Ros," he whispers, though there's no need to whisper. "Look at everything they brought. They were all so hopeful."

Wheeler barely grimaces. "I know, bud. Let's just get through it and get out of here."

"I don't want to just get through it." Yang's puppy-dog eyes are truly something to behold, but Wheeler must be immune to them after so many years. "It's better to feel these things fully, right?"

"LOL," Wheeler intones, without a trace of laughter in their voice. "That's, like, the Abe-iest thing you could have said."

Yang frowns. But Wheeler is already moving on without him, so he puts down the cleats he was holding and follows.

A handful of the passengers were family units. Here's where Yang will get even more weepy. There are holographic photo albums full of mountaintop nature shots and birthday party candids that blink out of their memory sticks to light up the dusty darkness. There are baby blankets and very small shoes—never worn, just packed for the little ones that would have been born along the way. There's a jean jacket covered in enamel pins of cartoon characters and a worn-out copy of Heresies by John Gray, with notes scribbled in every margin.

Those last two are from the same bunk, actually. Yang and Wheeler are searching through it now. In a moment, Yang will find a name scrawled on the inside cover of the book: Elijah Lucas.

ARCHIVED: *Providence* Intracrew Messaging System
Conversation — Capt. Wilhelmina Lucas and Dr. Kristoff
Halvorsen, June 2, 2041

WILHELMINA LUCAS
Hey, Kris, congrats on the all-systems-go

KRISTOFF HALVORSEN
Thank you, Billie. It's a joy and a relief.

WILHELMINA LUCAS
I'm sure
I bet your team has been desperate for some R&R, too

KRISTOFF HALVORSEN
Absolutely. Larson was telling me just yesterday how
    she couldn't wait to sleep for 72 hours straight!

WILHELMINA LUCAS
Ha. Speaking of: Did you see my email? I asked you
    to call me

KRISTOFF HALVORSEN
Must have slipped through the cracks. What's up?

WILHELMINA LUCAS
I was wondering if there's anything you can tell
    me about Jefferson and the others who got sick a
    while back
Obviously, everything's fine now
But if there's any chance that the problem could
    reoccur . . .
Do you understand what I'm asking

KRISTOFF HALVORSEN
You know that I can't share classified info you don't
    have clearance for. The board would have my head.
    We've been over this. I've told you absolutely
    everything I'm able to.

WILHELMINA LUCAS
Yeah, yeah, fine
Okay, just answer me this: Is there anything I should
    be worried about?

KRISTOFF HALVORSEN
Absolutely not, Billie. You can quote me on that.

WILHELMINA LUCAS
Alright, thanks.
In other news: More to come, huh?

KRISTOFF HALVORSEN
Ha!
Also highly classified, I'm afraid.
But I'm sure there's no harm in simply telling
    you that I've started work on further potential
    applications of the engine. Renewable energy, etc.

WILHELMINA LUCAS
[. . .]
Energy?
I thought the engine didn't produce any energy

KRISTOFF HALVORSEN
Right, yes. It's complicated.
And classified, of course.
But it's going to be big, my friend. I only wish you
    could be here to see it.

WILHELMINA LUCAS
Right
[. . .]
Alright, I'll let you go take a nap.
Or get back to work, more like

✳

BILLIE STOPPED IN FRONT of a well-loved whiteboard, and Cleo
watched as she reached, seemingly without thinking, for the

marker sitting on its bottom ledge. Of course, her hand phased through. The little frustrated sound she made in the back of her throat almost made Cleo take pity on her all over again.

"What do you need the marker for, Billie? Maybe I can help."

Billie shoved her hands into her pockets. "It's not," she stammered, "it's just—I was going to explain the, uh. Dark matter engine. And writing things out always—but it doesn't—"

Cleo's heart did a little twirl. Finally, a real explanation. "What if I take the marker and you tell me what to write?"

Billie's face pinched. "That's stupid."

"I'm doing it." Cleo grabbed the marker, uncapped it, and grinned at Billie, standing at the ready.

Billie squinted at her. "Fine," she grumbled. "Sketch our solar system and the Proxima Centauri system."

"I think I can manage better than a sketch," Cleo said. The marker squeaked as she drew.

"Big words for a woman who just gave the sun a smiley face."

"That's my uncommon artistic vision shining through. You're squashing my genius."

"Mm-hmm." Billie leaned over Cleo's shoulder and traced a finger between two of Cleo's polka-dot planets. "Now connect the stars, and the planets, and make it so the lines join together in the space between systems. Like strands of a frayed rope coming together."

Cleo did as she was told, then stood back. Two solar systems, joined together by a thick line that branched at either end to send out a strand to each celestial object. "It's the dark matter web," she said, realizing. "The filaments that connect planets and galaxies and stars to each other and everything else."

"Exactly." Billie's hand did a funny thing, almost like she meant to touch Cleo on the shoulder, but then she thrust it back into her pocket. "This is how Kris explained it to me. The flow of dark matter and dark energy along these filaments is what powers the ship. The engine doesn't burn dark matter. Rather, it *rides* the filaments, so to speak—latches on to one, lets the WIMPs flow through the reactor, and you've got a moving ship."

Weakly Interacting Massive Particles: the stuff dark matter was made of. Cleo had a million questions, most of them along the lines of *How did Kris Halvorsen figure it out?* and *Do you have any of his notes in your computer brain, maybe?* and *When did he find the time to film* Dr. Dark Matter *in between making some of the most groundbreaking quantum advances in the history of mankind?*, but she thought maybe she should start at the beginning.

"So the vortex I saw in the middle of the engine ring—"

"—is the core of our dark matter filament, yes, flowing through and powering the engine." Billie leaned across Cleo again to point at one of the smaller strands emerging from a planet. "Right now, we're here, riding the filament that connects Earth to the larger pathway between our sun and Proxima Centauri." She traced along the line to where it joined the others. "Once we leave the Oort Cloud, we'll reach the dark matter superhighway, if you will, and then it's off to the races."

Cleo tapped the marker against her mouth. She had only vague memories of news stories and interviews that had revealed bits and pieces of this explanation. Hearing it all together now, however, something didn't seem right. "So the engine transforms the kinetic energy of dark matter into kinetic energy for the ship. The reaction doesn't actually generate any energy."

"Yes."

"But they built and tested the engine before it was attached to the ship. So where did the kinetic energy go?"

Billie frowned at the whiteboard. "I don't know."

"And right now," Cleo said, starting to pace, waving the marker in absentminded loops as she went, "we're not moving at our final, near-lightspeed rate yet. Does the dark matter start moving faster as soon as we're out of our solar system? That seems awfully convenient."

"What are you saying?"

"And the light!" Cleo pointed the marker at Billie like a smoking gun. "What was the flash of light on Launch Day about, if no energy is being generated?"

"I'm not—" Billie gave her head a little shake like she hoped it would dislodge something. "I must be missing something. It must not have loaded yet. Kris explained it better . . ."

Cleo chewed on the marker cap, feeling unsettled. "Did you ever actually work on the engine? Or even see it?"

"No. It was so secret, so proprietary. They just told me the basics of how it worked, to relay to the press."

"Did Dr. Halvorsen ever explain how they were testing it?"

"No, that was also classified."

"Did you ever feel like something didn't add up?"

Billie ran a hand over her mouth, her gaze growing distant. "I'm trying to think."

Cleo flung her arms up in desperation. "Alright, I don't know, did you ever notice *anything* weird going on with the engine?"

Billie gasped. She froze, staring unfocused at some point past Cleo's head as her eyes buzzed fast enough to become bright green blurs. And then she exhaled, and looked at Cleo.

"Four engineers on Kris's team got sick."

Cleo dropped the marker. "*What?*"

Billie pinched the bridge of her nose tighter than ever, like she was trying to keep the memory from escaping out her eyes. "They wouldn't tell me what happened, the board just quietly put them on leave. I remember now."

"Sick how?"

"I don't know. I know they all got evaluated, but that—that

was the last I heard of it. I had to—" Billie stopped dead. "I didn't see the results until I started going through Kris's classified files."

Cleo dragged both hands through her hair. "Why were you going through his files? Wasn't he your partner?"

"He was my *friend*—" Billie's mouth fell open, her eyes fixed on some point in the middle distance. "But he—he said something. Something about using the engine for renewable energy."

Cleo's eyes flew back to the diagram of the dark matter web. "But the engine doesn't generate energy."

"That's what Kris told me." Billie ran her hand over her mouth again. "But it wasn't—it wasn't true, there was *something* wrong—"

As Cleo watched Billie's fingertips tremble, watched more wispy bits of golden hair escape from her ponytail, watched her shoulders clench and unclench with every bit of memory that revealed itself, she realized: There had to be a reason why Billie was an asshole. Why she could cry. Why Captain Lucas had made such a perfect, lifelike copy of herself.

Cleo clenched her fist around an idea and pounded the whiteboard triumphantly. "Billie, this might be a little forward of me, but let's go to the flight deck. I'm going to need to look at your code."

Billie frowned at her again, but this time it was tinged with something like fear. "Why?" she asked, her voice smaller than Cleo had yet heard it.

"Because I think I know what you were built for. I think Captain Lucas knew there was going to be a mystery that she might not be around to solve." Cleo jabbed a finger at the air right in front of Billie's forehead. "So she tapped you."

✳

THEY FIND A LOT in Elijah's bunk. A desiccated succulent in a tiny pot. An ancient copy of The Joy of Cooking *with three different sets of handwriting marking up the recipes. A vintage ukulele, with signs of a meticulous polish job still shining through.*

All that, and Wheeler gets distracted by one of Elijah's uniforms. Outwardly, it looks just like every other one they've seen; every crew member had a few breathable blue-gray shirts, matching pants, and an official Providence *bomber jacket, and the ones that weren't being worn when they all disappeared in a flash of light were mostly folded neatly on the shelves at the base of each bunk. Elijah's uniform was no different. It was folded a little more sloppily, maybe.*

But Wheeler notices something: a second jacket, with a sleeve that isn't lying quite the way the other ones did. They pick it up, see the name printed on its breast, and frown. And when they turn the strangely stiff sleeve inside out, they gasp. They run after Yang, who's already walking away, scrubbing the cuff of his hoodie under his nose. And Wheeler shows him the name, the sleeve, peels back the lining to reveal a layer of something silvery.

"It's Dr. Halvorsen's jacket, in Elijah Lucas's quarters," they say. "This is some sort of protective lining. I think someone knew the crew was in danger." Yang frowns, still not understanding, and Wheeler says:

"I don't know if we can trust Billie."

CHAPTER 4

ARCHIVED: *Providence* Intracrew Messaging System
Conversation — Capt. Wilhelmina Lucas and Mission
Specialist Elijah Lucas, June 30, 2041

WILHELMINA LUCAS
Hey, Jar Jar

ELIJAH LUCAS
Thought we were addressing each other professionally
  on our work comms, Captain!!

WILHELMINA LUCAS
You're hilarious
But if you can contain your glee at my hubris for
  the next 45 seconds, this is important

ELIJAH LUCAS
OK shoot

WILHELMINA LUCAS
Alright
so
[. . .]

ELIJAH LUCAS
Any time now, Bilbo

WILHELMINA LUCAS
Shut up

Whatever okay so you're going to find a jacket with
    Kris's name on it with your stuff tomorrow
The jacket might feel stiffer and a little heavier
    than yours, maybe
But it is extremely important that you wear Kris's
    jacket instead

ELIJAH LUCAS
Um
That's weird. Why

WILHELMINA LUCAS
Listen
Please
I literally cannot tell you anything else but I need you
    to PROMISE me that you will put that jacket on before
    they activate the engine and you will NOT take it off

ELIJAH LUCAS
Oh
Yeah sure I promise
Is everything OK, Bill?

WILHELMINA LUCAS
[. . .]

ELIJAH LUCAS
Baby brother classified. Got it

WILHELMINA LUCAS
Hey
You know I love you, right

ELIJAH LUCAS
Yeah
Love you too, Captain

✳

CLEO WAS ELBOW-DEEP IN Billie's source code, so to speak, trying to
ignore the woman herself, pacing behind her and gnawing loudly

on her glasses (the *detail!* the *realism!)* while Kaleisha fiddled with the radio and ignored them, when the elevator dinged and a voice rang out across the flight deck.

"*Billie!*"

Cleo turned away from the console to see Ros storming out of the elevator, Abe close behind them. They had a blue jacket in their hand, for some reason, and were brandishing it in Billie's shocked face before Cleo could form any thought besides: *Ros is angry, and that means there's been a war crime.*

"What did you know?" Ros snarled.

"I don't know what you're talking about, Wheeler, I—"

"I'm talking about this." Ros peeled back the lining from the cuff of the sleeve, and Cleo saw something flash matte silver inside. "I can't say for certain, Billie, but this sure looks like Dr. Halvorsen's special radiation-resistant jacket that *someone* stole and gave to her brother and no one else. Did you know the engine was dangerous in some way? Did you care at all about the lives of everyone else on your crew?"

Cleo knew that Ros and Billie couldn't hurt each other if they tried, but the ready-to-pounce bent of their bodies had her rushing into the space between them anyway, thinking of her parents, thinking of screaming matches in the kitchen and fragile things thrown as warning shots, thinking of raging galaxies threatening to collide, and she held a hand out in front of each of them, uselessly.

"*Fuck you*," Billie hissed at Ros over her head, and Cleo flinched at the furious shell that had once again snapped closed around Billie, even after Cleo had just seen something of her soft insides. "Fuck you for even suggesting—"

"Hey," Kaleisha said, taking Ros's wrist and pulling them away. "You don't get to talk to them like that. Do you know what Halvorsen's jacket was doing with Elijah's stuff or not?"

"I don't—" Billie stared at the jacket, her voice almost shaking. "I'm not—*fuck*."

She hit herself in the forehead with the heel of her hand, and Cleo was reaching out—to do what? Pull Billie's hand away, to shake her by the shoulders? *What?!*—before she knew what she was doing. "Hey, hey—"

"Whose side are you on, Cleo?" Ros said through gritted teeth. They looked even paler than usual, their freckles standing out starkly in the dusty-gold light of the flight deck.

"Since when are there sides?" Cleo cried. "She's having trouble accessing all her memories right now. They're coming back slowly, though, so just give it a goddamn minute."

Ros crossed their arms. "I'll believe it when I see it."

"Okay, look," Cleo said, hopping back over to the pilot console to scroll through Billie's code. "Captain Lucas's whole life and personality and everything are encoded here. I don't know enough about AI at this level to tell specific memories apart, and maybe I couldn't even if I was an expert, because this is, like, just an ungodly amount of data. And Billie has had to sort through an entire lifetime of memories in just a couple of hours, but she's doing it. It's basically the sexiest programming I've ever seen."

Billie went inexplicably pink in the face. "I, uh—"

"So what have you already remembered?" Kaleisha asked.

"Um." Billie blinked hard. "Kris lied to me—and by extension, the world—about how the dark matter engine works. And about whether it was safe."

Kaleisha, Ros, and Abe all broke out into a clamor of questions.

"Why the *ever-loving*—"

"Does that mean he knew, like, what was going to—"

"Why would he do that? What was he hiding—"

"I don't *know*," Billie shouted, hands at her temples. "I'm trying, but I don't—I don't remember."

"Do you think," Abe said slowly, nodding his head like he always did when he was thinking through a problem, "that maybe, if you did find out why Halvorsen lied, it would be a more recent memory? Closer to Launch Day, I mean."

"A newer memory would have had less time to form neural pathways to the rest of the brain," Ros added begrudgingly. They were sweating now, weirdly enough. Clammy-looking. Cleo wondered if they were already motion sick, even though the ship hadn't jumped to near-lightspeed yet. "Which would make it harder for Billie to access right away."

"Right." Billie dragged her hands down her face, her eyes flicking around haphazardly. "A newer memory—"

"You said you'd accessed Halvorsen's classified files after he let his plans to use the engine for energy slip," Cleo said. Billie nodded distantly. "Maybe there was something in his notes. Something you didn't find until just a couple days before the launch."

"Something—"

"Something about the engine? About what it did to those engineers?"

"I—" Billie looked almost close to tears again, her eyes buzzing faster than ever. "I feel close, I feel—"

"Hey," Cleo said quietly. "You can do this, remember?"

Billie's eyes went still, and for a split second Cleo almost thought Billie was looking at her softly, like her frantic mind had stilled just for her. But then Billie gasped, and she clamped her hand over her mouth.

"I knew," she whispered.

Cleo stopped breathing. "What."

"Knew *what*?" Ros said, voice going hoarse.

"I knew that it was radiation from the engine that made those engineers sick, that Kris—" Billie fisted her hands through her hair, knocking her ponytail off-kilter and leaving loose tufts hanging by her ears. "Oh God, the engine was generating energy somehow, dangerous amounts of it, and I found out, and I didn't know why he was covering it up, but I knew it wasn't going to be good if everything went ahead as planned—"

"So why didn't you tell anybody?" Abe cried.

"There was no time," Billie said. "I only found those last notes a couple days before the launch."

"You were the captain, you couldn't have pulled some strings?" Kaleisha looked shocked more than anything.

"The board wouldn't have listened." Billie's eyes were wet again, bloodshot again. "You can't understand how much pressure we were all under, to get the engine working and the mission underway. Everything was riding on it—the fucking future of humanity, yes, but also Erebus's bottom line, and presumably whatever other *incredibly* lucrative applications of dark energy they were planning with Kris. The board would never have canceled the flight, not for my hunch, not if they put those engineers on leave instead of doing anything about it."

"So you didn't even try?" Cleo said, scaring herself with how small she sounded.

Billie looked at Cleo like something was slipping out of her hands. "Maybe I could have," she said. "I should have. I don't know why I didn't."

They were all quiet for an inhale, for an exhale, trying to grasp the enormity of what had happened as Neptune, just a bluish prick of light, slid out of view.

"Billie—" Cleo said, not sure what would come next. But then Billie's eyes widened, and she never found out.

"Brace yourselves," Billie said.

And then the fabric of space *bent* around them.

Cleo felt it heavy in her cells, the acceleration to some horrible, impossible speed. She was a car speeding off a cliff, a plane getting swept up in a hurricane.

Motion. Sick. All the way down to her soul, like Billie had said.

Nothing moved around her, but the stars outside the flight deck window started sliding by faster and faster, as everything in front of the ship blurred into hazy white. Cleo stumbled like she'd been punched in the throat. She grabbed at her knees, trying to remember how to think. She was underwater, entire nebulae sparking at her peripheral vision, and she was only mostly sure her guts hadn't been blown out from between her shoulder blades.

"*Breathe through it, McQueary,*" she heard, as if from a universe away. She blinked, trying to get the lightspeed fuzz out from the space between her ears. There was a pair of glasses, she thought, possibly attached to a worried face and a body in a black sweater, crouching in front of her—

"*Ros!*"

Abe's scream cut bluntly through the fog. Cleo turned away from Billie and managed to focus her eyes, at last, on the cardigan-clad heap on the floor that was supposed to be her friend.

"Med bay. Now." Cleo reached with all her scrambled molecules for the sound of Billie's voice, and she remembered how to move.

✳

THE THING ABOUT DARK matter is that nobody knows very much about it. The universe is chock-full of it, we know that. Nothing else could exist without it—it was the framework that the first stars built themselves on, it keeps galaxies spinning long after they should have stopped, and the web that it forms between every object in existence is the closest thing anyone has to empirical evidence that everything is, as the hippies say, connected. The scientific community is also marginally sure that dark matter is made up of Weakly Interacting Massive Particles—or WIMPs, if you want to be cute about it—and that these can pass through matter, maybe spacetime, and possibly even dimensions without doing anything. Except, of course, when they want to, like when they hold galaxies together with their gravity. Or when people force them to, like they did with the dark matter engine.

But that's the most anyone can say with any degree of certainty. Even the Providence scientists—the ones who, if you'll recall, staked 203 lives and the continued survival of human civilization on their applied knowledge of dark matter—couldn't have said for sure how the engine worked. They invented it the way Alexander Fleming invented penicillin, or Ruth Wakefield invented the chocolate chip cookie: accidentally. In retrospect, a lot of those guys were morons. One time, one of the physics team leaders put a sweet potato wrapped in two layers of tin foil in the office microwave. That's the kind of talent they had working on the most ambitious space program in human history.

But that's not the point.

The point is that, instead of ruining everything, the scientists stumbled into a replicable reaction. Dark matter in, face-melting amounts of energy out. They ran all their tests, they peer-reviewed the shit out of it, and the engine worked the same every time. They didn't need to know how it worked, they figured, to trust that it would deliver the crew of the Providence to Proxima Centauri B, make Erebus Industries truckloads of cash, and maybe even save the world. Good enough, they all collectively shrugged, and went back to work.

But the thing about trusting in something you don't fully

understand is that you can't. Not when it comes to science, not when it comes to people's lives, and definitely not when it comes to the darker parts of the universe. Halvorsen understood this, for better or for worse. (Those engineers that got put on medical leave understood it too, very much for worse.)

So Halvorsen started running his own after-hours tests, with the board's blessing, to answer all the countless questions he still had. Where was all that energy coming from? Was it scalable for a world desperate for a way to both halt the climate crisis and maintain the relentless pace of capitalism? And what was happening—off the record, of course—when that energy came in contact with a human body?

Halvorsen got some answers. First, he learned that the energy was coming from Somewhere. Second, he found out that this Somewhere was not going to keep giving up its energy indefinitely. And third, if you want to talk about things that science wasn't yet capable of understanding, this place was on a whole new level.

This is one more reason why he had to lie to Lucas. He knew her. He knew that the minor risks (of hurting some people, of dabbling in horrors beyond human comprehension) would over-shadow, in her mind, the globally redemptive benefits.

But Lucas, who (for better or worse) knew Halvorsen right back, caught on to him. Halvorsen was too obsessed with his work not to let something slip. He was just single-minded enough to brush aside safety concerns if he thought he was on the verge of a breakthrough. And Lucas, never one to let something like an all-the-way-to-the-top security clearance stop her, knew that he would never stop taking notes, no matter what questionable shit he was getting up to.

So. Let's recap what we know so far. In more or less chrono-logical order, so the whole class can follow along:

In the months leading up to the launch, several engineers

get sick. Nobody talks about it. Halvorsen implies to Lucas that there's more to the engine than he's let on.

Lucas spends the month before the launch growing suspicious and uploading her suspicions into a hologram that will be able to figure out what happened if, by some astronomical chance, Lucas wasn't there to do it herself. She hacks into Halvorsen's notes; she discovers the radiation-resistant lining he's sewn into his Providence jacket. And at the last minute, she finds out exactly what Halvorsen knows.

Just before launch, Lucas steals the jacket and gives it to her brother, who doesn't fucking wear it like she told him to.

Launch Day is—well. It's Launch Day. You don't need it spelled out for you again.

Twenty years later, McQueary touches the engine and a wave of energy knocks her and her friends off their feet.

Now, Wheeler is comatose.

Have you figured it out yet? Shout it out when you do.

✳

ROS'S CURLY RED HAIR puddled around their head when Abe placed them on the hospital bed. That's what Cleo's lightspeed-addled brain chose to focus on, *had* to focus on, because the alternative was looking at Ros's slack, washed-out face, and that just wasn't an option.

Hope there's some curl cream on this ship for us both, bud, she thought fuzzily. She let Kaleisha squeeze the blood out of her arm once, twice, before Billie's voice made it to them through the haze.

"Reid," she said, her voice crackling tensely, "I think we need epinephrine. Do you remember where it is, from before?"

"I think so."

"Great. Please get me a dose."

"Is there, uh." Abe swallowed thickly. "Is there anything I can do to help? Scan their vitals, maybe?"

"The bed does it itself." Billie's eyes immediately started flicking through whatever data the bed was feeding to her. "Body temp is 109, pulse is 190, blood pressure is 210 over 160—"

"That doesn't sound right," Abe said, hugging his arms around himself. "They would be dead, right? Or dying? Because that sounds like a massive fever and maybe heart failure?"

"Well, they're not dead."

"Can you check again?"

Billie's right eye twitched. "The numbers are plugged straight into my head, Yang, I don't know what more you want—"

Cleo swayed on her feet as her vision went misty. Her head pounded with every heartbeat, and her nose felt oddly stuffy. Kaleisha's hand on her back as she arrived with the epinephrine was the only thing Cleo could feel with any clarity. Again, she wished that she was unconscious instead of Ros. Ros would probably tell her that this was a normal physical effect of near-lightspeed. Surely they would assure her that she wasn't, like, having a stroke.

Kaleisha pulled Ros's pants down by a few inches and carefully slid the needle of the syringe into their thigh. "God, they *are* burning up," she said, voice trembling even as her hands stayed steady. "Are the numbers going down, at least?"

"No," Billie said. "They're rising."

"*What?*"

"You heard me. Maybe I should do an EEG, the bed does that too—"

"Is there a defibrillator?" Abe asked, frantically opening cabinets. "If their heart stops—"

"Yang."

Billie's voice was suddenly quiet, full of alarm and awe. Abe removed his head from the cabinet he'd been rummaging through and froze. Cleo realized she was going to have to look away from the spot on the wall she'd been fixating on and look at Ros.

When she managed it, she thought she was seeing stars again. Except no, everything around Ros was clear. It was just her friend's eyes were open, and glowing gold.

What.

Kaleisha dropped the empty needle, and by the time it landed with a clatter she was already reaching for Ros's face. She winced, though, and froze, like the air around Ros had sizzled at her fingers.

"They're cold," she stammered. "Like, freezing. Billie, what the ever-loving hell is—"

And then Ros sat up, with a rattling gasp. Their blank, golden eyes stared past all of them. Cleo realized that their hands, clenched in the bedsheets, were crusted over with frost.

"Ros—" Abe cried, reaching out to them.

And then Ros screamed, and they were all knocked backward by a burst of icy air.

Cleo scrambled to her feet first. Ros's eyes were blue again, but bloodshot and petrified like a caged animal's, and they were struggling for breath, unable to look away from the icy mist pouring from their hands.

"Ros." Cleo stepped forward, shivering almost as badly as Ros was. If their positions were reversed, Ros would be helping, examining, saying soothing words, *something.*

"Cleo, no," Ros gasped, every word sounding like it had to be ripped out of them. "Don't—you shouldn't—"

But Cleo didn't listen, because her friend was in pain, and

something had to be done. So she reached out, ignoring the halo of biting cold that surrounded Ros's body, and closed her hand around their wrist—

Everything went black. And then blacker than black.

And then Cleo was somewhere else. Somewhere wavering and dark gold and slow, where time felt different, or maybe where time didn't exist at all. A cavernous room she'd never been in, with snow (*snow?*) drifting languidly past her eyes. And there, standing in front of her in the low light, was Ros.

Except their eyes were gold again. Glowing gold, and angry. And as they raised their hand in the air, bits of ice and snow latched onto their hand, forming an icy projectile that they reared back, and *threw*—

Cleo gasped and fell backward, right on her ass. The world was right again, fluorescent white instead of honey-thick, but nothing felt okay. Her body ached like it had been ripped apart and put back together proton by proton. She was pretty sure her nose was bleeding, but she didn't have the energy to wipe it away. It was all she could do to heave herself up onto one elbow and swallow the bile threatening to rise up in her throat—

And then Ros was screaming again. And the air was bending again, like rubber, like lightspeed, and the med bay was impossibly, kaleidoscopically folding over on itself in a way that made Cleo's eyes hurt. For a split second, beds and walls and floors were bending up and *over* Cleo's head; some instinct told her to look toward Kaleisha, who was staring at the phenomenon with a wild, wide-eyed interest. She stepped forward and into the fold— and with a deafening crack like thunder, everything unfolded, and Kaleisha vanished from the side of Ros's bed and reappeared across the room.

"What—"

It was too much. Cleo squeezed her eyes shut. She heard

frantic sounds and delayed fear spilling incoherently out of Kaleisha's mouth, heard Abe stumble toward her, heard them both stumble toward Ros. And then she heard something else.

"What happened, McQueary?"

She opened her eyes. Billie was crouching beside her, her breathing heavy and her eyes blown wide.

Cleo blinked. She watched distractedly as Abe helped Ros pull their hands out of the frozen bedsheets. "I saw something."

"Saw what?"

"Um." Cleo shut her eyes again. She was sure she was imagining the sound of electrons humming all around her, miniscule waves of energy coursing through everything. Everything except Billie, who was just empty space and the faintest buzz of photons. "Ros. With the golden eyes. Looking very angry. It was snowing."

Billie's fingers twitched, like she was dying to write it all down, make the connections, solve the equation. "So it wasn't here."

Cleo shook her head and swallowed around her leaden tongue. "I don't think it was now either," she said. She glanced again at Ros and the unformed ice falling from their fingers. She knew in her bones that the skilled, furious Ros she had seen was a vision of—well. "I think it was—"

"The future."

Cleo nodded silently. Billie's green eyes swept over her face, searching.

"There's one piece left," Billie said. "One more memory that will explain this. It's on the tip of my tongue. Help me remember."

Cleo finally sat all the way up. She squared her shoulders so her voice wouldn't come out as shaky as she felt.

"Why did I just see the future?" she asked.

Billie sucked in a shaking breath. Her irises went blurry, then still.

"The dark matter engine," she whispered. "This is what it does to people. Gives them . . . abilities." Billie fell back on her heels, gripping her hair with a white-knuckled hand like she could get her skull out of her head if she pulled hard enough. "This is what it did to those engineers. Kris knew. And so did I, at the end."

✳

WELL, THEY FIGURED IT OUT.
I wish there could have been a better way.

✳

ARCHIVED: *The New York Times*, July 9, 2042, "Providence Chief Engineer Presumed Dead in Apparent Suicide"

ST. AUGUSTINE - To most of the world, Dr. Kristoff Halvorsen was the face of the Providence I disaster. If that blinding flash of light is the first thing anyone remembers from Launch Day, the second is the now-infamous video of Dr. Halvorsen, who had been tasked with the countdown, watching first in shock, then horror, then anguish as it became clear that the entire crew was gone. His lack of composure in those first terrible moments was deeply relatable to viewers around the world; his honesty and stoicism in the following months would prove indispensable to a grieving people.

Halvorsen, 52, was reported missing from his St. Augustine home on July 1, a year to the day after the Providence disaster. On July 9, following eight days of searching, state and federal officials declared the renowned scientist dead in absentia.

"We have found no evidence whatsoever of foul play," said St. Johns County Chief of Police Wilson

Connolly at a press conference Wednesday morning.
"All evidence suggests that Dr. Halvorsen took his
own life. We found a note suggesting as much in his
home, alongside several items of recovered tech from
the Providence."

"I cannot begin to speculate what he was trying to
do with the tech, no," Connolly continued. "That's way
above my pay grade. Our experts have confirmed that it
seems to have been modified, but to what end remains
unknown."

"Dr. Halvorsen will be remembered for his quiet
charisma and endlessly giving disposition as much as
for his contributions to the Providence mission and
to the fields of mechanical engineering and quantum
physics," said Professor Jillian Darbandi, Halvorsen's
former colleague at Stanford University. "He wanted
nothing more than to make the world—make the whole
universe, actually—a better place."

CHAPTER 5

leo didn't sleep that first night.

(Not that there was such a thing as night, in deep space. But the ship's lights had gone from white to gold to a deep, gritty orange, to trigger the passengers' circadian rhythms. The Erebus people really had thought of nearly everything.)

Every time Cleo let herself drift off, she was plunged into half-waking dreams of a life that wasn't hers. The same person was in all of them, a blond-haired white boy, then teen, then man whose face grew more and more familiar as the night wore on. She saw him in grubby cargo shorts that didn't quite cover his scraped-up knees, in a graduation gown, in a welding suit. She watched as he meticulously arranged his Thomas the Tank Engine tracks; then as he wrote op-eds about the urgent need for a radical new approach to eliminating fossil fuels; then as he adjusted a rooftop telescope, the stars reflecting in his eyes as he looked, smiling, at Billie, who smiled back.

Cleo watched his hair get grayer, watched his wall fill up with degrees and awards, watched his arms stay sinewy and strong as he got his hands greasy in the guts of the *Providence* beside his colleagues. She felt his ambition, his curiosity, his shameless desperation for knowledge. It was so easy to lose herself in him. After all, she had always felt the same.

Every time she woke her headache deepened, and it was harder and stickier to come back to herself. So she held her eyes open until they felt dry and tacky, and she kept herself awake by pinching at the insides of her elbows and pulling at the sweaty tufts of her hair. And in the early hours of the morning, when the orange lights were just barely bleeding blue and Cleo could feel her heartbeat in the blood vessels of her eyes, his name vibrated through her head, no longer avoidable: *Kristoff Halvorsen*. Billie's partner, the head engineer, who had done this, who was gone.

✳

ARCHIVED: *Providence* Intracrew Messaging System
Conversation — Abraham Yang and Ros Wheeler, July 13, 2061

ABRAHAM YANG
Aren't these communicators cool?? Glad we found them
    in the crew quarters
So we can still talk without waking up Kal

ROS WHEELER
For sure. Providence Intracrew Messaging System sure
    is a mouthful though

ABRAHAM YANG
It shall henceforth be known as PIMS
Texting is now pimming
Pim me, baby

ROS WHEELER
[. . .]

ABRAHAM YANG
You feeling okay bud?

ROS WHEELER
Yeah
Might run another round of vitals checks on all of us

ABRAHAM YANG
No!!
ILLEGAL
You should be resting, I shouldn't even be keeping
   you up

ROS WHEELER
Fine
It's fine

ABRAHAM YANG
[. . .]
Will you PLEASE tell me how you're doing I can't
   take it

ROS WHEELER
I just
[. . .]
I didn't hurt anyone earlier, did I? With the ice?

ABRAHAM YANG
No not at all!! You saw us we're all fine

ROS WHEELER
Are you sure though

ABRAHAM YANG
Yes 100%

ROS WHEELER
Okay
I'm still gonna run another check

✳

NEIL THORNE HAD BEEN a writer. Captain Lucas's Erebus Industries colleagues and grad school friends, knowing Lucas's penchant for Shakespeare and very serious poetry, often assumed that her fiancé wrote stuff like that, or groundbreaking reporting for The New Yorker at least.

But Neil wrote what many serious poets and staff writers for The New Yorker would call fluff. He wrote lightly comedic science fiction that once led a reviewer to call him "his generation's answer to Douglas Adams," about which Neil would never shut up. He wrote short stories about love and trees and talking gorillas that taught blowhards the meaning of life; and his publishing credits in The New Yorker were fourteen winning submissions to the cartoon caption contest, each of which was framed at the place of honor above his desk. He also wrote letters, which Captain Lucas would read and reread until they were coffee-stained and soft at the creases, and keep in her pockets until she inevitably forgot them and washed them with her pants.

(Later, when she was furious at everything, she would be especially furious with herself for ruining them. Particularly what turned out to be the last one.)

Once they got over their surprise that Neil wasn't the kind of writer who would ever even be longlisted for the National Book Award, people moved on to surprise that Lucas was marrying him at all. Most (not all) were polite enough not to make that face that Lucas knew to mean, Didn't you used to date women? I've forgotten that bisexuals exist. Some (not most) were polite enough not to stare pointedly at her crisp ponytail next to Neil's overgrown poof of curls, at her pressed slacks next to his perpetually ripped jeans. But very few (not even some) were polite enough not to ask some version of the question "How did you know you were going to marry him?" by which they meant, "Why are you marrying him?" by which they meant, "Why are you marrying him?"

At which Lucas would put a hand on Neil's chest, glare murderously at everyone else, and say, "He makes me laugh." And everyone who had only met her in the lifetime after her parents died would shut up at that, as they tried to remember if they had ever seen Captain Lucas laugh.

✳

WHEN CLEO CAME INTO the med bay the next morning balancing two coffees, a chai latte, and a green tea from the replicator in her arms, the buzzing in her chest decelerated, just a bit. Kaleisha and Ros were passed out in adjacent cots, and Abe was nodding sleepily in a chair between them. Battered, all of them, but alive. Cleo too.

Abe twitched all the way awake when Cleo thrust his coffee at him. He took Kaleisha's chai and Ros's green tea too, and put them carefully on the bedside table. "Did you sleep okay?" he asked, lifting the mug to his face like it was the Holy Grail. "You look—"

"Slept fine," Cleo muttered, turning away before Abe could read any more into her bleary, bloodshot eyes. "The bunks are comfy enough, so if we all wanna pick a room once we—"

"—stop being genetically modified abominations?" Cleo hadn't realized Ros was awake. Their voice was rough and bitter in a way Cleo had never heard before, though they still emerged from their blanket cocoon with a tiny smile to accept their tea from Abe. "I don't think that's gonna happen, Cleo."

"That's not what . . ." Cleo blinked back the prickly feeling behind her eyes. "I was going to say, once we're all feeling better. Whatever that ends up looking like."

Ros just looked at her for a long moment before closing their eyes to breathe in the tea smell. Their fingers, wrapped around the mug, were a little pink and flaky, but not frostbitten or otherwise damaged. Their eyes were still blue too—another relief. Cleo wondered how long she would have to wait for them to turn that terrible, glowing gold again.

A loud groan made her turn around. Kaleisha was stirring on her cot, stretching her arms over her head before wincing and putting them back down.

"All the money they spent on this ship and they couldn't pay up for comfier hospital beds?"

Abe put his coffee down so fast it spilled a little, and ran a soothing hand over Kaleisha's face. "Hey, baby. How are you feeling?"

Kaleisha smiled up at him, like she'd forgotten all the soreness and confusion the second he'd touched her. "Best guess? Like my molecules can't decide whether they want to be here or somewhere else. And also like I just decided that bench-pressing would be a cool hobby to try."

"Well, not that I have any frame of reference, but it makes sense that teleporting or whatever it was you did last night would have taken an unprecedented toll on your body," said Ros. A muscle clenched in their jaw. "But I checked your lactic acid levels last night, and they're not too far out of the ordinary. You should heal up just fine."

Kaleisha leaned around Abe to smile at Ros. "Thanks for checking. How are you, though?"

Ros still looked pale, a bit green even, and the tendons in their hands were straining as they gripped their mug like they wanted to break it.

"Totally fine," they said unconvincingly.

Kaleisha squeezed Abe's hand. "What about you? Any changes?"

"Nope, nothing." Abe shrugged, though it looked more like a wince to Cleo. "Sorry if any of you were hoping for Fantastic Four vibes."

"Better no powers at all than the ability to accidentally drop the air temperature in a pressure-controlled ship traveling through the vacuum of space, is what I always say," Ros muttered.

Abe smiled at them sympathetically. "Yeah, not to be insensitive or anything, but I'm happy not to be adding to the dark matter weirdness."

"This must be why Billie took Dr. Halvorsen's jacket," Cleo said, gnawing on the inside of her cheek. "To stop her brother from getting freaky powers."

A shadow crossed over Ros's face again. "Has to be."

Kaleisha pursed her lips. "Why don't we ask her? I really want to hear her explain herself."

"No." Cleo didn't realize she'd shouted until she saw Kaleisha frowning at her. She took a deep breath. What she wanted was to shout at Billie—for dooming the *Providence* and the world and Cleo's dreams—which was exactly why she desperately wanted not to see her. "I mean, I don't think we should. You were right, Ros, we really don't know if we can trust Billie."

"Oh, I've changed my mind." Ros sipped their tea delicately. "I don't think she's lying to us. In fact, she was actually very honest with us as soon as she was able to be. I'm still extremely curious, though, about why she thought protecting her brother and no one else was in her crew's best interest."

Abe nodded energetically. "She's probably the only one who can answer all our questions, Cleo. I'm gonna call her."

"Abe, don't—"

"Hey, Billie?"

Pop. Billie appeared at the foot of Kaleisha's bed, apparently halfway through cleaning her glasses on the hem of her sweater. She looked up at all of them in surprise. Cleo wondered whether her hologram glasses actually got hologram smudges on them or the wiping was just a nervous tic. Then she remembered that she was furious at Billie, and didn't care.

"Hey," Billie said, having enough sense to sound sheepish, at least. "You're all, um. Conscious."

Cleo slurped her coffee loudly. "No thanks to you."

Billie's mouth opened soundlessly, then closed again. Her eyes were sunken, like she hadn't slept, or recharged, or whatever it was she did. The tangible air of remorse around her made Cleo want to grind her teeth down to nubs.

Billie frowned, chewing on the inside of her cheek. "You look tired."

Cleo's headache flared. "You're not exactly the picture of effortless beauty yourself."

Billie's mouth twisted, and she turned pointedly to Abe. "Did you need something?"

"I, uh." Abe blinked back and forth between Billie and Cleo. "It's not that important. But we were all kind of wondering what you knew about these powers that have, uh, manifested?"

Kaleisha stretched an arm across her shoulder and grimaced at the bone-cracking pop. "Yeah, I'd appreciate knowing what's going on with, you know, our bodies."

"And brains," Ros grumbled.

"And I would still love to dig a little deeper into how you got to be a captain when your decision-making process sucks so many balls," Cleo said through her gritted teeth. At least she wasn't yelling. She counted that as a success.

Billie placed her glasses carefully back on her nose and sighed. "Anything else?" she asked flatly, as if Cleo was an annoying waste of time, and not the only person who saw Billie for who she was.

Cleo's throat tightened. "You're such a dick."

"I'm just checking," Billie snapped, "whether there's anything else you want to interrogate me about, McQueary."

"Oh no, I wouldn't want to impose any further. Especially since looking at my hideous, bedraggled face is obviously such a struggle for you—"

Kaleisha cleared her throat, but when Cleo looked at her she just blinked back pointedly.

"Fine," Billie said, shooting one last glare at Cleo before directing her attention to the other three. "I'll go in order, then. Yang, I spent all night sorting through my memories, my files, and the ship's archives, and it looks like I don't know anything I haven't already told you. Reid, Wheeler, I've also been running simulations, and I still haven't figured out exactly how your powers work, but I'm making progress. And McQueary, I agree that my actions represented a horrific lapse in judgment, and if there were still a space agency with any jurisdiction over me, I would obviously accept my dismissal without contest."

Cleo tried not to visibly vibrate with fury. "Ha. As if they wouldn't have given you an award for your generous sacrifice in the name of their profit margins."

Billie sucked in a breath and held it. "I'm *sorry*. I fucked up. I understand if you're not inclined to forgive me."

Abe dropped his head onto Kaleisha's shoulder. "I forgive you, Billie."

"Whatever." Ros rolled their eyes and downed the last of their tea.

"What do you mean by 'progress'?" Kaleisha asked. "What have you learned about our powers?"

Cleo felt like she was going crazy. "I'm sorry, did I miss something? Or are you all actually ignoring the fact that Billie's apology would barely fly if she'd left dishes in the sink and now we have ants?"

Kaleisha closed her eyes like Cleo was giving her a headache too. "Clo, I swear to God, just drop it."

"Drop what, the teeny-weeny mistake that's defined our entire *lives*?"

Abe shifted nervously in the bed. "Look, Cleo, I know it's hard to accept, but there's nothing we can do about the past, so. Like. Maybe we can stop fighting about it and just figure out where we go from here?"

Cleo dug her fingernails into her biceps, bracing against the stabbing pain behind her eyes. She needed to either keep fighting or never see Billie's face again, but neither seemed like an available option. "Be my guest, Abe. I'm going to go lie down."

"Wait," Billie said, her voice pulling Cleo's eyes away from the gut-churning look of concern on Abe's face. Cleo barely had time to formulate a properly rude deflection before Billie was turning and stomping soundlessly past her toward the elevator. "There's something else I need to teach you about the ship. It's the, uh. Thrusters."

Cleo kept her feet planted where they were. "It can't wait? I thought we were on autopilot—"

"*Now*, McQueary. It's urgent."

Cleo turned to the other three, ready for them to defend her. But Abe still looked worried, and Kaleisha was murmuring something sweet to him, and Ros was rolling over in bed, pulling the sheets up to their ears.

Cleo, feeling very ignored, threw her hands up and trudged after Billie.

✳

ARCHIVED: Halvorsen, Kristoff & Lucas, Wilhelmina, *International Journal of Theoretical Physics*, Mar/Apr 2039, "A Conterminous Dimension Hypothesis for the Reconciliation of the Lambda-CDM Model with the Sangupta-Romanov Paradox"

ABSTRACT: It has long been theorized that dark matter, as it exists in our universe, is made up of Weakly Interacting Massive Particles (WIMPs), the nature of which is still largely unknown but which are understood not to interact with matter except in certain cases involving weak nuclear force and gravity (Kamionkowski, 1997). It has separately been put forth that WIMP theory is fundamentally incompatible with special relativity and quantum field theory, as spacetime and anything occupying it must interact with the electromagnetic force, and dark matter does not (Sangupta & Romanov, 2029). We will attempt to reconcile this paradox, incorporating observations made by the *Providence* Exploratory Team in their attempts to create an engine for interstellar space travel, by hypothesizing that dark matter and its constituent WIMPs exist not in our own spacetime but in an alternate dimension. This alternate dimension would not be "parallel" to our own, as is the common verbiage in the popular imagination, but conterminous—that is, occupying the same four-dimensional manifold but differentiated by a border of unknown nature—allowing dark matter to pass into and through our spacetime without resistance from electromagnetic forces.

※

SPECIFICALLY, NEIL WAS THE first person since the death of her parents who had proved capable of making Captain Lucas laugh so hard that she forgot to pay attention to whether or not she was snorting. She, against all odds, made him laugh too, and Neil's laugh ranked somewhere just above Jupiter's Great Red Spot on Lucas's list of Wonders of the Universe. She had always been drawn to sunshine people—to the people who managed to light up the dark corners of her frantic crank of a mind—and Neil was all light. With him, for the first time, Lucas could almost see beyond her ten-year plan, to a life of laughter and love letters and folding laundry side by side as their favorite podcast played.

When the end came, she couldn't imagine a future that encompassed the next day, let alone the rest of her life. There was just that hospital bed, and endless papers to sign, and Neil's once-strong hand slowly losing its grip on hers. She tried to be his sunshine for once, but all she could come up with was "It's going to be okay," and "I'm not going anywhere," spoken over and over, back and forth, like the most useless spell in the world. The last time she said it, she made Neil laugh, because they both knew by then that it was a lie.

When Neil was gone, everything contracted again. And Captain Lucas, furious that she had so willingly been tricked into wanting—into trusting the universe, given everything it had already taken from her—knew that she would never fall in love again.

"Love makes you stupid" became her mantra, and by "stupid" she meant "sad," and by "sad" she meant "weak," and by "weak" she meant "daring to believe, despite all evidence to the contrary, that the universe has anything to offer but darkness."

✳

BILLIE COULD MAKE THE elevator run with her stupid computer brain, which was good. It meant Cleo didn't have to push any buttons, which might have put her in danger of accidentally making eye contact. It meant she could keep her arms crossed and her gaze fixed on the doors.

"Alright," she grumbled, "what's so important with the thrusters that it couldn't even wait until the caffeine absorbed into my nervous system?"

"There's nothing important with the thrusters. We're on autopilot."

"Then what, pray tell, the *fuck*?"

The elevator door dinged open. Billie had taken them not to the flight deck, but to her lab. She stomped out, leaving Cleo with no choice but to follow.

"You have something to say to me, McQueary. I suggest you get it out of your system now, instead of continuing to snipe at me and push your friends away."

"I'm not pushing anybody away."

"The look on Yang's face just now would beg to differ."

"You're just kind of a garbage person and I know that now. Happy?"

Billie loomed closer. Cleo had the same disorienting sense as before that Billie was an empty space where something should be, that everything else around her was suddenly twice as solid and Billie was just a quietly buzzing void. Listening for the emptiness made her head hurt worse, though, so she tried not to.

"Listen, I guess you're still hung up on how I was your childhood hero or whatever, and you can't deal with the fact that I'm just a person who's made mistakes, but—"

"Oh my God." Cleo dragged her hands through her hair. "You *need* to get over yourself."

"*I* need to get over myself?"

"Do you think I care about your boring fame complex right now?" Billie's eyes went round. Cleo felt a few hairs pull free of her scalp and reluctantly loosened her grip. "Try to keep up, *Captain*. You ruined countless lives because you were scared, and you don't even seem to care. That's what I'm hung up on."

Billie was holding her breath. Cleo tried not to notice the red that was creeping up her face from the neck of her sweater. "So that's what you think of me," she whispered. "That I don't care? About my crew, about my brother?"

"And the entire human race, dude. You have no idea what the last twenty years have been like."

"Even worse than the previous twenty, I'd assume."

"After the *Providence* mission failed, Erebus Industries pretty much shut down. No one will even talk about the possibility of space travel anymore." Cleo felt the buzzing in her chest again, the prickle behind her eyes, but she couldn't stop talking. "Everything gets worse every day. We don't even know how much longer any of us can live on Earth. And *still* no one wants to do anything about it now that it's not profitable anymore. It's like the whole world is just willingly going quiet into that good night."

"Dylan Thomas."

"I don't know who the fuck that is."

A tiny smile twitched at Billie's lips, and she looked away. "Those bastards on the board always were useless."

"You're the original bastard here." Cleo wished she could shove Billie in the chest. "That's my entire goddamn point. All subsequent bastardly behavior is because of you, the first bastard domino."

"I would argue that Halvorsen seems to have been the first bastard domino."

"Yeah, but he's dead, so I don't get to yell at him."

"I'm dead too."

"Don't say that." It was out of her mouth before she could overthink it, but Cleo knew that regardless of what had happened to Billie's physical body, she was undeniably, vividly alive in front of Cleo's eyes.

Billie blinked. She took a tentative step closer. "If I'm not dead, can I at least be sorry?"

Cleo should have stepped away. Instead, she found herself laser-focusing on the pink in Billie's cheeks. "You tell me."

"I'm sorry, McQueary. God, I'm so fucking sorry it feels like I'm drowning." Billie looked away, like Cleo was the sun burning her eyes. "I'd say I can't believe I did something like that, but that would be a lie. It's true that we were under unbelievable pressure, that the entire human race was counting on us, but—but I was also just selfish. I cared too much about my work because I felt like I didn't have anything else. Anything except Elijah, that is. So when I found out on the *eve* of the launch that Halvorsen was playing with dark matter and the lives of our crew, I panicked and I was selfish and I tried to save my work and Elijah and I ended up"—she swallowed, then sucked in the smallest, softest gasp—"I ended up losing both."

Cleo was holding her own breath now. She couldn't say what she was waiting for.

"So," Billie continued, dragging her eyes back to Cleo and looking, for a second, almost like the starship captain Cleo remembered, "I will do everything in my power to fix this mess I helped create. I promise you that."

Cleo exhaled. The buzzing was still there in her chest, but it had changed tenor. It was warmer, Cleo thought, almost like anticipation. "That's—thank you," she said.

Billie narrowed her eyes, but in that way that was closer to a smile, Cleo was quickly learning, than a scowl. "For what?"

"For revealing that you're not just an asshole but an asshole with a heart of gold, which is way cuter." *What? What are you saying, Cleo?* "I mean—you know what I mean. You can hang. Opening up is Abe and Kaleisha's whole thing."

Billie looked dangerously close to laughing again. "Of course. Speaking of, are you going to tell them whatever it is you're hiding?"

"You're changing the subject. Also, what?"

"Answer the question."

Cleo was going to pull the rest of her hair out if she kept spending time with this woman. "I don't know what would make you think I'm hiding anything."

Billie circled Cleo slowly, looking her up and down. "You were irritable with them. Defensive. And, as I previously noted, you're tired. You didn't sleep last night."

"Brilliant, Holmes."

"If I had to guess," Billie said, coming to a halt and looking very self-satisfied, "you had another vision last night."

Cleo was officially too tired to keep pretending. "So what if I did?"

"*So*, if you saw the future again, that would probably be helpful to know."

"Wasn't the future."

"What?"

Cleo internally kicked herself. "It was the past, okay? I saw Halvorsen."

Billie blinked, her glasses sliding down a bit in surprise. "Kris? You mean you saw his, what, his past—"

"Yeah. He doesn't have a future to see, obviously." Cleo felt tears threatening again, and looked around for something to distract herself. "I saw his childhood. Grad school. You two stargazing together at Erebus."

"Yeah, we did that a lot."

"Were you actually friends? Or was that just for the cameras too?"

Billie's fingers clenched around her biceps. "He was a friend.

He was a genius. He was the only person on the crew I could have a real conversation with, because he didn't just see me as the child genius astronaut hero or whatever. I had so much respect for him. Until the end, I guess."

"We still don't know exactly what he hoped to do with the engine," Cleo said, pressing on the tip of her own nose in thought. "Is there any world where he had good intentions?"

Billie seemed lost in thought too, her gaze fixed on Cleo's finger on her nose. "God, I want to believe that, but—good intentions, gambling with the lives of everyone on our crew? He was so—" And then Billie frowned. "Now you're changing the subject."

"And you're still flinging wild accusations around."

"You had more visions!" Billie reached her arms out like she wanted to grab Cleo by the shoulders. "And they kept you up all night, by the looks of it. Why didn't you tell anybody?"

Cleo mumbled something about "more important things," and Billie scoffed so loudly that Cleo stood up straighter. "Everyone has a lot on their minds, okay? I wasn't about to bother them with Baby Halvorsen and his trains when Ros, for example, is trying to figure out how not to uncontrollably shoot ice out of their hands."

"And you don't think that your powers are equally worth figuring out? Visions so aggressive that they kept you up all night aren't worth your friends' time?"

"I didn't—"

"Come with me." Billie turned on her heel and marched deeper into the lab. "We're going to figure this out."

Cleo heaved a sigh and followed. "How are we going to do that, exactly?"

"Same way Wheeler is going to have to learn to control the ice. I'd bet anything that, if you learn to summon your visions deliberately, they won't keep seizing you involuntarily. Here."

Billie stopped in front of a bookshelf and pointed at an ancient copy of *My Side of the Mountain*. "Pick that up."

"Um. Why."

"Last night, your visions of Kris were loose and undefined. But yesterday, you saw Wheeler's future when you touched them, and that vision was contained and specific. If I'm right, which I probably am, touching something allows you to focus your powers on the past or future of that person or object."

Cleo pulled the book out and flipped through the yellowed pages. "So what am I going to see?"

"Me, in theory. I've had that book since I was five."

"Adorable." Cleo's hands clenched around the book. "I don't feel anything."

Billie rolled her eyes. "Try harder."

Cleo closed her eyes and tried to listen. It made her headache even worse, hearing that infinitesimal buzzing of every molecule around her. But as she pushed deeper, strained her awareness past the surface, she could hear more: the golden-dark thrum of *something else*, something flowing through her like a thundering river, something streaming through and under and around everything. It was fundamentally different from the world around her—but it was also inside her, shimmering strangely in her bones. And Cleo knew, without knowing, that if she could just trace the flow of it, if she could just *focus*, like Billie said, she might be able to grasp it, ride it, take control of it, even.

"Billie," Cleo said through gritted teeth. "Say something. Anything, to block out everything else."

"Okay." And even though Cleo was sure that Billie had no idea what she was talking about, she stepped closer, her voice suddenly right in Cleo's ear. "Focus, McQueary. Focus on the book, and everything it's connected to. Let it all move through you."

The book. The bonds of all its atoms. "Keep talking."

Billie chuckled. Cleo should have felt a puff of breath across her cheek, but of course there was nothing. "Remember how it felt, seeing Wheeler's future. Let the feeling take you again. But this time, it's yours."

Mine—

Black, then blacker than black—

And Cleo's eyes flew open, and the lab was gone.

A different room, smaller, but just as cluttered with bookcases and tools. A window for sunlight to stream through and a regular, wooden door. A gauzy, off-white curtain and a twin bed. Everything was golden and slow again, but Cleo could tell that the real room would have been bright and cozy. A homey room. A room where someone—

Cleo turned, and there was Billie. Not hologram Billie: flesh-and-blood Billie, only about eight or nine years old but still looking exactly like herself, glasses and blond ponytail and all. She was lying on top of a child-sized work desk stacked with abandoned precalculus and physics workbooks, head and hair dangling upside down off the edge of it, and she was reading a book with the same scowl of concentration that Cleo had already come to know. The book was *My Side of the Mountain*, the same edition, but less yellowed and less dog-eared.

There was a sound outside the door, a child's giggle followed by a crash. Billie's head popped up. She dropped the book, leapt down from the desk, and ran right *through* Cleo—

And then Cleo gasped back into her body. Everything was spinning; the book, now old and tattered once again, fell to the floor. She reached for Billie instinctually, for something to ground herself, but her hands found nothing.

"McQueary. Hey, McQueary. Breathe."

Cleo froze, gulping air as her head slowly settled back securely on her neck. She blinked and managed to focus on Billie, who was still staticky from having Cleo's arm swiped through her.

"Sorry about that," Cleo panted.

Billie waved her apology away like it was a dragonfly buzzing around her nose. "Never mind, McQueary. What did you see?"

"Well." Cleo swallowed, trying to get her sand-dry throat back to normal. "I saw what I would have to assume was your childhood bedroom. Which was only marginally less cluttered than this lab."

"Did you only absorb enough to insult me, or did you see anything else?"

Cleo stuck her tongue out at Billie. "I also saw you as a kid, maybe eight years old, reading that book. And then it sounded like your, uh, brother hurt himself out in the hallway and you went after him. Did your parents leave you home alone or something?"

"Probably. They both always had to work. Eli would have been three. Always throwing himself into walls and tables full of fragile things, especially when it was just me watching him." A smile began to crinkle around Billie's eyes. "You saw an event twenty-one—I mean, forty-one years ago and a million miles away. Impressive."

Some of the exhaustion drained out of Cleo's chest at that, and she stretched her neck to crackle out some of the tension. "It was a team effort."

Billie eyed her over the tops of her glasses. "Speaking of, what did you mean when you said you needed me to block out everything else?"

"Just that, like, I can kind of hear molecules vibrating now? And also something underneath it all? It's like a river. Outside of everything else. I just needed to listen to it."

Billie smacked herself in the forehead. "You didn't think the fact that you can *hear dark matter* was worth mentioning before now?"

"I don't—I didn't fully realize that's what it was, Billie. It's not like they taught us about this in undergrad astrophysics—"

"Jesus. Come on." Billie reached out a hand like she wanted Cleo to take it, and Cleo almost did. "I think I know how all your powers work."

✳

MCQUEARY IS BRAVE. I'll give her that. She has to be, not to crumble in the face of all these changes, all these unknowns. All that power.

There's also the fact that she seems, despite everything, to actually like the hologram. And the hologram is, for all intents and purposes, Captain Lucas, and I could count on one hand the number of people who have ever been brave enough to care about her.

✳

"A VISUAL AID IS going to be useful," Billie said.

She waved her arm, and suddenly the hospital bay was filled with oversized, bright blue holographic atoms, their misty electron clouds overlapping. Cleo heard herself gasp, heard Kaleisha's murmured "whoa" and Abe's excited laugh. She drew closer to the nearest nucleus, which was the size of a basketball, and brushed a finger through it. It was carbon, connected to a few relatively tiny hydrogen atoms. An organic molecule of some kind—Cleo had slept through most of undergraduate chemistry. It flickered when she touched it, just like Billie.

"Holy hell, Billie," Cleo said. "What happened to making me draw on the whiteboard for you?"

Billie smirked. "I told you, I learned a lot about myself last night."

Ros sat up a little straighter in their bed. "Cute trick. Now, will you *please* tell us what's going on with our bodies?"

"Right," Billie said. "So, the thing about dark matter is that it's slippery." She waved her hand again, and tiny, dark gold particles flowed into view, passing easily through and between the atoms. "It acts like it's part of our universe, but only sometimes, and only in certain situations, and other times it's like it's not here at all." The image zoomed out, making Cleo dizzy, until they were watching the solar system spin around the sun, golden tendrils connecting the planets to the sun like spokes of a wheel. "Kris and I had a hypothesis that might have explained it all: that dark matter exists somewhere else. A conterminous dimension that occupies the same fourth-dimensional manifold as our own."

Kaleisha paced between the planets, rubbing at the frown lines in her forehead. "Can we assume that the botanists in the audience need working definitions of gonzo theoretical physics words like *conterminous* and *manifold*?"

Billie smiled. "Of course." She swiped away the holographic universe and replaced it with just a circle, filled in blue. "This circle is a two-dimensional object, but it exists in a three-dimensional manifold, our universe."

"Okay."

"Now, say you draw a square that intersects the circle." As Billie said it, she did it, tracing a solid purple square with her finger so it sat inside the circle, perpendicular to it. "These two-dimensional objects now occupy the same three-dimensional manifold."

Kaleisha was nodding now, frown lines loosening. "Got it."

"Now, here's the thing. Imagine both shapes are a universe. Imagine there are two-dimensional beings living in the circle *and* in the square."

"Sure, why not."

Billie moved to indicate the line where the square and the circle intersected. "The inhabitants of the circle would have no way to see the square, because they can't think in three dimensions. The only evidence they would have of the square's existence is this inexplicable line running through their universe."

"Oh!" Kaleisha's hand flew back up to her forehead. "Dark matter is the line!"

"Exactly." Billie rubbed her hands together excitedly, shooting a look at Kaleisha that was almost proud. "If our universe and this conterminous dimension exist in the same *four*-dimensional manifold, then they intersect each other in ways our three-dimensional minds can't truly comprehend. All we can see are the points of intersection: dark matter."

Cleo realized she had been gaping at Billie the whole time she'd been talking, and clamped her mouth shut. "So this, um, other place—"

"Conterminous dimension."

"Just for that, I'm officially naming it the Other Place. Capital *O*, capital *P*."

Billie raised an amused eyebrow. "Fine. Go on."

"The Other Place is *maybe* where the energy from the dark matter engine is coming from."

"Correct."

"And maybe where our powers came from."

Billie nodded, squishing and un-squishing the circle-square into the outlines of three human bodies, coursing with and connected by those golden tendrils. "I believe, based on the simulations I've been running, that when the engine went off you were all blasted with something—dark matter, or dark energy, or radiation of some kind we have yet to comprehend—that altered you. I believe your abilities are rooted in this newly forged connection to the dark matter dimension."

"Damn." Kaleisha's eyes were wide. "How can we be connected when the, uh, shapes—the universes—are barely connected themselves?"

"I'm not completely sure," Billie admitted. "But it was McQueary who gave me the idea. Tell them what you told me."

"Oh, uh." Cleo swallowed. "I felt this, like, river? Of energy or particles or maybe both? Running under and through everything else. Focusing on it helped me focus my visions."

"Felt it how?" Kaleisha asked.

Cleo's face got hot. "I just focused really hard. I can show you how, since we are all connected to it."

"Not all."

Cleo realized guiltily that it was the first thing Ros had said since Billie had begun her speech. They were sitting up straighter in their bed now, looking accusingly between Billie and Cleo.

"I don't feel anything," they continued. "And I don't want to."

"Maybe that's why you don't feel anything," Billie said blandly.

"Ros, your eyes were, like, gold last night," Abe said. "I think you felt the connection to the Other Place before Kal or Cleo did."

Ros crossed their arms, bunching up the blanket around them. "Then maybe you guys should stop trying to commune with it or whatever, because if you didn't notice, it kind of messed me up."

"Listen," Billie said, with the air of someone trying to herd cats, "there's got to be some kind of scientific explanation for all of your powers. And once we learn how it works, you'll all be able to control them better."

Cleo's fingers started to twitch. "What do you think the explanation is?"

"I only have hypotheses, but: Reid." Billie pointed at Kaleisha, who raised an eyebrow. "I think you're folding spacetime itself along the intersection lines."

Kaleisha's mouth fell open. "Dope."

"McQueary." Billie's gaze fell on Cleo, and Cleo could feel herself practically vibrating from the attention. "I believe your consciousness, like a WIMP, is now only weakly interacting with our universe. Like dark matter, your mind can now exist outside of space and time, allowing you to see the past and the future, matter and dark matter."

Cleo thought of the distant, golden river, of the vibrating under-energy of the Other Place. Of how her head had felt like an untethered particle, bouncing helplessly around in time, until she had figured out how to ride that wave. "Feels right. I can even call my visions 'wimping,' since everything needs a cute name now, I've decided."

Billie's mouth twitched into an almost-smile, but then she dragged her gaze away from Cleo. "Wheeler."

Ros slid further down into their sheets, like they were trying to dissolve away into the pillows. "What."

"Your powers are, possibly, the most interesting."

"Gee, thanks."

"To freeze the air around you, you have to remove energy from it. But, since energy can't just disappear, and nothing else was getting correspondingly warmer—"

"I must be diverting the thermal energy out of this dimension and into the Other Place." The revelation didn't seem to do anything to improve Ros's mood, and they reached for their mug to slurp at the last dregs of tea. Cleo wanted to give them a hug. Or she would have, if she wasn't so afraid of getting thrown into another terrifying vision of their future.

"Exactly," Billie continued, oblivious. "What's interesting is that your powers are the only ones that seem to involve the Other Place directly. I'm fascinated by what the purpose of all that diverted energy might be."

Ros glared daggers at Billie over the rim of their mug. "Well, good to know you're *fascinated*."

"Damn it, Ros," Kaleisha said sharply, making Cleo jump. "Can you chill, please? You're not the only one going through it right now."

"Right, sorry. I forgot that the fact that we're all miserable is actually great news. I'm all cheered up now."

"Come on, babe, that's not what I—"

Ros slammed their empty mug down on the bedside table. "Whatever! Whatever. It's fine. Forget it."

Kaleisha frowned, blinking hard. Ros threw up their hands.

"Oh my God, ignore me. I'm such an asshole. I'll stop talking now."

"Get the *fuck* over yourself," Kaleisha seethed, her voice suddenly quiet, halting. "Because you're right, we're all screwed straight to hell. We just don't all have the luxury of dissolving into prickly puddles of self-pity at this particular moment."

"Dissolve away, Kaleisha," Ros said through gritted teeth. "It's not myself I'm gonna fucking pity when I lose control and crush the *Providence* like a tin can."

Kaleisha sucked in a breath and held it, her chin jutting out.

"Babe," Abe said softly, "are you—"

"Jesus, get me off of this *goddamn ship!*"

And Kaleisha turned and ran to the elevator, swatting away one of Billie's holographic atoms as she went.

Billie raised her eyebrows at Cleo, but Cleo focused on Abe. Abe mouthed *You go* at her, inclining his own head toward Ros. Cleo went.

✳

CLEO FOUND KALEISHA IN the greenhouse, of course. It was the one level of the ship that, if the launch had gone as planned and the crew remained alive to work and water the plants, might have smelled like Earth. Like the botany lab at the university. Like Mr. Reid's house. Now it was just rows upon rows of planters filled with twenty-year-old dirt, dry as dust.

"Hey."

"Do you think there are any microbes left in the soil? From the air, maybe?" Kaleisha asked, her back still to Cleo. "Or are we going to have to, like, shit in it?"

Cleo snorted before she could stop herself. "We could do a sign-up sheet. A shit schedule. I'll take Wednesdays."

She drew even with Kaleisha and saw that she hadn't cracked so much as a smile. In fact, she was staring at the large pot in front of her with tears in her eyes. It held the remnants of a sapling that might have almost been a tree by now, its slender trunk and sparse branches twisted and desiccated.

Cleo could count on one hand the number of times she'd seen Kaleisha looking so lost. No, one finger—winter break, sophomore year of undergrad, when she'd told Cleo under their Christmas Eve blanket fort that she'd hooked up with Abe and it was perfect and she was terrified to blow up the friend group. Cleo had an easy answer to her worries then: *Finally. Please just go for it. You've been painfully in love with each other since we were fourteen and I'm exhausted.* Now, with her best friend staring down over a decade without smelling a flower or hugging her dad, what could Cleo possibly say? What was the thing to say that would make it all make sense? What was she supposed to do if she couldn't fix it?

"We can test the soil for a microbiome," Cleo said, desperate to at least get that look off Kaleisha's face. "And there must be something on board to help the soil out. Can chemical plant food do that? I bet some of the seeds are still good, and the botanists' notes are probably in the—"

"God, just—just stop." Kaleisha sniffed wetly and rubbed her nose on the sheer black sleeve of her dress. "It's not gonna make this okay."

Cleo shoved her hands in the pockets of her coveralls, which now smelled noticeably of nightmare sweat. What were they going to wear for the next seven years? Dead people's *Providence* uniforms? "I know."

Kaleisha blinked hard, tears streaming down her face. "It's not gonna make Ros's Virgo ass process their feelings."

"Oh, trust me, I *know.*"

"They're lashing out at everyone because they're scared." Kaleisha scrubbed her hands over her face, the last remnants of her blush and foundation coming off on her fingers. "Can't blame them for that. I mean—"

She closed a hand around the air in front of her and pulled like she was tugging on a rope. The room folded, creasing like a piece of paper, until the pot and the sapling were perpendicular to them. Now that it was directly in front of them, Kaleisha plucked the sapling out of the dry soil. The room snapped back with a shuddering crack, the little trunk still in her hands and the pot now empty.

Kaleisha drew a shaking breath. "It's so weird. Why—why is it so—"

And she broke down crying, the sapling falling forgotten to the floor and full-on sobs racking her body. Cleo carefully folded all the soft curves of her friend's body into her arms.

"Fuck this. Fuck our fucking drunk idea. Fuck everything."

"I know. I'm so sorry this is happening. And I'm sorry I was being such a dipshit last night."

Kaleisha made a strangled little sound into Cleo's T-shirt. "Thanks."

"And I'm sorry about Ros. And the dark matter powers. And the incomprehensible mysteries of the universe we're now forced to contend with."

"Okay, you don't have to be sorry for all that." Kaleisha let out a gurgle that might have also been a laugh, which Cleo took as a win.

"Well, I am."

"I don't actually need you to be sorry. I need you to help me find out what the hell is going on."

"Oh my God, of course. Of course." Cleo rubbed Kaleisha's back, up and down, up and down. The fabric of her dress was silky, and her hand slid over it so easy. "We'll figure it out, babe."

"How?"

"Oof, you're the one with the plans. I'm just the muscle."

Kaleisha reached a hand up and thumped Cleo on the forehead. "You're too tiny to be the muscle. You still gotta contribute with your brain."

"Okay, we start with the basics, right? How much HRT does the med bay have?"

"Ros says, like, decades' worth."

"Thank God." Cleo hooked her chin over Kaleisha's shoulder. She still smelled like her moisturizer from home, just a little. "Do you think they've got coconut oil for you on this ship?"

"There were Black people on the crew, dummy. Next question."

"The *Star Trek* back catalog?"

"Natch."

"Then our most pressing order of business is listening up for the response to your radio message."

Kaleisha pulled away, looking snotty but hopeful. "You think we'll get one?"

"Heck yeah. We've only been moving at near-lightspeed for, what, eighteen hours? So a radio message will take even less than that to get back to Earth. The farther away we get, the longer it'll take, but—"

Kaleisha shook her head, wiping her eyes. "Good enough for now. Now we just have to figure out the next fourteen years."

Cleo smiled and brushed the last tear off her friend's cheek. "I really am sorry. For getting us into this. For being so starry-eyed."

Kaleisha rolled her eyes, and she was almost herself again. "Nuh-uh, don't go changing that now. We're gonna need you to be extra obsessed with space if we're ever gonna get through this."

Obsessed. "Oh man! That reminds me! I had more visions."

"Cleo!"

"I'm sorry! They were last night. I saw the chief engineer—Halvorsen."

"Oh man." Kaleisha raised an eyebrow, and for the first time since takeoff she looked the way she did when she was writing: like the past was an origami crane that just needed a few more folds to take shape. "Then you gotta have more visions. See if you can find out what Halvorsen was up to."

Cleo bit her lip. "I guess I could work on it. With Billie's help. She was really good at helping me focus my powers."

Kaleisha smirked. "Of course she was."

"What does that mean?"

"Nothing." She grabbed Cleo's hand and pulled her toward the elevator. "Let's go replicate some wine and start planning, babe."

✳

LATER, THEY ALL STOOD huddled around the console on the flight deck as a recording of a very familiar voice crackled out of the speaker.

"Christ, baby. It's like you're trying to give me a heart attack." Mr. Reid chuckled, half in relief and half in barely disguised terror. Cleo pictured him pacing around the disused Erebus control center, rubbing his bald head the way he always did when he was agitated. "I love you. You and the other kids too. But I do have to say that this is the last thing on Earth I ever expected. Or—or off Earth, I suppose."

Kaleisha rolled her eyes. It didn't hide how close she was to crying.

"Listen up. The NASA folks are on the job, and they told me to say"—he cleared his throat, shifting into a tone that sounded like he was peering through his reading glasses at a notecard someone had scribbled on for him—"that you're going to have to reprogram the ship's planned orbital pattern. If you do it right, instead of falling into orbit around Proxima B, you should be able to swing around the planet, then Proxima C, and then you'll be angled back toward Earth. There's a lot of math involved. They said the ship's computer should be able to figure it out."

They all looked at Billie, who was staring at the speaker and chewing on her bottom lip. She met Cleo's gaze, her eyes flickering briefly, and nodded.

"That's—that's all they really have, baby." Mr. Reid's voice was thick, his words coming in a choked-out staccato. "I know it's going to take years, but there's nothing else they can do. There's no way to come after you."

"Yeah, Dad," Kaleisha whispered. "I know."

"You're going to have to be strong, like I know you are."

"I know." Abe and Cleo wrapped Kaleisha up in their arms as she wiped her eyes. "I know."

✳

THAT NIGHT, CLEO CHANGED into some very soft Erebus-issue pajamas, wrapped her dad's NASA jacket around herself, and slept in the med bay with the others. She still had visions, this time of Mr. Reid and another man she couldn't quite make out, but those dreams slipped away easily. A few times, she was gripped by scenes of Halvorsen staying up late into the night writing, making adjustments to the dark matter engine, and pulling out his hair. But when these visions woke her, Cleo had Kaleisha's rumbling snores to listen to until she drifted off again.

CHAPTER 6

I t didn't take long for Cleo to start going a little nuts.

It started in her chest: a flutter, a catch, a bit of tightness around her heart that made itself known any time she wasn't actively focusing her attention on a task or a TV show or a conversation. She could still ignore it, usually. She could still breathe around it, most of the time.

But then came the absolutely fist-clenching need to be around her friends, all the time. If she found herself alone in a room, just her and the walls and the vacuum of space outside, she couldn't breathe around the lump of tension in her chest anymore. Going to bed, which had once been in her Top Five Favorite Parts of the Day, became, well, a nightmare, her pulse racing and stuttering at the thought of waking up tomorrow to this same ship, these same walls, the same emptiness all around them. Cleo started bugging her friends whenever she could, asking Kaleisha to start a new show with her, Abe to work out in the gym with her, Ros to try a new dish from the replicator with her.

Billie she didn't have to bug, since exploring her powers and the *Providence* with her was the closest thing Cleo had to a schedule. They had started a training regimen, with Billie as a coach of sorts, guiding Cleo, Kaleisha, and Ros toward a slightly better understanding of their abilities. Practicing extra-dimensional feats of magic and mayhem worked up quite a sweat, it turned out, but that still didn't stop the twitchy malaise from setting in the minute Cleo stepped into the water-recycling shower.

It helped, she quickly learned, to think of the passing days aboard *Providence I* like a montage in an eighties movie—a training montage, a getting-the-team-together montage, a "dancing and sock-sliding through the empty rooms" montage. Quick shots of her and her friends learning how to use their nascent superpowers interspersed with shots of Kaleisha working in the greenhouse and Ros treating Abe's allergic reaction to an avocado from the replicator. Montages had no in-between time. Montages had no endless, fluorescent days. Montages had an end, the next plot point always just around the corner.

※

ON DAY 15, AFTER hours of training that felt more like treading water than swimming, Cleo announced that she was going to go watch a dumb movie in the rec room.

"Ooh, I'm down," Abe said through his shirt, which he'd lifted up to wipe off his face. Despite his resolute lack of any supernatural abilities, he had found a way to be helpful: throwing small objects across the room so Kaleisha could fold them through the air.

"I'm sorry, what was that?" Kaleisha held a hand up to her ear mockingly. "Did you say 'I'm going to take a shower immediately so I don't stink up the bed later'?"

Ros shook a few stray ice crystals off their *Providence* jacket disgustedly. They had just spent an hour struggling to conjure any ice at all—and when they did, it had been in a jagged, unwieldy burst, one icicle even ricocheting off the ceiling and forcing Cleo to dive out of its way. "I'll join you."

"Alright." Abe made pouty lips at Cleo. "Watch something extra stupid for me."

"Aye-aye, Captain." Cleo gave an exaggerated salute, but the other three were already walking out of the mess hall. She caught Billie's eye. "Sorry."

Billie puffed out an almost-laugh. "If you ever unironically called me 'Captain,' McQueary, I think I'd die." She crossed her arms and looked at her feet. "What are you going to watch?"

"I don't know. Didn't think that far ahead. Something dumb." Cleo thought for a second. "Something happy."

Billie chewed on the inside of her cheek. "Have you ever seen *While You Were Sleeping*?"

"No, but that sounds like a rom-com, and rom-coms are garbage."

"It was my mother's favorite movie. And rom-coms are great."

Cleo blinked, trying to picture Billie swooning at some AI-generated straight couple falling in mind-numbingly predictable love while a pop song played too loud. "I'm sorry, I think my brain just broke a little."

Billie rolled her eyes. "We're watching it. Come on."

The rec room was surprisingly cozy, full of plush sofas and richly patterned carpets; one wall held a massive TV screen, and the others held bookshelves. Some of the coffee tables had holographic board games built in. Cleo was shocked that Erebus Industries had expected the crew to ever spend time anywhere else.

They started the movie in not quite companionable silence, Billie sitting in a not quite relaxed position on the floor and Cleo sprawled across the couch with her feet not quite touching Billie's shoulder.

Corny voice-over, love at first sight, a mushy-faced male love interest—it was a rom-com, all right. The only redeeming factor so far was the sight of a young Sandra Bullock in an oversized sweater. Cleo was practically vibrating from the effort of not sighing derisively when Billie announced, with absolutely no preamble, "My parents are dead."

Cleo jerked her head up from the armrest so fast she thought she might have twinged something. "Um," she said, rubbing her neck and thinking vaguely that she should pause the movie, "I know?"

Billie sighed in frustration, her eyes still locked on the movie. "Right, I know you know, because you had my *Time* magazine profile hanging in your locker or whatever. I wanted to bring it up the way a regular person might, however."

"With no warning, while I'm trying to understand what you see in this movie?"

Billie gestured at the screen like a lawyer revealing an incontrovertible piece of evidence. "It's my dead mom's favorite movie, asshole. And Sandra Bullock's parents are dead, aren't they? It felt like as good a segue as any."

Cleo sat up, tucking her legs under her butt. She peered at Billie, who was still determinedly watching Sandra trying to haul a Christmas tree through the window of her walk-up. "Do you want to, I don't know, talk about it?"

"No."

Cleo flung her arms in the air. "Then why did you bring it up?"

Billie finally turned to look at her, a small frown on her face. "It's something I want you to know about me."

Cleo blinked. "Oh. Why?"

Billie shrugged. "It's an important part of knowing me. You should know that my parents were killed by a drunk driver when I was nineteen and Elijah was fourteen. You should know that he had to move into my shitty college-student apartment with me, and I had to learn how to make gluten-free pancakes because he has—had, that is—celiac. And you should know that the most alone I'd ever felt is when I cracked open my mom's box of recipes for the first time and realized that she hadn't written detailed enough instructions on most of them for someone else to follow, because she thought she'd have so much more time to teach me how."

Cleo let out a breath. "I'm sorry."

Billie scoffed. "Don't be."

"No, for real." Cleo scooted a little closer. Billie tensed up, but didn't look away. "You've lost so many people. Your parents, your fiancé, now your brother and your crew. It's not fair."

Billie's eyebrows twitched, like she had never expected to hear those words in that order. "No, it's not."

Her hands were clenched so tightly in her lap that every blue-green vein stood out against her knuckles. Cleo wished she could reach down and gently untangle her fingers. "Thank you for telling me, Billie."

A tiny smile played at the corner of Billie's mouth. "No problem, McQueary."

Cleo smiled back, wide and toothy. Billie suddenly tensed up again and turned back to the movie. Cleo stared at the side of her face. Why had Billie pulled away again? How many times had she watched this movie, thinking of her mother? Why had she wanted Cleo, specifically, to watch it, and love it?

Finally, Cleo turned too, shifting into crisscross-applesauce right next to Billie's head. On-screen, some guy was hitting on Sandra Bullock and being pushy about it. "Uh. Who's this dipshit?" Cleo asked. "Why is he bothering Sandra?"

"That's the super's son. He's there to be creepily convinced that Sandra's in love with him, so that later he and Bill Pullman can have a big misunderstanding about it."

"Who's Bill Pullman?"

"The actual love interest. He's coming soon. He's hotter than the guy in the coma, don't worry."

"I'll be the judge of that."

"Aren't you a lesbian?"

"Yeah, and that makes me the perfect impartial evaluator. Obviously."

✳

ON DAY 20, THEY got another message from Mr. Reid.

"Damn. When I tell you the science guys have no idea what's happening to you kids—I'm sorry. I wish we had more answers for you. I'm glad you have the, uh—hologram, was it? Of Captain Lucas to help you out. I remember always thinking she seemed like a real smart cookie."

In the following days, Cleo often caught Kaleisha replaying the recording over the greenhouse loudspeakers as she worked on reviving the garden. Billie had, to Kaleisha's ecstatic relief, pointed out the flash-frozen earthworm eggs in storage, and Kaleisha had wasted no time in thawing and hatching them as Mr. Reid's voiced echoed through the space.

"Remember, Kallie, soil wants to be alive. If you can print any greens out of the food-printer whatsit and chop them up for compost, that'll make a world of difference. Be sure to check the pH levels regularly. I'm so proud of you, baby. I'm glad you're growing life where you can."

✳

THERE ARE A LOT of things that can go wrong on a spaceship. Some of them, Cleo was learning, sounded like the pulse-pounding climax of an Oscar-nominated astronaut movie when you said them out loud, but turned out to be just minor annoyances once she'd hauled her tools into the maintenance shaft of the day. As a result, she was learning to respond to Billie's bored messages with less of a hyperbolic, sprinting-through-the-ship, *I'm giving it all she's got, Captain* energy.

"McQueary, there's an ammonia leak in cooling loop theta," Billie had grumbled at her over the intercom that morning while she was trying to make her *Providence* uniform look cute.

"Lame," Cleo replied, settling on tying the jacket around her waist so the tank top and baggy pants combo could really shine. "Think I've got time to grab a coffee to go?"

"Sure. And when you're puking your guts out from bringing an open Dixie cup into a vent full of ammonia gas, be sure to tell Wheeler that I was the one who let you poison yourself."

"You're no fun," Cleo said brightly, making sure to put a respirator mask in her toolbox on her way out of her quarters.

It was, of course, a tiny leak and an easy fix, but that didn't stop Billie from hovering in the open access panel—she couldn't come into the maintenance shaft because there were no hologram projectors inside—and backseat-repairing like her life depended on it.

"That's not—McQueary, I swear to God, if you don't pull out a torque wrench right now—"

"I've got it handled, Billie." Cleo scrubbed her dripping forehead with the back of her hand and pushed down harder with her trusty old combination wrench (which she had made sure to put in Abe's backpack for the Space Heist, thank God). "Where I come from, physicists know not to condescend to engineers about torque."

Billie smirked at her through the sweating coolant pipes. "They absolutely do not."

"Fine, maybe not. But I once built myself a car with nothing but this wrench and an entire pallet of green apple Hi-Chews, so you'll forgive me if I ignore your expert guidance." Billie was now staring at her straining biceps in what Cleo could only assume was a pointed manner. "Stop that."

Billie might have gone a little pink, but it was so hard to tell when she was silhouetted in the panel opening. "I didn't say anything."

"Your eyes speak volumes."

"Poetic."

"How dare you."

Billie narrowed her eyes, fixing Cleo with that curious stare of hers. "Who taught you how to build cars and hate poetry? I want to have a word with them."

"Cars? My dad. Hating poetry was all my dear mother."

"Hmm. Because she was a philistine and passed it on or because she was a poet and you hate her?"

Cleo blinked a drop of sweat out of her eyes and wished her mouth wasn't covered by the respirator, so she could send Billie her best stuck-out tongue of disapproval. "You're asking a lot of personal questions for someone who wants this leak patched as soon as possible."

"Fine, I get it. You're a closed book. A woman of mystery. No one may fathom the depths behind those hooded eyes—"

"Damn straight."

Billie fell quiet, her face deliberately, infuriatingly placid as she watched Cleo struggle with the pipes. Cleo glared at the bolt beneath her wrench and ground her teeth into the silence for one breath. Two. Three.

"My mother was an English professor. She left when I was seven."

If Billie was feeling satisfied with herself, it didn't show. Not that Cleo was looking at her. "I'm sorry to hear that."

"That was a fun year. The *Providence* disaster, the woman who birthed me deciding she never wanted to see me again, my dad forgetting how to talk to me like a fucking person."

Billie looked almost—sad, was it? concerned? pitying?—and Cleo couldn't stand it. "So he just taught you how to build cars."

"Yup, he was great at explaining how a shock tower worked. Not so great at treating me like I wasn't going to up and leave at any moment too."

"Sounds hard."

Cleo finally got that goddamn bolt secure and huffed out an angry, relieved breath. "Yeah, well. I spent a lot of time at Kaleisha's in high school."

Billie peered through the access panel at the coolant pipe, the golden glow from the room behind her lighting up her hair like a sunrise over water. "So you did up and leave."

The wrench nearly slipped out of Cleo's sweaty hands. "Excuse me?"

Billie just raised an eyebrow at her, infuriatingly. Cleo thought she deserved some credit for resisting the urge to toss the wrench through her.

"You're such a piece of work."

Billie smirked. "'How noble in reason, how infinite in faculty.'"

"If that's a poem, I'm going to throw this wrench—"

"It's *Hamlet*. My God."

Cleo groaned explosively, swiping her damp hair out of her eyes. *Yes, I left,* she could have said, *and I made a life for myself where I could mostly avoid looking at my father's face and only seeing how much we both missed her. And now I've completed the job and left the whole planet.*

"You don't get to judge me," she said instead. "You of all people."

A tiny breath, sucked in through the nose. Billie probably

thought Cleo wouldn't notice such a small gasp, but she did. "I know."

"Then don't look at me with those judgmental eyebrows," Cleo grumbled. She threw her wrench back in her toolbox and sat back on her hands. "*Now* can I go get coffee?"

The corner of Billie's mouth danced up again. "No one's stopping you."

"Come with me." Cleo had said it without thinking. But, despite how much she hated talking about her parents, something about saying all that to Billie had shifted something inside her. She felt lighter, in a heavy way. Tender, in a terrifying way.

"Sure," Billie said, and smiled for real. Maybe this was what making a new friend felt like, Cleo thought. It had been so long since the other three had become her family, she'd probably just forgotten. Surely it was always this uncomfortable, and incongruent, and electrifying.

※

ON DAY 35, KALEISHA became fixated on the climate of Proxima Centauri B.

"If the worst-case scenario goes down and we have to survive on the planet," she told Cleo as she bustled around the greenhouse, checking the height of every seedling and the moisture level of every pot of soil, "we need to know what we're facing."

The *Starshot* probes had gathered seemingly endless data on their missions to Proxima B in the decades leading up to the *Providence* missions, and Cleo was refreshing her memory by poring over a virtual stack of Abe's old documents that Kaleisha had seemingly already memorized. "Looks like it's going to be cold as balls."

"*Half* cold as balls," Kaleisha corrected her as she tenderly repotted a basil sprout. "Its orbit is tidally locked, so one side is actually boiling hot, the other is *colder* than balls, and there'll be an itty-bitty strip in the middle where we probably won't die."

"Lovely." Cleo swiped through the twenty-year-old Erebus-brand tablet and found a table of temperatures recorded by the long-suffering *Starshot 5*. "At least if I'm hankering for a tan, I can walk right up to the edge of the Hot Zone and take a little sun bath."

"Have fun dying instantly."

"Yeah, yeah."

"Remind me how cold the terminator line is?"

"Minus thirty, on average." Cleo showed Kaleisha a photo, a panorama taken by *Starshot 2* from the top of a mountain. There was nothing, as far as the camera lens captured, but snowy purple-gray mountains, blanketed in shadow from the perpetual sunset. "The star's a red dwarf, so not hot to begin with. And the atmosphere is thick enough to stand up to the solar flares."

"Nut me." Cleo reached into the bowl of chocolate-covered hazelnuts that Kaleisha had replicated, and popped one into her friend's mouth. Kaleisha crunched down on it as she frowned at the picture. "Does that mean we won't have to worry about dying by solar storm?"

The sky in the photo was a darkening red, shot through with fuzzy, iridescent streaks of color. "Those auroras," Cleo said, "mean that the planet's atmosphere will protect us." She let herself smile, thinking about it. She'd never seen the northern lights, back on Earth. Not that they would have been worth a trip to the disaster zone that was the Artic Circle, even if she'd had the funds. "Should be pretty."

"Gorgeous. We can be sure to enjoy the rainbow sky as we freeze to death, subsisting on lichen."

"Hey now." Cleo bumped their shoulders together. "We're never gonna see the surface of Proxima B."

Kaleisha rubbed one of the tiny basil leaves between her fingers and sighed. "I hope not."

"In other news, the dirt smells dirt-y again."

Cleo could hear the smile in Kaleisha's voice. "The baby earthworms are doing so good."

"And we didn't even have to shit in it."

"Hear, hear," Kaleisha said, and they went back to work.

✳

"BILLIE!" CLEO CALLED, STRUGGLING with the stack of books she was keeping in place with her chin.

Pop. "Oh my God. You couldn't make two trips?"

Cleo set the wobbling pile down on one of the coffee tables. "You asked me to bring up books from your lab when there are already, like, a billion books in here. You don't get to ask me to also take the elevator twice. Anyway, it worked out."

A few of the books tumbled from the less-stable top of the tower to the floor. Billie raised a perfect eyebrow. "Clearly."

"Listen, bucko, you should treat me nicer. I did all this for you."

Something like the beginning of a laugh twinkled across Billie's face as she watched Cleo sit on the floor to restack the books into smaller piles. "Thank you."

"Whoa, stop the presses, did the great Captain Dr. Wilhelmina Lucas just thank me for a favor?"

Billie raised an amused eyebrow at Cleo, then got distracted by the book in her hands. "That one."

Cleo looked down at the heavy white hardback. She turned it over, flipped through the pages. "Is this just poetry?"

"It's *Mary Oliver.*" Billie sat down on the carpet next to Cleo. "She's just one of the greatest poets of all time."

"You dastardly bastard. You're trying to trick me into reading poems!"

Billie rolled her eyes so hard her entire upper body followed. "She was also queer."

"Let it never be said that I'm not easily tricked." Cleo flipped through aimlessly. "Is there any one in particular you want me to read?"

Billie leaned back on her arms, her long legs stretching in Cleo's direction. "Something about the world."

"Thanks for narrowing it down there, chief."

"That's what Oliver was a master of, McQueary. The gorgeous little mundanities of being a person in the world."

Cleo landed on a page titled "To Begin With, the Sweet Grass," which was so long that it was divided into little numbered chapters or something. Billie was probably into that, the freak. Cleo looked up at her for confirmation, but Billie was watching the stars fly past the little electronic window—a smaller version of the one in the mess hall—in the wall, so Cleo just started reading.

It was nice, she supposed, though she didn't really get it. There was something about larks singing, and bread being yummy, and nature being reliable.

"*And someone's face, whom you love, will be as a star both intimate and ultimate,*" she recited.

As Cleo read, Billie closed her eyes and didn't move except for the calm, slow rise and fall of her chest. Cleo had the impression that she was softer than usual, less prickly, less encased in armor, and if she reached out to touch her she would feel the difference.

"*Love yourself. Then forget it. Then, love the world.*"

Cleo stopped, her throat suddenly tight. She blinked at the words, trying to will the tears to stop gathering in her eyes. Billie crawled forward and put her hand over the top of the book, making

Cleo put it down. Cleo avoided her eyes, but could still feel them boring into her.

"Let me read another one."

"No."

"This is how you're supposed to engage with poetry, right? Cry about it?"

Billie sighed out, hard, through her nose. "You've cracked it."

"Here, this one's called 'The Dog Has Run Off Again'—"

"Do you miss Earth?"

Cleo glowered at Billie over the top of the book. "No."

"Your dad? The sky? Dogs, maybe?"

"Not really, not at all, and yes, but I'll live."

Billie leaned back again, her head tilting up so she could watch dust motes swirling around the lamp overhead. "*I* miss Earth."

"But you were prepared to live on Proxima B forever."

"Well, McQueary, a lot has changed since then, if you haven't noticed." The sound of Billie's slow, measured inhale reminded Cleo of the ocean in the distance. "And now I'll never stand on Proxima B *or* feel the sun on my skin again, so I think I'm entitled to a little wistfulness."

That thick feeling in Cleo's throat got thicker. "Fair."

Billie tilted her head to meet Cleo's eyes. "You'd be happy never going back to Earth?"

"I—" Cleo blinked hard. It didn't make the prickle at the corners of her eyes go away. She thought about *While You Were Sleeping*: how Sandra Bullock's character worked in the Chicago subway, how Chicago had closed down its subway system a decade ago thanks to all the flooding from the Great Lakes. "It's really hard to overstate how much Earth sucks, Billie."

"So much that you've spent your whole life wanting to escape it. I know the feeling."

"If you could drop just the tiniest hint about where you're going with this, I'd appreciate it."

Billie shrugged, her eyes flicking over Cleo's face. "The poem got you emotional, McQueary. Just trying to figure out if there's anything you and your emotions need from me."

Cleo's mind went buzzy. What did she need from Billie? Why would she need anything from Billie? Her needs were—had always been—concrete and therefore achievable: she needed to go to space, she needed to learn everything she could about the universe, she needed to figure out how it all worked so that yawning hole inside her would stop wanting everything— knowledge and freedom and a new world—so badly it threatened to swallow Cleo and everyone she touched whole.

What could she possibly need? She needed Billie to stop looking at her like that, like she was a connect-the-dots puzzle in the stars. She needed Billie to stop looking so real that Cleo was half convinced she could reach out right then and tuck that loose strand of hair back behind her ear. She needed her own fingers to stop itching to do that.

"I need," Cleo said slowly, "for us to stop reading sad poems and watch another stupid, happy movie."

Billie stared at her for another long moment, long enough that Cleo started worrying she was going to argue with her.

"Gladly," Billie said, and just like that, she was turning the TV on with a flick of her head. "Let's do *Independence Day*."

"Another Lucas family favorite?"

"My dad's. And it's also got Bill Pullman in it. He's the president who leads humanity through the alien invasion. And he's practically a poet, anyway. Wait till you hear his speech at the climax."

※

Nearly 80 years ago, during the original Space Race and the Cold War that precipitated it, President John F. Kennedy gave a speech at Rice University that is still quoted today. "We set sail on this new sea because there is new knowledge to be gained, and new rights to be won, and they must be won and used for the progress of all people," he said. "We choose to go to the Moon . . . not because [it] is easy, but because [it] is hard."

But in private, JFK sang a very different tune: "I'm not that interested in space," he said in a meeting with NASA leaders in 1962. What he was interested in was war, and gaining the upper hand over the Soviet Union.

Science has long walked an uneasy line between the high-minded ideals it is supposed to support and the earth-bound evils it often ends up serving. Every scientist must grapple, in some way, with the fact that even their best-intentioned work may one day be used for harm. In the words of Robert Oppenheimer, the Manhattan Project researcher who later became a vocal opponent of the nuclear proliferation he had helped kick-start: "The physicists have known sin; and this is a knowledge which they cannot lose."

On its surface, the Providence Project seems as pure of intention as anything can be. Its mission is nothing more or less than to give the human race its salvation: to put a colony on an exoplanet, and in so doing prove that life and civilization are possible beyond this Earth that we've so rapidly turned uninhabitable. Providence captain Wilhelmina Lucas said as much in a speech last year, acknowledging the troubled history of space exploration in the same breath: "We take to the stars, this time, for ourselves. Not as some kind of a militaristic chest-puffing, or as a grab for unclaimed resources, or as an excuse to build bigger and better rockets with which to kill each other. This time, we're going to space so we can save each other. We're going to space so we can all go on, together."

As a physicist, however, I am interested in something else that Captain Lucas keeps saying: specifically, that the dark matter engine is proprietary, and this is why the public cannot be allowed to see it in action. Lucas and her team claim to have discovered a new type of reaction, one that does not follow previously established laws of physics; they claim to have circumvented the Rocket Equation problem; they claim that this is all entirely safe and reliable, with no negative side effects or possibility of catastrophic failure.

And the rest of us have, for many reasons, no choice but to believe them. What would we gain, anyway, from attempting to forestall our own salvation? But history shows us that it rarely ends well when science, human welfare, or the fate of the world are left in the hands of capitalists. Profit and growth will always, always come before truth or safety.

I ask again: Why haven't we seen the dark matter engine in action? Why hasn't Erebus Industries invited the scientific community to witness this unprecedented, energy-neutral phenomenon? Is it possible that we aren't getting the whole story, in the name of slick marketing and a corporation's stock prices?

Oppenheimer had something else to say about the bomb and the conditions that created it: "Our own political life is predicated on openness," he said in 1950. "We do not believe any group of men adequate enough or wise enough to operate without scrutiny or without criticism." Here is my criticism: I do not believe, absent concrete evidence, that Providence I can travel to Proxima Centauri B without any fuel. A spaceship carrying 200 people cannot fly from one solar system to another without something burning, or being consumed.

I don't know what Providence I is running on. Neither do you. Maybe the Providence team doesn't, either. All I know is that, one day, we will find out. And if Erebus Industries continues to operate without scrutiny, continues to whisper sweet nothings to us about sailing new seas while privately caring less about salvation than about their bottom line, the results will not be revolutionary. They will be catastrophic.

※

ARCHIVED: *Providence* Intracrew Messaging Service conversation — Program WL2-Mk1.4 and Abraham Yang, August 17, 2061

PROGRAM WL2-MK1.4
Yang
Hey, Yang

ABRAHAM YANG
WHOOOOAAAA WHO IS THIS

PROGRAM WL2-MK1.4
It's Billie. Obviously

ABRAHAM YANG
Oh my god hi!! I didn't know you could pim!!

PROGRAM WL2-MK1.4
Well, I can
[. . .]

ABRAHAM YANG
What's up, Billie?

PROGRAM WL2-MK1.4
You're watching something in the rec room. What is it

ABRAHAM YANG
Star Trek Voyager!

PROGRAM WL2-MK1.4
Oh
I always liked that one
Even though my dad always said "everyone" "agreed" it
   was the "worst series"

ABRAHAM YANG
YESSSSSSSS BILLIE I AGREE
Like, who cares if some of the storylines are silly!
   It's about the found family even out in the dark
   reaches of the unknown!!

PROGRAM WL2-MK1.4
Plus, Captain Janeway is hot

ABRAHAM YANG
EXACTLY
Okay Kaleisha wants to know if you consider yourself
   a Torres or a Seven of Nine

PROGRAM WL2-MK1.4
I consider myself a Janeway, obviously. I'm offended

ABRAHAM YANG
I'm so sorry
But Kaleisha says, and I'm quoting directly here,
   "Bullshit. Absolute nonsense. Tell her I know
   she's an Aries and she can't pretend she's not the
   most B'Elanna Torres-ass bitch to ever be born"
Sorry

PROGRAM WL2-MK1.4
That's okay, Yang
I'll concede that I am MAYBE a Torres sun, Janeway rising
(That's how you use astrology words, right? Elijah was
   the one who knew about that stuff)

ABRAHAM YANG
You're doing great!!

PROGRAM WL2-MK1.4
[. . .]

ABRAHAM YANG
Do you want to come watch with us? We're about to
    start the episode where Janeway and Paris get
    turned into lizards
And I'd love to hear more about your brother, if
    you're up for it. I know he was so important to you
But no pressure

PROGRAM WL2-MK1.4
[. . .]
Yeah?
That sounds nice
Thanks, Yang

✳

DAY 38: ABE MADE Cleo and Ros stand back farther from Kaleisha than was probably strictly necessary, though none of them, Cleo thought as they all crowded against one wall of the mess hall, had any frame of reference for what was probable, strict, or necessary in this particular case.

Kaleisha turned back to look at them from her position at the center of the room. "Ready?"

"Ready!" Abe snapped his goggles on and gave a vigorous thumbs-up. Cleo and Ros, only rolling their eyes at each other a little, did the same.

Kaleisha faced the opposite wall again. Cleo saw her take a deep breath and raise her arms, palms out—

And there it was again, that uneasy too-tight sense that the universe itself was being stretched like a rubber band, and the mess hall was folding in half the way three-dimensional space wasn't supposed to and the far wall wasn't so far anymore. And Kaleisha stepped forward, and for a split second she was standing on the slanted ceiling, which was actually the floor—

And with an echoing, bone-shaking crack, space snapped back into place again, and Kaleisha was across the room, striking a showy pose. Cleo broke into applause along with Abe and Ros. She took her goggles off, saw Billie nodding approvingly, and smiled a little wider.

"You beat your best distance, babe!" Abe looked to Billie for confirmation. "That had to have been, what—"

"Seventeen meters of spatial distention," Billie said. "Not bad, Reid."

Kaleisha was trotting back across the room toward them, smiling harder than she had in a fair while. "Thanks, Billie. And everything still looks good with the ship?"

"All systems operational. You wouldn't think anything had changed." Billie pushed her glasses up her nose as her eyes started vibrating. "I still can't quite figure out the physics of it, but you really are folding space, not matter."

"And I think that's very sexy of me." Kaleisha raised a hopeful eyebrow at Ros. "You're up, Rozzy."

Ros's face immediately fell. "No thanks. Rather not waste everyone's time again."

"Hey, Ros, don't get discouraged," Abe said. "No one expects you to totally figure out your powers overnight."

"Cleo basically did." When they looked at her sidelong, Cleo realized that Ros's eyes were bloodshot, like they hadn't been sleeping. Or like they'd been crying. Or both.

"McQueary's abilities work when she passively allows extra-dimensional forces to flow through her." Billie was looking at Ros sternly, but not unkindly. "Your abilities, as far as I understand them, require you to be more active, deliberately siphoning energy into the other dimension. It makes sense that you require more practice, but your powers will probably be more precise once you master them."

The hard edges of Ros's face got even harder, their shoulders ratcheting up to their ears. "That's all speculation."

"Sometimes it's okay to start with speculation and work from there."

"Easy for you to say, when you don't have a body to be frozen to death if I cock it up."

Billie blinked in surprise, reeling back like Ros had tried to slap her. She opened her mouth angrily, but Kaleisha intervened before she could let her retort loose.

"*Cleo*," Kaleisha said in her fake-calm tone, "I think me and Abe can help Ros take it slow. Do you want to take Billie down to the engine bay and do that thing?"

Billie's gaze snapped to Kaleisha at lightning speed, her jaw still jutted out in frustration. "What thing?"

"I was telling Kal last night that I wanted to wimp the engine, to see if I can find out anything about the crew or why it started on its own when I touched it." It occurred to Cleo that it was panic turning Billie's cheeks pink, and she thought she knew the reason. "And if it energy blasts us again, it probably won't matter, right? So you don't have to worry."

Billie licked her lower lip absentmindedly, which made Cleo blink very hard several times, for some reason. "And you want me there for, what, my effervescent personality?"

"Because if I learn anything you might have supersecret memories about, I'll need to ask you."

"I told you, I went through everything. I've remembered everything I can."

"Then we'll just have a fun science adventure, damn."

A tiny smile twitched at the corner of Billie's mouth, but Cleo was distracted from how almost-cute it made her look by Ros making the gagging noise they usually reserved for Abe and Kaleisha when they were being gross.

"Go on, then," Kaleisha said, elbowing Ros in the ribs.

*

LET'S DO A THOUGHT EXPERIMENT:

Is falling in love ever a bad thing?

Some people, like Sandra Bullock in While You Were Sleeping—*the kind who have never been really, tragically in love—would say no. Love is great. Love is all one-liners and gently falling snow and proposals at the subway station. Love is always a net positive.*

But anyone with half a brain—like, say, tiny lesbians with mommy issues and a fear of commitment, or starship captains who have lost everything—knows that love can hurt too. Your closest friend could betray you. The person you planned to spend the rest of your life with could die. You could fall for someone who's (literally, physically) incapable of loving you back.

And that's just people. There are other things to fall in love with, plenty of chances to be crushed from the inside out. Captain Lucas, to pick another totally random example, transferred most of her affections to her job after Neil died. And man oh man, did she romance that job. Late nights together. Fairy-tale vacations to the moons of Jupiter. You're the only one for me, baby, there will never be anyone else.

Which is why, when Lucas found out about the flaw in the dark matter engine on the eve of the launch, she reacted stupidly. Because love makes you stupid. She assumed that no one would take her seriously. She assumed that it wouldn't be as bad as she feared. Worst of all, she assumed that Halvorsen had been working to fix the engine, because that would be the reasonable, rational, right thing to do.

That was not what Halvorsen did.

You see, Halvorsen was also in love. He was in love with an idea, a plan, a dream: that the human race could one day understand more than we ever thought possible. That, through knowledge, we could avoid the consequences of the coming environmental collapse, and then focus on better things like exploring the cosmos, ending unnecessary suffering, even achieving enlightenment. That Halvorsen himself, through discovery, could make humanity a better version of itself.

That idea was the love of Halvorsen's life. He wanted nothing more and nothing less. And, at first, the Providence mission was everything he wanted—people traversing the galaxy, advancing science, working together to make the impossible possible. What's not to love?

But then he did want more, because he found something better. Because he fell too hard. Because sometimes love makes you stupid, and sometimes it makes you a monster.

✳

THE SHADOWS IN THE engine bay had a gold tint to them, thanks to the endlessly spinning vortex of dark matter at the center of the engine. It was dead silent now that they were sliding frictionlessly through the vacuum of space, but Cleo's head was full of the other kind of sound, the whooshing roar of the dark matter, of the Other Place, as it slipstreamed around her.

Billie was a little hazier here, a little less opaque and a little more prone to flickering out, like she was running on an upstairs neighbor's Wi-Fi signal that didn't quite reach through the floor.

"You okay there?" Cleo asked. "Does that hurt, or—"

"No, McQueary. It's just annoying."

"If you say so." They stopped in front of the engine and Cleo craned her neck to look up at it. It was easier to look straight at the vortex now that she had dark matter in her blood or whatever, but it was still weird to be seeing something that people weren't supposed to see. "Hey, Billie?"

"Mm."

Cleo swallowed around the sudden clench in her throat. "If I find out what happened to the crew . . . do you want me to tell you?"

A muscle twitched in Billie's jaw. "Of course I do."

"Even if it's, like—"

"Even if it's bad. Even if it's terrible. Even if it's the worst thing you've ever seen, McQueary, you have to tell me."

Cleo chewed on the inside of her cheek and wished she could put a hand on Billie's shoulder. "So you'll know."

Billie's eyes dragged over Cleo's face like there were answers to be found there. "So I'll know."

"Okay." Cleo took a shaky breath. "I'm gonna touch it."

"Be my guest."

"Do the thing."

Billie's mouth softened. "You're so much better at this already," she said, though she was already stepping behind Cleo to speak in her ear. "You really don't need me."

Cleo shivered involuntarily. Probably because her fingertips were a centimeter away from the surface of the engine, and the energy coming off it was already pulsing into her skin like static electricity. "I think that's for me to decide," she said, trying to sound less breathless than she felt and failing miserably.

She heard Billie huff out a laugh. "Close your eyes, McQueary. Reach out with your feelings, so to speak."

Cleo did as she was told. She set her hand on the engine, spreading her fingers over the just-warm metal, feeling the frequencies of two dimensions vibrate through her.

"Listen for them," Billie whispered, her voice shimmering along the strands of the universe. *"Where did they go?"*

A flash of light, then a shimmering golden darkness—

Cleo opened her eyes. The engine was still in front of her, looming up toward the shadowy ceiling. But it was off, and when she turned, Billie was gone.

The engine bay was almost unrecognizable. It was well lit, for one thing, softly glowing lamps scattered among the cluttered aisles of desks and build stations that lined the floor between the server stacks. And at the front, standing behind a hulking control console, was Dr. Kristoff Halvorsen.

At last, he appeared not as an overbright kid or a pimply postgrad, but just as Cleo remembered him: blond but graying, strong-shouldered, friendly lines around the eyes. He fiddled with some dial as she watched, muttering to himself, and despite knowing that he'd lied to Billie and put their crew's lives in danger, Cleo swelled with fondness. This man had been the first to demonstrate to her what being an engineer meant. How big a girl with a wrench was allowed to dream.

"Test number 5.3, December first, 2040," he said, and Cleo realized that there was a small recorder clipped to his jacket pocket. "Flux fields set to 30 gigawebers. Acceleration stable at 55 MeV."

And Halvorsen twisted some toggle, flipped a few switches, and slammed down hard on a large button.

This time, of course, the massive wave of energy that came out of the engine didn't knock Cleo over. She was nonetheless surprised to see Halvorsen blasted into the air and slammed into the desk behind him, just as she had been on the vibrating

Providence floor the night of the Space Heist. She almost ran over to help him, before she remembered she wasn't there. Instead, she could only wince as she heard Halvorsen groan.

"Jesus." He rolled over and slowly pulled himself up by the edge of the console. "What in the damn—"

HALVORSEN.

Cleo jumped in shock. Halvorsen did too.

The voice, or maybe it was a thousand voices, had come from everywhere and nowhere all at once. It rattled Cleo's bones and made the air shift in a way she sensed even through all the intervening layers of time, like every quark in every molecule was spinning the opposite way now. Halvorsen also seemed to be feeling it; suddenly he was trembling.

WE CANNOT ALLOW YOU TO CONTINUE.

Halvorsen dragged himself to his feet, elbows quivering. "Who are you?" he called, spinning to take in the whole engine bay. "Where are you?"

YOU MUST ABANDON YOUR MISSION.

Halvorsen's eyes landed on the center of the engine, where Cleo saw a tiny, pulsing spark that her eyes refused to focus on correctly. A small frown creased his forehead. "What? Why?"

YOU BELIEVE YOU HAVE DISCOVERED A SOURCE OF LIMITLESS ENERGY. THIS IS UNTRUE.

"Are you speaking from somewhere else?" Halvorsen stepped slowly toward the engine, his hands half raised like he was trying to settle a rhinoceros about to charge. "Does this mean my conterminous dimension hypothesis is correct?"

WE ARE ELSEWHERE.

"Brilliant," he breathed. Cleo recognized the gleam in Halvorsen's eyes. She had seen it in every one of her friends', and Billie's, and her own. He lived on discoveries, on the thrill of pulling back the curtains of the universe. They all did. "And let me guess. The energy comes from wherever you are. And our activity is depleting it."

The gold-dark point vibrated. *WE WILL ONLY GROW WEAKER IF YOUR EXPERIMENTS CONTINUE.*

"I see." Halvorsen approached the engine and extended one hand, palm out, toward it. He was very close to Cleo now; she could see the creases deepening around his mouth as he tried not to smile. "I didn't know. I would never wish to hurt you deliberately. But you must understand: this engine is crucial to the continued survival of my species. If you tell me how you work, I could try and remedy the issue."

THAT IS NOT POSSIBLE. YOU CANNOT COMPREHEND US.

Halvorsen's face fell. "I can't just stop. My planet is on the verge of irreversible disaster. I don't know if you can comprehend this, but there are billions of lives that will be at risk if I don't at least attempt to put this energy source to use. It sounds like we have more in common than not. We could work together. If you could just tell me how we might reach a compromise—"

YOU SEEM NOT TO BE LISTENING. WE TOLD YOU THAT YOU ARE KILLING US. IS THIS AN ACCEPTABLE CASUALTY IN YOUR QUEST FOR PROGRESS?

Halvorsen hesitated. It was too long a pause, too callous a deliberation, and Cleo would have silently yelled *What are you doing, the answer is obviously no* if a sickening sort of shock hadn't taken up residence in her throat.

"Of course not," Halvorsen finally said, and if Cleo was finding it hard to believe him, she knew the voices wouldn't either. "But I have to think of my own home, my own people—"

A deafening roar of bass and feedback ripped its way out of

the engine. Cleo clapped her hands over her ears right as Halvorsen did the same. She felt the sound vibrating her bones, leaving
an unshakable sense that this was a scream of frustration.

CEASE YOUR EXPERIMENTS, HALVORSEN, OR THE
CONSEQUENCES WILL BE BEYOND YOUR UNDER-
STANDING.

Halvorsen's hands fell to his sides. Cleo watched as the soft,
hopeful Dr. Dark Matter face she recognized slipped into something grim and determined, the lines around his mouth made
hard by the shadowy not-light.

"No."

Cleo stumbled back to reality like she'd been drop-kicked in
the ass. Billie was right there, though, stooping to meet her eyes.

"McQueary." Billie's hand twitched toward Cleo's face, like
she wanted to brush the hair out of her panicked eyes. "What did
you—did you see—"

Cleo did it for her, tucking her curls back behind her ears as
she tried to steady her breathing. "You didn't happen to know that
the dark matter engine could talk, did you?"

"Could *what*?" Billie's eyes went wide. The glow from the
engine made them a deeper, fluorescent green. "Absolutely not."

"Well, Halvorsen knew." Cleo ran her hand through her hair
again and kept it there, clenching it between her fingers as she
looked up at the engine. "The voice—voices, maybe—told him to
stop the *Providence* mission."

"Why?"

"They kept talking about energy being depleted. I think the
voices were from the Other Place."

The muscles in Billie's jaw seized. Cleo practically heard her
teeth grind. "And he didn't tell *anybody*—"

"Billie, there's more." Billie clamped down on whatever
creative insult she'd been about to call her old friend. Cleo

chewed on her lip. "They said the engine was—I think it was *hurting* them, and Halvorsen—it almost seemed like he didn't care—"

And then Billie held up a hand and froze, staring right through Cleo at something only she could see.

"Tell me later," she growled. "Wheeler is about to break the goddamn ship."

✳

WHEN CLEO AND BILLIE tumbled out of the elevator, they saw Abe doing his best to keep Kaleisha back from the edge of the spiraling ice storm that had almost engulfed the cafeteria.

"*Ros!*" Kaleisha screamed over the howling wind and the deafening rattle of hailstones bombarding the walls. "*Come back to us!*"

Cleo squinted through all the white and, sure enough, there was a figure at the center of the storm, knees curled against their chest and arms over their head, curly hair white with frost and whipping violently in the wind. Cleo ran to Abe and Kaleisha and grabbed them both by the arms.

"Oh, thank God," Kaleisha yelled, looking ready to cry with relief at the sight of Cleo and Billie. "Billie, can you counter their powers with the ship's climate control?"

"I'm trying!" Billie shouted back. "It's not enough, they're draining too much heat—"

"What happened?" Cleo asked.

"They were trying to freeze a pitcher of water," Abe replied, tears gathering in his eyes and being whipped away by the wind before they could fall, "and they couldn't, and they got frustrated, and just—they lost control, and the ice kept spreading—"

"We need to get to them." Cleo wrapped her arms around

herself and took a step toward the maelstrom. Growing up in the over-warm, over-wet levee towns of the Florida islands, she had never even seen snow, let alone anything like this shredding whiteout of a storm. There was ice everywhere: clinging to the tables, forming drifts on the floors, clumping over the see-through wall and blocking the stars. "We could talk them down if we can get through."

"Reid." Billie filled the space between Abe and Kaleisha, and suddenly the starship captain was back. Kaleisha looked at Billie, eyebrow raised. "Can you fold your way past the ice?"

"I don't know. I tried earlier, but it's hard when I can't see where I'm going, and the wind keeps messing me up—"

There was an ear-splitting groan of shifting steel. Kaleisha and Abe flinched, and Billie's frown deepened.

"If it gets any colder in here, it'll threaten the structural integrity of the hull!" Cleo bellowed. She considered just walking into the ice storm. Her skin would heal. Probably.

"Reid, you need to bend yourself over to Wheeler, now."

"Me too." Abe gripped Kaleisha's arm so hard he was probably cutting off circulation.

"And me." Cleo took Abe's other hand and definitely didn't notice the stricken look on Billie's face. "You can do it, Kal."

Kaleisha squeezed her eyes shut and reached forward with her free arm. The space in front of the three of them wavered, rippling like lines of rising heat. Kaleisha twisted her fingers around the air, and for a moment the sideways hail was flowing in impossible, fractal directions—and then Kaleisha grimaced, and everything went straight again.

"Nuh-uh," she grumbled, clenching her fist toward where Ros was as the ceiling moaned again. "This is not how we go down."

"Feel for the dark matter web, Reid."

"What do you think I'm trying to do, Billie?"

"Here." Cleo moved to Kaleisha's side and guided her fisted fingers open, until her friend's hand was resting in hers. "Do it with me."

Cleo breathed in, and Kaleisha did too. And something happened, something like a static shock passing from Cleo's fingers into Kaleisha's, something like osmosis, something like power flowing from where it was to where it was needed most. Something entirely new.

And Kaleisha stretched out her fingers once again, snow and ice flecks pummeling her dark skin, and made a motion like she was ripping a massive hole in the curtain of ice between them and Ros—

And Abe was grabbing them both by the waist, and the wind and the floor and Ros's distant form were bending up and over and closer, and as they all stepped forward together, Cleo was struck with an overwhelming sense that she was being pressed into diamond and stretched like dough all at once—

And the three of them, with a deafening snap, were standing in front of Ros. The storm resumed like it had never stopped, but Kaleisha and Abe fell immediately to their knees, ignoring the needles of ice tearing into their exposed skin, and wrapped their arms around Ros. Cleo followed suit, and tried not to tense up at how cold Ros's skin was to the touch.

"You heard Kal," Abe murmured. "Come back to us."

Ros shivered, not lifting their head from their knees. Their frost-caked hair crunched against Cleo's cheek. "They're angry," they whispered.

"No, baby, never," Kaleisha cried, tears gathering in her eyes, "no one's angry at you—"

Ros raised their head and Cleo saw (*thank God thank God*)

that their eyes were still blue. But Ros wasn't looking at Kaleisha; they were staring somewhere else, at something only they could see.

"They're angry," they said, more to the middle distance than to the other three. "And tired, and hurting."

Something nagged at Cleo, some vague sense of recognition at what was happening to Ros. She took their freezing face between her hands, blinked the snowflakes out of her eyes, and made Ros look at her. She tried to flow energy into them too, if that was in fact what she'd just done to Kaleisha, but it wasn't working; everything she gave to Ros seemed to slip away immediately.

"What you're seeing? It's not real, buddy," Cleo said instead. "I'm real, though. Feel that? I'm here."

Ros's pupils contracted, just a bit, like they were trying to shift their focus. Cleo almost thought that the roaring of the storm dropped in pitch.

"The others are safe," Ros breathed. "But *they*—they're still angry."

"Okay," Cleo whispered back, absolutely unable to think of anything else to say. "They are, though. They're safe."

A tear leaked out of Ros's eye. They blinked it away, and it traced a warm path through the ice on their cheek. "Cleo?"

"Yeah, Ros." Cleo laughed, and Abe and Kaleisha laughed in relief, tears streaming freely down both their faces. "Yeah."

✳

HERE'S ANOTHER THOUGHT EXPERIMENT: *Is going through something traumatic ever a good thing?*

That's an easy one: no. But the aftermath, the way people deal with it, might not always entirely suck.

To give one totally random example: After they all make sure that Wheeler just needs sleep and some warm fluids, Yang and Reid shuffle them off to bed and McQueary goes down to the lab with the hologram. ("I need to warm up too, Billie, and I bet the captain's quarters has fancy blankets.")

And it does. McQueary immediately makes herself a cocoon on Lucas's bed and looks up expectantly, like she wants the hologram to sit next to her. And the hologram does.

"No harm in warming up in here for a few minutes," McQueary says. "I need to preheat the blankets with my flesh before I bring them to my bed."

"Whatever you want," the hologram says softly, "considering you stepped into an ice storm with no hesitation today."

McQueary shrugs, her cheeks going pink, her freckles standing out stronger as a smile crinkles her nose. With her round face poking out from under her blanket hood, she looks precious. Cute, almost disarmingly so. Happy, despite it all. "It's no big deal," she says, as if risking your life for your friends isn't the biggest deal in the universe.

"Stop that." The hologram glares at her, though anyone who knows Lucas would recognize that as her affectionate glare. McQueary probably knows, by now. "You were—" The hologram clears her throat. "You were incredible."

"Damn, Captain, what did I do to earn this commendation?" McQueary can't think she's fooling anyone with that sarcasm, not with her dark eyes shining, blinding and contagious and beautiful, from the praise.

"It's true. My only censure would be that you entirely failed to prioritize your own safety. But you're not going to listen to me, so."

"I don't know, Billie. I'm so cozy right now I might just do anything you say."

It's dark in there, so McQueary doesn't see the hologram blush. Stupid idea, programming a hologram to blush.

✳

WHEELER HAS A DIFFERENT way of dealing with their trauma. Specifically by sneaking into the lab, long after McQueary and the hologram have talked themselves to sleep, and stealing Elijah's jacket. You know the one. With the anti–dark energy lining. That one.

CHAPTER 7

There was always a reasonable explanation for things. That was just science.

For example, Cleo was starting to order more and more salads from the replicator, just so she could smell something green. Abe and Billie had started inhaling every nature documentary in the ship's database. Ros was skipping movie nights to take longer and hotter baths, during which they would go through an entire bottle of lavender- or pine- or orange-scented bubble soap. Kaleisha was spending every available moment in the greenhouse with her nose practically shoved into the pots to absorb as much damp soil smell as possible.

There was a well-documented phenomenon, Ros grumblingly told them all one morning, first recorded among submarine crewmen, and later studied and named in the era of long-distance space flight: *biophilic deprivation anxiety*. The crews of the Erecura Deep missions had reported near-constant arguing over the available shifts in their greenhouse labs. Upon their return to Earth, astronauts had been known to cry at the sight of puppies, or rivers, or the changing of the leaves. With nothing around her to touch but metal walls and synthetic materials, and nothing to see out the window but black punctuated by the occasional streaking star, it was understandable that Cleo's absentminded thoughts were filled increasingly with the smell of the ocean, and the feeling of grass under her toes.

There had to be a similar explanation, then, for The Dream.

The first time she had it (Day 39), Cleo assumed it was a honey-sweet fluke. A bungle. A random chaos-theory twist of fate. Dreams were just your brain doing word association. Nothing less, and *definitely* nothing more.

After the second, third, and fourth times (Day 40 and, annoyingly, *twice* on Day 42), Cleo had to admit that it was becoming less of a fluke and more of an observable pattern. There was still a rational explanation, though—they'd been spending a lot of time together, obviously, and there was nobody else on this stupid ship besides Cleo's friends, who were more like her family, and therefore not exactly featured players in her frisky dreams. And, unfortunately, Billie *was* always reaching out like she'd forgotten she couldn't touch Cleo, and scooting up closer than was maybe strictly necessary while they were training or watching movies or tinkering in the lab. So it made some kind of sense that Cleo's unconscious mind would want to extrapolate, out of purely scientific interest, how Billie's breath would feel against her ear, how her long fingers would feel trailing up her back, how her hair would feel if Cleo released it (*finally*) from that fucking ponytail and twisted it between her fingers as Billie kissed her way down her—

Okay, well, maybe *scientific interest* was a bridge too far. Maybe Cleo just hadn't gotten any in—when had they started planning the Space Heist? A long time, anyway.

The fifth, seventh, *eleventh* times (Day Who Cares), though, there was only one explanation left: Cleo was losing her mind. Something had to be done about it. She couldn't keep waking up like this, desperate and pissed off and, worst of all, unable to properly start the day without touching herself to the thought of a woman with no body. It was untenable.

✳

KALEISHA WAS ALONE IN the cafeteria, serenely sipping her chai latte and watching the stars in the viewing wall. Cleo almost turned right back around, since she hated to disturb her friend's quiet morning with her nonsense, but Kaleisha saw her and smiled, so Cleo decided it was okay to sit across from her.

"Morning," she said. "Are Abe and Ros—"

"Still sleeping, per usual."

"Hmm." Cleo slumped into her seat with her head propped on her fists, making her cheeks squish pathetically in a way that unfortunately seemed to have no effect on Kaleisha. "I guess Abe sleeping a lot makes sense, with all the training he's doing with us, but Ros—"

"—shouldn't be so tired all the time, I know. I worry about them." Kal eyed Cleo over the top of her mug. "What's up with you, though?"

"Kal," Cleo said though her guppy-fish lips. "I think I'm going crazy."

"Mm." Kaleisha took a loud sip. "How so?"

Cleo was finding it hard to look Kaleisha in the eye, and realizing that she hadn't thought this far ahead. "I've been having. Uh. Weird dreams."

Kaleisha, to Cleo's horror, snorted into her mug like she knew exactly what Cleo was trying to hide. "Aww." Kaleisha raised her eyebrows amusedly. "Are you getting horny, babe? It's been, what, three months since that girl at the Stardust Lounge, and we all know that's your absolute upper limit—"

"I come to you *baring my soul* and this is how you treat me?"

"Oh boy." Kaleisha set her mug down. "Maybe you need a project."

Cleo scrubbed her thumb over the surface of the table.

Someone had already left a scratch there, long ago. "I'm trying. I've memorized every system on the ship, I've learned a frankly upsetting number of chess moves with names like racehorses. I've even started reading Billie's poetry books, which has to be the definition of insanity—"

"What about Billie's lab?" Kaleisha asked, and Cleo's dumb heart skipped a dumb beat. She didn't like the smile on Kaleisha's face, that little knowing smile that made her look exactly like her dad when he understood something the four of them didn't and wasn't going to wait politely for them to figure it out. "She's got so many books. And all those tools, and piles of junk you could build stuff out of."

"I don't know. Billie's junk is fine for fooling around with— I mean, ha, *fooling around*, not, um"—*stop talking stop talking abort abort abort*—"but there's nothing in there that'll keep me occupied for seven years. Seven years, Kal. It's barely been a little over a month. Do you know how long seven years actually is?"

Kaleisha gripped her mug tighter. "Yeah."

"Seven years ago we were *twenty.* Sophomores in college. Still hitting up that senior from my fluid dynamics class to buy us vodka. In seven more years we'll be thirty-four. Can you even imagine being thirty-four?"

Kaleisha kicked Cleo gently under the table, which made her realize she'd been jiggling her leg frantically. "Of course I've imagined it, Clo. When I thought about getting a teaching gig, and having a home with Abe, and maybe a kid."

"Oh." *Haha. Fuck.* "I forgot you actually like to plan that far ahead. Can't relate."

"Just because the world was falling apart doesn't mean I didn't want things."

All thoughts of The Dream wiped from her head, Cleo reached out and took Kaleisha's hand. Kaleisha laced their fingers together and squeezed. "You can still have those things," Cleo said, even though as soon as she said it she knew it wouldn't sound anything like the truth.

Kaleisha knew it too, and smiled sadly at her. "Fourteen years from now, on the off chance we're able to pull off this maneuver and get back to Earth? Maybe. But I'm not counting on it." She rubbed her thumb over Cleo's, staring glumly into her coffee. "I'm going to have to make new plans."

Cleo watched as the stars streaked by in the viewing wall. "Me too, I guess."

"Any ideas?"

"Oh, please. I was about to ask you to plan for me, like always."

Kaleisha snorted. "Like I could come up with anything that would keep you busy for seven whole years."

Cleo imagined a dark matter tendril seven years long. An endless rush of gold, the *Providence* swept up in its current like a tadpole in a river.

Seven years.

She pictured the water curving upward, bending and looping until it flowed straight up and then straight back down.

The tadpole could just leap from the start of the curve to the end.

Kaleisha, folding space. The three of them, stepping across the loop she'd made. Kaleisha, getting to have that house and that job and that adopted little munchkin she'd always wanted.

"What if it wasn't seven years?"

Kaleisha frowned at her. "We would have to go faster, which isn't physically possible."

"Not for mere mortals." Cleo felt her leg start to tap again, but this time with purpose. "But you know how you can fold space now?"

"*Oh.*" Kaleisha's eyes widened. "I can't make a fold big enough for the ship to cross, though."

"I think you could, actually." Cleo was already out of her chair and pacing back and forth in front of Kaleisha, she realized with a start. "But, um. You remember when we saved the ship from Ros's ice storm?"

"Not at all. What a forgettable experience."

Cleo stuck her tongue out at her friend. "Did you feel something . . . different, when I took your hand? Like energy flowing from me into you, maybe?"

Kaleisha frowned. "I guess so. I didn't think much of it at the time, but—"

"There was that energy, and then you were able to use your powers in ways you hadn't even come close to."

Kaleisha's eyes widened, and Cleo could tell they were remembering the same moment: that electric current flowing between them, that feeling like, all of a sudden, Cleo was no longer alone in that golden river. "What are you saying, Cleo?"

"I'm saying—" Cleo stopped pacing, her eyes coming to rest on the stars outside the window wall. "I've been thinking I'm just helplessly floating along on these channels of dark matter, but I don't think that's true. I think I can direct the flow. I think I'm a conduit."

"Oh my God." Kaleisha pressed a hand to her forehead, her brow furrowing in thought. "You flow out, and Ros flows in."

"*Yes.*" Cleo's mouth fell open at the simplicity that hadn't even occurred to her. Dark energy coming out of the Other Place through her, thermal energy replacing it through Ros. A closed circuit. A perfect system. "Kaleisha Reid, you're a genius."

"Duh. Okay. How fast do you think we could move?"

"Depends on what we're both capable of, but maybe we could cut down the journey by months, if not years."

"That's *huge*, babe. But"—Kaleisha pressed her fingers hard against her temple—"if we jump ahead by light-years, won't that mean . . . Will we be able to send messages to my dad anymore?"

Cleo slumped back into her chair. "Probably not. Moving faster than lightspeed would mean we'd outpace the radio waves."

"But we'd get home faster?" Cleo nodded. Kaleisha blinked forcefully and squared her shoulders. "Then it's worth a shot."

Cleo punched the air. "*Hell* yeah."

"Let's get Billie in on this."

For Christ's sake. "Should we? I mean, she's already so busy with—"

"Helping us hone our powers so we can maybe do something like this?" That smile crept onto Kaleisha's face again, like she knew something Cleo didn't, or at least was very close to figuring it out.

"Okay, sure, but—"

"Hey, Billie?"

Pop. "Morning, Reid." Billie looked at Cleo before she could pretend to be busy watching the stars, or sprinting away, or asking Kaleisha to teleport her out into the blissful vacuum of space. "McQueary."

Cleo gave what she hoped was a cool, nonchalant nod. Kaleisha kicked her under the table. She kicked back, harder.

"Billie, *Cleo* was *thinking*," Kaleisha said, "that we could use my powers to get to Proxima Centauri B faster."

"Huh. Near-lightspeed not fast enough for you?" Billie was teasing, but Cleo could tell from the deepening crease between her eyebrows that she was probably already running calculations in her head.

"Yeah, you know me. Cleo McQueary, infamous speed demon," Cleo teased back, because that's what they did. They teased each other in a totally normal, platonic way. "No, it's just that some of us would like to not spend the next three-quarters of a decade doing sock slides through the empty corridors and endlessly rewatching every *Star Trek* property. Which I normally wouldn't complain about, but eventually I'll be forced to watch that *Wrath of Khan* prequel with the English guy who looks like a naked potato, and who knows what that'll do to my deteriorating psyche."

Billie waved her hand and conjured up a panel of holographic equations and diagrams, flicking through them faster than Cleo could track. "Theoretically, it's possible, but Reid, you don't have anywhere near the capabilities for something like that."

"Right. Well." Cleo's fingers twisted around themselves. "I think I might be able to help her."

She explained her hypothesis to Billie, who just nodded mildly all the way through it, making adjustments to her simulations. "That makes sense," she said. "I wondered if there was an explanation for your sudden increase in ability, Reid."

"You don't seem surprised," Cleo grumbled. "Or, like, impressed."

Cleo realized she'd made a horrible mistake when Billie and Kaleisha both snapped their eyes to her. "Do you want me to be?" Billie asked softly.

Yeah, Cleo, Kaleisha mouthed behind a cupped hand, *do you want her to be?*

"I didn't—*ugh*." Cleo let her face fall forward into her hands, just for a second. "So we'll all have to train with you a lot more, won't we?"

"Yes?" Cleo refused to look at Billie's face, but she could hear the confused, mouth-twisting annoyance in her voice. "Is that a problem, McQueary?"

"No. Not at all." Cleo straightened up and gave her best everything-is-fine smile. Everything *was* fine. Would be, anyway.

Sometimes you just had preternaturally persistent sex dreams about people you had to see every day. Life went on.

"Let's get on it, then." Kaleisha clapped Cleo on the shoulder as she got up to go wake Abe and Ros, and Cleo could have sworn that she flashed her that knowing smile again, angled exactly so that Billie wouldn't see.

✳

WHY HAS WHEELER BEEN so tired lately, you ask? Well, I'll tell you.

Since the incident with the ice storm, Wheeler has been spending every night in the bio lab, trying to replicate the compound in the lining of Halvorsen's jacket that makes the material impervious to dark radiation. It's difficult, given that the jacket is twenty years old and many of its components have sublimated or decayed.

But Wheeler is—will be, would have been, whatever—an excellent doctor. So they're making good progress. Or bad progress, if you're the kind of person who thinks that trying to make a slapdash, dark-matter-infused, DNA-altering medicine to use on yourself is a bad idea.

McQueary would definitely think so. And though I don't really have a moral leg to stand on here, I think I'm inclined to agree with her. God, it's like Halvorsen all over again.

✳

ARCHIVED: *Providence* Intracrew Messaging Service Conversation — Capt. Wilhelmina Lucas and Mission Specialist Elijah Lucas, September 23, 2040

WILHELMINA LUCAS
Happy birthday, Jar Jar :)

ELIJAH LUCAS

Is that . . . is that an e m o j i

WILHELMINA LUCAS

Yeah, don't get your panties in a twist about it
When's your break, I want to drop off your present

ELIJAH LUCAS

A present? For moi??? Whatever could it be??? The
    anticipation is killing me
(1400h)

WILHELMINA LUCAS

See you then, shithead
How's your day so far

ELIJAH LUCAS

Pretty good! The guys managed to strongarm the mess
    hall into giving me a slice of gluten-free cake
    for breakfast
Dr. Meynier figuratively kicked my ass in the psych
    session this morning, though
She grabbed onto the "dead parents" thing early on
    and she's riding that ship into the sunset, baby

WILHELMINA LUCAS

Ugh. Want me to literally kick her ass

ELIJAH LUCAS

It's my birthday I think you're legally required

*

ON THAT FIRST DAY (Day 52), Billie focused on testing the limits of
Cleo's new ability. She had her practice channeling that slippery
Other Place energy into Kaleisha until Cleo's fingers tingled, and
Kaleisha could turn space into an accordion and fold herself from
the cafeteria to the flight deck and back. And in between Gatorade
breaks and Kaleisha accidentally sending herself shins-first into
a table and several doses of aspirin between the two of them,

they slowly, surely started to get the hang of it. By evening, Cleo's head was pounding and Kaleisha was sweaty and shaking with exertion, but smiling.

(Cleo had The Dream again that night. Given the fact that Billie had spent most of the day focusing on Kaleisha instead of standing just behind Cleo and whispering huskily in her ear, Cleo may have expected her brain to have chilled the hell out, but no such luck. Still, it was fine. Being around Billie was still easy. Nice, even. Everything was fine.)

A few days later—were they really making such quick progress?—Kaleisha graduated to folding the space just outside the ship. While Cleo stood behind her, one hand on Kaleisha's shoulder pulsing ever-larger sparks of power through her, Kaleisha folded pockets into the space just ahead of the *Providence*. None of them were very big, or lasted longer than a few fractions of a second, but Billie was able to track them through the ship's computer, and assured the two of them that the folds were stable and gradually getting larger.

"Am I doing enough?" Cleo found herself whispering, while Kaleisha collapsed into the captain's chair for a breather. "Should I be giving her more? Is she making enough—"

"You're fine," Billie whispered back, raising an eyebrow. "You and Reid have already made so much progress, working under such unprecedented conditions, I'm surprised you both haven't had a breakdown by now."

Cleo rolled her eyes. "Thanks for the vote of confidence. You sure you're not just saying that?"

"Oh my God, McQueary. If I've ever done *anything* to make you think I would coddle you like that—"

"Right, sorry. Perish the thought."

And Billie's holographic eyes crinkled in that almost-smiley way, and as they stood together watching the stars, her shoulder drifted toward Cleo's, almost like she wanted to bump them companionably together.

(But again, everything was fine. Having frisky, golden-hued dreams about someone didn't have to be weird unless you made it weird. Granted, The Dream started to morph and multiply into something more like a Rotating Roster of Dreams. Variations on a theme, so to speak. Successive movements in the *What Billie Would Feel Like Inside Me* Symphony.

If anything, it just made Cleo focus harder on the training. Because no way was she letting her brain spend seven Gregorian years trying to convince her that she was into Billie, who she couldn't fuck even if she'd actually wanted to.)

✳

ARCHIVED: Providence Intracrew Messaging Service Conversation — Program WL2-Mk1.4 and Abraham Yang, September 11, 2061

>   **PROGRAM WL2-MK1.4**
>   Yang I have a question
>
>   **ABRAHAM YANG**
>   Hit me
>
>   **PROGRAM WL2-MK1.4**
>   [. . .]
>   [. . .]
>
>   **ABRAHAM YANG**
>   Take your time bud
>
>   **PROGRAM WL2-MK1.4**
>   [. . .]
>   Do you know why McQueary is acting weird around me
>
>   **ABRAHAM YANG**
>   Weird how?

PROGRAM WL2-MK1.4
Talking less
Acting nervous

ABRAHAM YANG
Hmm! I don't know. Maybe you should ask her what's up?

PROGRAM WL2-MK1.4
[. . .]
Never mind forget about it

ARCHIVED: *Providence* Intracrew Messaging Service
Conversation — Abraham Yang and Kaleisha Reid,
September 11, 2061

ABRAHAM YANG
[screenshot of previous conversation]
AHHHHHHHHAGHJGSHJGSHHSDKQKGHERGF

KALEISHA REID
Oh my GODDDDDDDDDD
YES
Yes yes yes
Cannot WAIT to see what plays out here
Mwahahahaha

ABRAHAM YANG
I hope they can talk it out:)

KALEISHA REID
This is gonna be DELICIOUS
Oh speaking of talking it out, I meant to ask
Has Ros said anything . . . illuminating to you at all

ABRAHAM YANG
:(no :(

KALEISHA REID
Yeah me neither

ABRAHAM YANG
I'll keep trying, don't worry love

ARCHIVED: Providence Intracrew Messaging Service
Conversation — Abraham Yang and Ros Wheeler,
September 12, 2061

ABRAHAM YANG
Hey!! Where'd you go? Heard you get up

ROS WHEELER
Oh hey didn't realize you were awake

ABRAHAM YANG
Only barely
What are you up to?? I also can't sleep

ROS WHEELER
Just needed to walk around

ABRAHAM YANG
You can always tell me if you're feeling bad, you
  know

ROS WHEELER
I know
I will

ABRAHAM YANG
[. . .]
But, like
You haven't been
Telling me, I mean. Or anyone

ROS WHEELER
Who says I'm feeling bad

ABRAHAM YANG
[. . .]
Do you really think I haven't noticed that you're not
  talking to us

ROS WHEELER
I talk to you guys all the time
Not like there's anything else to do on this goddamn
  ship

ABRAHAM YANG
You know what I mean

ROS WHEELER
[. . .]

ABRAHAM YANG
Come on
Whatever it is, I want to help
I love you
[. . .]
[. . .]
Ros?

✳

SEVERAL MORNINGS LATER (DAY 74), with training having grown more intense and more productive each day, Cleo arrived at the cafeteria before Kaleisha, feeling tired and on edge. She clutched her replicator coffee for strength and called out to Billie for some company.

Billie didn't appear. No *pop*, no snark, no nothing.

"Billie?"

Still nothing. Cleo started to panic—the ship's computer was down, Billie was gone, they were going to career off course and the engine would malfunction and explode them all into quark dust—

"Billie, if this is some kind of joke, let me be the first to tell you—"

Pop.

"What?"

Billie said it though gritted teeth, around clenched fists and bloodshot eyes. She was practically trembling with tension, about to go supernova, all the long lines of her threatening to collapse, then explode.

"Jesus," Cleo breathed. "What's wrong?"

"Nothing."

"Um, bullshit. You look like death. What took you so long to answer me?"

Billie turned and stalked away across the cafeteria. "What am I, your secretary? Your servant?"

"Billie, *what*?"

"I don't have to come like a . . . like a *dog* every time you call me, McQueary. I have other . . . I have my own . . . fucking—"

Billie kicked at one of the benches and *yelled* when her foot passed through, her whole body flickering.

"Okay, okay, stop." Cleo trotted after Billie and shooed her away from the table. "Sit down, take a goddamn breath. Tell me what's going on with you."

To Cleo's mild surprise, Billie did as she said, collapsing cross-legged onto the floor and dropping her face into her hands, elbows in her lap. Cleo waited for her to speak, counting her deep, harsh breaths.

"I was double-checking the date on Earth." Billie's voice was muffled in her palms. "It's, uh. Complicated. With the relativity."

Cleo sat down facing Billie. It was so hard to know what to do with her hands. She thought of the way Abe, when Kaleisha was sad, would rub her knees soothingly as she cried. She realized, with an accompanying heart palpitation, that she wished she could do that for Billie. Their knees were so close together. "What day is it?" she asked, instead.

"September twenty-third. Elijah's birthday."

"Oh." Cleo twisted her fingers in her lap. "Do you want to, like, talk about it?"

"No."

Cleo waited. She watched Billie take off her glasses and rub at her eyes, hard. She heard Billie sigh, almost imperceptibly.

"His favorite cake was carrot. He used to get sad when our

parents would send him to school with cupcakes and the other kids wouldn't eat them because of the raisins."

Cleo chuckled morosely. "Yeah?"

"And he never—he couldn't stand not knowing what I'd gotten him for a present, so he'd always bully me into ruining the surprise. I tried, for a few years, to pretend I hadn't even gone shopping, but he always saw through that."

Cleo thought back to her wimp, to the little boy careening joyfully down the hallway. To the look on Billie's face when she heard him trip and fall, like making sure that Elijah was safe was what she'd been made for, and everything else was just bonus features.

"He really loved Neil," Billie continued, and Cleo felt her stomach fall like a rock. "They had the same stupid sense of humor. They both cried whenever a dog died in a movie. And they were both so happy all the time, happier than I ever thought it was possible to be, like they had sunshine living inside them. That was what I loved about them most. The sunshine."

Billie opened her eyes. Her eyebrows knit together briefly like she was surprised to see Cleo still sitting in front of her. Cleo saw that muscle in her jaw work, as she chewed on her tongue or whatever she was about to say.

"Eli would have liked you," Billie finally whispered. Cleo's breath hitched in her chest. "And Neil too. I think he would have wanted—he was always telling me, toward the end—"

Billie's words were cut off in a strangled sound—*what,* Cleo wanted to scream, *what did he tell you, in the end*—and she looked down at her hands again. Cleo ignored all the particles in her body screaming at her to *not do that,* and scooted herself forward, until her knees were only atoms away from Billie's knees. She thought she heard Billie inhale sharply, just a little, thought she felt Billie lean in just a little closer. But her thoughts had been traitorous lately, and were not to be trusted.

"They both would have told you," Cleo murmured, "that it's okay to feel your feelings. It's okay to be sad, or angry, or whatever this is. It's okay to grieve. To just do your best. Because that's enough, you know?"

Billie shook her head infinitesimally. Their foreheads were almost touching—or would be, if they could touch.

"No, listen, we don't have to train today," Cleo continued. "I could just tell the others that you're, I don't know, running diagnostics on the ship's mainframe. They won't even ask me what that means."

Billie breathed out an almost-laugh and looked at Cleo, her mouth slightly open. Cleo didn't look at her mouth. And Billie definitely didn't look at hers, or inch even closer like Cleo was a star and Billie was just letting herself succumb to the gravity—

"No," Billie said. "Let's get to work."

And she stood up very suddenly, so that Cleo had to scramble backward on her ass to avoid phasing through her, and marched toward the open center of the room.

"Get up, McQueary," she called, with barely any roughness in her voice to betray what had just happened. "We have to go help Reid, or she'll never fold this old wreck through space and time."

Cleo rolled her eyes, but heaved herself to her feet and followed Billie. And, even though her blood was buzzing furiously, by the end of the day she was, in fact, helping Kaleisha move large machinery from one end of the ship to the other. When she did it, Billie smiled, and it was fine. Everything was fine.

✳

WHEELER IS GETTING CLOSE to isolating the compound. As they make progress, they work even harder, they sleep even later, and they brush off questions about how they're doing even more brusquely.

They show up at training even less often. Eat dinner with their friends less often. Laugh at McQueary's and Yang's jokes less often. Once they have the compound, a serum won't be far off, and I'm worried.

If only they would just talk to the others! It would kill McQueary to know what they're doing. She cares about Wheeler so damn much—

Wheeler is better at containing their powers now. Having this harebrained scheme to focus on has helped. But sometimes, late at night—like now, right this second—their powers still take them by surprise. Their hands clench up, the air in the lab goes cold, and their mind—well. It's hard to explain. If they would just think, for one moment, beyond their terror, Wheeler would realize what they've seen, and what they know. They would remember who they were talking about, when the other three were holding them in the eye of that storm and all they could say was "They're angry." It might even occur to them that Yang is up too, watching them on the security feed in the flight deck, finally realizing where they've been going every night. Worried at first, and now terrified.

They don't understand yet, but they've seen the truth. It just won't make sense until—

(Until what, idiot? Stop getting your goddamn hopes up.)

✳

ARCHIVED: Transcript of Radio Message from *Providence I* to Erebus Headquarters, September 26, 2061

> **KALEISHA REID**: Hi, Dad. So, we've got a new plan. It's going to sound crazy—or maybe it's not, no more so than everything else I've told you, anyway. I'm going to fold space so we can move faster than light.
>
> **CLEO MCQUEARY**: Did you hear that? Faster than light, make sure that gets in the papers—

KALEISHA REID: [Laughter] Hush. Billie—Captain Lucas—thinks I might be able to get us to Proxima Centauri in a matter of months, meaning we'd be home by next Christmas rather than a decade and a half from now. So, obviously, that's a good thing. But it does mean that this will be my last message that's able to reach you.

ROS WHEELER: [whispering] Fuck.

KALEISHA REID: We've got everything we need. The ship is running well. The plants are doing great, better than we ever expected.

ABRAHAM YANG: The cookies that the replicator makes aren't anywhere near as good as yours!

KALEISHA REID: Seconded. Point is, Dad, we're going to be okay. I love you so much. I miss you so much. I'll take a picture of this other planet and send it to you, even though it'll get home after we do, because I'll be thinking of you so hard when we look at that alien sun.

CLEO MCQUEARY: Also, um. If anyone has, like, I don't know, gotten in touch with my own dad, could you let him know—you know, if he's paying attention or whatever—that I'm alright, I guess. Ahh okay bye.

✳

THE FIRST TIME KALEISHA brought the *Providence* through a breach, Cleo was 97 percent sure they weren't going to make it.

There were so many ways it could go wrong. Billie could flub the timing, interpreting the readings on the dashboard incorrectly and giving Kaleisha the signal too soon, making her cut the ship in half and kill them all instantly. Cleo could gauge her own powers badly, giving Kaleisha only enough energy to make a too-small fold in space, sending just the middle of the ship forward and leaving the *Providence* cored like an apple and killing them all a little slower. Or Cleo could finally get her comeuppance for meddling in space magic she didn't understand, accidentally crack open the Other Place, and release some kind of lightning-voiced dark matter monster that would kill them all as slowly as possible. All of these possibilities had haunted Cleo's dreams, among other things.

But when Kaleisha actually did it—actually bent a ripple in spacetime big enough to launch the ship forward a full quarter of a light-year, by Billie's readings, with a jolt and a deafening crack—it felt almost anticlimactic. The *Providence* didn't shudder apart beneath them. Kaleisha didn't collapse out of exhaustion. There were no dark matter monsters to be seen. They were still, beautifully, on course. Everything was fine.

Still, Cleo let Kaleisha pull her by their linked hands into a grasping, enveloping hug, and she laughed as Abe, and even Ros, joined in and squeezed them both like they'd just been saved from certain doom. Which, maybe they kind of had, Cleo thought as Abe twirled her off her feet and around the flight deck. Maybe none of them had ever quite dared to say aloud how likely it was that seven or more years in space with nothing but their thoughts and their terrifying powers would have been the death of them. Not of their bodies, necessarily, but of the softer parts of them—the parts that needed a planet under their feet, and a sky to look up at.

Cleo saw those soft parts of her friends come back from a brink she hadn't realized they'd all been standing on. She saw it in Abe's shining grin, in the gentle squeeze of her hand from Ros, in the way Kaleisha's killer high five turned into another desperate, brink-of-tears, rocking-back-and-forth hug.

She didn't quite see the same change in Billie. Cleo had never asked her how she felt about the plan to get to Proxima Centauri faster. She didn't have a glimmer of a clue what she would have done with the answer. But even if Billie wasn't looking quite as ecstatic as the others, she was still watching Cleo with *something* in her eyes, something gentle and deep that Cleo suspected she would never climb out of, if she let herself fall.

Still, she found herself drifting ever so slightly away from the tightly packed joy of her friends, and toward Billie. "Don't look at me like that, man," she said quietly, even though she probably wanted Billie to never stop looking at her like that. "We both know that getting sappy makes your brain short-circuit."

Billie snorted. "Alright." She leaned in close so Cleo could hear her over Abe's renewed, happy shouting. "Then I won't tell you how brilliant your plan was," she said against Cleo's ear. "Or how amazing you are."

Cleo let her eyes flutter closed for an instant, maybe to memorialize the final moment in which she could still pretend she had anything resembling a self-preservation instinct.

"No," she whispered back, "tell me."

Alright, so. Turns out, nothing was fine.

✴

ARCHIVED: Medical Report — Veronica Ruiz, MD, to Chief Engineer Kristoff Halvorsen, PhD, June 3, 2041

> Kris—Got the tests back. Don't think the jacket worked. Or it was already too late when you made it, anyway. Give me a call ASAP.
> V

CHAPTER 8

They make record time.

Well, any amount of time getting to Proxima Centauri B would have been a record, since they're the first. But you know what I mean. With Reid and McQueary working together, they're over halfway there in about three weeks. It takes a lot out of both of them, of course, so they can only make a jump every few days. But in between, they get to rest a lot, and Yang brings them coffee and tells them stories and they all watch movies late into the artificial nights. Even the hologram. McQueary always makes sure to include the hologram.

I wish I could say that McQueary is getting less jumpy now that they're moving faster, but she seems more agitated than ever. I wish I knew what was wrong with her.

I think I want her to feel better. I think I want her to be happy. That's not weird, is it? I've been watching her long enough. Makes sense that I've gotten a little invested.

✳

SOMETIMES, WHEN SHE WAS feeling particularly out of her mind with post-training exhaustion or unresolved tension or biophilic deprivation anxiety, which she'd taken to calling by the much snappier name of The Deep Space Blues, Cleo fell into day-dreams about how each of her friends would respond if she told them she had a whatever-she-had on Billie. She'd never had a crush to tell them about. Her longing tended to take other forms.

Abe, she imagined, would stare open-mouthed at her for a full six to eight seconds. *Well, uh, that's. Thank you for telling me,* he would stutter, rubbing the back of his neck and nervously smiling at a point just over Cleo's left ear. *I mean, I guess I can see how you would—'cause you guys are always, you know—but, like.* And Abe would take a deep breath, cringe with every muscle in his body, and look directly at her. *Isn't Billie kind of . . . made of light?*

And Cleo would say, *Yes, Abe, you're right, and I'm made of dumbass. Crush discontinued, thank you for your insight.*

But then Abe would get that twinkle in his eye that he got when he was thinking about Kaleisha. *I don't know, buddy. You really like her?*

I think so.

Then you gotta go for it, right?

Okay, forget Abe.

Kaleisha would sigh and do her absolute best not to laugh at her, for which Cleo would be grateful even though she would know she deserved it. *What's the plan, babe?* she would say, closing whatever book she was reading. *How exactly are you going to be in a relationship with a hologram? I don't see that being enough for you.*

And Cleo would say, *You're so right, Kal, thank you for your wisdom. I'll stop fantasizing about climbing Billie like a beautiful, grumpy tree right away, because that's all it is: a fantasy.*

But then Kaleisha would say, with that little smile she usually reserved for talking about Abe, *That's not what I asked, babe. It's*

not just about wanting to jump her bones, right? She makes you happy.

Hey hey hey, you just said—

I know what I said. And Kaleisha would take a matter-of-fact sip of her coffee and say, *Love should feel like sharing your whole heart with someone, not tearing it in half. Only you can decide which one this is.*

So Kaleisha was off the table too.

(Once or twice, late in the night—"night," that is, there was no night in the space between stars—Cleo drew her dad's NASA jacket tighter around herself and imagined Neil. Faceless, dead Neil, who she couldn't help but picture as having dark, curly hair like hers, either because of a dim childhood memory of photos on the news or because of a vain, stupid hope that Billie had a type, and Cleo was it.

I feel like I'm not allowed, she would say.

Of course you are, he'd say, because by all accounts he was a nice guy. *Just take care of her, okay?*

I don't know how, Cleo would say, to herself or to Neil or to the empty space around her. *I don't know why she'd ever let me—*)

Ros. Well. Ros was a little harder to talk to these days. But if they were feeling up to it, they would probably say something like *I don't know, Cleo. If anyone can figure out how to make it work with a hologram, it's probably you.*

And Cleo would say, *Thanks for your faith in my, uh, software engineering skills, but I think I must have missed the How to Make Love to Your Computer Girlfriend unit in Heuristic Programming.*

And Ros would say, *Listen, not that I'm not thrilled to be asked my aroace opinion on this very pressing issue, but some of us are a little too busy being slowly consumed by our extra-dimensional ice powers to really sink our teeth into a problem like this—*

And Cleo would say, *Come on, you know I didn't—*

"Clo?"

Kaleisha was standing at the foot of Cleo's bunk, Abe hovering nervously behind her. Cleo sat up in her bed and put on her best "What, no, I wasn't just arguing with you in my head" face. "Hi, hey. Hello."

"Hi." Kaleisha's hand twitched at her side, and she thrust it into the pocket of her *Providence*-issue trousers. "Are you busy?"

"I had a pretty full night of just lying here and staring up at the ceiling planned, but I think I can squeeze you in."

The corner of Abe's mouth twitched, but he didn't smile. Cleo wasn't sure she'd ever seen him go so long without smiling, and it had only been a minute. "It's Ros," he said. "I'm worried about them."

"Oh man, okay, what—"

"They're in the bio lab," Kaleisha said. "You should come see for yourself."

"Um." Dread settled heavy in Cleo's chest. "You got it. Lead the way."

✳

THE BIO LAB WAS a carefully organized disaster—beakers and bottles crowded on every surface, rows and rows of petri dishes arrayed in various states of incubation, concentric circles of test tubes spiraling around the centrifuge. Cleo had seen Ros in the throes of an obsessive project enough times to immediately recognize the signs. Usually, though, they told the other three about it before they got this deep, so Abe could bring them late-night cookies and Kaleisha could convince them to go to sleep occasionally and Cleo could be a sounding board for all their cluttered ideas.

But Ros had kept this from them all, as evidenced by the way

they jumped and spun around when the elevator dinged open, arms spread like they could hide the entire lab behind them.

"What are you guys doing here?" they asked, eyes bloodshot and betrayed.

Kaleisha took a tiny breath and held it. "What do you think, love? How long did you think you could go without telling us anything?"

Ros's eyes flicked to Abe, whose shoulders folded in on themselves even as he maintained eye contact. "I saw you on the cams, Ros," he said.

"So you spied on me."

"No, not really, we've just been so—"

"So this is why you've been sleeping all hours of the day, I guess?" Cleo interrupted Abe, taking a step deeper into the lab and looking around. "Are you going to tell us what you've been working on?"

Ros watched Cleo out of the corner of their eye as she bent down to peer at a rack of test tubes. "You wouldn't understand."

Kaleisha shot a warning look at Cleo, but Cleo straightened up to look Ros in the eye anyway. She thought of Billie. She thought of how many times Billie had simply given her permission to tell the truth, and so she had. "Try me."

Ros's nostrils flared. For a long moment, Cleo thought they were going to refuse, kick them all out of the lab, and never talk to them again. But then they turned to rustle through a cabinet. And from it, they pulled a neatly folded crew member's jacket. It was almost the same as any other, as the ones they'd all been wearing themselves for weeks. But Cleo would have recognized that one anywhere.

"Halvorsen's jacket," she said grimly. "Ros, do I even want to—"

"I've almost replicated the compound in the lining that neutralizes the effects of dark energy." Ros squared their jaw, fixing them all with their ready-to-fight look, which Cleo would have found endearing under any other circumstance.

"Ros." Abe stepped forward, ready to—well, Cleo didn't know what, but she guessed that he was full of the same feeling that Ros was about to fall, and that one of them had to be close enough to catch them when they did. "You can't."

"Yes, I can." Ros's nostrils flared again. Cleo winced, bracing for a spray of ice shards, and hated herself for it. "I knew you wouldn't understand."

"We don't have to be doctors to understand that injecting yourself with some kind of untested dark matter medicine is a *bad idea*." Kaleisha's voice was getting louder than she usually let it. "You gotta at least check that you got it right with Billie, whose head I seem to remember you almost biting off, by the way, when you found out that she tried to slip this jacket to her brother—"

"Billie's not a medical doctor either. And that was different—"

"You don't even know if it'll work!" Cleo felt like pulling her hair out, and realized she already was. She loosened her fist from her scalp. "The lining was supposed to *prevent* the dark energy from affecting Elijah, and now that you've already been affected you have no idea what it'll—"

"You think I haven't accounted for that?" Ros's breath came in short bursts, like they were wounded. "You think I haven't taken every precaution—"

"Every precaution except telling us!" Kaleisha shouted. "Every precaution except letting us know what you were feeling, or letting us help you, or letting us at least be there to drag your unconscious body to the med bay when you go into convulsions!"

"I knew you'd react this way." Ros's eyes brimmed with furious tears. Their fingers tightened, white-knuckled, around the jacket, and Cleo could have sworn the temperature dropped a few degrees. "I'm going to do it whether you approve or not. I can't wait anymore. I need to cure myself."

"Ros." Abe curled a hand around their shoulder. Ros flinched. Cleo saw Abe's heart break a little. "It's not about—you're not sick, you don't need a cure, you just need to come back to training and—"

Ros shrugged him off. "Easy for you to say, when you don't have to deal with any of this—and you, Kal, with your phenomenal cosmic powers, and Cleo gets to see the future. You don't get it, any of you, you *can't,* because you can do amazing things, and all I can do is lose my mind and nearly kill us all."

Cleo reached a hand toward Ros, as if it could make any difference. "Buddy, I—"

"Stop." One of the tears finally fell from Ros's eye onto the jacket, where it fractured into ice crystals. "Don't make me lose control and hurt you. Don't you dare."

And they shoved the freezing jacket into Cleo's hands, and her vision went black.

✳

ARCHIVED: Notes on the Conterminous Dimension, 06/15/41 by Dr. Kristoff Halvorsen

> Last communication from Conterm. Dim. was 3 wks ago; assume they could no longer justify expending the E
>
> How much E required for voices to traverse Conterm. Dim. boundary?
>
> How much E required, hypothetically, for humans to traverse boundary?
>
> Still feeling ill—dark m. levels still elevated— condition progressing—Dr. Ruiz has been handled—more tests to come

✳

IT TOOK LONGER THAN usual for the darkness to loosen its grip on her. Almost like she was wimping someplace farther or deeper or more forbidden. Almost like she had to swim through more layers of the universe.

Eventually, Cleo opened her eyes. She was in a small, empty room flooded with flat, golden light. Empty, that is, except for the chair next to the window, and the young man with blond hair sitting in it.

He turned to look at Cleo—no, *through* Cleo. Because she was wimping, and he couldn't see her, because she wasn't there.

"What are you doing here?" he said. His voice was clever and kind, and his eyes were a bright, familiar green.

Cleo twisted around to look for whoever he must have been speaking to. There was nobody there. Just a closed door.

"I'm talking to you."

She whirled back around to face the man. "You can see me?"

He inclined his head curiously, and his eyes narrowed in thought. "Should I not be able to?"

"No. Usually this is a one-way-mirror deal." The eyes. The searching expression. "Are you Elijah?"

The man frowned, like he had to think about it. "I think so." Then his frown lifted, and he beamed at her. "No, you're right, I am. Thanks for reminding me. It can be easy to forget, and it's been so long since—I haven't spoken to—"

He glanced toward the door, like he had suddenly remembered that he'd lost something.

Okay, what?

Cleo stepped closer, trying to gauge exactly how old he was, when in his life this might have been, and whether Billie would have told her if Elijah had ever had some kind of amnesia situation going on. Or a *psychic connection to the fucking multiverse* situation.

"What do you mean, Elijah?"

"I mean, I think it's been a long time. Time works differently here." Elijah blinked at her, whatever he'd lost behind the door forgotten again. "Do you know how long we've been gone?"

Cleo's heartbeat kicked into overdrive. "Who's 'we'?"

Elijah also had the same *you're an idiot, McQueary* face as his sister. "The crew of *Providence I*, of course. You guys *have* noticed we're gone, right?"

No.

What?

No way.

Cleo blinked, trying not to betray how much she felt like she'd been blown apart into particles and poorly reassembled. Her insides were scrambled. It was like jumping to sub-lightspeed all over again.

Breathe through it, McQueary.

"You mean . . ." Her mouth was so, so dry. "You mean you're all—"

"We're all here, yeah." Elijah glanced distractedly out the window, then toward the door again. "The others are around, somewhere. I have to find—"

The others. If Cleo let herself contemplate the full implications of that, she was not going to be able to stay on her feet. "Elijah," she said slowly, urgently, "where's *here*?"

He fixed his eyes on her again. "It's hard to explain."

"Can you try?"

Elijah chewed the inside of his cheek. "You found me. So you already know, even if you don't realize."

Cleo breathed in. Breathed out.

Billie, in the med bay: *Dark matter exists somewhere else.*

A conterminous dimension that occupies the same fourth-dimensional manifold as our own.

In, out.

Ros, in the eye of the storm, looking through her at something only they could see. *They're angry. And tired, and hurting. The others are safe. But they're still angry.*

In—

Halvorsen, facing that chorus of voices from everywhere and nowhere, voices like thunder and hurricanes and the rush of dark matter past her ears—

WE CANNOT ALLOW YOU TO CONTINUE.

"This is the Other Place," Cleo exhaled. "And it—it took you. It took all of you."

Elijah nodded slowly, like he was trying not to disturb something. "They had their reasons," he whispered. "But—"

And then Cleo was struck by lightning.

That's what it felt like, anyway, as her vision crackled apart into painful white shards, as her whole body fizzed like a radio tower in an electrical storm, as she felt her mind being *squeezed* in the fist of something big and angry and broken—

And she thought she might have been back in the lab, and Ros was standing over her mouthing something terrified that she couldn't hear over the tempest in her head—

And she might have been back with Elijah, who was scrambling from his chair to reach out to her—

And she might have been somewhere else, where the air was cold and glistening with all the colors of the rainbow, and a deep, discordant voice was growling in her ear:

Good. You're on your way.

And then Cleo gasped back to the golden room. She was on her hands and knees, and Elijah was indeed kneeling by her side, his panic making him look even younger than he was. When he tried to touch her face, his hand phased through her.

"Come find us, Cleo." His voice echoed softly in her head, in her chest, everywhere. "I think you're the only one who can."

✳

ROS WAS ALREADY IN full doctor mode when Cleo crashed back to awareness on the floor of the bio lab.

"Oh, thank God," they said when they saw her eyes fly open. "Can you hear me?" Cleo nodded, blinking hard. "You collapsed during your wimp and went into convulsions. Your nose—" Cleo automatically reached up to touch her face. Her fingers came away covered in blood. Ros ran a hand over their mouth and gestured to Abe and Kaleisha, who were also leaning worriedly over Cleo. "Help me get her to the med bay. It could have been a seizure, and I need to rule out an aneurysm—"

"It's not any of that." Cleo sat up, surprising Ros enough to knock their fluttering hands off of her chest. Everything hurt. She didn't care. "I need to talk to Billie. Right now."

Ros made tense eye contact with Kaleisha. "Cleo, what you need is to—"

"Trust me." Cleo gripped Ros's shoulder hard, shocking them into silence. "I'll meet you in the med bay afterward. Just—just don't make any major decisions without me, okay?"

A frown creased Ros's forehead. They let out a trembling breath, and nodded. "Promise."

And Cleo trusted them with every particle in her body, even if that made her a fool.

She let Abe and Kaleisha pull her to her feet and staggered into the elevator. As the door dinged shut, she leaned against the wall to stay upright. She wiped at her nose, and blood smeared darkly all along the sleeve of the uniform she was wearing. She made sure not to get any on Elijah's jacket, clutched safely in her other arm.

The elevator deposited her on the flight deck, and Cleo gripped the back of the captain's chair for support before calling out.

"Billie."

Pop. "Hey, what's—"

Billie froze at what must have been the deeply upsetting sight of Cleo's bloody, sweat-drenched face.

"What in the *hell*, McQueary? Are you—"

"I'm fine." Billie's mouth flattened into a skeptical line. Cleo made herself hold Billie's gaze, suddenly unsure if she could handle what was coming. "There's something I need to tell you. I thought you might not want all the others to be around when you heard it."

"Jesus." Billie crossed her arms like her hands would have vibrated away if she hadn't. "Spit it out, then, so I can get you to the med bay."

Cleo held up the jacket. She could still feel it resonating faintly with all the strange, golden frequencies of the Other Place. "I wimped Elijah."

Billie's face fell. "I was present for most of his life, McQueary, I don't need you to tell me—"

"Listen to me, Billie." Cleo inhaled as deep as she could, air rattling through her blood-choked nose. "I wimped where he is *now*. He's alive."

Cleo saw the exact moment when Billie stopped breathing. She went so still that Cleo might have thought one of her projectors was malfunctioning, if her eyes hadn't been raking desperately over Cleo's face.

"Don't." Billie's voice was barely any louder than the thudding of Cleo's heart in her ears. "You can't—you're not allowed to say that to me, unless you're sure."

"I'm sure." Cleo was sure of so few things. This, at least, was one of them. "He's in the Other Place. Him and the rest of the *Providence* crew."

Billie pressed a hand over her mouth and stumbled back like Cleo had shoved her. Cleo heard the exact moment when she started breathing again, big, wracking, sobbing breaths that bent her double. Cleo dropped the jacket and fell to her knees in front of Billie, and through a series of gentle but firm hand gestures got her to lean up against the pilot console. Cleo settled against it too and let Billie cry, wishing there was literally anything else she could do.

After a long while, Billie sniffed loudly, pressing the heels of her hands under her glasses and into her swollen eyes. "Is he, uh." She swallowed thickly. "Is he older? Older than me?"

"No." Cleo brushed a sweaty curl out of her eyes. "He still looked the same age as he would have been on Launch Day, anyway. He said time was weird in there."

Billie nodded, then lowered her hands. Her ponytail was coming undone, pieces of golden hair falling in tangles around her face and shoulders. And her eyes, the same eyes Elijah had, were shining with tears, but she didn't look sad, exactly. She looked like she had never seen the sun before, and Cleo had just thrown the curtains open and given it to her.

"Tell me everything," Billie whispered.

Cleo did. The creepy room, Elijah's apparent fear of saying too much, the Other Place having its "reasons," the mysterious interference that had broken her vision and the blood vessels in her nose. Billie listened quietly, the fluttering rise and fall of her chest getting steadier the more Cleo told.

When she finished, Billie swallowed again, and Cleo saw her

sifting through all the infinite questions being generated in her head. "Eli looked safe, at least? Healthy?"

"Not a scratch on him."

"Good." Cleo got the distinct impression that, if she'd given any other answer, Billie wouldn't have let anything so simple as quantum physics stop her from challenging the dimension that had taken her brother to a fight out back. "Do you think the interference came from the Other Place?"

Cleo remembered the rainbows, and the voice that had sounded all too human. "No. It was from someone, somewhere else."

"Hmm." Billie's gaze fell to the blood on Cleo's lips. "Whoever it was, I won't let them hurt you again."

Cleo tilted her head at a teasing angle, but the smile that spread across her face was painfully genuine. "Big words, Billie."

Easy as anything, Billie reached for Cleo's face like she was going to wipe away the blood, or run her hand through her hair, or or *or*—but just before her fingers would have flickered through Cleo's cheek, she stopped. She closed her hand into a fist, pulled it back, and brought it briefly to rest on her mouth. She squeezed her eyes shut again and bumped the back of her head soundlessly against the console.

"You said—" Billie hissed in a breath like whatever she was thinking was hurting her from the inside. "You said the *whole* crew."

"Yeah." And Cleo was pretty sure she knew what Billie was asking, because it had also been her own first thought. Because how could it not be. But she had already decided not to think about that, because all the possibilities she knew Billie was considering had already slid, slippery and hazardous, through her own head. And she wasn't about to lose herself in that danger zone when Billie—*this* Billie—was right in front of her, being as real as she knew how to be.

"Hey," Cleo said. Billie grumbled an acknowledgment, not opening her eyes. Cleo tipped her head upward, for strength. "I'm not, um. Concerned. About that."

Cleo saw it in her periphery and felt it in her blood when Billie opened her eyes to look at her. She kept trying to burn holes in the ceiling with her own eyes as she continued. "Let's just figure out how to get back into the Other Place. How to get Elijah home."

Cleo faced Billie, who was looking at her *like that* again. And if Cleo had been worried about keeping her heart in one piece—well. She pictured twisting her hands in Billie's sweater and reeling her in as close as she could get. She let herself imagine, outside the confines of her insufferable dreams, whether Billie's mouth would taste like salt or sarcasm or something sweeter. How it would feel to breathe comforting words against her lips. Whether Billie would gasp softly through her nose when Cleo kissed the tear tracks off of her cheeks.

If some of that made its way onto her face, Cleo was past caring. She was tired of not letting herself want. And Billie—if Cleo was right, if she wasn't still imagining, Billie kind of looked like *not* wanting had never even occurred to her.

"Thank you," Billie murmured. "Cleo."

Cleo was sure of so few things. One of them was that it was too late for her torn-up, idiot heart.

＊

IT FEELS IMPOSSIBLE, FROM *so far away, to get a good look at her eyes. But, for one perfect moment, I'm basking in that kilowatt happiness*

she's directing at the hologram. And then, just as quickly, everything contracts, and I'm back.

I open my eyes, and at first I can't see anything but that damn
golden light. I blink once, again, a few more times, and through
the haze I can absorb two things: my old tape recorder pressing
annoyingly into my leg through my pocket, and a face uncomfortably close to mine.

"Holy hell," Elijah says. "You're awake."

As disoriented as I am, I can't help but smile. "Yeah. Unfortunately."

I expect Eli's face to fall at that, but he pulls me to my feet,
something even more manic than usual in his smile. "Something's
happened," he says. "Someone was here."

"I know, shithead." I shove him in the shoulder, and he only
grins wider. "I saw."

"You saw—"

"And I cannot believe you didn't come get me."

Eli waggles his eyebrows. "So that was the same Cleo you
were muttering about."

I feel my face grow hot. Which is surprising, because it's hard
to feel anything in this place. "Shut up."

"I think your girlfriend's going to need our help."

"She's not my girlfriend, Eli."

"And since you've been in some weirdo trance for who knows
how long, it's lucky I have a plan."

Teasing forgotten, I pull him into a hug. If it's too tight, he
doesn't say anything. "Not if I come up with a better plan first."

Eli laughs. "It's good to have you back, Bilbo."

CHAPTER 9

My name is Wilhelmina Lucas. I had forgotten, for a while. Or I didn't want to remember. But now I do, because I need to. Now I do, because of her. So no more of this third-person-omniscient garbage. From here on out, I tell my own story.

My name is Wilhelmina Lucas. My crew calls me Captain. Eli calls me Bilbo. And Cleo calls me Billie—or she might, once she knows me.

BILLIE HAD REFUSED TO let Cleo call the others straight up to the flight deck, insisting instead that they convene in the med bay.

"You and Ros, I swear to God," Cleo grumbled as they walked to the elevator, "I think I'd know if I was having an aneurysm—"

"Maybe. But you should still get a checkup after being brain-blasted by a mysterious, evil space entity, Cleo. That's the first thing they teach you at astronaut school."

And Billie had looked so tenderly down at Cleo—riding the elevator with her even though she could have just popped down to the med bay herself—that Cleo had found it very hard to argue with that.

So, when they had all finally gathered in the med bay, Cleo explained what she'd wimped to all of them from her cot, with Abe and Kaleisha sitting at her bedside, Ros bustling around her running tests and gently wiping the blood from her face, and Billie parked against the wall by the headboard, watching Ros's hands. The concern on all their faces melted into confusion, then shock, then even deeper confusion.

"So. Wait."

Cleo looked up at Abe, watching the gears churn behind his eyes.

"You're saying that the Other Place," Abe continued, "is actually not a place, but a . . . consciousness?"

Cleo would have nodded, but Ros was shining an otoscope in her ear. "It seemed like maybe it was both? Elijah was definitely in a room, in a house of some kind. But he also said 'they had their reasons' for taking the crew. Didn't elaborate any further."

"Oh, so the unfathomable space entity that carjacked our lives is nonbinary? Love that." Cleo looked up at Ros in surprise, knocking the scope out of her ear. "Sit still, bucko," they said. "I can still make jokes."

"Rozzy, that's music to my absolute ears."

"Whatever. So is it a single consciousness or a collective of some kind?"

"I feel like we're glancing over the fact that we just got confirmation of *extra-dimensional life*," Kaleisha said. "And they apparently have the ability to just, like . . . slurp people out of this dimension?"

"And talk to us through dark matter engines and redheaded med students." Cleo glanced back up at Ros without moving her head. "I think you saw them, Ros, or felt them, when you were lost in the storm. 'They're angry,' you said."

Ros put the otoscope down and reached for some other

device, not looking at her. "I don't remember feeling anything. A vague sense of dread, maybe, but who among us isn't always filled with—"

"Well, that's not nothing," Cleo pressed on. "That could be, I don't know. Useful. We could work with that."

Ros glared at her then, because they knew exactly what she was suggesting. "I'm not coming back to training," they snapped. "I'm not going to nearly destroy the ship again just so I can spout cryptic nonsense about these extra-dimensional kidnappers' *feelings*—"

"Stop." Kaleisha stood up, and everyone fell silent. "You've all skipped a thousand steps ahead. Has it occurred to either of you that, if the Other Place has a mind of its own, it gave us our powers for a reason?"

"*Gave* us—" Cleo started to argue, before she remembered a gentle graze, a deafening roar, a blast of energy from everywhere and nowhere. "The dark matter engine. It's their connection to our dimension. *They* started it up when I touched it."

"And used the energy blast to alter us," Kaleisha said, watching the realization spread across Ros's face. "Just like they used it on Launch Day to take the crew."

"Whoa," Abe breathed. "So you think they've got a—a plan?"

A muscle clenched in Kaleisha's jaw. "They've got to."

"What's your point, Kal?" Ros snapped. "Why should I care what the space demons who trapped us on this ship want us to do?"

"My powers helped breach us to Proxima a million times faster, and Cleo's just helped her find the missing crew; you don't think that's something?"

Ros's nostrils flared. "Sure, Cleo's powers are unambiguously awesome, the fact that they've left her in a hospital bed with blood pouring out of her skull notwithstanding."

"Well," Cleo said weakly, "that wasn't the Other Place, it was the rainbow voice—"

"You'd better not be implying that I think we should go along with their plan just for shits and giggles, Ros. You know I'm not." Kaleisha's voice was quiet, her mouth set in a restrained line, her eyes burning. "All I want is for us to get out of this. And if figuring out how to play the game they've set up for us is what'll keep us and the *Providence* crew safe, then—"

"I don't want to play any game where all I do is go crazy and hurt the people I *love*, Kal—"

"Jesus Christ, Ros." Kaleisha grabbed Ros by the shoulders. "If you can feel what the Other Place is feeling, you might be able to help Cleo find the crew."

Ros went silent. It was the killing blow, Cleo knew: appeal to the med student's desire to help people in trouble. For a long moment, it seemed like Ros couldn't do anything but stare at Kaleisha in shock.

"But they took the crew," they said finally. "And they changed us. I don't want to accept their terms."

"You might not have to."

Cleo twisted her neck to look up at Billie, who was staring at her glasses in her hands. Like she'd intended to clean them, but got lost along the way.

"Billie, what—"

"I don't think," Billie continued, "that we should be accepting this as some sort of divine, all-knowing plan. I don't think the Other Place is that infallible."

Kaleisha dropped her hands from Ros's shoulders and clasped their hand tightly. "What do you think they are, then?"

"I think," Billie said, putting her glasses back on, "that the Other Place is scared."

Ros got a faraway look in their eyes, just for a moment. "They're tired, and hurting."

"Exactly." Billie waggled a finger thoughtfully at Ros. "When Cleo wimped Halvorsen talking to the Other Place, they said something about growing weaker, about the engine draining their dimension of its energy. It stands to reason that they took the crew, not to punish us, but to prevent the mission from moving forward and depleting their life force, for lack of a better word, even further. Given that it seems they can only make things happen in our dimension via the engine, they may have felt it was their best available option."

"Doesn't really justify it," Ros muttered.

"Oh, believe me, I agree." Billie clenched and unclenched her fingers, and Cleo thought of her tears for her brother. "But if we understand their motivations, it might help us figure out a plan of our own."

"So. Wait." Abe bit his lip. "If they took the crew because they were scared of the mission going forward, why did they start the engine back up? Why did they risk depleting themselves again? Why did they give you these powers?"

Cleo rubbed at her aching temples, thinking back to her realization about herself and Ros, that closed loop of energy. Except that Cleo was drawing on the Other Place so much more now, and Ros—Ros who, when Cleo looked up at them, smiled a small, tired smile—hadn't used their powers in weeks. They couldn't possibly be replacing all the energy that Cleo was using. So what would motivate someone, or someplace, or whatever the Other Place was, to push themselves toward the breaking point like that? What took precedence over the fear of that slow annihilation?

"They're scared of something new," Cleo heard herself saying. "Something even more dangerous than last time."

Everyone turned to look at her.

"Sorry," she muttered. "Not to darken the already dismal mood."

"No, Cleo, you're right." Billie crouched down at Cleo's bedside so their faces were level, and Cleo felt herself leaning gently toward her as if being pulled by a string. She was so busy watching Billie that she almost missed Kaleisha turning to Ros and mouthing *Cleo?* with a smirk. "What could scare them more than the engine depleting their remaining life force?"

Cleo's mind returned again to the freezing rainbows, the voice crackling through her like an electric shock. *Good*, it had said. *You're on your way.*

"Here's a wild guess," she said, "but it could be the creepy voice that just broke my brain so bad you all thought I was dying."

"Damn it." Billie looked like she wanted very badly to bang her head against the bed frame. "Seems like a strong contender."

"Could you try and wimp the voice again?" Kaleisha asked. "Get a little more intel?"

"Maybe? I don't know where it came from, though. I wouldn't know where to look."

"The Other Place, then. To see if we can find anything else out from them or the crew."

Billie turned from Kaleisha to Cleo and frowned. "No. Not if you'll get hurt again."

God, I love—

"I can try." Cleo swallowed. "I will."

She felt a hand on her shoulder. "Let's wait till tomorrow," Ros said. "I'll monitor her, Billie. Keep her safe however I can." Cleo put her hand over theirs and tried to say *thank you* with just her eyes and her closed-up throat.

※

LATER THAT NIGHT, AFTER Billie had left to run simulations as if she could solve for Elijah like an equation, and long after Ros and Kaleisha had fallen asleep cuddling one cot over, Cleo let the thought that had been itching at the back of her head all evening rise to the surface.

"Abe," she whispered, "what are you scared of?"

Abe blinked up at her from where he'd been dozing in a chair between the two beds. His hair stuck up in odd places, and his face was more drawn and drained than Cleo had ever seen it. "What do you mean, Clo?"

"I mean I've never seen you look, like, hopeless, but you looked close to it today."

Abe bit his lip. "I mean, yeah, I'm scared."

Cleo just waited. She thought about one night when they'd been in high school and weathering a hurricane at Kaleisha's place, and they'd gone for a walk as the eye passed overhead because they were sixteen and stupid and losing their minds. And they'd climbed up one of the levees, which was very illegal, and Abe had looked hard at the rest of them—at Ros's exhausted face, Kaleisha's brow furrowed toward the turbulent horizon, and the pitifully studied vacancy in Cleo's own affect—and he'd said, *Fuck this.* And he'd leapt ungracefully off the wall and into the water, and they'd all cried out in concern, and he'd surfaced with a laugh and a flick of his hair out of his eyes, and he'd said, *Come on in, the water is fine.* And Cleo dove in after him without a second thought, followed by Kaleisha and finally Ros, and for one shining moment they all believed him when he said, *It's going to pass.*

Eventually, Abe sighed and looked at her with wet eyes.

"I've been doing a pretty good job of staying positive, right? About you guys all having this crazy, profound experience that I can't really fathom? I've gotten pretty good at helping out any way I can. But finding out that the Other Place gave you guys powers on purpose . . . and that it didn't give me anything, also on purpose . . . Did they just not have a use for me? Do I not have anything to contribute?"

"Whoa, now. I thought we decided not to care what the Other Place thinks."

Abe wrinkled his nose at her. "I'm not as good at compartmentalizing as you, Commander Compartmentalizer. It's hard to ignore all these big, cosmic things happening around me, and all I can do is try not to get in the way. It's like the Other Place didn't even think of me."

"Or you're already perfect and the Other Place didn't need to change a thing." Abe scoffed, but Cleo sat up straighter on her pillows. "No, for real. What could the stupid Other Place have done to improve on Abe Yang, the kindest, caring-est guy in the whole universe?"

Abe chewed on the inside of his lip. "Thanks. But how is being kind going to help save you from the rainbow voice, or the crew from the Other Place?"

"It's gotten us this far, Abe. Seriously, I don't know how me and Kal and Ros would stay sane without you. And Billie, honestly. Your bromance means a lot to her, she just doesn't say it."

Abe looked at the other two and sighed. "Maybe."

"No, listen, think of it like physics." Cleo made grabby hands at Abe, and he cracked a tiny smile and put his hand in hers. "What if the four of us, our powers, I mean, are, like, the basic building blocks of the universe. I'm time, Kaleisha is space, Ros is energy, and you're mass."

Abe frowned. "So, dense and boring?"

"No no no. Oh my God, *no*. Mass is *not* boring. You know the strong force?"

"Yup, it's the strong one."

"Exactly. It's what holds quarks together into protons and neutrons, and protons and neutrons together into atoms. It blows every other physical phenomenon out of the fuckin' water. It's ten to the *thirty-eighth* times stronger than gravity, dude. Nothing would exist without the strong force. Space? Empty. Time? Meaningless. Energy is bouncing around with nothing to do. It's miserable."

Abe squeezed her hand. "So you're saying I'm the strong force? That's my power?"

"Yeah." Cleo squeezed back. "The stuff that holds the rest of it together."

✳

SHE DRIFTED OFF HOLDING Abe's soft hand. Asleep, Cleo dreamed of rose-gold rivers. Of washed-out fields of waist-high grasses and an off-white house in the distance, windows locked. Of icy mountains and sunset skies. Of the *Providence* crashing, empty, into a night-black desert of ice.

She woke with a start, pulled the NASA jacket that Kaleisha had brought her tight around herself. Dreamed of her father, watching the news with his jaw clenched tight enough to snap, knocking on a door and demanding entry, breaking down into racking sobs halfway through making himself a cup of coffee. She startled awake again. Drifted off again.

She dreamed of Billie, Billie with a body, Billie who was solid enough to touch, to kiss, to hold on to for dear life. Billie, in her arms, moaning and sighing as Cleo tasted every inch of her skin. Billie, who smiled at her, just before dissolving into particles of rainbow light and drifting away into the—

Cleo's eyes flew open like a switch being flicked, her heart pounding like she'd just leapt out of a plane. But before she could cry out, maybe to Billie, maybe to the universe, there was a finger over her mouth.

"Sorry," Ros whispered, wide-eyed. "Sorry. I didn't mean to scare you."

"You didn't." Cleo heaved herself up onto her elbows. "What's going on, bud? You okay?"

Ros gnawed warily at a cuticle. "Do something for me?"

"Whatever you need."

"Tell me again about your very first vision."

Cleo's stomach convulsed, just a little. She tried to do the calculations—probability that she would make Ros cry, probability that Ros would run straight back to the lab, probability that the gods were currently striking her down for her prophetic hubris. "Well. Uh. Your eyes were all gold."

"And? Where were we?"

"In a . . . big, dark room. Or something. You were making it snow."

Ros finally ripped the hangnail off with their teeth. "And?"

"You were throwing ice at—" Cleo collapsed back onto the pillows. "Someone."

Ros looked less despairing than Cleo might have expected. They frowned, clearly thinking through something very carefully. "Did I look," they said slowly, pausing to suck at the sore spot on their thumb, "like I had lost control?"

"Huh," Cleo said. The glowing eyes had been so disconcerting that, in her sick and frenzied state, she had assumed that the Ros of her vision wasn't fully Ros, but was there actually anything indicating as much? "I don't think so. You looked angry, furious, but you were fully in control of your powers."

"Okay." Ros nodded. "I can work with that."

Cleo squinted up into her friend's round face. She could

count on one hand the number of times she had ever seen that face contorted in anger. And as much as the vision had scared her, she knew that the idea of being that angry—of hurting someone in anger, of hurting someone due to any unchecked emotion at all—was Ros's biggest fear.

"Cleo," they whispered, "if it comes true, if it looks like I'm putting any of you in danger . . . will you stop me?"

Cleo froze. Something in Ros's face broke a little.

"I'm not asking you to, like, put me down," they said, a whimper creeping into their voice. "I trust you to figure it out. All I want is to not be a liability. I could never forgive myself if I hurt you guys."

"You're not a liability," Cleo whispered. "And you didn't, like, take the Hippocratic oath the day you sat at our table in the high school cafeteria."

"Still." Ros paused, deliberating, then crouched down and took Cleo's hand in theirs. Cleo suddenly felt ready to cry—she could also count on one hand the number of times Ros had ever been this tender. "Please?"

Cleo nodded. "Okay."

A bit of tension leaked out of Ros's shoulders. And they squeezed Cleo's fingers and went back to bed, curling up against Kaleisha like they had never left. And after some sleepy amount of time later, just when Cleo was starting to think she heard their breath slowing down, Ros whispered:

"Cleo?"

"Yeah."

"I think sometimes I mask my feelings with humor."

And they both stifled their laughter behind their hands, shaking silently at each other across the space between their beds.

"Me too, bud," Cleo said, once she had control of her diaphragm again. "Me too."

They were both quiet then, for good. Cleo listened until she could hear two pairs of soft, even breaths under Kaleisha's snores, and slipped out of bed.

✳

ARCHIVED: *Providence* Intracrew Messaging Service Conversation — Capt. Wilhelmina Lucas and Dr. Kristoff Halvorsen, December 4, 2040

KRISTOFF HALVORSEN
If your brother ever tries to talk philosophy at
    lunch again, I might have to formally censure him.

WILHELMINA LUCAS
Hey, you are not allowed to tease him about being a
    useless liberal arts hack
Only I am allowed to tease him about being a useless
    liberal arts hack

KRISTOFF HALVORSEN
Noted.
I'll concede that he did have some interesting
    points to make about the myth of progress, though.
    What was that line he quoted? John Gray, was it?
    "Progress is an illusion with a future"?

WILHELMINA LUCAS
Would've thought you'd have hated that sentiment,
    Mr. Progress Man

KRISTOFF HALVORSEN
Dr. Progress Man, to you.
And I do. Everything I've devoted my life to, not
    to mention everything we do here, is meaningless
    if we don't believe that we are moving toward a

better future. But dissenting opinions are still
valuable in their own right.

WILHELMINA LUCAS
Sure, but I take it you won't be converting to Eli's
cyclical theory of history anytime soon

KRISTOFF HALVORSEN
Nothing cyclical about what we're trying to do here,
Billie.
The work we do is not only going to enable
interstellar travel, it's going to end our current
crisis and put humanity back on the path toward
prosperity and happiness. "Enlightenment," I guess
Elijah would call it. I have to believe that.

WILHELMINA LUCAS
"Back," ha
We were never on the path, Kris
But it's good to think that way. No point in any of
this if we're not trying to help people

KRISTOFF HALVORSEN
Thank you, I appreciate that.
[. . .]
As long as we're getting philosophical
What would you say is any appropriate price to pay
for such progress?

WILHELMINA LUCAS
Um
What do you mean, Kris
Don't tell me you're, like, regretting never having
started a family

KRISTOFF HALVORSEN
Ha, no.
Just contemplating what could be worth giving up if
it meant securing a safe, peaceful future for the
human race.

WILHELMINA LUCAS
[. . .]
Have the goons on the board asked you to give
   anything up?

KRISTOFF HALVORSEN
No, nothing like that.

WILHELMINA LUCAS
Then what's it like?

KRISTOFF HALVORSEN
Forget it. I've had my head a bit in the clouds
   thinking up projects to busy myself with once you
   and the crew are gone.

WILHELMINA LUCAS
[. . .]
Fair
But for what it's worth, I think Eli would say that
   prioritizing progress over everything else, with
   no thought to the consequences, is what got us in
   this mess in the first place.
Not that I'm warning you about anything. Just, you
   know, speaking of cyclical history

KRISTOFF HALVORSEN
You have nothing to worry about, Billie. My
   priorities remain the same as ever.

＊

THE GREENHOUSE SMELLED OF hyacinths and lavender and countless
other green, growing things. It smelled like Mr. Reid's house.
Which was, Cleo knew, the whole point.

She was burying her nose in a sunflower when she heard a
small *pop* behind her. She smiled.

"How did you know I was just about to call you?"

"I can come, sometimes, without you asking me to," Billie said softly. Cleo heard her move closer from the way her breath stuttered softly. "I saw you in here and figured you'd want company."

"You figured right." Cleo turned to find Billie's face just inches from her own, and her own breath went still in her chest. For a moment, she just looked at Billie's face, memorizing the geography of the faint smile lines around her eyes. "Got too many thoughts bonking around in here to just lie in bed alone with them."

For a moment, Cleo thought Billie was going to step closer, but she stayed planted where she was. "Like what?"

Like, I think I love you, Cleo didn't say. *Like, I'm pretty sure you love me back.* "Like, today I found proof of extra-dimensional life, and it's nowhere near the top of my mind."

"Mortal danger can do that to you."

"I've just—" Cleo realized she was twisting her fingers together, and dropped her hands by her sides. "I've spent my whole life wanting to go to space and discover new worlds, and now I've done it, I'm *doing* it, and—why doesn't it feel good?"

Billie narrowed her eyes at Cleo for a single, taut moment, then stepped past her toward a pot of sunflowers. "This is how it feels. At least that's how it was for me, on the Erecura Deep mission. Space is anticlimactic, Cleo. You pile into a tin can with a few other dipshits, you spend a year bouncing off the walls and trying not to kill each other, and then you get there, you get to Europa, and then—what? What now? The first time I saw Jupiter, I stared at it for a minute, and it was beautiful, and then all I could think was *What do I do with this?* You're still the same person after you see Jupiter, with the same problems. It's just that now you've seen Jupiter."

Cleo worried a sunflower leaf between her fingers. "Then why did you keep doing it? Why did you sign up for the *Providence* mission?"

Billie reached a hand up to trace a line along the golden-yellow petals above her head. She glanced at Cleo, her eyes a dark olive in the dim, orange light. "You know how some people have to move when their partner dies, because the house has too many memories?" Cleo nodded, and Billie blinked back up at the bloom. "I tried to do that, but with the Earth. First my parents, then Neil—there was nowhere to go that didn't hurt. So I had to move."

Cleo thought, inexplicably, of her dad. Of his suffocating grief, of his fear that Cleo would leave him too becoming a self-fulfilling prophecy. Of her childhood home that she abandoned for Kaleisha's at every opportunity. Of the smoke-yellowed sky on Earth and her lifelong hope that, if she could just break through it to the stars, her escape would be complete, and the wanting would finally let her rest.

"I think," Cleo said slowly, "I know what you mean."

Billie smiled, just a little bit. "Yeah. I know."

Looking at Billie's lips, Cleo's recurring dream popped unbidden back into her head. Talk about wanting that wouldn't let her rest. But this was different, she supposed. Billie wasn't like the stars or a disappointing view of Jupiter. She was here, she was real, and loving her—*loving* her, like Cleo had never loved anyone before—was, or could be, maybe, worth everything it took.

"Did I ever tell you that there's one poem I actually kind of like?" Cleo blurted.

Billie raised an eyebrow. "Oh?"

Cleo tried very hard to contain the pink rising up in her cheeks. Maybe Billie couldn't see it in the near-dark. "It's that one called 'The Old Astronomer to His Pupil,' I think."

"I know it."

"Someone read it at the memorial for the *Providence*."

Cleo cringed the moment she said it, but Billie just nodded. "Makes sense. That's what I would have chosen."

"It just always stuck with me, you know? *Though my soul may set in darkness, it will rise in perfect light; I have loved the stars too fondly to be fearful of the night.* Even though everyone did get fearful, after that."

Billie stepped close again, then. "What made you think of it now?"

Cleo let her eyes flutter closed, just once, and forced herself not to lean into Billie. "I guess I was just wondering—if you could do it over again, would you still choose to get on the *Providence*?"

"I don't know." Billie licked her lips, and Cleo nearly had a heart attack right there. "Would you?"

"I think—"

I think I could learn to be less fearful, with you—

"I don't know."

✳

"SO," ELI SAYS CONVERSATIONALLY, leading me through door after door with edges that don't quite line up right, "how did you figure out how to see back into our universe?"

"It just kind of happened." I rub my eyes. There's a lingering feeling of disorientation, like part of me is still back with Cleo, even though I'm fully, solidly here for the first time in ages. It's like arriving here on Launch Day again, my eyes unused to the gold-black tones and the not-quite-Euclidean lines of it all. Eli leads me down each twisting, yellowing hallway like he knows the way; for my part, I think we've taken five left turns in a row, and it's making me dizzy. "I spent so much time letting my mind drift that eventually I just drifted into—"

"—the cute girl who happened to be in the process of stealing our spaceship?"

"She didn't steal it, this place did. And shut up."

"I'm just saying." Eli pushes open the front doors, and I'm blinded by the off-white sunless sky. Unnerved all over again by the field outside that extends out forever toward an impossible horizon, by the tall, flaxen grasses that wave slowly in time with each other in the still, staticky air. "I wonder if there's, you know"—he wiggles his fingers to denote the unexplainable—"some kind of reason you started seeing her when you did."

I scoff, even though I've wondered the same thing. "Like true love?"

"You said it, not me."

"Why would that be how any of this works?"

"Why not?" Eli asks, dead serious. "Why is it so impossible to believe that the thing that pulled you home was the person that reminded you how to love?"

"Love isn't a force of nature, Eli." As soon as I say it, I realize I don't quite believe it.

He blows me a giant, nasty raspberry. "More things in heaven and Earth, Horatio."

(Doubt thou the stars are fire, I think, seized by the memory of the way Cleo's freckly nose crinkles up when she smiles. But never doubt I love.)

"Fine," I say. "Let's say you're right. What good is all that if I can't help her?"

"I thought you'd never ask." Eli plops himself down on the porch swing, and I lean against the railing so I can cross my arms at him. The wood looks bleached, desiccated. I have to remind myself that it's not going to break under him. "That's what my plan is for."

"Alright, lay it on me."

"Step One: Bully the Other Place into letting us go."

"Needs some work."

He starts pumping his legs. The swing doesn't creak, or make any indication at all that friction is a law of physics here. "Step Two: Save your girlfriend and her friends from whatever was breaking her brain."

I groan. "Brilliant, Eli. Real actionable."

"Wait, wait." He swings forward and kicks me in the ass before I can walk away. "In all seriousness, Bill, I think we have a chance if we talk to them. I've seen other crew members talking to them. I have a sense of how they operate now."

"And how is that?"

"We appeal to love. See how it's all coming together now?"

"This place has taken everything from us. They don't get to also have my love."

"Yeah, well." Eli kicks the swing higher, faster, and for a second I can imagine him arcing up and away from here. "If you figure out how to physics your way out of this place outside of time and space, let me know."

Damn it, he's right. Maybe.

"Alright, loser, I'll follow your lead," I say. "Don't make me regret it."

✳

THE NEXT MORNING, WHEN she could walk with only a slight wobble in her knees, Cleo held Halvorsen's jacket in her hands once again, feeling for the dark matter tendrils shooting off of it and into the void while the others stood around her bed and watched. Cleo closed her eyes so she wouldn't have to see their worried faces.

"Pretend I said something clever about performance anxiety," she mumbled, right before she was yanked into the darkness.

She opened her eyes and knew immediately that she had not, in fact, managed to wimp the Other Place, because everything was dully honey-toned instead of that uncanny gold. She saw

Elijah, his breath ragged and his floppy blond hair dripping with sweat as he ran on a zero-gravity treadmill.

No, this is wrong. Take me deeper.

Cleo *pushed* against the vision, trying to find the dark matter filaments that would let her peel back the layers between universes. And it worked, maybe—everything went black and then blacker, and she opened her eyes and saw—

Also wrong.

Elijah again, still gold-dark and liquid slow, but this time strapped into his bunk in his *Providence* quarters. Halvorsen's jacket was folded, forgotten, on his shelf. And even though his eyes were closed, there was an expression of anxious rapture on his face, like he was waiting for something extraordinary and unfathomable. Cleo emerged into the hallway and saw that every other room was also filled with passengers staring up at the ceiling and clenching their hands around the straps of their safety harnesses.

"*Three.*" A deep voice boomed from the intercoms and oh, *of course,* that's what everyone was waiting for.

"*Two.*" The voice sounded familiar, painfully familiar, just familiar enough that Cleo forgot what she was about to see—

"*One.*"

There was a blinding flash of light. Cleo cried out and covered her face, but not soon enough to avoid the burning and the spots of color spreading across her retinas.

She blinked. Rubbed her eyes. And when she lowered her hands, Elijah's bed was empty, the harness lying limp and the sheets bearing just the faintest impression of the body that had been there.

Damn it. Somewhere, up in the flight deck, there was another empty seat, with a Billie-shaped—

No.

Fuck.

Alright, that was closer. Give it just a little more juice.

Deeper. Darker. Cleo felt herself flying again through the molten boundaries between universes. She thought she was close, could feel the Other Place just out of reach, knew that if she opened her eyes she would *be there—*

And then it happened again. Static shattered through her nervous system, blinding her, threatening to tremble her molecules apart. Everything was black, and white, and blue-gray steel and dry gold grasses and Ros's hands as they held her down through the spasms racking her body—

And then it was the rainbow light again, hazy shifting spectrums in a dark red sky. And the voice, that painfully familiar voice, was whispering curiously in her ear.

You don't give up, do you?

Cleo gritted her teeth against the pain, trying not to slip back to the med bay just yet. *Why? Should I?*

A wheezing chuckle. *Not at all. I've always respected tenacity.*

This doesn't feel like respect.

I'm sorry. Doing what needs to be done can sometimes come at an unfortunate price.

Vibrations, jagged and blistering, crackled through Cleo's body again, and she felt the Other Place slip further away.

No—

I'm sorry, Ms. McQueary. But I can't let you keep visiting the Conterminous Dimension. They've been a hindrance to me since the beginning. I can't have you scheming together to out-maneuver me.

You're still calling it the "Conterminous Dimension"? What a mouthful. All the cool kids are calling it the Other Place now.

Cleo felt a shadow fall heavy around her, like someone somewhere was drawing closer to spit their words in her face.

You won't mock me, the voice said, *when you learn of my plans. Then you will see, as I have, that I only want what is best for humanity.*

Oh, yeah? And what exactly is that?

Progress, Ms. McQueary. Enlightenment. Nothing more or less than salvation, in fact.

Cleo plunged back to the med bay, gasping for air. Ros released their pressure on her shoulders and grabbed a damp cloth to wipe down her face.

"You absolutely cannot do that again," they said, their voice clipped with concern. "I can't even begin to speculate what kind of damage it's doing to your nervous system."

"Preaching to the choir, Ros." Cleo looked around dazedly, past Abe and Kaleisha just releasing their frantic grips on each other. "Billie."

Billie gripped the side of the bed, looking pale and pained. "Yes?"

Cleo took a rattling breath. "Remind me," she said, though she already knew the answer, "who did the countdown on Launch Day?"

Billie frowned. "Kris did."

"Yeah, okay." Cleo slumped back into her pillows and squeezed her eyes shut against the throbbing ache building in her head. "So, fun fact. Halvorsen's not dead. He's the rainbow voice."

feel the difference in the air even before Elijah comes running. Someone new, taking up space where there's none to spare, like a stone dropped into a bucket of water about to overflow.

It's been nineteen years since I felt anything like this. It's lighter than the last time, less intrusive, but I know the panic still registers on my face. Because when Eli skids soundlessly into my doorway, the first thing he says is:

"Don't freak out, but I think one of your girlfriend's pals is here."

I blast my way through the uncomfortably weightless double front doors of the house. A crowd of my crewmates has already gathered on the plain outside, but they barely notice me as I sprint past them, wading through the grass that's at my ankles, then my knees, deeper and deeper, as fast as I can.

There's a figure standing waist-deep in the grass, red hair gleaming in what's supposed to be the sunlight. They're staring at the gathered crew, at our house-prison, at the one wizened tree that marks the point past which none of us have ever tried to go, because there's nothing, because the arid fields would swallow you up. Their mouth is open in awe even though they're shaking with the effort of something. And when I get close enough to see that they're wavering, they're not really here, the *ripples I felt weren't a body but a mind and so I can almost see through them to the hazy horizon behind—they look at me, and say, "Billie."*

"Ros, wait—" I start to say, but they're gone.

✳

ROS BLINKED THEIR EYES open, ice crystals falling away from their ginger eyelashes, and Cleo could tell it had worked.

"What did you see?" Billie asked. Cleo shot her a *wait for them to catch their breath, butthead* look, but Ros was already brushing the frost off their uniform and looking excited.

"I didn't lose control," they said, and smiled contagiously.

"No," Cleo said. "You did so good, dude. Told you I wouldn't need this."

She indicated her back pocket, where the tranquilizer gun that Ros had adamantly told her *not* to put in her back pocket was. But Ros had also insisted that she and Billie build the tranq gun in the first place, so.

("You haven't aligned the striker right, Cleo, you've got to—"

"I've aligned it perfectly, actually."

"No, it's going to catch on the side of the chamber, knocking your aim off by at least three degrees."

"It's aligned perfectly, Billie, which I would prove by tranqing you right now, if that wasn't such an obvious waste of a dart."

"You're just threatening me because you *know* the striker is—"

"Hey, Billie?" And Cleo had turned so their faces were just centimeters apart. She heard Billie's breath hitch, and let her gaze easily and obviously drop down to Billie's mouth. "Shut up." And Billie had.)

"There was a house," Ros said. "Just this off-white house in a big, empty field."

"Spooky."

"And I saw—" Ros hesitated, glancing at Billie, at Cleo, biting their lip. "I saw the, uh, crew."

A muscle clenched and unclenched in Billie's jaw. "All of them?"

Ros nodded slowly. "As far as I could tell. I don't know their faces, of course, except—"

There must have been a warning in Cleo's eyes, because Ros shut their mouth.

"Right," Billie said quietly, her throat working. "Well, Ros, if you're done for the day, I'd say we made good progress, so—"

"Actually, I think I'd like to go again." Ros raised their eyebrows at Cleo. "If that's okay?"

"Um." Cleo could practically feel the anxiety coming off of Billie in waves. "I think, since we're on a roll, yeah, we should keep going."

Billie made an indignant noise at the back of her throat but didn't argue. "Fine. Close your eyes."

Ros did. Billie paced wide loops around them, and Cleo watched as she squared her shoulders and lifted her chin, a bit of the old starship captain demeanor returning to stifle that nagging nervousness.

"I think we have to zoom out," Billie continued. "The house and the field are illusions. You should try and see past them, to what the Other Place really is."

"Okay," Ros said slowly. "So, in practical terms, Billie, what does that mean?"

"Feel for the dark matter web," Cleo said. "That's the true structure of the Other Place. If you can get a feel for that, maybe we can understand the boundary and how to pass through it."

"Right." Ros stood up straighter. "Dark matter web. Boundary. Got it."

"Remember, Ros, focus on shifting your awareness, not on the energy flow." Cleo saw Billie smile, soft and infinitesimal. "You're in control."

Ros smiled too, eyes still closed. "I'm in control."

Ice crystals crept along Ros's fingertips and the ends of their hair, but they didn't seem to notice. Their breathing stayed even.

"Excellent," Billie said. "Do you see anything?"

"Um." Ros screwed their eyes up tighter. "It's a layer removed, like it's shining at me from behind my eyelids. But there's a golden light? Maybe? It might not be light, it's different, it's *darker*—"

"That's it," Cleo said, balling up her fists. "Keep going, Ros."

Ros lifted their hands, freezing air curling off them around their feet. The frost climbed farther up their hair, and snowflakes began to swirl around them—but in gentle eddies, not a storm, not a hurricane.

"You're doing it," Billie said, something like pride in her voice. "Stay focused."

"I am," Ros said. "I can—Billie, I think I—"

Ros opened their eyes. They were glowing solid gold.

"Whoa," they said with an incredulous laugh. "That was easier than I thought it would be."

"Ros!" Cleo wasn't thinking, she was running toward them, she was reaching for the tranq gun to stop them before—

Ros blinked, and their eyes were blue again. They frowned. "What the hell, Clo?"

"Your—your eyes." Cleo stared at Ros's face, waiting for something to change, for everything to go wrong again. "They were—they were gold, like in the vision."

Ros lowered their hands, and the cold wind around them died down. "Oh."

"Billie, we have to stop."

Billie opened her mouth, but Ros cut her off. "Cleo, it's all good. Does this look anything like the big, creepy room you saw?"

Cleo tried to breathe around the pounding of her heartbeat in her ears. "Negative, doc."

"Maybe the color in their eyes isn't strictly a bad thing, Cleo," Billie said, crossing to Cleo's side and hovering a hand over her shoulder. "It could just be a side effect of a deeper connection with the Other Place."

"Hey." Cleo felt a hand actually come to rest on her other shoulder, and turned to see Ros smiling at her. "I'm here. And not attacking anybody."

They weren't. They looked happier, really, than Cleo had seen them in a long time.

She nodded. "Alright. Can we take a break, at least?"

Ros clapped their hands together. "Absolutely. Let's go see if Kal and Abe have any popcorn left."

✳

COMMUNING WITH THE OTHER *Place doesn't require any kind of training montage, something I'm sure would disappoint Cleo immensely. Eli and I don't have to climb a mountain or learn karate or light candles around a big Erebus logo on the floor. The Other Place is all around us, after all, and they've spoken to us before. We just have to ask them.*

I've seen other members of the crew talk to them. They take the faces of people we love, and some people need that in here, even if it's a lie. I've never summoned them myself. Because they do dead people too, I've heard, and I couldn't be less interested.

Twice, they've spoken to all of us. The first time was right after they stole us, and they put on the president's face to tell us they were our saviors.

"Halvorsen has taken so much, without regard to our safety or yours," they said, "and would have done much worse if we had not stopped him. You are safe now, as are we. We will watch over you here."

We hated it, of course. Hated that keeping us locked in our little gilded cage was apparently the only solution. But we didn't say that out loud, because we still believed that the Other Place would put us back soon. And that they were watching.

The second time was nineteen years ago, a year to the day—on Earth, anyway—after we'd been taken. No matter how hard they tried, the Other Place couldn't stop us from seeing when Halvorsen used stolen Erebus tech and the powers that had been growing in him since before the launch to shatter through the boundary. So we all watched as they shattered him, and cast him back out.

"You see," they said to us, breathing a little too hard, Mr. Rogers's face slipping a little because they'd put it on too hastily. "It's still not safe for you out there."

They couldn't stop us whispering to each other, after that.

A part of me expects Eli's room to feel different now that Cleo has been there—a thrill where she stepped, a glamour in the air denoting a shift in the polarity of my world—but it looks the same when I walk through the door. Except Eli's got that look on his face like he's ready to fight the whole universe. People always told us it makes him look like me. None of them ever knew that, actually, he has Mom's fighting face, and I have Dad's.

"You ready?" Eli says, taking my hand.

I nod, grateful as always that we can still touch each other, at least, even in this nothing place. "Remember," I say, "no matter whose face they take—"

"We're not letting it get to us." He squeezes my hand. "I won't, Bill."

"Alright. Eyes closed, then."

Eli closes his eyes, and I only take a second to look at his almost-calm face before closing mine too.

"Hey, you," I call out. "We need to talk."

There's no pop, no ding, no Windows 98 boot-up sound. We just open our eyes, and he's there.

They're there, I mean.

It's Neil's face. They're wearing Neil's face, the motherfuckers.

✳

"OH HEY, BY THE way"—Cleo crunched around a mouthful of cheesy popcorn—"what did you see in there, Ros?"

They had found the other two in the rec room, Kaleisha retwisting her locs with Abe's occasional assistance as they watched *The Watermelon Woman*. Now, all five of them sat on the floor, passing around the bowl of popcorn while Billie stared hungrily and insisted she didn't even want any, actually. Ros munched thoughtfully as their gaze went soft.

"Nothing I could really parse. That same dark-golden light was all around. And I felt like I was, I don't know, suspended in this pool of molasses, and I was looking down on something I couldn't make out. A lot of points of light. In some kind of network, it looked like."

"Maybe the molasses was the boundary," Cleo said sagely, spitting popcorn bits into the carpet.

Billie's head perked up. "We should try and get you further through it next time. Ros, what did you mean when you said it was easier than you thought it'd be?"

Ros frowned. "I meant that the Other Place feels . . . closer. Like, during the ice storm it was like getting dragged through something thick and substantial, and that's why I felt so far away when I was on the other side. But now . . ." They shrugged and popped more kernels into their mouth. "I don't know. It's easier to move by myself."

"Huh." Cleo twisted a kernel between her fingers contemplatively. "Practice makes perfect, I guess?"

Billie frowned the way she did when she thought Cleo was wrong, but she didn't say anything.

"Billie," Abe said suddenly, "can I ask you a question?"

"Shoot."

"Were you looking forward to living on Proxima B?"

Billie's eyebrows flew up, like no one had ever asked her that question, like it hadn't even occurred to her to think up an answer. "I was, uh. Proud to be chosen. And hopeful about what the mission meant for—"

Cleo took a deep breath and blew a fart noise into the palm of her hand. "Try again, Captain."

Billie crinkled her nose at her. "I don't know if I was looking forward to it, per se. I was eager to get off Earth, that's for sure."

"So you didn't think at all about what your new life was going to look like?" Kaleisha rested her head in her hands and peered at Billie. "No apprehensions about eating space bugs?"

Billie snorted. "The probes didn't find any space bugs, so no." She looked at Cleo, and something in her eyes made Cleo's heart do an even twistier backflip than usual. "I guess I was looking forward to the perpetual sunset."

"How romantic," Cleo heard herself say, like an idiot.

Kaleisha cleared her throat, and Cleo and Billie both snapped their attention back to her. She looked so smug, it was practically indecent. "Yes, Billie, tell us more about how hot and heavy sunsets get you."

Billie harrumphed and busied herself with cleaning her

glasses. "I *was* excited to see the sky, if nothing else. The auroras. The red sun."

"Hope it was going to be decent compensation for living in a freezing tundra for the rest of your days," Ros said, rolling over to stare at the ceiling.

"I hoped so too, Ros."

"I'm sure we'll get to see the auroras from orbit," Cleo said. Billie smiled at her, and Cleo's toes curled in her boots. "The sunset too, if we angle it right."

"Auroras," Kaleisha murmured, her gaze going soft. "Like, rainbows in the sky?"

Cleo frowned at her. "I guess that's one way to describe them?"

"No, like—" Kaleisha suddenly scrambled up onto her knees, as if she sensed she was about to have to run for her life. "The air will be full of rainbows, Clo. And it'll be cold, and the sky will be red and dark—"

Abe and Ros were still looking at Kaleisha like they were completely lost, but Billie—something was dawning behind Billie's eyes, just like Cleo assumed something was dawning behind her own. She knew (*loved*) that look so well, but it was horrible to watch this time, because it was a horrible thing to know—

"Halvorsen," Cleo whispered. "I've been wimping him on Proxima B."

✳

I HEAR ELI'S BREATH catch in his throat. I assume mine has too, because I don't seem to be breathing.

"You wish to speak with us, Captain Lucas?" they say, with Neil's voice.

My breath returns, patchy and diluted with a fury that pitches my voice low. "No," *I manage to grit out.* "You don't get to have his face, you cowards."

Out of the corner of my eye I see Eli shoot me a warning glance, and I don't care because Neil's body is taking a step closer and it's taking everything I have not to jump out the window. "Is there another you would prefer? Anyone else that you care for?"

I think of Cleo, of course. And then I make myself stop thinking of Cleo, because I'm pretty sure they can read my mind, and if the first time I saw her face in front of me was because my depraved space warden was wearing it, I might actually fight the whole universe.

"No," I say. I can tell they know I'm lying, because Neil had a face he made when he knew I was lying. But they don't transform, which is, I guess, a good thing. *Gather ye rosebuds while ye fucking may.*

"Very well." They incline Neil's head. That one infernal curl flops out of place onto Neil's forehead, and I feel my heart drop into my knees. "Say what you must, then."

Elijah, possibly sensing how pitifully compromised I am, clears his throat. "We need you to let us go," he says, and his voice only trembles a little.

"You know we cannot do that." They fix Eli with a look that's too stern, too patronizing for Neil, which helps nudge me out of my stupor. "It is not—"

"Not safe. Yeah, you said." Elijah crosses his arms aggressively at the Other Place. I'm so proud of him. "But the people headed for Proxima Centauri B, the ones that you inexplicably turned the engine on for and gave abilities to, even though those were big enough no-nos to trap us here for all eternity? They're in danger. You saved us, or so you keep insisting. Let us save them."

The Other Place narrows Neil's eyes at Eli. Which is how I learn that interdimensional dark matter gods can still have terrible poker faces. "What danger do you speak of?"

I remember how to say words again. "There's someone, somewhere, with the power to hurt them. Who's already hurting them. Who's already hurt Cleo."

Neil's face rearranges. His eyes go hard as steel, his mouth twists into a pained snarl, and I instinctively fling an arm out in front of Eli. Not because I think the Other Place will attack, necessarily, but because he shouldn't have to see the mask of Neil's face like this. I shouldn't either, but that's beside the point.

"How do you know this?" the Other Place hisses through Neil's teeth.

I square my jaw. "I figured out how to see back into our universe. I thought you'd have noticed, what with your all-knowing gaze."

They look absolutely wild with rage and panic, and I swear the air grows thicker with static electricity than it already was. I can feel them probing around in my mind, trying to dig out what else I've done and seen. That's unacceptable.

"How?" they growl.

By accident. Because I was bored. Through the power of love, per Eli's theories. They don't get to know that.

"Who is it?" I counter, hoping to distract them. "Who's scary enough to get you all rattled like this? Someone capable of throwing a wrench in your infallible plans?"

"You cannot comprehend our plans, no matter how omniscient you think you have become." Neil's voice is practically a whisper. Maybe they think it sounds threatening, but it just sounds scared.

I laugh, short and devoid of humor. "No, you're right, I can't. Because you don't actually know what you're doing."

They get right up in my face, which is something that Neil used to do sometimes, in entirely different contexts. But Neil never bristled with inhuman anger like this, hair on end and hands curled into claws. And where he smelled like coffee and pine trees, this thing smells like copper wires sizzling with a too-strong current, so it's not as hard to stand my ground as I thought it would be.

"Dr. Halvorsen escaped with his life," they spit at me. "He will be dealt with."

I stop breathing. Everything I might have said slides away, static buzzing at the blurry edges of my brain.

Kris.

Kris is gone. I thought I watched them kill him.

But—

"So you tried to eliminate him as a threat, and failed," Eli says softly. "Now you have something planned for the four of them, but he's getting in the way."

"Once again, you reveal your shortsightedness. You cannot comprehend—"

"Fuck off." I'm getting a few words back, apparently. Just the basics. "Try us."

The Other Place hesitates, blinking slowly. "Dr. Halvorsen will be dealt with," they repeat.

"How?" I ask, because I honestly want to know. "Who's going to deal with him?"

Neil's eyes flicker to Eli. "You were close to the truth. You had it the wrong way around."

Christ. I realize what they mean, just as—

"Oh." Eli shudders out the word, taking none of his usual joy in having solved the puzzle. "He's planning something, so you need the four of them to get in the way."

The Other Place nods, regal and infuriating. "We bestowed

their abilities upon them and set them on their current course so that they may arrest Dr. Halvorsen's plans."

Something flashes red behind my eyes. "You're going to sic them on Kris like trained dogs."

They turn their arrogant glare back on me. "Nothing so crude as that, Captain Lucas. Their abilities are precisely calibrated to make them collectively a perfect match for Dr. Halvorsen."

"Bullshit. He's already hurting Cleo, even from a light-year away."

They frown at me. "The one called Cleo McQueary is the key. If the pain makes her stronger, it is a necessary sacrifice."

It's Eli's turn to hold me back. It's probably for the best, because who knows what would happen if I clocked the Other Place in the jaw like I so, so desperately want to. I struggle against his grip, though, just to make it clear that I would if I could.

"Fuck you," I hiss in Neil's face. "Let us go. Let us help her."

"We cannot."

"Why?" Eli shouts at them. "We understand the scope of the danger now. Why can't you let us protect ourselves?"

The Other Place deflates, just a bit, which surprises me into stillness. They chew up the inside of Neil's cheek in a way that looks almost worried.

"Dr. Halvorsen," they say softly, "has not been wasting away these nineteen years. His powers did not disappear when we cast him out; they only changed, becoming twisted and wild. Quietly, in ways you cannot understand, he has been working. Chipping away at us, and deflecting our every attempt to stop him. If we free you, if we open even the smallest gap in the boundary between our universes, he will break through. That is why you must remain."

I feel my breath thick in my lungs, ready to seize up and run away from me again. "Kris is trying to get back in here?"

"No." They look at me, and Neil's eyes are almost pleading.
"This time, he plans to do much worse."

✳

ARCHIVED: Transcript of Recording by Capt. Wilhelmina
Lucas, June 20, 2041

WILHELMINA LUCAS: Hey, Kris.

KRISTOFF HALVORSEN: Billie. I thought you had a
press conference. What's up?

WILHELMINA LUCAS: It's just the two of us in here,
Kris. Please tell me what's going on. I swear I won't
breathe a word.

KRISTOFF HALVORSEN: I don't know what you're
talking about.

WILHELMINA LUCAS: Cut the bullshit. I know that
you lied to me about the engine.

KRISTOFF HALVORSEN: Excuse me?

WILHELMINA LUCAS: I know there's something wrong
with it. I know whatever it is has something to do
with your sick engineers. I don't know if the board
has you covering it up for the investors, or if you
just care about this mission too much, but I need to
know what we're getting into. You can tell me, or I
can figure it out myself, but either way—

KRISTOFF HALVORSEN: You should go home. Get a good
night's rest. You're clearly not thinking straight if
you would accuse me of . . . whatever you're accusing
me of.

WILHELMINA LUCAS: Fuck off, Kris. I know you lied
to me. I know you made me lie to the public, to my
crew, to my brother. I'll go to the board if you
don't—

KRISTOFF HALVORSEN: You won't.

WILHELMINA LUCAS: You don't know that.

KRISTOFF HALVORSEN: Yes, I do.

WILHELMINA LUCAS: I . . .

KRISTOFF HALVORSEN: Something wrong?

WILHELMINA LUCAS: It's—it's nothing, I just—

KRISTOFF HALVORSEN: I hope you're not recording.

WILHELMINA LUCAS: What?

KRISTOFF HALVORSEN: It's very inappropriate to record a colleague without their consent, Billie. Especially while pressing them to reveal company secrets. I hope your tape recorder isn't in your pocket . . . But I'm sure you'd never even think to do such a thing.

WILHELMINA LUCAS: If you're trying to scare me—

KRISTOFF HALVORSEN: You look like you have a migraine coming on. And, oh dear, is that a bit of a nosebleed? Please go home, Billie. I worry about you sometimes.

[A door slams.]

✳

BILLIE HAD A ROCK in her lab that one of the earliest *Starshot* probes had taken from Proxima B decades ago, and she showed it to Cleo like it was the last thing in the universe she wanted to do. It felt like any other rock, when Cleo held it in her hands. No one would have suspected that it had traversed the galaxy. Or that, with any luck, it was about to confirm exactly how fucked they were.

Ros hovered behind her, medical supplies at the ready. Billie chewed the knuckle of her thumb as she watched Cleo run her hands over the stone's rough surface. Cleo wondered how many times, at this point, she had made Billie watch as she leapt into the ravenous mouth of the multiverse. Too many, probably. But there was nothing else for it.

Cleo closed her eyes, and opened them on Proxima B.

It was the place Halvorsen's voice had come from, she knew that immediately. Even through the golden haze of her vision, she could see dry snow drifting across a sky lit up with auroras shimmering in every color of the rainbow. She stood on a mountain, icy and craggy. She turned and saw its peak stretching above her, the valley below, the tiny red sun setting over a frozen lake in the distance, and she kept turning and saw—

A man, tall, not as tall as he had once been. He was now hunched a little with age, though still broad-shouldered and proud, stepping surely over the rocky, slanting ground. Streaks of ashy blond were still woven through his gray hair. Cleo followed him, even though she couldn't think of anything she wanted to do less. She kept a healthy distance, to split the difference.

The man led her to an outcropping in the mountainside that turned out to be the wide, oddly circular mouth of a cave. The walls were smooth and mossy (*more life, there's life everywhere, I'll have to tell Kal*), and the floor tilted down as Cleo and the man walked, taking them deep under the mountain.

The tunnel grew wider as they went, and Cleo could feel the air getting warmer, see the moss growing thicker. In fact, right as the last light from the surface faded out, the moss began to blink with its own bioluminescence. Softly, then brighter. Blues and purples and greens, all around the walls and the ceiling of the tunnel, each patch of moss glowing with a pulsing light like it had its own little heartbeat.

Cleo couldn't help it. She gasped.

The man stopped. He half turned like he was listening, like he was sniffing the air. Cleo froze, even though this was a wimp, she wasn't really here, she couldn't be seen or heard or smelled—

But that rule had been broken before.

Cleo crept backward on the tips of her toes, willing the wimp to be over, trying to feel her way back to the world and the stone and Billie—

An unsettling smile crept across what used to be Dr. Dark Matter's cheerful face.

I must admit, I didn't think you would figure it out. Halvorsen turned fully toward her, casting his eyes around the tunnel—he couldn't see Cleo, then, just sense her presence somehow. Great. *But you are cleverer than, perhaps, I have given you credit for. Bravo.*

Cleo's insides twisted with the urge to spit insults back in Halvorsen's face—*I used to admire you, I wanted to be you, every kid on Earth wanted to be you, and now look what you've become, how dare you*—but she just kept fumbling backward through the tunnel, through the layers of time and space separating her from her body.

I wish we could work together, Ms. McQueary. Halvorsen's voice was older, rougher, more unstable than it had been twenty years ago, but Cleo could still hear the vestiges of the kindly engineer she'd watched obsessively on TV. *You're already bringing me something I desperately need, after all, and I know that we want the same things, at the end of the day. A livable planet. A better world. A happier universe. I don't know why you're so resistant to that.*

Halvorsen reached out a hand as if he could grab Cleo by the hair. And Cleo was already meters away and getting farther, and she knew Halvorsen couldn't touch her, and she knew she could probably take an old man in a fight anyway, but she also knew she really, *really* didn't want to find out what happened when Halvorsen closed that hand.

Halvorsen sighed, looking disappointed in her. It was awful. And he opened his mouth and answered, impossibly, her thoughts:

Unfortunately, no. You probably don't.

And he closed his hand, and Cleo's mind shattered. Again.

CHAPTER 11

ITEM: Urn

DIMENSIONS: 9cm H x 6.5cm D

WEIGHT: 181.4 g

SIGNIFICANCE: It's an urn

[REJECTED. PLEASE ELABORATE ON: SIGNIFICANCE]

SIGNIFICANCE: It's an urn containing my dead
fiancé's ashes

[REJECTED. PLEASE ELABORATE ON: SIGNIFICANCE]

SIGNIFICANCE: It's an urn containing my dead
fiancé's ashes that I would like to scatter on
Proxima B, if that's not too much fucking trouble

[REJECTED. PLEASE ELABORATE ON: SIGNIFICANCE]

SIGNIFICANCE: It's an urn containing my dead
fiancé's ashes that I would like to scatter on
Proxima B, if that's not too much fucking trouble,
because I guess we can't cure cancer but we can put
people on a goddamn exoplanet. And I couldn't save

him, and neither of us ever believed in any kind of
heaven, and this is the best I can fucking do for him
and it's not even a fraction of what he deserved

[REJECTED. WORD COUNT EXCEEDS LIMIT ON:
SIGNIFICANCE]

ARCHIVED: *Providence* Intracrew Messaging Service
Conversation — Capt. Wilhelmina Lucas and Travis
Onyango, March 13, 2041

WILHELMINA LUCAS
Trav did you code this infernal baggage request form

TRAVIS ONYANGO
I did! What's the issue, Cap?

WILHELMINA LUCAS
I need you to manually approve my stupid request

TRAVIS ONYANGO
What went wrong exactly? I know some folks have
    reported problems at the input level

WILHELMINA LUCAS
Just look at the transcript

TRAVIS ONYANGO
[. . .]
ah
Okay yes I'll get that approved right away Cap
Sorry

✳

*I DON'T GET A wink of sleep that night. Not that I've ever slept particu-
larly well in the Other Place. Not that my body seems to have any
physical needs here at all. But that night, I feel particularly awake
in a way I haven't in what should have been twenty years.*

I need to help her. I need to save her. I need to do everything

I can, even if the Other Place explodes me into molecules for the crime of it.

I just don't know how.

I pace back and forth for hours, knowing Eli can hear me in the next room, not caring. My footsteps become a second-nature rhythm, just an ambient ebb and flow like the gentle heartbeat of the ocean. And, right when the heartbeat becomes indistinguishable from my own, I slip away back to the universe. Back to her.

✳

CLEO WOKE UP IN the med bay feeling like her head had been pressed through a pasta machine and boiled to a nice al dente. But the first thing she saw was Billie, leaning against the wall by her bed and watching her with tired eyes, so it wasn't all bad.

"Cleo." Billie bent down to her eye level. "Are you—are you alright, do you need anything, should I get Ros—"

"'m fine, Billie," Cleo mumbled, even though she wasn't, not really. Anything to get the gasping panic out from between Billie's words. "My head just hurts."

Billie reached out like she was going to touch Cleo's face. But this time, she didn't draw back, letting her fingers hover like Cleo was a butterfly that would flutter away if spooked. Cleo held her breath, almost forgetting, almost leaning into Billie's not-touch. But then she remembered, and stopped herself. And she remembered other things too, like what had gotten her into this bed, and what was waiting, and what she had to do.

"Where are the others?"

Billie dropped her hand, and Cleo could practically hear it when her jaw clenched tight. "Off working out a plan for how to deal with Kris when we arrive at Proxima B. They want to enter the planet's orbit and then maybe send a *select* team down to—"

"I should go help them."

"*No.*" The force in Billie's voice was enough to push Cleo back against her pillows. "You need to rest. And also have as little to do with Kris as possible."

Cleo crossed her arms. "What, so you want me to let my friends face him down by themselves? No chance, Billie. He said I—I have something he wants, or something, and I need to make sure I don't let him get it."

"What you *need* is to take your own safety into account, for once." Billie's voice was all rough edges, and Cleo tried not to think about all the different, better, impossible ways she'd imagined it taking on this low and desperate tenor. "You promised you wouldn't wimp Kris again, and yet here we are."

"What else was I supposed to do? You know I didn't have a choice."

"There's always a choice."

"Not when our lives are on the line."

"*Especially* when your life is on the line." Billie leaned closer, the pain on her face enough to whip Cleo's blood up to fever speed. "What happens when we get to the Proxima System? He already has the power to hurt you and enter your mind and teleport himself across the galaxy somehow—what happens when there isn't a light-year of space between you and Kris?"

Cleo swallowed. "I don't know."

"But you do. You have something he wants, and Kris—he has never, not once, been dissuaded in his pursuit of what he wants. I've seen him in action. He doesn't stop. Whatever it is, he'll take it, he'll use it, he'll use you up for whatever his idea of *progress* is now. And the closer we get to the planet, the closer he'll get to making good on that promise."

Cleo turned in the bed to properly face Billie, standing up on her knees so their faces were level and Billie's green, green eyes were glaring right into her own. "What's your point, Billie? You gonna turn the ship around?"

"Maybe."

"We can't do that! That was the first thing you ever said to me, that we can't do that."

"Not right now, maybe. But what happened to the orbital schematics from Erebus? What happened to just swinging around the system and heading back to Earth? You and Kaleisha could get us there in a matter of weeks, we know that now."

"Are you shitting me?" A sweaty curl fell in Cleo's face, and she tugged it back, nails scraping across her scalp. "We can't just let Halvorsen do whatever it is he's going to do. Look how that turned out for you last time."

Billie reeled back. "This is different."

Cleo threw her arms in the air. "How, Billie? How is this not the exact same shit you pulled twenty years ago? Except this time, the consequences are *even more* dire, and I know that, and you know that, and if we let him get what he wants, that'll be on us for the rest of—"

"I can't keep watching you *break apart, Cleo!*"

Billie shouted it like the words were being dragged from her throat. Cleo went quiet.

"I can't watch him hurt you. I promised—" Billie hung her head. Pounded her fist into the wall soundlessly. "*Fuck* me, I want to be different this time. I would do anything to be better, to protect my crew. But I promised I wouldn't let him hurt you, and look how useless at that I turned out to be."

Unbidden, Cleo's mind went to Neil. How had he died, again? Cancer, wasn't it? Another hospital bed, another love withering away before Billie's eyes?

"Hey." Cleo raised her hand up to Billie's chin, just close enough to make Billie look up at her. "Don't say that, okay? You are the opposite of useless."

Billie gave a tiny shake of her head. "I couldn't save a mug if it was falling off a table, Cleo, let alone save you, or Eli, or anyone else. I was built to solve a mystery, and I've done that, so what am I? What am I *for*?"

Cleo brought her other hand up to frame Billie's face, her fingertips just atoms away from dipping into Billie's light, and leaned in close. If she listened really hard, she could almost imagine that the buzzing of Billie's photons was a heartbeat.

"You're not *for* anything, Billie," she whispered. "You just *are*."

Billie's gaze fell down, maybe to Cleo's mouth. "I'm not, though."

"Yes, you are. And you're going to help us kick Halvorsen's ass, and you're gonna help us get your brother back and save the *Providence* crew—"

Billie stepped back, and Cleo almost lost her balance, almost like she'd actually been holding Billie tight. There were a million emotions working their way through Billie's face, it looked like, and none of them were good.

"The crew," she whispered.

"Uh, yeah?" Cleo fell back on her heels. "The crew that we've been trying to save from their interdimensional dark matter prison, that crew. Elijah's there, as well as two hundred and two others, in case you—"

Billie cut Cleo off with a watery, terrified, furious look. *Oh. The others.*

The other*, that is.*

"Hey," Cleo said, hopping down from the bed and only swaying on her feet a little bit, "I told you, I don't—I'm not thinking about her."

Billie clenched her fists. "I don't believe you."

"What—well, I'm not, and unless you've figured out how to read minds I don't know how you expect me to prove that."

"But she's me, and she's *real*, and that's—that's everything you want, right?" Billie scrubbed a hand over her mouth, looking around the room frantically, desperately. "Why wouldn't you be thinking about her?"

Cleo tried to ignore how much she felt like her lungs had just been punched out of her body. "Why *wouldn't* I?"

Because the other Billie doesn't know me, she could have said.

Because every moment I've spent with you has been lightning in a bottle, she could have said, *and you know what they say about lightning striking twice.*

Because I don't think I could stand to be around a version of you that doesn't love me back, she could have said. *Because I think that would actually end me.*

"Because *you're* everything I want, Billie," she said instead.

Billie squeezed her eyes shut and inhaled. "Don't lie to me, McQueary," she said, and with a *pop*, she was gone.

✳

FUCK, I THINK, FALLING out of my trance too suddenly, an upside-down vertigo feeling scraping in my stomach.

This isn't—

What am I supposed to do if—if she doesn't—

✳

CLEO WENT TO THE mess hall fully intending to help the others with their plan. But apparently something of what had just happened still showed on her face, because as soon as she walked in Abe gasped.

"What's wrong, Cleo?"

And Kaleisha and Ros turned and saw whatever her stupid face was doing, and the deep concern in their eyes was too god-damn much. So much that Cleo started crying, which was not at all what she had intended to do.

The other three had wrapped her up in a warm, tangly group hug before she knew what was happening. There was a lot of Cleo sniffling into Kaleisha's jacket and Ros awkwardly patting Cleo's hair and Abe cooing comforting nonsense. And then Kaleisha had somehow gotten her into a chair, and the rest of them were sitting around the table looking at her, some horrible combination of worried and expectant.

For a moment, Cleo considered lying again. But her head hurt, and her heart hurt, and they were hurtling through space toward a freezing planet, population one brain-shredding madman, and these people were all she had in the universe right now. And, really, who had the energy?

So Cleo took a deep breath, because everything was about to change, and it seemed the thing to do. "I think," she said, staring very carefully at her hands on the edge of the table, "that I'm in love with Billie."

Kaleisha snorted.

Ros let their head drop forward onto the table with a *clonk*.

Abe smiled sweetly and said, "Wow, really? Thank you for telling us."

Kaleisha elbowed him in the side. "We talked about this weeks ago, you goober."

"Yeah, but I wasn't going to *say* that because I'm trying to be *supportive*—"

Cleo covered her burning face in her hands. "God, was it really that obvious?"

She felt Kaleisha's hand on her arm and reluctantly peeked through her fingers. "Yes," Kaleisha said. "We were waiting for you to figure it the fuck out, frankly."

"Since when?"

Ros straightened up and pulled a sarcastic thinking face. "Since—hold on, let me consult my records—about the second day on the ship."

"But," Cleo spluttered, "that means you guys knew before I did."

"Duh."

"We know that matters of the heart take you a little while to figure out," Abe said.

Kaleisha snorted again. "That's one way to put it."

Cleo felt more tears gathering in her eyes. God, she hated crying. The snot. The puffy face. The deep-down, unsteady, *I don't have time for this* feeling of it all.

"Hey. Hey. I'm sorry. I didn't mean to roast you." Kaleisha took her hand, and Cleo gave up on containing the snot. "What's bringing this up? Did you and Billie have a fight?"

Cleo wiped her face on her other sleeve and nodded. "She's, uh. She's really upset about being, you know. A hologram."

Abe nodded sagely. "Because you guys can't bone."

"Oh my God. No. Oh my *God.*" The other three all raised their eyebrows at Cleo in unison, so Cleo just plopped her head onto the table. It had looked so satisfying when Ros had done it, but it just made Cleo's head hurt worse. "I mean, *ugh, maybe.* But there's also a lot of other. Um. Stuff."

"I'd be shocked if there wasn't." Kaleisha rubbed little circles on the back of Cleo's hand. "What are you gonna do about it?"

Cleo twisted her neck to look up at her. "What is there *to* do, Kal? Other than suck it up and get over possibly the most ill-advised crush in history?"

Kaleisha smiled at Cleo like she was being very, very dense and Kaleisha loved her very, very much. "I'm not going to tell you to stop loving her, Clo. Not when it's been obvious from the jump that you two just . . . fit."

"But *how*? How do I love her right?"

"Listen, Cleo," Kaleisha said softly, "if there's anything I've learned from this whole clusterfuck, it's that you can plan and plan and turn everything over in your mind until you pass out, and the universe still doesn't care. Sometimes, we just gotta fly by the seat of our pants, baby. So just, you know, fly your pants on over to Billie and see what happens from there."

"She's right," Abe said. "You guys, when you're around each other—we can feel, in the air, how much you want to be together. So, if you want to, you'll be able to make it work."

Cleo found herself looking at Ros, who had been quiet while Kaleisha and Abe talked. Cleo hadn't expected them to have a ton of input, but they raised a ginger eyebrow at Cleo's searching expression.

"Just try to let her in, Clo. I know it's hard, but, like. It's so worth it." A sly smile tugged at the corner of their mouth. "No more jokes."

The tugged corner turned into a full, blinding smile, and Kaleisha ran around the table to wrap Cleo up in another crushing, basil-scented hug, and Cleo felt her heart go *Oh. Oh yeah.*

＊

THE OTHER PLACE WAS *right about Kris chipping away at the boundary. Now that I know what to look for, I can feel the places where it's weaker, thinner, more pliable. Like I could break through if I poked at just the right spot.*

Or Cleo could, if I showed her where.

But I can't—I need to focus. Focus on the plan. Stop letting thoughts of her distract me, for now.

✳

THE LIGHTS IN BILLIE'S lab were that viscous nighttime orange. Winding her way through the shadowy corridors of junk, Cleo found herself tiptoeing, even though there was no reason to. Maybe it was to compensate for the ear-piercing pounding of her heart. Maybe it was because she felt ready to vibrate off the floor and out into the stars.

She stopped in front of the door to Billie's quarters. It had always opened so easily in her dreams. "Billie?" she whispered.

Nothing, for a breath. Then a *pop*, startling in the heavy silence, and Billie was there, leaning against the door and not looking at Cleo.

"Billie," Cleo said again, and it sounded like *please.*

Billie ran a hand over her mouth, and Cleo felt her whole body throb like a plucked guitar string.

"Cleo, I . . ." Billie swallowed. Her whole throat tightened with the movement. "I'm sorry, Cleo. But I can't."

Cleo took a small step closer, close enough that she would have been able to smell Billie if she'd had a smell, feel Billie's heat if she'd had a body. "Can't what?"

"You know what." Billie looked down at her feet, still not at Cleo. "I can't be what you need me to be."

"I don't need you to be anything."

Billie squeezed her eyes shut like something had hurt her from the inside out. Cleo wanted her, needed her, was going to explode if she couldn't wrap her arms around her, pull her close, and kiss her hair until neither of them remembered what they'd been crying about.

She wanted, she needed. But there were other things to want.

"Billie," Cleo murmured. "Spend the night with me."

Billie finally looked at her then, with such a sudden flare of fear and shock and hope that Cleo was surprised to find herself unburned. "What—what do you—"

"I mean I'm going to lie down in your bed, and you're going to lie next to me, and we'll be close to each other. And that'll be enough."

It sounded true, when Cleo said it. It almost felt true too.

They settled into the bed in the captain's quarters: facing each other, hands almost touching, breathing the same air, sort of, if Cleo didn't think about it too hard. Billie seemed stiff at first, scared to move, scared to disturb the equilibrium, but then Cleo shuffled even closer until their noses were dangerously close to brushing. And Billie gasped against Cleo's mouth, and her long fingers curled near Cleo's collarbone, and Cleo felt the spark of it tremble all the way through her.

"See," she murmured, "this is perfect. I get all your good blankets to myself."

Billie puffed out a breath that was almost a laugh and almost a sigh. "You're doing it again."

"Doing what?"

"Making jokes instead of feeling."

Cleo breathed in and out, letting the electric buzz spread into her belly and curl her toes. "Am not."

Billie took off her glasses. Seeing her like this was like looking up at the night sky, Cleo thought. She wouldn't get tired of counting the details if she lived for a million years.

"I love you, Cleo," Billie whispered.

"I love you too," Cleo said, and wondered at the ease of it.

They stayed like that, breathing together, their lips just photons apart, until Cleo's eyes started to flicker closed. She was tired. She ached all over—from Halvorsen's attack and from the wanting—but she didn't want to sleep. She couldn't let her body forget that Billie was there.

"Billie," she said softly, thinking of what her friends had said. "When did you know?"

Billie blinked her eyes open, her face completely untired. "Know what?"

"That you loved me."

"Hmm." Billie smiled, her eyes searching Cleo's face. "You first."

"You're deflecting, but whatever." Cleo trailed a finger over her own palm, imagining the light touch was Billie's. "I knew when I told you Elijah was alive. I should have realized earlier, but I've never been in love before, hindsight is twenty-twenty, et cetera, et cetera."

"That *was* pretty late in the game."

"Alright, Dr. Love, tell me how soon *you* knew."

Billie slid her hand just a hair closer to Cleo's, her eyes following Cleo's fingertips as they traced the lines of her hand. "From the beginning."

Cleo's blood pounded in her chest, in her cheeks. "Bullshit."

"Is that so hard to believe?" Billie murmured. "That I could know I was going to love you from the moment I saw you giggling to yourself about Newton's third law of motion and that goddamn sneaker?"

Cleo squeezed her eyes shut again, just for a moment, so she wouldn't do something stupid like try to kiss Billie's brains out. "No way you knew that after knowing me for, what, fifteen minutes—"

"I did." Billie's voice was so rough. So soft. "It was—"

"Love at first sight?" Cleo was scared that if she smiled, her happiness would be too bright, too blinding, but she did it anyway. "Gross."

Billie gave Cleo as exasperated a look as she could manage with their foreheads practically touching, and didn't deny it.

✳

"BILL, ARE YOU OKAY?" Eli asks me, after I've been in another trance, picking at the boundary and utterly failing to find a way through for God knows how long, making him worry about me again.

No, I could say. No, because I thought I would never see Neil's face again, and when I did it was because a monster had put it on to threaten me, and you, and the woman I love.

No, I could say, because Cleo is in love with the hologram, the one that I was an idiot and gave my face to, and my mind, and my weakness for people who shine like the sun. So when—if—I meet her, she's not going to want me. Because she already has me.

No, I could say. Because still, despite everything, all I want to do is help her. And I don't know if I can.

"I'm fine," I say instead. "Let me get back to work."

CHAPTER 12

Cleo didn't sleep, that first night. She kept waking with a start, terrified to her unconscious core that she would roll right over and through Billie. That Billie wouldn't be able to stand that reminder. That Billie, finally unable to ignore this one thing they hadn't been honest with each other about, would leave. But every time Cleo opened her eyes, against all odds, Billie was still there, curled up on top of the blankets, snoring lightly.

It made Cleo's heart swell up to an uncomfortable size, seeing her like that—quiet, calm, looking just like anyone else. She wanted to wrap her arms around Billie's middle and burrow into her chest. She wanted to brush that stray lock of hair out of her face and kiss the tip of her nose. She wanted Billie to make some soft sleepy sound at her touch and pull her in tighter, barely awake enough to know what she was doing.

This is good enough, Cleo told herself over and over, her heart fluttering in time with Billie's gold-shot eyelashes. *I can live on this, if I have to.*

It occurred to her, briefly, that Billie didn't need sleep and was feigning it for her benefit. Cleo brushed the thought away, and lost herself again in imagining warm arms.

✳

"ALRIGHT, EVERYBODY, LISTEN TO my beautiful girlfriend," Abe said.

"Thanks, babe." Kaleisha flashed him a brilliant smile and snapped open the extendable pointer she'd unearthed from somewhere in Billie's lab. The rest of them were all gathered around Billie's whiteboard: Ros sunk into a beanbag chair, Abe perched on a suitcase that Cleo happened to know was full of varying sizes of Rubik's Cubes, and Cleo sitting next to Billie on the floor. Abe had covered the board in color-coded diagrams that Kaleisha had surrounded with instructions. "In a few days, we'll officially begin our deceleration in preparation for arrival in the Proxima System. I'll be going over the plan as it stands, with the standard caveat that every plan I've made this year has been immediately dashed to pieces on the rocks of fate, et cetera, so please hold your questions until after the presentation."

Cleo leaned toward Billie. "Hear that?"

The muscles in Billie's jaw were already working overtime, but she shot Cleo a fond look anyway. "You're one to talk. I think I can control myself."

Kaleisha rapped the whiteboard pointedly, and Cleo jumped back to attention, grinning.

"Step One," Kaleisha said, indicating the first diagram, a cartoonish sketch of the *Providence* surrounded by arrows, "Cleo and I make the last jump to Proxima B."

※

THE MED BAY BEDS did EEGs all by themselves, which freed up Ros's hands for skittish wringing while the bed scanned Cleo's brain.

"Just as I thought," they said as soon as the machine beeped. "The scan is showing even more unusual brain activity."

Cleo sat up and rubbed her temples. "Meaning what, exactly?"

"Meaning that Halvorsen's influence is fucking you up more and more every day. I think Billie was right."

"Of course," Cleo muttered as she pressed her thumbs against her eyes. "She's gonna be even more insufferable."

"She just wants you to be safe." Cleo heard the sad little smile in Ros's voice, even without looking at them. "We all do."

"I know."

"Do you?" they said, putting a hand on Cleo's shoulder. "Cleo, all this—stopping Halvorsen, saving the crew, getting back home—none of it is worth very much if we lose you."

"Don't you think that's a little shortsighted of you, Dr. Wheeler?"

Ros grinned bleakly. "Maybe. But I really couldn't care less."

*

"STEP TWO." *THWACK*. In red marker, Abe had drawn three stick figures clearly meant to be Kaleisha, Abe, and Ros with a rainbow over their heads. "While Billie and Cleo navigate the ship into orbit around the planet, I will fold us three down to the surface."

"What if Cleo has another seizure, and Ros isn't there to—"

"Whoa there." Cleo cut Billie off with a finger almost against her lips, and Billie went quiet and a little bit cross-eyed. "Listen to the lady, Dr. I-Can-Control-Myself."

Kaleisha rolled her eyes, obviously stifling a grin, and swung her pointer in Ros's direction. "You take this one."

"I've rigged up one of the hospital beds to auto-inject the phenobarbital," Ros said modestly. "Once we're gone, get Cleo in that bed, Billie, and you won't have to worry."

Billie nodded, flashing Cleo a look that made her heart grow a size. Cleo lowered her finger.

Thwack. In yellow, a cloud full of *pow*s and *bam*s and *kabloo*ies. "Step Three: The three of us subdue Halvorsen."

✳

CLEO HADN'T SEEN HER friends sweat so much since early in their training. They were all practically dripping, though, as they ran drills in preparation for the inevitable fight with Halvorsen. Ros had flung icicles through half the pillows on the ship and Kaleisha had made several folds in space so intricate that a rope flung through her distortion came out in a Celtic knot when they finally sat down for a breather.

"Guys." Cleo laughed incredulously. She had just watched Ros create a volley of lethal ice spears for Kaleisha to fold across the cafeteria and shatter on a wall. Her concerns about how they would fare without her and the dark energy boost she gave them were beginning, finally, to slip away. "Halvorsen literally won't know what hit him."

Abe frowned, fiddling warily with the pulse blaster Kaleisha had unearthed from one of the ship's escape pods. "We do have to hit him, don't we."

"Uh, yeah. I mean, he's old, but he also has psychic death powers, so I don't think you'll be able to take him out without at least a minor scuffle."

"No, I know." Abe sighed the world's tiniest sigh. "But, I guess I've been thinking . . . what if we can't restrain him? Are we gonna have to kill him?"

Cleo's stomach plummeted, through the floor and out into the universe. "I don't know," she said hoarsely. "I hope you don't have to."

"Yeah." The stars from the viewing wall reflected blankly in Abe's eyes. "Me too."

Ros slung a tired arm over Abe's shoulders. And Cleo locked eyes with Kaleisha, knowing they were both having the exact same thought:

We can't make those two into killers.

✳

THWACK. A DEVIL-HORNED STICK figure with a pouty face and a syringe in his arm, followed by an arrow pointing to the same figure trapped in an awkward oval. "Step Four! Ros injects Halvorsen with the cure, and I fold him into one of the escape pods for confinement."

✳

"SO." KALEISHA HELD UP the syringe and peered at the colorless liquid inside. "This is it."

"Yup. A serum designed to sever Halvorsen's connection to the Other Place, developed with Billie's help." Ros met Cleo's eyes, and almost smiled. "Plus a hefty dose of sedative, for good measure."

Concern creased Kaleisha's forehead faintly. She seemed unable to look away from the syringe. "Guys," she said softly, "what if this doesn't work?"

"It'll work, Kaleisha," Billie said. "We've isolated the dark-matter-resistant compound in Kris's jacket lining, and combined it with a prokaryotic enzyme that we engineered to splice the modified DNA out of his—" Billie stopped talking at the *stop talking* look that Cleo flashed her. She cleared her throat and pushed up her glasses. "Oh, you mean the—the everything. It—it'll work. It'll work because you won't accept anything less."

Kaleisha smiled at Billie then. And when her shining eyes found Cleo's, Cleo said "Rocks of fate, who?" and Kaleisha pressed her hand to her heart.

*

KALEISHA LANDED THE POINTER on the final diagram—the *Providence*, which had a smiley face, following a loopy arrow around Proxima B—with one last *smack*. "Last, but certainly not least, we turn this ship around—using momentum and gravity and a lot of equations that Billie and Cleo can figure out—and we head back to Earth faster than Cleo started flirting with Billie."

Billie choked on something—spit? holographic spit?—and Cleo felt her face go up in flames. "Kaleisha Grace Reid, how dare you?"

Kaleisha winked at her. "Hold your questions."

*

"BILLIE."

"Hmm." Billie didn't look away from the whiteboard (they were rapidly running out of boards in Billie's lab) that Cleo had been covering with orbital trajectory equations.

Cleo swallowed, rubbing the heel of her hand over a square root she'd miscalculated. "What happens when we get back to Earth?"

She felt Billie's eyes burning into the side of her head. "Well, having handled Halvorsen, we keep working to free Eli and the crew from the Other Place, obviously."

"No, I mean"—Cleo kept scrubbing, *stupid board stupid marker*—"I mean, like, with you. And me. And, you know, you and me."

"Cleo." Billie stepped closer, and Cleo put the marker down like it had burned her. "How much of your free time do you spend thinking up new and exciting things to be anxious about?"

"Excuse you. My anxieties are extremely reasonable and not at all arbitrary."

"Really? Because I, like most reasonable people would, I believe, have placed that particular bridge firmly in the 'to cross when we come to it' category. Because, and I don't know if you know this, Earth is very far away."

"Har har." Cleo turned to face Billie. Looked up into that beautiful face that was always one wrong move from flickering away. "Must be nice, to be so clearheaded."

Billie smiled like she couldn't help it, or didn't want to. She reached out to hover her fingertips just molecules away from Cleo's cheek, and Cleo felt her spine turn to jelly.

"Cleo," Billie murmured, "it's going to be okay. I'm not going anywhere."

✳

"BILL," ELI SAYS TO me at last. "I don't think you can break through by yourself."

"Watch me."

He sits next to me on the floor of my stupid, empty room that looks the same as his, and every other room in this stupid, empty place. "I think we both know that Cleo has to be the one to do it."

I sigh, and the strands of the multiverse I'd been coiling around my mind fall away. I'm not Cleo, and I'm certainly not Kris—I don't have their DNA-level connection to the Other Place's power, I can only surf its intersections with our own dimension from within. It doesn't seem fair, given that I know what's going on, Cleo doesn't, and Kris is—well, the goings-on.

"There has to be another way."

He narrows his eyes at me. "Why are you convincing yourself you've lost her before you two even meet?"

I want to splutter, scream, deny it all. But Eli sees right through that shit. "You know why," I say instead. "Easier."

He nods sagely. "Then I think I speak for myself and for Neil when I say: You're a fucking idiot."

I noogie him on the arm, but we both know it's half-hearted.

"Dude, I can feel just by looking at you how much you care about her. And I don't even have psychic powers like Cleo. So there's no way she won't feel it too."

As I watch him walk out the door, his words churn around in my head.

And all at once, I know what I have to do.

*

THE NIGHT BEFORE THE last jump to Proxima B, they danced.

Abe put on the dress that Kaleisha had worn to the Space Heist, and Kaleisha and Ros painted flowers and crescent moons on each other's faces, and Cleo doused her body in glitter from the rec room craft closet, and they danced. Billie dimmed the lights and blasted the twenty-year-old music. She smiled as Cleo shimmied and bounced around her, laughed as Cleo tried to grind up on her, responded to Cleo's bellowed "come on, baby" by wrenching her hair out of its ponytail—*oh*, Cleo thought, *oh no, oh yes*—and joining their tangled four-person rave as best she could. And they danced, and Cleo accumulated three sets of lipstick prints all across her face, and in the barely orange glow of the room the waves of hair tumbling over Billie's shoulders looked like sunset, and as she twirled and raised her hands to the stars (in every direction, because the stars were all around), Cleo thought: *Right. This is what the world is.*

*

ARCHIVED: Emergency Response Protocol for the Crew of *Providence I*, February 9, 2041

> **ONBOARD FIRE, EXPLOSION, OR BIOHAZARD EXPOSURE**: All affected levels must be evacuated, depressurized, and inspected by the emergency repair team for damage or continued danger before repopulating.
>
> **DECOMPRESSION**: The *Providence* pneumatic delivery system will automatically dispatch air masks to affected levels. All personnel should affix their own masks before helping anyone else, and immediately evacuate to unaffected levels.
>
> **DAMAGE TO SHIP'S INFRASTRUCTURE OR MINOR ENGINE FAILURE**: All personnel must report to their launch stations in the quarters and flight deck. If repairs are needed and possible, the emergency repair team must complete them ASAP.
>
> **ESCAPE PODS**: ESCAPE PODS ARE ONLY TO BE USED IN THE EVENT OF CATASTROPHIC ENGINE FAILURE OR HEAT SHIELD MALFUNCTION WITHIN 400,000km OF EARTH OR PROXIMA CENTAURI B. PODS HAVE LIMITED FUEL STORES AND ARE NOT EQUIPPED FOR LONG-TERM SURVIVAL.

✳

"KALEISHA, CLEO, GET YOURSELVES into position," Billie called.

"Aye-aye, Captain." Cleo, wearing her NASA jacket for luck, stood next to Kaleisha in front of the flight deck window, stance wide and knees bent. She closed her eyes and listened to the space in front of them. She found and latched on to the feeling-sound of the dark matter filament surging ahead of them, the shimmering undercurrent of dark-gold energy. "Abe, what's our velocity?"

"Twenty thousand kilometers per second and dropping fast," Abe answered. "We'll reach our, uh, target orbital speed? In twenty-three seconds."

Cleo took Kaleisha's hand, letting a tendril of power flow through her—it was so easy, now, whether from practice or something else she didn't know—and into her friend. "Ready?"

Kaleisha stretched out her other hand toward the vacuum of space. "Ready."

"Kal, Ros, be ready to fold down there as soon as we enter orbit," Abe said. "Ten seconds to jump, guys . . . nine . . . eight—"

Cleo glanced back at the console, even though she knew it could break her concentration. Abe was sitting in the copilot's seat like he'd been born there, and Billie was sitting in the captain's chair. Her eyes were half elsewhere, scanning through the numbers and trajectory simulations deep inside her mind, but she still smiled, just a bit, when Cleo looked at her. And Cleo turned back to the sparkling nothing in front of them, satisfied, and lost herself in the river flowing through her.

"—two—*one*."

Cleo's spine snapped straight as the dark river, stronger and more overwhelming than ever, rushed through her and into her friend. Kaleisha closed her fist and *ripped*, and the stars bent around them. For a moment, the *Providence* wasn't moving, or maybe it was free-falling through the impossible kaleidoscope of darkness and light around them, and Cleo felt small and enormous and tired and unstoppable as she and Kaleisha held the fold in the universe together—

And then, with a thunderous crack, everything unfolded, and for the first time since they'd left Earth there was something in the window.

Cleo and Kaleisha practically collapsed against the glass, their legs and breath stuttering, and stared. Abe, Ros, and Billie crowded in around them, even though they were supposed to be in ready positions.

Proxima Centauri B hung in front of them, all of it still easily visible in the window, its dark surface a craggy red brown under a vibrant blanket of auroras. As they curved slowly around, the planet pulling them into orbit, the light side came into view, and the twilight zone, the strip of icy mountain between the day and the night. And there, in the distance but nowhere near as far away as Cleo had expected, was Proxima Centauri, tiny, red, and raging, spitting looping strands of plasma into the ink-black sky.

Cleo fingered the logo on the arm of her dad's jacket. "We're in another solar system, guys," she murmured, in case saying it helped her believe it.

"You're the first humans to lay eyes on an exoplanet," Billie said behind her. Cleo would have shivered at her voice in her ear if the sight of Proxima hadn't already prickled her skin into goose bumps.

"Halvorsen doesn't count?" she whispered.

Abe snorted. "I'll make sure he doesn't, even if I have to write the history books myself."

Cleo grinned at him. "Don't you three have somewhere to be?"

She followed Billie back behind the console, hoping nobody saw the wobble in her knees as she watched the planet grow to fill the window. She could pick out wispy clouds now, the wrinkled lines of frozen riverbeds. She pictured the cave where Halvorsen was hiding, with the valley below and the impossibly high peak above. The frozen lake in the distance, multicolored light glancing off its surface. She scanned through the ship's tracking system, searching for anything resembling what she'd seen.

"Alright," she said, landing on a set of coordinates. Kaleisha leaned in close so Cleo could point them out. "I hope that's it.

Please don't be mad at me if you end up on a *different* weirdly tall mountain, though."

Kaleisha wrinkled her nose at her. "I forgive you in advance, babe."

She joined hands with Abe and Ros, the three of them standing swaddled in parkas and silhouetted against the window.

"Ready?" Billie said.

"As we'll ever be," Kaleisha said, and she reached out her hand—

And then the world *lurched*, and they all fell to their knees.

Cleo gasped, the pain from the impact flaring up her thighs. "Billie, what the *fuck* was that—"

"I don't know, I'm not getting any—"

A siren started blaring, harsh and matched by a flashing red light that cut right through Cleo's aching head like a knife—

A flash of somewhere else, an icy rocky mountainside where a man stood, raising his frail arms to the rainbow-red sky, and his eyes screwed in concentration as he opened his mouth and said:

"Dear old Billie. Bless her for turning the Providence *into a mind."*

And Cleo slammed back to the flight deck, where Abe and Ros were struggling to stay on their feet, Kaleisha was punching buttons, and Billie's eyes were flicking back and forth so fast they blurred and the *sound*, God, the too-familiar roaring of the ship crashing through an atmosphere they'd never intended it to—

"It's Halvorsen," Cleo said between heaving breaths. "He's bringing down the ship."

Kaleisha, Ros, and Abe all started shouting at once, but Cleo blocked them out.

"Billie," she said, pulling herself to her feet by the edge of the console, "what's he doing to the systems?"

Billie groaned, clutching her head in her hands. "*Fuck.* He's inside, he's wrecking everything, I can't I can't I—"

She cried out, and Cleo stumbled toward her over the see-sawing floor of the bridge. "He's messing with your head like he's been messing with mine. Don't fight it, you don't have to—"

"*No!*" Billie gritted her teeth and clenched harder at her temples, her face turning red with the effort. "He's taken out one of the thrusters," she boomed over the cacophony, the way she had the first time she'd ever spoken to them. "And he's"—she winced, like something in her own head had burned her—"he's hijacked the autopilot."

"He can *do that*?" Kaleisha yelled, tapping frantically at a screen that refused to cooperate. "Did we know he could do that?"

"Doesn't matter." Billie half looked at Cleo again. "What does he want?"

Cleo reluctantly reached for the white-hot simmering at the back of her mind, letting herself fall into it—

Rage, and exhaustion, and a plan so much worse than she'd expected, though he wouldn't have to do this, would he, if you would just cooperate, Ms. McQueary—and an image in her mind's eye, or maybe Halvorsen's, of a dark-bright swirling hole between two dimensions—

"He wants the dark matter engine," Cleo gasped.

"What for?" Ros shouted.

"Its power. Its direct connection to the Other Place. Doesn't *matter.*" Billie stood, and her eyes were bloodshot and clear. "He's not going to get what he wants. He's not going to hurt anyone else on his way to a *better world.*"

"Billie," Kaleisha said, "can you get the autopilot back under your control?"

"No, he's got too—ahh!—too firm a grip." The floor lurched

again, and Billie flickered. "But if I disable all systems entirely, the ship will crash to the surface, destroying the engine."

The air tightened, as they all realized.

"And the ship along with it, right?" Kaleisha's voice was smaller than Cleo had ever heard it. Maybe she was trying to remember the last time she'd heard her dad's voice. Maybe she was trying to remember what a warm breeze felt like on her cheeks.

"Unless you have a better idea," Billie said, her voice strained but not unkind.

"If Halvorsen gets the engine, it'll be bad?" Kaleisha asked Cleo. Cleo closed her eyes and saw screaming and suffering and the fabric of a universe unraveling, knowing it meant death without understanding why, and she nodded grimly even though she'd already seen the resignation in Kaleisha's eyes.

Kaleisha breathed in, breathed out. She gave her head a little shake, like maybe that would dislodge any memories of Earth that were keeping her from making a call. "Okay," she said. "Do it, Billie."

Billie braced her hands on the console, and her breath might have hitched a little, or Cleo might have imagined it. "The escape pods are outfitted with survival packs—more coats, food, water, meds, everything you'll need." There was silence as they all stared at her. "Well, get going!"

Kaleisha grabbed Ros's and Abe's hands and tugged them toward the elevator. Cleo went too, holding her hand out for Billie as if she could have pulled her along.

"Come on, dude, I want a window seat," she joked, because there was nothing else for it.

Billie put an arm out, stopping Cleo in her tracks. Their eyes met, and that was when Cleo should have realized what was about to happen, because Billie's were wet and miserable and very, very sure.

"Cleo," she said. "I can't go with you."

Cleo was only dimly aware of the other three freezing in place behind Billie, even though the elevator had just dinged onto the flight deck. "Sure you can."

"No." Billie winced and took a shuddering breath. "The escape pods aren't connected to the ship's computer."

"So we'll download you." Cleo's mouth was full of wool, and so was her head, and she hadn't known it was possible to feel so dry and dumb and desperate. "We'll transfer your program to the pod computer, no problem—"

Billie laughed, empty. "You said it yourself, I'm just an ungodly amount of data. You don't have time to download me."

"But." The other three, over Billie's shoulder, were looking at her with so much pity she was sure it would shatter her apart. "If the ship is destroyed, you will be too. I'm not leaving you here."

"You have to."

"No, I—" She reached up to hold Billie's face between her hands but she couldn't get close enough, the floor was shaking too badly. "I'll stay here with you, then."

The line of Billie's mouth went hard. "Don't be an idiot, Cleo. You would die."

"Maybe."

"*Definitely.* And I'm not worth it. I'm not real."

Furious tears dripped down Cleo's face, and she didn't care. "What are you talking about, you are real, you *are*—"

"Not real enough to leave this ship." Billie was so close that Cleo should have felt the vibrations of her voice on her own lips, but she didn't. "Just real enough to save you."

Cleo shook her head endlessly, out of words. Billie ran her fingers over the space above Cleo's hair.

"Let me save you, Cleo," she said, her voice going rough. "And you'll survive, and you'll stop Halvorsen, and you'll—you'll find her."

Cleo's heart clenched around the words. "Her?"

"Her. Me. The other me." Billie squeezed her eyes tight, just for a moment, and when she opened them again she looked almost calm. "You'll find her, Cleo. And she'll love you, because she's me, and there's no version of the universe where any version of me doesn't love you."

Cleo was never going to stop crying, just like she was never going to be able to move her feet from that exact spot. She looked up into Billie's eyes and leaned closer, listening for something, anything but empty space and sirens and the ship plummeting through alien air—

"Find her. Find me," Billie whispered. "Go."

And Cleo opened her mouth to say *no*, to say *not on your life*, to say *you said it was going to be okay, that you weren't going anywhere, you promised me, Billie—*

But before she could say anything, there was a pair of strong arms around her middle, and before she knew what was happening she was in the elevator, kicking and scratching against Abe's grip on her. And through the door she could see Billie, silhouetted against the rainbow light, raising a hand in farewell like they were going to see each other again.

And the door was closing, and Cleo was screaming, and that was the end of it.

The others watched from the escape pod as *Providence I* burned through the atmosphere. Cleo curled up in her seat, as far away from the window as she could get, and tried to forget how to exist.

＊

I SWIM THROUGH THE golden edges of two dimensions, my mind diving deeper and deeper with every push. I've learned how to see back into the universe, how to hear, how to watch from the outside as time unravels before me in its twisting, knotted skeins. But it's only now, thanks to Eli—thanks to Cleo—that I think I've figured out how to feel my way back into the universe.

The boundary, despite what Kris has done to it, is still strong, and my mind was never meant to cross it. I can touch it, though. I can poke around the places where it's cracked and the light is bleeding through. And when I find the right spot, I can put my mouth right up to the keyhole, so to speak, and whisper across time and space and everything else between us:

Come find us, Cleo. Come find me.

CHAPTER 13

J ust before the pod went into its landing pattern, Cleo felt
something, and looked up.

A featherlight stroke of a finger over her heart. Familiar,
somehow, like it belonged to a hand that had touched her before.
But before she could parse it, before she could remember, the
feeling was gone.

"Cleo?" Abe said softly, reaching over from the opposite seat
to put a hand on her shoulder. "Are you—"

"Don't touch me, Abe," Cleo hissed, and folded back in on
herself.

*HERE ARE SOME THINGS they didn't tell us about Proxima B, because
they couldn't have known from just the probes and the telescopes:*

*The terminator zone is really fucking cold. I mean, we knew
that going in, but we didn't know. It's cold enough that the air
burns going down. Cold enough to drive you a little crazy, if
you're here long enough.*

*With the tidal locking giving you endless sunset and the
tepid red dwarf star giving you endless winter, it starts to feel*

like time is meaningless and nothing matters. However, that's nothing compared to being trapped in a conterminous dimension, where time actually is meaningless. And I've managed not to become a supervillain, so what's Kris's excuse?

The Starshot *probes found life, of course, but they couldn't have predicted how weird it would be. Like how the purple-gray flora that we might call lichen tends to grow in incomprehensible spiral formations that look almost intentional. How those little furry four-legged things that we might call moles turn out to have poisonous fangs and dead, black eyes. And those oddly circular tunnels? They lead down to the much warmer underground where many more things live. Some of them are less terrifying because they live in the warmth; some of them are more so because they live in the darkness. Whatever made the tunnels went extinct a long time ago. Probably. That's what you have to believe to live there.*

(God, come on, Cleo. I hate waiting. I really do get bored easily.)

※

LATER, CLEO WOULD REMEMBER Ros handing her a thermoregulating face mask and a pair of heavy snow boots but not how she managed to put them on; she would remember Kaleisha flinging open the escape pod hatch but not where she'd found the pulse rifle she thrust upon Abe. Cleo only faintly registered the biting blast of wind that rushed in, and barely saw the landscape around them when she followed the other three out.

If she cared enough to look, though, Cleo would have seen the snow-streaked mountains reflecting the Technicolor sky, the red sun twinkling in the barren distance, the clouds catching shades of scarlet she'd never seen before. She would have seen Kaleisha and

Ros and Abe staring, mouths open and heads swiveling hungrily, as they crunched through the snowbanks coating the valley the pod had landed in. She would have seen an alien world, for the first time, just like Billie had said—

Goddamnit, Billie—

But Cleo couldn't see anything except the memory of Billie, lit up every which color against the alien sky as she went to her death. So she stood numbly while the others stared, pain occasionally slashing across her head and her heart.

Abe's voice wobbled through the haze. "Kal, what—what's the plan?"

Kaleisha adjusted her pack on her shoulders. "I think," she said slowly, "we should focus on finding shelter and fuel for a fire. Then we can go from there."

"What about Halvorsen?" Ros's voice was quiet, as if saying the name would cause an avalanche.

"What about him, Ros? I don't think we're in any kind of state to take him—"

Lightning crashed across Cleo's mind, bending her double. *Bone-deep weariness and cave walls glowing mossy blue; anger at yet another setback but not despair, never despair—*

Cleo felt Kaleisha's hands on her back, at her temples. "See, Ros?" Kaleisha said. "We can't go after Halvorsen with Cleo like this."

"But he's *making* Cleo like this, don't you think we should—"

"Stop that," Cleo said through gritted teeth. She straightened up, blinking Halvorsen from her eyes. She was more awake now, to the world and to what she needed to do. "Stop talking about me like I'm not here."

"Sorry, love." Kaleisha rubbed circles between her shoulder blades. "I just don't think we should get any closer to Halvorsen, for your own—"

"I think I should." The other three looked at Cleo with that same corrosive pity, obvious even through their masks, that made her want to climb out of her skin. "I want to finish this."

Kaleisha rubbed her forehead wearily. "Okay, but let's think about this, because there has to be a way we can do it without putting you in any more danger—"

"What happened to flying by the seat of our pants, hmm? I'm the one who knows where he is. I'm going to lead the way."

"Or maybe you could tell Kaleisha where he is?" Abe looked Cleo in the eye tentatively. "And she could fold the three of us over there, and we could take care of Halvorsen, and you could stay here and be safe."

Cleo clenched her teeth against the anger that was either hers or Halvorsen's or both. "You gonna stop me from doing this too, Abe?"

Abe inhaled sharply, like Cleo had burned him. "Come on, Cleo, you know I didn't have a—"

"What I *know* is that you and Halvorsen are both the reason Billie's gone, and since I can't kick *your* ass—"

"Cleo." Kaleisha's hand tightened on her shoulder. Cleo tried to shrug it off, but she just squeezed harder. "Watch yourself. This is *not* his fault."

"What was I supposed to do, huh?" Abe spread his arms helplessly. "Let you stay there and die? So we'd have to lose you *and* Billie?"

"I could have *done something*," Cleo shouted. "I could have figured something out, you know I could've."

"What would you have done, Cleo?" Abe was close to tears, tears that reflected the shifting rainbow light as they threatened to spill over. "In the *four minutes* between when we left the flight deck and when the ship crashed, with Halvorsen messing with your head *and* Billie's, what would you have done?"

Cleo opened and closed her mouth. "Something. I could have *tried*."

"I wasn't gonna risk it—"

Cleo wrenched herself forward and shoved Abe in his down-covered chest with the hand that Kaleisha wasn't holding back. "It wasn't your risk to *take*!"

With a *crack*, Cleo and Abe were suddenly fifteen feet apart, both of them stumbling into the snow where the fold in space had dropped them. Between them, Kaleisha was panting, her arms spread, Ros standing frozen behind her. Kaleisha looked at Cleo, angry and scared and tired, her eyes wet.

"Cleo," she said, "you need to stop. I know how much you're hurting right now—"

"Like *hell* you—"

"We *all* lost Billie, Cleo!" Kaleisha shouted, and Cleo fell silent. "I know it's different for you, but we cared about her too."

"And lashing out at Abe won't fix anything," Ros piped up from over Kaleisha's shoulder.

"We all have to take care of each other." Kaleisha blinked hard. "Especially now. If I never get to see a flower again, you can bet your ass I'm going to do everything I can to take care of you people."

Abe made a quiet snuffling sound, and Cleo looked over in time to see his eyes crinkling at her, in spite of the tears finally falling down his mask and into the snow.

"Fuck," Cleo said, and she crossed the distance between them. She launched herself into a hug, and he caught her. "I'm sorry, Abe."

"I'm sorry too," Abe said, giving her a squeeze that lifted her feet off the ground. "You know that all I want is for you to be okay."

"I know," Cleo said in his ear.

Abe put her down gently. "Then tell me you're going to be okay."

"I'll work on it," Cleo said, "but you're gonna have to let me brain-blast Halvorsen into next Sunday. Because my seizures will keep coming, and none of us will be safe"—*and Billie's death won't fucking mean anything*—"until I deal with him."

Ros clapped a hand onto Cleo's shoulder. "Until *we* deal with him."

Kaleisha's eyes got smiley too. "Yeah, you're not getting rid of us that easy."

Abe wrapped them all up in a bear hug. "Can you find him without hurting yourself too badly, Clo?"

"I think so."

"Then what are you waiting for?" Kaleisha said. "Lead the way."

※

A SHUDDER RUNS ALONG the boundary, like a subway shaking the dust loose from under your feet. It's all I can do to hold on, and not get knocked back to my empty body in my empty room.

Kris.

He's still working, whatever the hell that means. Pounding on the doors of the Other Place with his messed-up mind powers. And it's clearly paying off—every second there are more places where the boundary is so thin that I worry I could punch right through. I can't, of course. But someone else could. Kris could, with Cleo's help.

I should reach out for her again. It's been too long, I think.

My feelers go out again, through the widening gaps in the

*honey-viscous membrane between the two universes. But then
there's another quake, and I'm thrown, almost knocked off-kilter—*

*And I almost slip, then I do, then I'm tumbling through nothing
and something's dragging me away from her—*

*And I'm on my back in my room, Neil's snarling face looming
over me.*

*"What have you done?" the Other Place screams, forgetting that
Neil's voice doesn't sound like the screeching of steel getting struck
by lightning.*

*"I think you know," I say, and I reach out one last time, just for
the space of a breath—come on, Cleo, follow the feeling of me—
before they cut me off.*

✳

THERE IT WAS AGAIN. That faintly swelling *something* in Cleo's chest
that felt almost like happiness. Something like a hand in hers,
pulling her forward, away from the cold and the grief and the
near-certainty of death—

"I can go again."

"Are you sure, Cleo?" Ros put their hands out to catch her as
she stood on wobbling legs, but she waved them away. The feeling
had cut off sharply, gone as quickly as it had come, but she still felt
the strength of it in her blood.

"I'm sure," she said, and shuffled through the snow to stand
on the crest of the hill Kaleisha had folded them to. It was closer to
the hot side of the planet, a few degrees warmer, the snowflakes
bigger and softer. The escape pod was hundreds of miles behind
them now, and Halvorsen still hundreds ahead, but Cleo could
already feel him more clearly, sharper at the back of her throat,
and she knew they were getting closer.

She reached for Halvorsen again, letting the burn overtake

her for just a moment—it was getting easier, too easy, to fall into the inferno at the end of her mind—

That's right, Ms. McQueary, keep coming, and you'll see how much better it can be if we work together—

"That way," Cleo gasped, and pointed between two mountains in the distance.

Kaleisha nodded, taking Cleo's hand and waiting for Abe and Ros to link up too. "All secure?" she asked, and as soon as they nodded, space bent around them, mountains and snow and rainbows folding and flowing—

And with a thunderclap, it was over, and they were standing by a frozen lake. And Cleo's head hurt worse than ever, because it was the same lake she'd seen in her vision, and there, against the horizon, was that tall arrowhead of a mountain where Halvorsen was hiding himself.

"Okay, break time," Ros said firmly, pushing a groaning Cleo and a panting Kaleisha over to some rocks they could sit on. While they both ripped their masks off and ate a small pile of the nutrition bars Ros had pilfered from the other survival packs in the pod, Kaleisha eyed Cleo piercingly.

"Are you good?"

"Sure." Cleo's head was between her knees, so she knew she didn't look particularly convincing. "Peachy."

"Somehow, I'm having a hard time believing that."

"Alright, Kal, no, I am extremely not good." Cleo straightened up, and Kaleisha's face wavered hazily red and gold before coming into focus. "Probably never been worse, actually."

Kaleisha took Cleo's gloved hands in her own and started rubbing them, so they could both get the feeling back. "I guess a better question would be: Are you going to be able to keep going?"

Cleo looked past her, toward Proxima Centauri casting long red shadows over the lake.

("I guess I was looking forward to the perpetual sunset."

"How romantic.")

She pressed her eyes shut. "Big question, Kal."

Kaleisha squeezed her hands. "You know, once we take care of Halvorsen, we can figure out how to get back into the Other Place. Then you could—"

Cleo groaned and let her head fall forward into Kaleisha's lap. "Let me stop you right there."

"Why?" Kaleisha extracted a hand to brush the hair out of Cleo's face. "What are you scared of?"

Of a Billie that doesn't know me.

"I just don't want to think about that right now," Cleo said into their joined hands.

Kaleisha kept stroking her curls, slow and soft. "Okay."

Of a different Billie, changed by the Other Place, or just not quite my Billie, because maybe she never was.

"Kal." Cleo's voice was so small, she was surprised it wasn't carried away on the freezing wind. "I'm such an idiot."

"Babe, no, not at all—"

"I just—" Good thing her face was hidden in Kaleisha's coat, because Cleo was dangerously close to crying. "It was never going to be okay, the thing with Billie, and I *knew* that, because it was a fluke, but I wanted so badly—"

Of losing her all over again because God, Kal, it wasn't real—

"Hey." Kaleisha pulled Cleo up by the coat and looked her right in the eye, deeper and clearer that she had ever looked at her before, maybe. "Nothing about the two of you was a fluke. You loved her, and she loved you back. That was real, okay?" Cleo nodded, but Kaleisha pressed on. "Billie is still out there, in the Other Place, and she's the exact same person who you fell in love with. She loved you once, and she can love you again."

"It just feels like it was an accident. Like an experiment I'm not going to be able to replicate." Cleo looked up at the stars that peeked hazily through the darkest parts of the sky, wondering which one was the Sun, wondering whether anyone had ever given names to these slightly askew constellations.

"Yeah, yeah, your mom left and your dad checked out and it convinced you that love can't be safe and reliable," Kaleisha said, with so much tenderness behind the sarcasm that Cleo couldn't even think about sticking her tongue out at her. "Are you going to believe that forever? After everything we've been through?"

Cleo's lip trembled, and she let it. "I feel like the answer you're fishing for is *no*."

"Of course not, dummy. Give love a little more credit. Give *Billie* a little more credit. Love—real, honest love—*is* safe, and it *is* reliable, and you're so fucking lovable that there's no way Billie won't really, honestly love you. *I* love you. We all love you— not because you lucked into it, and not because you ply us with jokes to keep us happy, and not because you've managed to hide your true, unlovable nature or whatever. You care so much, and you want so badly for things to be good. You help me believe that things *can* be good, even when the plan's gone to shit and I don't know how. I love you so much, babe. Here at, like, the end of all things, especially."

Cleo pressed her face back into Kaleisha's coat and let the tears fall. "Fuck, Kal."

Kaleisha squeezed her tight. "It's gonna be okay."

Cleo swallowed. Nodded. Breathed until the tears dried up.

"I can go again," she said, and her voice was bigger this time.

Ros and Abe looked over from their rock, Abe's mouth still stuffed with protein bar. "Are you sure?" Ros asked.

"I'm sure."

✳

"WE TOLD YOU, you cannot leave."

Before, I might have laughed in their face just to piss them off, but now I just state the facts plainly. "I wasn't trying to. Just trying to show Cleo how to bust us out."

The Other Place snarls. "Did you not listen when we told you that doing so would destroy everything?"

"Agree to disagree."

They sit back on Neil's heels, then, with a lost look in their eyes. "Captain Lucas, our plan is well on its way. You must let us see it through."

I scramble to my feet. "What are you talking about?"

"Cleo McQueary and her companions are at Halvorsen's doorstep. They will reach him any moment now."

"No." I try to see back into the universe, try to see what could have gone so horribly wrong since the last time I checked. I can only get flashes—Cleo crying, the Providence burning through the multicolor atmosphere of Proxima B—before the Other Place cuts me off again. "You have to let me—"

"We do not have to do anything except wait. Do you not understand? To do otherwise would mean the end of us all."

I grit my teeth, ready to fight or run or dive back into the boundary. "You can't let them die fixing your mess for you."

The Other Place rises to Neil's feet, radiating power and terror, panic twitching that muscle in Neil's jaw. "You misunderstand the situation again, Lucas."

"No, I understand perfectly." I clench my fists. Elijah's not here, this time, to hold me back. "You just don't want to admit that you fucked up. That you can see everything and do anything, and you're still losing control."

"Do you forget so easily how this all began?" Electricity crackles through Neil's eyes and the air around me. All the breath leaves my body. "We did not create this conflict. You did.

You creatures, who destroyed your own world in your never-ending quest for profit and progress, who could not devise any solution but seeking out new worlds to conquer, who would have drained us of everything we have if we had not stopped you— what makes you think that you know any better than us? How are we to know that you are capable of anything but devastation?"

All the breath leaves my body, because they're right. They're so right. And at last, I really do understand. Appeal to love, *Eli said.* Doubt thou the stars.

"I'm sorry," *I say, sucking in a shaking breath.* "I know how it feels to lose your home."

The static around me relaxes a bit. The Other Place eyes me warily.

"We were stupid," *I continue.* "I was stupid, and Halvorsen was stupid, and every human that ever came before us was stupid. We're stupid, shortsighted creatures, and I used to think that I could somehow cure myself of it if I just didn't let myself feel anything, and look how that turned out." *I think of Eli, of Neil. Of Cleo.* "I don't know if you have a concept of love. You must be feeling something like it, to care this much about saving your home and all your . . . selves."

"Self." *Neil's face grows thoughtful.* "Selves. Is there a difference?"

I nod, frantically latching on to this scrap of understanding. "For us, there is. But love is the feeling you get when two separate selves get less . . . you know, separate."

I suck at this. Eli should be here. I scrub a hand against the furrows in my brow and keep going anyway.

"It's like—it's like when someone else's needs become just as important to you as your own. When that other person becomes more important than your fear, or your anger, or your selfishness. And the thing is, I think love is the antidote to everything

*you've described: our greedy, universe-conquering impulses, and
our worst, most self-serving behaviors, and absolutely everything
that Kris has going on. He forgot that the worst atrocities happen
when you're only thinking of yourself. He forgot that progress is
worse than nothing without love.*

*"For a while, I thought that love made you stupid. But now,
I see that it's entirely the opposite. I'm in love, and I've never felt
less stupid. I think I need to follow that feeling. And I hope you'll
let me, if only because love is the opposite of destruction."*

*The Other Place blinks Neil's eyes at me. "What is your love
telling you?"*

"That Cleo can save us all. Including you."

*"Do you really believe that she could release you without
allowing Halvorsen to destroy the boundary?"*

*"Yes." My hands relax. "I think she and her friends can do
anything."*

*The Other Place looks out the window, at those infinite fields
that must mean something to them, even if they look like nothing
to me. "Then you may do what you will. But we will be watching."*

❄

CLEO KNEW WHEN THEY reached the cave. Not because she recognized
it immediately—it looked too much like every other eerily round
tunnel mouth they'd passed—but because the crackling interference in her head disappeared. The others noticed it too, even,
because her spine uncurved, her jaw unclenched, and her whole
body unwound for the first time in weeks.

"Cleo?" Ros said.

"He's here." Cleo could feel it, even without the constant
burning assault on her mind. "I guess he's letting us approach
peacefully, or something."

"Yikes." Kaleisha shook the snow out of her locs and squared her shoulders. "I guess we always knew a surprise attack was out of the question. So we're gonna go in slowly, and Cleo, let us know if you sense any shift in Halvorsen's vibe."

Cleo nodded. She got three nods back, and they started moving.

It was all the same as in her vision—the monstrous mouth of the tunnel, the slow warming of the walls that let them lower their thermoregulating masks, the gradual replacement of the rainbow-red light from outside with the cool pulsing of the mosses. Kaleisha, Ros, and Abe all gasped at it, just like Cleo had the first time. She would have told them to be quiet, if she thought it mattered. If she hadn't been distracted by something, something that *wasn't* the same, that she hadn't felt when she'd been here as a specter—

"Don't touch it, Abe!" Ros whispered, pulling Abe's hand back from a patch of moss. "Not without . . ." They trailed off and drew closer, the tip of their freckled nose reflecting the thumping blue-green glow. "Kal, do you think it's a fungus? The stem structure looks more bryophytic to me, but there's no way they photosynthesize, not all the way down here—"

"Can we focus up, please?" Kaleisha whispered, cringing like the effort of not inspecting the alien moss was physically paining her. "We are, tragically, in crisis mode at the moment."

"Sorry—"

Kaleisha stopped walking. "Cleo?"

Because Cleo was standing with her hand on the wall, possibly pathogenic bioluminescent mosses be damned, with her eyes closed and all her senses reaching for the gold-dark vibrations she could feel just under the surface—

"It's the Other Place," she whispered. Because even though it was just a faint scent in the air, instead of a sea flooding her lungs like it had been when she wimped Elijah, it was unmistakable: the jangling weirdness, the upside-down light, the quarks in everything spinning just a little bit wrong. "It's—I don't know, it's like it's closer here, somehow. Like it'd be easier to break through."

"Easier," Ros murmured, their eyes going wide. "Like the last time I went in."

Cleo frowned, trying to dig deeper, trying to find the source. "Almost like—like the boundary is—"

Have you figured it out yet, Ms. McQueary? Can you feel what we could do together?

"*Fuck!*" Cleo yelled, even though the pain from Halvorsen's intrusion dissipated quickly. The other three rushed over to her, concerned for all the wrong reasons, and she waved them off to keep marching down the tunnel. "Come on, guys. I think I know what that bastard wanted the engine for."

The passage grew wider and wider as they walked until eventually, finally, it opened up into a massive cavern. Cleo could barely make out the ceiling, but the floor and the colossal stalagmites rising up out of it were so covered in the glowing moss that she had no trouble making out the slightly stooped figure standing in the middle of it all.

Kaleisha shoved past Cleo. Cleo could feel the space-collapsing power building between her friend's fingers.

"Hands up," Kaleisha called into the echoing cavern. "*Now.*"

The figure just laughed jovially and stepped closer, and as he did Cleo felt that same clattering chaos, that same discordant brokenness that she'd felt every time Halvorsen invaded her mind—it wasn't just in his head, it was in his skin, his heart, his whole body, veins of white-hot shrieking agony just barely held together by rage and resolve—

"Ms. McQueary," Halvorsen said. "And friends, of course. How nice of you to finally join me."

CHAPTER 14

Cleo had been seeing Halvorsen all her life, of course, even before the visions. There was one clip that was replayed on every retrospective, in every documentary, even though it was burned into her brain and probably the brains of everybody else on Earth: a blinding flash, and then silence; the click-burst of cameras over the face of a man watching his world disintegrate; then a storm of voices, of "What just happened?" and "Dr. Halvorsen! Dr. Halvorsen!" and the clattering of the countdown microphone as it fell to the floor; then a "Leave, all of you," and a "NOW!" and a door slamming shut for the final time.

But here, in the bluish light of the cave, Cleo saw Halvorsen as he was now: old, twitchy from almost two decades in isolation, and looking deeply, self-righteously baffled that four strangers weren't just teaming up with him, no questions asked. And seeing that look on his face, even though he'd caused so much pain, even though they'd stopped him from getting the engine, even though Billie had *died* to stop him from getting the engine—

"Nobody's joining anybody," Cleo shot back at him, her voice trembling with rage. Not her best—she probably should have been able to come up with a better opening line in the space between two solar systems—but she was past caring. "This ends now."

Halvorsen sighed, and the echo of it around the cavern almost drowned out Cleo's heartbeat in her ears.

"Oh, Ms. McQueary," he said, shaking his head. "I must say, I'm disappointed. Despite it all, I really hoped that this delusional optimism you seem to have picked up from Billie wouldn't win the day."

Cleo felt the other two draw up closer behind her and Kaleisha, Ros humming with dark energy and Abe readying the rifle with a mechanical whine, and she felt—well, not safe. But not alone either.

"You're the deluded one," she said, trying to draw strength from the river of energy churning just under her awareness. "I know what you're trying to do, and it won't work. We've already foiled your stupid plan."

"I see we're speaking like comic book characters instead of scientists." When Halvorsen raised an eyebrow, the dissonant buzz coming from under his skin slid even more slimily down Cleo's spine. "Tell me, then: What exactly is it that you've *foiled*, Ms. McQueary?"

Cleo stepped forward, ignoring Kaleisha's sharp intake of breath. Just close enough to see the atrophy in Halvorsen's face, the wrinkles like fault lines and the skin threatening to flake away into dust. His eyes, cold and nearly colorless, haughty but also unfocused, as if he was half somewhere else, straining against something only he could feel. It was too much, Cleo thought, too much deterioration to attribute just to aging or to the weathering of the elements. Halvorsen looked like a husk. Which is what he'd have to be, she supposed, to want what he wanted.

"You want to destroy the boundary between our dimension and the Other Place," Cleo said. "That's been your plan since Launch Day. You tried, nineteen years ago, but your janky powers just dumped you on this planet, I guess, and now you need the dark matter engine to finally punch that hole in the boundary. That's how you're going to get your unlimited energy source."

Halvorsen stepped closer too, sending ripples through Cleo's awareness that felt like rot and burnt copper wires. "Very good."

And then lightning split open Cleo's mind again, and she saw an unfathomable flood of light, a tear in the fabric of reality pouring the contents of one universe into another—

When we break open the Conterminous Dimension, Ms. McQueary—

Stop calling it that. Also, there's no "we"—

—we will have everything we could ever want. Unlimited energy, unlimited potential. Environmental degradation will be a distant memory. Every human will gain abilities like yours and mine. We will be better, stronger, we will reach a new step in our evolution, and we will live in a universe of endless creation and innovation.

But Cleo was watching this so-called progress, and the merging of the two dimensions wasn't creating anything in the Other Place, just destroying, just draining, just pouring out the golden guts of a living, breathing universe until there was no time or life or light left—

You're so fucking stupid, Halvorsen. The Other Place is alive, and you're going to kill it.

Progress always comes at a price.

That's not your price to pay.

Halvorsen's grip on Cleo's mind tightened, and like a spitting hiss in her ear came the words *I tried to come to them in peace—*

That night in the engine bay? People generally don't call it "peace" when you threaten to take their life force against their will.

No. Nineteen years ago. On the anniversary.

Cleo felt constricted, as if Halvorsen's mind was wrapped around hers like a python, and as she gasped for air there came flashes, bright and chaotic and unbidden, of memories that weren't hers: Halvorsen, swimming through the dark-golden honey of the boundary. Pulling himself straining and screaming into the Other Place. Breaking down the dry wooden wall of a house, coming face-to-face with something that looked like an all-wrong, eldritch Mr. Rogers and, before he could register the human faces behind it staring at him in horror—a terrible lightning strike through his mind and body, a tearing on the molecular level, a falling, a landing on the entirely wrong planet—

All that light, and they hide it away. All that power, and they only use it to play with us like toys.

Cleo swallowed down her nausea. *Ah, got it, so you're really just pissed that they kicked your ass.*

In the real world, Cleo was knocked off her real feet by a wave of white-hot energy ripping through her mind. She landed on her back, the moss not providing anywhere near as much cushioning as she would have hoped, and groaned as Kaleisha, Ros, and Abe closed in between her and Halvorsen.

"I would have brought the human race salvation!" he shouted, every crack in his voice reverberating around the dark corners of the cave. "And what did I get for my efforts?"

"What you deserved, I'd say," Kaleisha said, raising her hands into fighting position.

Halvorsen laughed again, lower and more unhinged. "Wrong, Ms. Reid. Because the Conterminous Dimension tried to kill me, and I survived. They tried to stop me, and they made me more powerful. They tried to tear me apart, atom by atom, and I still have not succumbed to their entropy."

Cleo's awareness briefly flickered into Halvorsen's body, where his bones and his blood were trembling with effort—*oh,* she thought, almost realizing—before she was slammed back again by the wall of Halvorsen's mind. She coughed, as if all the hurt could be dislodged from her body as easily as a wayward speck of dust, and hauled herself to her feet.

"I really don't want to hurt you, Ms. McQueary," Halvorsen rasped. "I want us to work together. Because another thing the Conterminous Dimension gave me was time to plan, time to see what must be done, and I need you to help me do it."

"Well, joke's on you." Cleo tried laughing, and almost managed to make it not sound sad. "The dark matter engine, the big key to your plan? It was destroyed along with the ship. Now there's no way you'll ever break into the Other Place."

Halvorsen smiled, slow and smug. Abe shivered and adjusted the rifle on his shoulder.

"You don't have it in you to kill me, Mr. Yang," Halvorsen said, barely glancing at him. "And, Ms. McQueary, I must say I am disappointed, though not surprised."

Cleo dug her nails into her palms. "What are you going on about now?"

"I have to say, letting Billie's contingency plan be destroyed was a maneuver I didn't anticipate from you."

"Yeah, because you're not as smart as you think you are—"

"That's not the case."

Cleo felt Halvorsen wrap himself around her mind again and tried to fight it. But he was too harsh, too probing, and his mind scalded her whenever she tried to push back.

I never needed the engine.

Cleo's veins went cold. *What are you—*

What I needed was something with a direct connection to the Conterminous Dimension. And that describes the engine, yes, but it also describes you, Ms. McQueary. And so I couldn't let you try and pull off your little coup. I needed you here, with me.

There was a storm building in Cleo's head, rage and fusion and solar wind gathering in her fingertips. *You mean—*

Yes. Your simulation of Billie sacrificed itself for nothing.

Don't—

I'm learning that you are, sadly, quite gullible. Despite your intelligence, you fall so easily—for an idea, for a pale imitation of a woman, for the notion that you and your friends can save the world like this is just a Saturday morning cartoon.

You're wrong—

Halvorsen's mind collapsed in on her own, and Cleo clenched her fists, reaching again for the Other Place, for the energy running just outside her reach, for anything but the knowledge that Billie—that she hadn't—

And *there*, there it was again, that tender something like a reassuring squeeze of her hand—

But in the end, Halvorsen echoed around her skull, breaking the feeling, *I suppose it's for the best. Because if you won't join me by choice, I'll unfortunately have to force you.*

"*No!*" Cleo shouted, and then all of the electron-spitting anger was flowing out of her, literally out of her hands, and an explosion of white-gold energy was blasting Halvorsen off his feet like a rag doll.

Then a crack, and Kaleisha was on Halvorsen, pinning him to the mossy floor. Abe and Ros quickly followed, ice dripping from Ros's fingers and Abe setting the rifle directly against Halvorsen's head.

Cleo strode forward, tendrils of light still snaking around her fingers. "Give it up, Doctor."

Halvorsen coughed, and that weird, brittle energy in his veins pulsed in time with his stuttering heartbeat. Then he looked at Cleo, seeming barely to notice Abe on top of him or the flecks of snow whipping up all around, and narrowed his eyes.

"Fascinating," he croaked. "You're drawing power from the Conterminous Dimension. And from—"

Then Halvorsen smiled. Cleo was really starting to hate that smile.

"Oh," he said through a flash of teeth. "How sweet."

Halvorsen swiped at the air, and Abe, Ros, and Kaleisha were falling to their knees, clutching their heads in their hands. Cleo reached out to do something, catch them, cushion their falls, anything—but then Halvorsen's real hand was around her real throat, pressing just hard enough to cut off her scream at the source.

"You will join me willingly, after all," he hissed in her face.

It took every ounce of willpower Cleo had not to struggle against Halvorsen's grip. The other three had hit the ground hard, so instead she tried to listen for groans, for any sign that they were getting back up.

"You *will* help me open the Conterminous Dimension," Halvorsen continued, "because that is the only way you can be reunited with Billie."

"No," Cleo rasped, but it sounded half-hearted even to her ears. What if it was true? What if closing off the Other Place from Halvorsen meant never seeing Billie again? Not the one who had died to stop this, and not the one Cleo was terrified of meeting but more terrified of living without.

"Don't you want to use all that power for good?" Halvorsen squeezed tighter, and the edges of Cleo's vision went red. She sucked in a too-shallow breath and tried to fight it, the mild oxygen deprivation and the not-so-mild temptation to fight back. She tried to focus on something else, anything other than how badly she wanted to give up—and there was a snowflake drifting past Halvorsen's ear, how weird—

"Don't you want the pain to stop?" Halvorsen whispered.

And Cleo felt it again, that feeling like the fingers of someone who loved her on her cheek. She let her eyes flutter shut, just for a moment, and thought again of Billie, whose love had made her stronger, not weaker. Both Billies, one who was counting on her not to fuck up the multiverse and one whose death wasn't going to be in vain, *goddamnit*, not if Cleo had anything to say about it. Billie, who would be calling her an idiot right now for even considering—

Cleo opened her eyes.

"I'll take the pain," she said. "Bring it on."

And then Halvorsen was knocked aside by a piercing burst of ice, and Cleo stumbled and gasped cold air into her hungry lungs. And there was *Ros*, frost-twisted hair swirling in the snowy wind they'd whipped up around them, eyes gold and angry and *oh*, Cleo thought. *There it is.*

Because there Ros was, just like in Cleo's very first vision, not lost to mindless violence but glowing with righteous rage, firing swaths of the blizzard blowing around them at Halvorsen to drive him back from Cleo. They coated his arms and legs with it, the weight bringing him down to one knee as the freeze climbed up his face.

And then Halvorsen was gritting his teeth and Ros was crying out as he tore through their mind again, but with an echoing burst of thunder Kaleisha had crossed in front of him and socked him straight in the face—

And suddenly Kaleisha had Halvorsen in a headlock, and Abe had the gun in his face again, the threat of blowing his brain into dust deadly clear, and Ros was reaching into their coat pocket for—

NO.

It was almost a scream and almost a hole in the universe, tearing harshly and haphazardly through Cleo's awareness. She doubled over in pain, only vaguely aware of Kaleisha falling to her knees clutching her own head, of Abe and Ros doubling over too, of all their bodies going rigid.

Make your choice, Ms. McQueary. Help me, or find out what grief really is.

Cleo gritted her teeth against the dagger aimed at her mind. *Never.*

I cracked the Providence *like an egg, Ms. McQueary. Do you really want to see what I'm capable of doing to your friends?*

Cleo dragged her eyes open and saw Kaleisha, looking at her through tears and bulging veins. *Don't hurt them. Please.*

The air pulsed with dangerous energy. *Your choice, Ms. Mc-Queary.*

Kaleisha's mouth was moving, just barely. *Do it,* she mouthed.

Cleo shook her head, or maybe she was just shaking. What did Kaleisha mean, what was she saying—

Kaleisha's eyes flicked over to Ros—Ros, who had the cure in their coat pocket—and then back to Cleo.

"Distract him."

Ah.

"Fine!" Cleo shouted hoarsely at Halvorsen. "Fine."

Halvorsen grinned, and Kaleisha, Ros, and Abe collapsed to the ground, unmoving.

"Very good."

And then Cleo was nowhere, and everywhere, and Halvorsen was dragging her through the viscous boundary between dimensions. She could feel the fractures in it, the threadbare bits where dark-gold light threatened to leak through, and she hated how fragile it all felt, how close the dam was to breaching.

You feel it? How simple the procedure will be?

Yeah, I feel it. Fuck you.

You need only push, Ms. McQueary. They will let you in.

It was so easy, too easy, to let herself fly forward into the light. The boundary was so thin. So easy.

But there was something else—too easy—something pulling Cleo along so firmly she didn't even have to try. That same hand over her heart, that same swelling, that pounding, that *feeling*, what was it—

It wrapped her up, drew her in, and it felt like home, felt like fitting into a slot that was made for her, felt like—

Almost like—

✳

I'M GOING TO TELL *you something, Cleo, and I'm going to choose my words carefully. Because, when you're psychically screaming something across the interdimensional void, it's important to get the phrasing right. And because—because I don't know if you're going to believe me. So I'm going to put it as plainly as I can.*

I lost myself a long time ago, even before all of us got lost in a more literal sense. Neil taught me how to be a person, and when he was gone I forgot again. For years, I didn't have anything in me but grief and work, numbers and missions, keeping Elijah safe and lying on television. I had nothing I actually cared about. Nothing but the memories.

So when we were taken here it was so easy, too easy, to let those memories go too. I spent these twenty years—or two thousand years, or ten seconds, or whatever—doing what I'd been trying to do ever since Neil died: forget.

And because I forgot myself, and because the rules of the multiverse are weirder than we'll probably ever be able to fathom, I drifted. I drifted out of my body and into the world again, from that space above and between. And eventually, I drifted into you.

And you—you brought me back to myself, with your mouth and your mind and that foolhardy way you have of caring for people until they can't help but care back. You helped me remember my name, and how to want something other than oblivion, and that I'm allowed to love ideas and stars and people who smile bigger than the space between solar systems. And I do, Cleo, I love you. It's stupid how much I love you. Except it's not stupid at all, because loving the light in the darkness is the only thing in this universe that makes any goddamn sense.

And I'm not just saying that because the fate of another universe depends on it. I mean, I am. But it's also true. I hope you can feel that. You've gotten so much better at feeling.

So feel it. Reach out for it. Reach out for me, Cleo, you're so close.

✳

CLEO'S EYES FLEW OPEN, the light from two dimensions colliding only burning her retinas a little.

—*almost like Billie.*

And it wasn't, couldn't be, she refused to let herself believe it was. But she knew what love felt like, because love felt like Billie, and someone, somewhere, was radiating so much love through the barrier that Cleo could follow the trail, right up to the gap she knew she had to widen just so—

And suddenly, Cleo saw the way.

A universe away, some part of her made eye contact with Ros, where they were playing dead on the ground behind Halvorsen. Cleo sent out those curling feelers of dark energy, and Ros felt it even through the space between them—they didn't have to be touching after all, Cleo realized, because of that golden web connecting everything—and the river poured through her into Ros.

Can you hold it? they mouthed.

And with the only energy left in her bones, Cleo nodded, and mouthed back:

Three.

From the deepest pocket of their coat, Ros drew a tiny syringe. Cleo stretched out in her mind for Kaleisha, for the energy coursing through her, and felt an acknowledgment. Cleo reached for Abe, linking up with him to complete their circle. She gave herself a split second to marvel at the feeling of holding hands with her friends across space and time, at the feeling of raw power and electricity and *love* coursing through them, at the sense that they could hear her thoughts and she theirs, so when she envisioned what they had to do, she knew that each of them saw it too.

Two.

Cleo reached out, back into the pulsing boundary, with some other part of herself. And wherever she was, there was another hand reaching through the door. Could it really be a hand? Could it really be—

Cleo grabbed on to it, but it couldn't really be Billie because it *wasn't*, even though that was exactly what she'd always imagined how Billie's fingers would feel wrapped around her own—

One.

And Kaleisha bent the fabric of the world, only this time she creased past the edge of what was and gathered up what was beyond in her hands, a wave of pure spacetime bursting out of her, enough to hold the dimensions apart and in place, for now—

And Cleo felt herself and Ros flowing up and into the Other Place, and where there had always only been strands of dark matter there was now an entire, endless tapestry—

And then, with a blinding flash of light, it opened.

CHAPTER 15

For one spectacular moment, I'm holding her hand.

Then, I'm falling down a glittering golden vortex, being swept through the boundary like a snowflake in the wind, and I'm vaguely aware of Elijah next to me and the rest of the crew tumbling just behind—

And then I'm lying face down on the ground.

The ground. It's rough, mossy, the opposite of the Other Place's frictionless surfaces. It smells like dirt, and plants, and moisture and cool stone and nothing like the lightning made solid that we've been breathing for twenty years. My fingers close around the pulsing purple tendrils of moss, and even though my head is aching with the sudden assault on the senses, I drink it all in. The colors, the smells, the textures. The world.

I hear Eli groaning as he pushes himself up to all fours beside me, and I heave myself up onto an elbow so I can look at him. His hair is in his face from our fall, and his nose is wrinkled up from the sensory overload, and he's smiling, wider and freer than he has in God knows how long.

"Hey, Bill," he says, and he laughs in wild relief. And I grab his hand in mine, and I laugh too.

And the others, all 201 of them, are lying and sitting and

staggering to their feet around us, in this cave full of shimmering columns of stone stretching up to a ceiling I can barely see. They're also laughing, and hugging and crying and touching everything they can reach.

Until they're not, until they're turning, pointing, yelling, because we aren't the only ones here. At the center of the cavern is a blazing ball of light, two figures at its core and three others around its periphery, and I don't have to scramble up and push my way through the crowd to know who they are, but I do anyway.

And I see Kris, heat rising off his skin and glowing from his eyes, looking too pleased with himself for how close he is to destroying a dimension and maybe himself.

And I see Cleo, and she's shaking with the effort of holding two universes together, and she's shining like the sun.

✳

THE TIME BETWEEN THE end and the beginning was only seconds, only a few vibrations of the universe, but to Cleo it felt like an eternity.

The end: A hole opened up in the Other Place, and Cleo was vaguely aware of 203 somethings streaming out of it. She was a bit distracted, though, by the strain of keeping all of existence from ripping apart along the weakened seam they'd just busted open.

Very good. Halvorsen's voice was too big, too happy, taking up too much space in Cleo's head. *Now let go, Ms. McQueary. Let it fall—*

Nope, Cleo thought, letting the refusal reclaim her mind. *It's over, jackass.*

Another end: Somewhere, outside of the *everything* that was burning through Cleo, she finished that countdown. And Ros knew what to do, because they could feel it, and they gripped the syringe tighter in their hand.

"*Kal!*" they yelled, and threw the cure into the air—

And with a crack, and a curdling scream, Kaleisha appeared at Halvorsen's side and plunged the needle into his neck.

Another end: Cleo breathed out, weary and triumphant, and waited for the light around Halvorsen to fizzle out. But instead it got brighter, shone more strongly through the cracks in the artifice of his body, even as his eyes dulled and his arms sagged—and Cleo's awareness was split, one last time, by a white-hot crackle of lightning.

The pain was unimaginable, every cell threatening to combust as the Other Place's mortal blast tore the very bonds of my molecules apart. So was the falling, falling away from paradise, through the golden river between, toward this frozen wasteland and certain death—

But no, not certain, never certain, because the dark energy was still coursing through my veins, and with the resolve built over a lifetime of wanting it was easy

(not easy, it was agony and nineteen years of sleepless feverish nights tying and retying the knots of a body that wanted to unravel, but what other choice did I have?)

easy to keep it together, to defy the entropy they'd planted in me, Ms. McQueary, long enough to see the plan through—

Cleo wrenched her mind away from Halvorsen's memories. And she saw, in the real world, that without his powers there was nothing keeping Halvorsen's body from unspooling into a stream of dark energy—

oh—

and Cleo knew, she knew how to fix everything, and it was

perfect. But it wasn't, not really, because she was watching Halvorsen's face breaking apart in front of her. She spared herself a fraction of a second—or maybe a long, uninterrupted moment—to recall what it felt like to be seven years old, watching Dr. Dark Matter hold the stars in his hands on television as he told her that anything was possible.

No—her dad watched those videos with her, every time. He was the one who had shown her the stars first.

And so she let that feeling slip away into the space between universes, leaving only the broken man before her and the knowledge of all the things she'd been wrong about.

Are you happy now, Ms. McQueary?

Not really, no. But I think I will be soon.

Hmm.

And somewhere, Halvorsen's body fizzled away into gold-dark light. And somewhere else, the light wrapped itself around Ros's fingers.

The beginning: Ros gently, ever so gently, let those strands of dark energy flow into the Other Place. Kaleisha, the muscles in her arms and the energy running through her straining, bent the boundary back into shape, and Cleo wrenched the door closed, particle by particle. There were hands—nothing like any hands Cleo had ever felt or seen—helping them, holding the edges together and drinking the light back into themselves. And when she put an ear up to what was left of the gap, she heard a voice, or voices, that sounded kind of like her dad and kind of like her mom and kind of like nothing at all:

Thank you, Cleo McQueary.

Of course. It's the least we could do. We'll do our best not to mess with your shit anymore, okay?

Something like a wry chuckle rippled through Cleo's blood. *Same to you.*

✳

CLEO OPENED HER EYES to a smothering feeling, and panicked for a split second before she realized that it wasn't Halvorsen's hands or the choking golden air of the Other Place—it was her friends. They were hugging her so tightly that she couldn't move if she'd wanted to, Abe laughing and ruffling her hair, Kaleisha kissing her cheek and getting her own happy tears all over her, Ros trying to cling to her and check for injuries at the same time. And Cleo clung to all of them right back, reveling in the realness of their bodies, their joy, and letting the seconds tick by just like that. There was no rush, now. No more countdowns.

Eventually, Kaleisha broke the group hug and, wiping her nose, pointed behind her to the sloping sides of the cavern.

"Look, Cleo," she said. Cleo grabbed her hand and, together, they stumbled forward.

An absolute host of people in blue-gray *Providence* uniforms were crawling to their feet and spreading out across the cave, eyes permanently wide and mouths permanently agape. Two hundred and three of them, if Cleo had to hazard a guess. And some of them were directing their awestruck elation at the cave or the moss or each other, but a lot of them were looking at Cleo and her friends—

And then the breath was knocked out of Cleo's body by a hurtling collection of golden hair and gangly limbs, and there were arms wrapped around her middle in a hug so forceful it lifted her feet off the ground and spun her around.

"Cleo," Elijah Lucas said in her ear, "you found us."

A smile spread across Cleo's face, and she squeezed him right back. "'Course I did."

Elijah pulled back, his green eyes shining, and started rattling off questions in a way that made Cleo certain that they would get along famously. "How did you do it? Did you speak to the Other Place? Where did Kris—"

But then he saw something over Cleo's shoulder and cut himself off. "I'm actually going to—I want to introduce myself to your—"

And Cleo only had a second to process what had just happened before—

"Hey."

She heard *that voice*, and felt a *hand* on her shoulder, and spun around and saw *that face*, and her body reacted before her brain even had a chance to put it all together. She scrambled backward, knocking the hand off her shoulder, and felt her breath go cold and hard in her lungs. Everything—the purple-green cavern, the crowd of crew members, Elijah determinedly talking the ears off her friends—fell away.

It was Billie. No, not Billie. But yes, *Billie*, and she looked exactly the same—scowly, beautiful, not a day older than she'd been when she disappeared in a flash of light—save for the *Providence* uniform she was wearing. Her hand was still outstretched, still frozen in the space where Cleo had been, and her eyes were wide open.

"Hi there," she said, the corner of her mouth almost twitching into a smile.

"Fuck," Cleo breathed.

Billie frowned at her. And God, if Cleo had ever thought that this Billie might be different enough that she could separate the two in her head, that dream was crumbling down around her. Cleo knew that frown so well, had loved that face so recklessly, and to see it pointed at her so uncomprehendingly was more than she could stand.

"Sorry." Cleo screwed her eyes up, just for the second she

needed to stop herself from doing something irredeemably pathetic like crying, and then opened them again. Billie—*Captain Lucas? Are we making distinctions again?*—had lowered her hand, but was still watching her warily. "I just—you wouldn't know, you can't, because you—you don't know me, Captain Lucas, but—"

"Cleo."

That stopped Cleo's rambling. How did—

Captain Lucas—*Billie?*—licked her lips nervously, which was one of the absolute worst things she could have done for Cleo's fragile resolve, and stepped closer. Cleo could feel—shit, she could *feel* the woman's molecules vibrating, and the dark matter flowing between and around them, all of it solid and warm and still glowing with residual dark-gold energy. *Real.*

"I do know you." Billie's voice was soft, and as close to tentative as Cleo had ever heard it. "I—I could see you from the Other Place. I saw almost everything."

Cleo's hands came up to cover her face of their own accord. She could feel the shame rising, hot and caustic, in her cheeks. "Jesus," she mumbled. "I am so, so sorry."

"What are you apologizing for?" Billie said, and for a woman who'd been put in the unenviable position of having to break up with her computer's girlfriend, she sounded so, so kind.

Cleo lowered her fingers an inch to see Billie still staring at her. She was close enough to reach out and touch. There was nothing Cleo had ever wanted to do more, and nothing she had ever known with more certainty would trigger the immediate heat-death of her universe.

"For being so embarrassing." Cleo hated how small her voice sounded. "I let things get way out of hand with"—*with you*—"with your hologram."

Billie nodded, slow and careful. "You loved her."

"Yeah. And I know that's insane, and I don't want to make things weird for you, so I'll just"—*launch myself back into space*—"I'll leave you alone."

Billie's eyes fell closed, and Cleo saw her take an unsteady breath. "Right," she said, and her voice was rough with emotion the way Cleo had heard it get just hours ago. "I understand."

Cleo blinked. She was seized suddenly by the overwhelming feeling that she was missing something. Her hands dropped to her sides. "Understand? Understand what?"

Billie rubbed a hand over her mouth, eyes locked on the ground between them. "That you don't, uh. Want me."

Something in Cleo's chest crashed down through her stomach and into her feet. Her heart, maybe.

"What." *Stupid.* She sounded stupid.

"*I* should be embarrassed," Billie said, "because I was watching you all that time and it was so hard to distinguish . . . I mean, I let myself"—she pinched the bridge of her nose—"I love you too, Cleo. That's how I—that's what you grabbed on to, to open the boundary. Me, reaching out for you. Except you didn't—*you* don't know *me,* so I can't expect you to—"

"Stop talking, Billie." Cleo's voice came out strangled and trembling, as she remembered. The hand on her heart. That gentle, insistent tugging. That feeling that had no words, except maybe it did, and they were *I do, Cleo, I love you, it's stupid how much I love you.* "You—wait. You love me? So much that I felt it across dimensions?"

"Of course," Billie said, like it was the simplest thing in the world.

Cleo was falling. Flying. Jumping to lightspeed. *Breathe through it, McQueary.* "Just like you said you would." Billie inclined her head curiously at that. "Holo-Billie," Cleo clarified. "She said that you'd feel the same way she did, but I didn't believe her."

Billie's eyes narrowed into that Rubik's Cube–solving stare that took all of Cleo's breath and doubt away. "I'm sorry, you thought *I* wouldn't want *you*?"

"I don't know why," Cleo said, taking a tiny step closer just to hear Billie's breath hitch in her chest, the way she'd known it would. "Something about lightning not striking twice?"

"Idiot." There was a smile creeping across Billie's face, wide and dimpled and full of desperate hope. "That's a myth. Lightning strikes twice all the time."

"Then I thought you'd be different, maybe." Cleo tipped her head up to look into Billie's eyes. "But you're not. You're still you."

"I've always been me, Cleo."

"Yeah, but most folks are okay only having one of themselves. You had to go and duplicate yourself just to stress me out."

Billie breathed out a chuckle, and the puff of air on her face was the most electrifying thing Cleo had ever felt. "Right. Just to stress you out. Not like my foresight saved the galaxy or anything."

"Hey now, I think *I'm* the one who just saved the galaxy." Cleo grinned at Billie for the first time, or the thousandth, and definitely not the last. "But distinctions aren't important."

The first part of Billie that Cleo learned how to touch was her chest. Softly at first, then firmer, she spread her hand out over Billie's heart, so she could feel it pounding for her. So she could shut up the tiny *this isn't happening* part of her brain with a *yes, yes, it is, feel that, she's alive.*

Billie, for her part, reached for Cleo's face like she had so many times before. But this time, she didn't stop herself, and she didn't flicker away into nothing. Instead, gloriously, her fingertips brushed Cleo's cheeks. Softly at first, tickling the tiny hairs there with featherlight strokes, then firmer, until Billie was cradling Cleo's head in her hands. Cleo's eyelids fluttered shut involuntarily when Billie rested their foreheads together. It was ridiculous, really, how hungry she'd been for this, how much the want had been burning through her, how close she was to doing something irredeemably pathetic like crying, now that it was finally happening.

But then she looked back up into Billie's Earth-green eyes, and saw that Billie was already crying. So Cleo didn't have to feel embarrassed about a goddamn thing.

There was nothing softly-at-first about it when she kissed Billie. It was fireworks and Cleo surging up on her toes to press closer, galaxies colliding and Billie tangling her fingers tightly into Cleo's curly hair. It was like stars exploding, Cleo thought as she learned how Billie tasted and touched and loved her, into the stuff the universe was made of.

※

(IF SHE'D WANTED TO, Cleo would have heard Kaleisha sighing happily and Elijah laughing triumphantly. She would have seen Abe looking away with an embarrassed grin, and Ros rolling their eyes fondly. But Cleo was busy. Time for all that later. No more countdowns.)

※

EVENTUALLY THEY ALL WANDERED away into the branching tunnels in search of soft places to sleep, because despite the crew's exhilaration at being free, they were all remembering how rough switching dimensions was on the human body. And Cleo and Abe and Kaleisha and Ros, muscles aching and minds overwhelmed with the *what next* of it all, agreed that sleeping for no less than fourteen hours before trying to do anything else was the best— "Nay, the *only*," Cleo said—course of action.

So Cleo gave Kaleisha what she hoped was a passable *don't come a-knocking* look, which Kaleisha of course returned with an even saucier eyebrow wiggle. And Cleo grabbed Billie's hand, which was just as strong and calloused and warm as she'd known it would be, and tugged her away down one of the glowing tunnels.

As soon as Cleo found the perfect little chamber off one of the minor passages, one with an extra-cushiony layer of moss on the floor, Billie dragged her inside and pushed her up against the wall. The luminescent moss felt warm against Cleo's back, but Billie felt even warmer as she planted one elbow next to Cleo's head and ran her other hand up her ribs.

"What do you want, love?" she said roughly, softly, like the words would shatter them both if spoken too insistently.

"Whatever you got." Cleo fisted her hands in Billie's shirt and pulled her down into another supernova kiss. "Could you tell, from over there?" she whispered against Billie's lips. "Could you tell how bad I wanted—"

Billie groaned into the kiss and pressed closer, so Cleo felt her all over—heart beating, atoms pulsing, everything about her radiating heat and love and need. "Wasn't sure," she said, and buried her face in the curve of Cleo's neck. "Couldn't tell what you were thinking."

Cleo couldn't stop the high, trembling sound that came out of her at the feel of Billie's mouth on her skin. "Well, can you"—Billie ran her tongue over the dip above her collarbone, and Cleo gasped—"*shit*, Billie, can you tell now?"

Cleo felt Billie smile, then press a leg between her own, right where she was burning hottest, then smile even wider as the back of Cleo's head thumped against the wall. "Might have some idea," Billie whispered.

It wasn't long before her hand was slipping under the waistband of Cleo's pants, and her fingers were slipping inside her. Cleo expected Billie to make short work of her from there, but instead Billie froze as soon as she touched wet, her breath stopping in her chest and her forehead dropping to Cleo's again, like she'd been at sea for years, and Cleo was her homeland.

"Keep going," Cleo whispered, her hands coming up to Billie's cheek, Billie's hair, Billie's mouth.

"I just—you feel—"

"I know." Cleo let her words hang between their lips. "I need to feel *you*."

In one fluid motion, Billie breathed in and moved her fingers. Cleo moaned and clung tighter to her, moaned as she stroked in deeper, moaned with each curve of Billie's hand. She hadn't realized how deep the feeling went, that feeling of needing to crawl out of her skin that she'd had for weeks, or months, or maybe her whole life. Now Billie was breaking her open, peeling back those layers of desperation one by one.

Cleo came faster than she would have thought possible, clenching around Billie's perfect fingers and muffling her cries in the curve of Billie's neck. Billie held her through it, letting Cleo tremble against her and running her other hand through Cleo's hair.

"*Fuck*," Billie whispered, and Cleo could feel her trembling too. "You're so beautiful."

Cleo smiled into Billie's skin, nibbled lazily at her earlobe. "Your turn."

She got Billie's uniform off in (if she did say so herself) record time, and got to work learning the body that had haunted her dreams. She learned that Billie was ticklish between her ribs and at the tops of her knees, which was hilarious, and when Cleo touched her there she would squirm and Cleo would giggle and Billie would roll her eyes and drag Cleo back up her body for another breathless kiss. She learned that Billie liked having her stupid ponytail pulled, just a little, just enough to make her gasp and dig her fingertips deeper into Cleo's skin. And she learned—once she had Billie spread out on the mossy floor, both of them naked and glowing purple, blue, and green together—that she could bury her head between Billie's legs and pull the most ungodly sounds she'd ever heard out of her.

She got Billie off like that, Billie's hands tugging at her curls and Billie's legs wrapped around her and Billie's taste filling her mouth. As soon as she was done, Billie rolled her over, kissed her deeply, and ran a hand between her legs. Cleo was already wet again, and Billie smirked at the feeling of it.

"Yeah, yeah, don't get too cocky," Cleo murmured.

"I won't." Billie ran the tip of her tongue over Cleo's nipple, and Cleo gasped. "But I *do* plan to keep fucking you until neither of us can see straight. If you're game."

Cleo groaned. "Hell yes. Yes, Billie. I think I actually need you to never *stop* fucking me."

Billie looked up from kissing her way down Cleo's stomach and grinned. "I think I can make that happen."

Cleo learned a lot of things that night: She learned that Billie was happy to drive her crazy with her mouth, with her fingers, with every tool in her arsenal designed to dissolve Cleo into a babbling mess; she learned that, once she asked for it, Billie could always find the spot inside her that would make her come like mountains crashing to the Earth. She learned that Billie sometimes needed it soft, needed it tender, needed Cleo's hand on her cheek and Cleo's mouth at her ear whispering, *I love you, Billie, I love you so goddamn much.* Most of all, she learned that Billie just felt right, like a home she'd grown up in, like a movie she could quote from memory, like a dream she'd had every night of her life—

Cleo's eyes flew open. "Shit!"

"What?" Billie looked up from eating Cleo out. It meant that she wasn't doing that thing with her tongue anymore, but the instant look of concern on her face was so endearing that Cleo couldn't mind too much. "What's wrong?"

"Nothing." Cleo ran her fingers through Billie's now loose and sex-ruffled hair with a small laugh. "I just realized that I wimped this."

Billie leaned into Cleo's touch and frowned. "This? This specifically?"

"Precisely that thing you just did with your tongue, yes."

"Then how did you not know I was—"

"I thought it was a dream. A series of dreams, actually." Cleo sat up. Billie did too, with just the faintest of grumbles. "A few weeks into our spaceflight, I started having these horny dreams about you. Like every night, Billie, it was absolute torture. I guess I just didn't realize they were visions."

Billie cracked a smile and brushed a curl out of Cleo's face. "Dumbass."

Cleo swatted Billie's hand away, but when Billie leaned in to suck at her neck again she tilted her head to give better access. "Sorry I didn't immediately assume that my wet dreams were a sign you were actually pining away for me from your interdimensional space prison. How silly of me."

"I forgive you," Billie said, her chuckle muffled in Cleo's skin. She bit softly at her shoulder. "Did you dream this too?"

"No, this part's all new," Cleo said, and she ran her hands down Billie's back to pull her closer.

CHAPTER 16

ARCHIVED: Transcript of Recording by Capt. Wilhelmina Lucas, c. November 5, 2061

WILHELMINA LUCAS: We never meant to set the record for Galaxy's Fastest U-Haul. But, looking back, there wasn't any other way it could have gone.

We settled into each other, Cleo and me, so quickly that it probably should have scared me. It would have before all of this. Before she saved me. Saved us all. But it turns out that cohabitation looks a lot less intimidating when you've already stared down the end of a universe.

This mountain is an absolute honeycomb of tunnels and caves of every size, so it's been easy to convert into an apartment complex of sorts. Cleo and I have a room, with a firepit and a blanket we made out of plant fibers. Eli has one, across the tunnel, just close enough to call out to Cleo when he has an idea he needs her to bounce back to him. Kaleisha and Abe and Ros are right around the corner.

All my crewmates have a space of their own. Families have what might be called wings. And the ones who came alone, who were ready to dive into this abyss without so much as a familiar hand to hold, have formed their own neighborhood in the

caves surrounding that massive cavern where it all
went down. It's a bit of a nonstop party in there,
actually—food always sizzling away on every fire,
Kaleisha always doing a tarot spread for someone or
other, songs and happy talk always echoing around the
purple-green walls. If you'd asked me before all this
how I'd feel about spending my evenings in a cave
passing skewers of charred alien meat around to my
smelly coworkers, I probably would have thrown the
nearest dry-erase marker at you. But all the talking
and laughing and sharing feels necessary now. Feels
good. So I let Cleo drag me down there most nights,
and I don't even pretend to argue.

Everyone has been working so hard to make this work.
Collecting snowmelt, keeping the fires going, cooking
and sewing and making music. The medical team—now
including Ros—are working around the clock to keep
everyone nourished, un-frostbitten, and away from that
one variety of fungus on the mountainside that spews
noxious spores if you touch it. Abe and the xenobiology
team have done a phenomenal job cataloguing which flora
and fauna are safe to eat.

(I'm partial to the meat of these fat little scaly
things that cling to the walls of the caves with their
mouths. Cleo started calling them "sucklizards,"
though, and I can't get her to stop. I wish I could
come up with an equally annoying name for those
berries she likes that grow by the lake and taste like
toffee. But they make her lips so sweet that I always
get distracted.)

It's almost gratifying, knowing how well the
Providence mission would have worked out if—well,
if everything had gone about as differently as it
could have gone. But the part of me that wanted this,
that wanted to be part of the first human colony on
an exoplanet, that was prepared to live and die here
making that vision a reality . . . that part withered
away somewhere between realizing my hubris had

imprisoned us all in another dimension and falling in love again.

Now, I just want to go home. Eat a burger. Start a queer commune that runs on wind power, so I can keep feeling this way. Get a dog, so Cleo can name it Chewie or something.

I know Cleo wants the same thing. She keeps sketching things—a carbon scrubber, an artificial reef, a starship powered by solar sails that she insists would get us to Saturn, at least. And Kaleisha and Abe and Ros are champs, but every time I see them the bags under their eyes are a little heavier and they're holding each other a little tighter. Then there's the crew, who signed up for this, technically. But they're exhausted, too. I thought some of them might want to stay, to keep that old original dream alive, but all of them are as over it as I am. And I wouldn't be any kind of captain if I let them keep going like this.

So we're going home. I don't know when, and I don't know how, but my crew is exceptional, and my brother is better at coming up with whackadoo ideas than anyone else in the universe, and the woman I love can do anything she sets her mind to. We're going to make it.

CLEO MCQUEARY: [unintelligible]

WILHELMINA LUCAS: Yeah, yeah, you caught me being a sap. You happy?

CLEO MCQUEARY: Very. Hey, future historians—

WILHELMINA LUCAS: Oh my God, stop it, I'm almost done, I—

CLEO MCQUEARY: What she won't tell you is that ten minutes ago she was crying because I wrote her a poem and—

[scuffling]

WILHELMINA LUCAS: Shut up, I [unintelligible]–
I hate you.

CLEO MCQUEARY: No, you don't.

WILHELMINA LUCAS: Nope, that's on the tape now,
recorded for all posterity, so—

[silence]

WILHELMINA LUCAS: Mm.

CLEO MCQUEARY: So's that.

[silence]

WILHELMINA LUCAS: Ahem. Anyway. The batteries in
this stupid tape recorder are dying. Funny how they
lasted for ages untold in the Other Place, but the
minute I take this thing outside in a snowstorm it
craps out on me. So this will probably be my first
and only Post-Other-Place recording, which is fine
by me. I tried to get everything important down so I
can remember what this time, on this world, with this
woman felt like. For my personal records, obviously.
No more press for me.

The one exception might be Abe, if he ends up
actually writing that book he's been thinking about.
So Abe, if you're listening: Sorry for all the rambling.
Sorry you had to listen to Cleo and me being gross.
And sorry for being such an asshole at the beginning,
there. I would ask you to forgive me again, but I
think—I'm pretty sure you already have. I think we're
friends. Family. Cleo keeps telling me that's what we
all are, anyway. And I think I finally believe her.

*

AFTER A COUPLE WEEKS of resting and making sure that the crew
hadn't escaped the Other Place just to die on Proxima B, Cleo
and her friends felt ready to reach out again. So they zipped each

other into their parkas, Abe grabbed a basket in case they saw any ice willow sprouts, and they all hiked up the mountain under the rainbow sky.

"Do we really need to be at the peak for this?" Kaleisha huffed as they climbed. "I doubt our powers work on cell phone physics."

"You don't know that." Cleo smiled, her breath shining reddish in the frozen air. "But no, probably not."

Kaleisha rolled her eyes and gave Cleo's gloved hand a squeeze. "So it's mostly for the cinematic aesthetic of it all, huh?"

"You know me so well."

(It was also—and Kaleisha knew this to some extent, because Cleo was still trying to be better about talking to the people she loved about her feelings—because Cleo wanted to remember the landscape for how beautiful it was, instead of as the backdrop to the visions that had nearly torn her apart.)

They reached the summit, and while Ros guided Kaleisha through some stretches, Cleo tested the waters, so to speak. The Other Place felt farther away now—which was good, it meant the boundary was holding—but it also meant that their powers had diminished. Cleo couldn't transfer energy to her friends without touching them anymore, nor could she shoot light out of her hands. Not that she had to, she supposed. It was just that, if she had known her first time shooting light out of her hands would also be her last, she would have savored it a little bit more.

"Alright," Kaleisha said, "you wanna try that thing we talked about?"

"You know it," Cleo said, and took both of her hands in hers.

It was almost second nature, at this point, for Cleo to let the undercurrent of the Other Place flow through her, belly to chest to hands and then into Kaleisha's fingers. She felt the river connecting them, their veins pulsing gold-dark together. They were almost like one body. Which was good, because that was the plan.

Kaleisha's theory—as she had explained it to Cleo a few days previous as they sat by a fire crunching on fried lichen-flowers like popcorn—was that if they focused hard enough, they could share not just dark energy, but other things. Things like thoughts, which they had already done during the Halvorsen thing. Things like Cleo's ability to see across space.

As she dug deeper, losing herself in the flow, Cleo squeezed her friend's hands tighter and thought of Earth. Her vision went black and suddenly she was falling upward into the universe, skidding along the dark matter filaments until Proxima Centauri was only a speck on her awareness and the Sun was a speck ahead—

And Cleo opened her eyes, and all she could see was green.

Plants. She was surrounded by plants.

She was in a dining room, a deeply familiar one, and so it came to her as no surprise when she turned and saw Mr. Reid sitting at the table, just as bald and bespectacled as ever, clutching a mug of coffee like his life depended on it and looking more tired than she'd ever seen him. He got up and walked toward the kitchen, so Cleo followed.

There was a viney plant dangling over the doorway. Cleo moved to brush it aside out of habit, but her hand phased through it. So she stepped forward, and then she froze.

Dad? she cried soundlessly.

Because there was her father in Mr. Reid's kitchen, making coffee in his vintage pour-over just the way he'd taught her. Mr. Reid walked in just as he was decanting it, and her father handed him a fresh mug wordlessly, like this was something they'd done a thousand times. Cleo racked her brain trying to remember if her father had ever spoken to Mr. Reid, if he'd ever even asked where she was sleeping all those nights in high school.

"Thanks, Connor," Mr. Reid said. *First-name basis.*

"Of course." Her father looked tired too, if she wasn't imagining it. And then he was turning and looking at Cleo, though she was definitely imagining that, and she couldn't take it, couldn't take the tears rising in her cheeks at the sight of those dark brown eyes she'd inherited, so she turned to leave—

And there was Kaleisha. Kaleisha, watching their fathers just like Cleo was. Kaleisha, getting all misty-eyed about it. Kaleisha, *wimping with her.*

Oh my God! Cleo cried, shocking herself and Kaleisha out of their sadness. *It worked!*

I know! Kaleisha took her hands and swung her around, and for a moment they were dancing, and Cleo was laughing, and they were home.

And then they were flowing out of Mr. Reid's house and up, over the whole wide world, and Cleo could feel those dark-gold tendrils that connected them and the planets and everything, and she knew her friend could feel it too.

Whoa, Kaleisha said, *space is big.*

Brilliant, Holmes. Now that I've brought you along for the ride, do you think you can reach this far?

I can try.

Back on Proxima, Kaleisha reached out her hand, and Cleo felt her straining toward the rippling emptiness around them, light-years away. Dark matter rushed all around them, gold and deafening, and Cleo could feel Kaleisha stretching, stretching as far as she could go, space tautening around them like a rubber band, threatening to snap at the tiny tears you hadn't noticed until it was too late—

"I can't." Kaleisha fell to her knees, breath belabored and tears welling in her eyes, and Cleo fell with her, the heavy material of their pants crunching into the snow. "I can't reach that far, Cleo."

She clutched at Cleo, gloved hands scrabbling for purchase

on her coat, and Cleo clutched her right back. "That's okay," she said helplessly. "It'll be okay."

"No," Kaleisha said through gasping breaths. "How? I don't know how. I don't know how we're going to—"

"We'll figure something else out," Cleo said. "We always do."

✳

ARCHIVED: *Providence* Intracrew Messaging System Conversation — Elijah Lucas, Wilhelmina Lucas, Cleo McQueary, Kaleisha Reid, Ros Wheeler, and Abraham Yang, November 12, 2061

ELIJAH LUCAS
Here's a philosophical question for you all: Did I
    miss my Saturn return while I was frozen in time
    in the Other Place or did I still experience it

KALEISHA REID
Oh shit.

ABRAHAM YANG
Man that IS a good question

KALEISHA REID
I would say no you did not experience it?? Given that
    you were in a different plane of existence than
    Saturn in 2044???

WILHELMINA LUCAS
What the fuck are you all on about

ELIJAH LUCAS
Okay but like. Is your approach to astrology more
    metaphysical or epistemological because Saturn
    very much DID return while I was in there

KALEISHA REID
Right right right but you were in a different timeline.
    I think??

And you are still functionally 25 and Saturn return
   is all about your late twenties and vibe shifts
   and leaving things behind and you've still got all
   that coming down the pike baby

ROS WHEELER
My brain hurts

ELIJAH LUCAS
Okay but then do I not get my return until 2073??
   It's all out of whack:(

WILHELMINA LUCAS
Has it ever occurred to you all that, even if the
   planets did have any material effect whatsoever on
   your life
(Which they don't)

KALEISHA REID
Billie.

WILHELMINA LUCAS
Your understanding of astrology might have to shift
   now that the existence of the Other Place has
   completely upended our conception of the universe?

KALEISHA REID
Shut up shut up shut UP
WHATEVER

ELIJAH LUCAS
Yes obviously that's what I'm trying to figure out
   right now

ABRAHAM YANG
We'll throw you an awesome Saturn return party in
   2073 Eli!!

ELIJAH LUCAS
Thanks bud
Wait Kal isn't your Saturn in Gemini
Does that mean you're experiencing your Saturn return
   RIGHT NOW

KALEISHA REID
OH MY GODDDDD
ELI YOU'RE
SATURN ENTERED GEMINI THE DAY BEFORE WE GOT ON THE
    PROVIDENCE

ELIJAH LUCAS
Now THAT'S what I call a vibe shift!!

WILHELMINA LUCAS
Saturn is 37 trillion kilometers away.

KALEISHA REID
Well it wasn't when I made the STUPIDEST ASTROLOGICAL
    DECISION OF MY LIFE, BILLIE

CLEO MCQUEARY
I love all you idiots a lot

※

THE COLONY COLLECTIVELY TRIED to ignore the truth for a while, but after several weeks in the mountain it became unavoidable: They were going to have to send an expedition to the wreck of *Providence I.* Kaleisha and Abe had collected all they could from their escape pod, but there still weren't enough coats for more than a small group of people to leave the moss-warmed caves at a time. Ros and the medical team were desperate to know if any of the med bay supplies had survived the crash; there were medications that they simply couldn't soldier on without anymore, and Kaleisha's emergency stash of hormones was running low. Plus, everyone's uniforms were getting undeniably rank. And when it became clear that Kaleisha and Cleo weren't going to be able to teleport them all home, the crew began to talk. They would probably be able to scavenge some parts, they said. A generator, maybe. A radio, if they were lucky.

(Any radio message would take four years to reach Earth, no one said. And any reply would take four more.)

"Do you want to come?" Billie finally asked Cleo the night before the expedition, as they lay naked on their bed of moss, tangled up in their blankets and each other. Billie was going, of course, because she was the captain, and Cleo knew she'd never forgive herself if something happened to any of the crew and she hadn't been there. But Cleo couldn't stop thinking about the twisted metal. The singed scraps of circuit board. The flight deck, and whether it would be worse to see it destroyed or still recognizable as the place where—

"I don't know." Cleo trailed her fingertips over the lines in Billie's palm. "I don't know if I can handle seeing it. But I'll still go, if you need me to guide Kal or—"

Billie kissed Cleo on the forehead so tenderly that she shut up. "It's okay, love. It can't be very far. Just tell Kaleisha where to go."

"Will you send me a postcard?"

Billie snorted, running her fingers through Cleo's hair. "We'll be gone two days at most."

"Still. If I'm gonna be staring mournfully out the window for forty-eight hours, I deserve a token of your affection upon your return."

"Of course. I'll make sure to stop and pick up a tacky magnet on the way back."

Cleo kissed Billie on her smirking mouth. "I'll clear a spot on the fridge."

✳

ARCHIVED: Transcript of recording by Capt. Wilhelmina Lucas, June 30, 2041

WILHELMINA LUCAS: Test 014—final test, actually, by necessity if not resounding success—commencing now. I've finally finished uploading, I think. And I patched the aforementioned vocal tic, so I should be able to ask her questions without getting cursed out. Initiating now.

[silence]

WILHELMINA LUCAS: Computer?

WL2-MK1.4: What in the goddamn—

WILHELMINA LUCAS: Shush. You're okay.

WL2-MK1.4: You're—you're me.

WILHELMINA LUCAS: Technically, you're me, but I'm not here to argue metaphysics.

BOTH: That's Eli's job.

[Both laughing.]

WILHELMINA LUCAS: Exactly. Now, who are you?

WL2-MK1.4: Captain Wilhelmina Lucas.

WILHELMINA LUCAS: Close. You're a perfect replica of my consciousness, but for all intents and purposes, yes, you can think of yourself as Captain Wilhelmina Lucas. Especially since you won't be needed unless I . . . well. Anyway. What happens tomorrow?

WL2-MK1.4: Um. Providence I launches, bound for Proxima Centauri B.

WILHELMINA LUCAS: Good. Who is Dr. Kristoff Halvorsen?

WL2-MK1.4: My friend and colleague. Or—wait.

[silence]

WL2-MK1.4: Maybe not. Not anymore. He's done something, something that—that endangers—

WILHELMINA LUCAS: Why wasn't that memory retrieval instantaneous?

WL2-MK1.4: Cool your jets. You've given me a lot to sort through.

[sigh]

WILHELMINA LUCAS: Fine. You'll have to do.

WL2-MK1.4: Can I ask you a question?

[silence]

WILHELMINA LUCAS: Sure.

WL2-MK1.4: What am I for?

WILHELMINA LUCAS: Jesus Christ. What kind of *I, Robot* shit—

WL2-MK1.4: Fine, don't answer. I just wanted to know if you had a directive in mind, so I can ignore it.

WILHELMINA LUCAS: You're for the worst-case scenario, okay? In case my suspicions are correct, and—and something happens to me

WL2-MK1.4: I'm supposed to figure out what Kris did?

WILHELMINA LUCAS: Yeah.

WL2-MK1.4: Then why do I remember Neil?

WILHELMINA LUCAS: Excuse me?

WL2-MK1.4: If I'm just supposed to solve your little mystery, what's the point of giving me all these—these memories that have nothing to do with that? Memories that might even get in the way, arguably.

[silence]

WILHELMINA LUCAS: Because, if you're going to figure it out, you have to be me. And you can't be me without those memories.

WL2-MK1.4: Well then, great job, idiot. You made a hologram capable of love. No way that's going to end in—

WILHELMINA LUCAS: Computer, disable interface.

[sigh]

WILHELMINA LUCAS: And wipe the last five minutes from the memory bank. Test ends.

✳

ARCHIVED: *Providence* Intracrew Messaging System Conversation — Abraham Yang, Kaleisha Reid, and Ros Wheeler, December 1, 2061

ABRAHAM YANG
My Dearest Dr. Wheeler:
Due to unforeseen circumstances, we are returning a day early. Our embankment will be brief, but Madame Reid and I will anticipate your presence in the upper hall forthwith. Captain Lucas will accompany us. Until then.

KALEISHA REID
Can you pim like this all the time? It's hot

ROS WHEELER
God, no thank you
Also, what????

ABRAHAM YANG
We'll explain in 2 min when we see you in the entry tunnel!! Bring Cleo!!!

KALEISHA REID
Can you also bring one of those lakeberry things Eli made? There's no good snacks out here

ROS WHEELER
Menaces, the both of you. See you soon

✳

THE MISSION HAD ONLY been gone a day—which was still enough time for Cleo to start conjuring up images of eldritch behemoths that lived under the ice and loved nothing better than the taste of twenty-somethings and snarky starship captains. Luckily, Ros rescued her from her umpteenth straight hour pacing the cave and trying to wimp Billie from their blanket, and dragged her into the rainbow-lit mouth of the tunnel.

There was a slight distortion of the space in front of them, a *snap*, and then Abe was grinning at them, Kaleisha holding his hand and Billie clinging to his middle, looking a little motion sick. Cleo leapt at Billie and kissed her, laughing, her toes barely brushing the tunnel floor as she dangled from her neck.

"Alright," Ros said, handing Kaleisha a lakeberry cake, "for real, to what do we owe the pleasure?"

"Two things," Abe said, helpfully raising two fingers. "Billie, you say your thing first."

"Okay." Billie licked her lips nervously, for some reason, and held up the knapsack Cleo hadn't realized she'd been carrying. "Cleo, I, um. I have something for you."

"You didn't, like, actually bring me a souvenir, did you?" Cleo watched apprehensively as Billie rifled through the bag. "I was (and I know this'll be hard to wrap your head around) *joking*, though I wouldn't say no to a shiny rock you found, or—"

Cleo's words died in her throat as Billie straightened up, holding a small, black box in one hand and a palm-sized, apparently equally indestructible steel urn in the other. She shoved the box into Cleo's hands, and Cleo turned it over slowly, finding an orange panel on one side, feeling the fire-roughened titanium under her fingertips.

"What is this, Billie?" she asked, even though she knew the answer.

"Exactly what it looks like." Billie's fingers flexed at her sides, like she wanted to touch Cleo again but wasn't sure if she was allowed. "The *Providence*'s black box."

"Oh shit." Ros went pink when Cleo looked up at them. "Sorry."

Cleo swallowed thickly. "So it has—like, it recorded—"

"It should have retained all the data generated by the ship's computer," Billie whispered. "All of her memories."

Cleo's knuckles paled around the box. She looked up at Billie, who was practically vibrating with uneasiness.

"So she's alive. In a manner of speaking," Billie continued around her stuttering breath. "I thought you'd want to know. In case—in case you—"

Cleo cut off whatever insecurity Billie had been about to choke out with another kiss, tugging her close by the collar of her parka and doing her damnedest to press all the reassurance she could muster into her mouth.

"Thanks for telling me," she whispered. "Now don't worry about it."

Billie exhaled slowly, finally letting her hands land on Cleo's sides. "We could bring her back, though. Back on Earth. Recode her program, build a portable projector—"

Cleo shook her head. "I don't think she'd want to keep being a hologram. Too much angst." She looked at the box in her hand, making sure to hold on to Billie with the other. "Any way we could build her a server and just let her, you know, *be*?"

The crinkles around Billie's eyes deepened softly. "She could travel the virtual world. Solve the Riemann hypothesis. Develop a new Grand Unified Theory."

"*Hell* yeah. She'd unravel all the mysteries of the universe before long. Just like you would if I wasn't here distracting you with all *this*."

Billie snorted, and rested her forehead on Cleo's. "Right. Though I was thinking we could—I don't know, only if you're okay with it, obviously—"

"Any day now."

"—we could code you in too. Give her a Cleo to keep her company."

Cleo blinked, her throat tightening happily. "Really?"

"Really. I think I can say, with a reasonable degree of certainty, that she wouldn't want to just *be* without a Cleo."

Cleo lost herself in kissing Billie all over again, and was seriously considering dragging her back to their cave to remind her how little she had to be insecure about when Kaleisha made a gagging noise.

"Nasty," Kaleisha said, though she definitely looked a little misty. Ros was actually wiping a tear from Abe's eye behind her. "Abe, darling, you had a second point, remember?"

"Oh man, I almost forgot." Abe sniffed. "Yeah, um, Cleo, you gotta come to the *Providence*."

Cleo's stomach did a backflip. "Why?"

"It's the engine. Or what's left of it, anyway? You'll see when we get there."

✳

PROVIDENCE I LAY CRUMPLED in a wide-open ice plain, like a discarded sheet of paper. Cleo tried not to think about what the greenhouse or the rec room or Billie's lab must look like. As Billie and Abe and Kaleisha led her and Ros through a split in the hull on the engine side of the ship, Cleo focused on hoping that the other crew members still exploring the wreckage were finding enough to make the trip worthwhile.

The engine bay, having been the farthest away from the nose of the ship when it hit the ground, was wrecked but still largely intact, though they had to walk along what had been a wall now that the ship was tipped on its side. It was darker than ever, hulking towers of steel, rubble, and contorted sections of paneling looming over them past the sliver of red starlight they had entered through. Abe shone his flashlight ahead, guiding them all through the piles of fallen server stacks. Billie took Cleo's hand and squeezed. Cleo squeezed back, forcing herself again not to think about what had happened here.

But then she couldn't, because—just as suddenly as it had that very first time—Abe's light landed on the dark matter engine.

It stretched from the former floor on their left out into the darkness in front of them, as hulking and breath-stealing as ever. It was buckled, now, the top of the loop nearly touching the wall at their feet. Wires spindled off of it in places like broken guitar strings, and large sections of ducts and tubing hung together only by a thread.

Miraculously, though, the circle was unbroken. And even more miraculously, the tiniest of golden sparks hung, suspended and twinkling cheerfully, at its center.

"Cleo," Kaleisha whispered. Cleo jumped, and closed her gaping mouth. "I think they want to talk to you."

"How on Earth would you know that?"

Kaleisha shrugged. "I felt it. You know"—she waggled her fingers—"the energy."

Ros rolled their eyes and leaned an elbow on Cleo's shoulder. "If you break your brain again, I'll kill you."

Cleo looked at Billie, who was frowning at the engine skepti-cally. "Any thoughts?"

Billie sighed. "I don't *think* they'll do anything shitty again. Probably."

"Probably?"

"You saved them." Billie laced her fingers into Cleo's and smiled a tiny smile. "I'm sure they're grateful."

Cleo took a deep breath. "Okay, then. Count me down."

"Absolutely not," Billie said, laughing, and Cleo reached up to lay her hand on the top of the engine.

Her vision went black, and then darkest gold, and she was standing knee-deep in a gently bubbling stream surrounded by tall, waving grass—each towering stalk looking dried out and dead except for the new, green shoots growing in at the base of each stem—and in front of her was *her.* Another Cleo, eyes glowing gold, wearing loose, white linen pants that billowed in the warm water.

Hello again, said the Other Place.

You're always gonna come off a little bit creepy, aren't you? said Cleo.

The Other Place laughed, seeming genuinely tickled. *It appears to be inevitable. Does it help to know that we also find your forms unnerving?*

It helps a lot, actually. What did you want to talk about?

The Other place frowned. *We have been watching you, from time to time. We believed we had returned your friends*—their mouth formed the word uncomfortably, because it was natural, Cleo supposed, for an incomprehensible hive mind not to have a solid grasp on the concept of "friends"—*to your shared home. But it seems we were wrong.*

Yeah, Cleo said kindly, *our home is on Earth.*

They nodded. *And Earth is beyond your reach.*

Unfortunately.

The Other Place trailed a hand into the river. *Then we wish to help. As one last favor, in gratitude for all that you and your friends have done.*

What do you mean?

We will send you all home. They straightened up, and Cleo saw that they were smiling. *And that will be the end of it.*

Holy shit, that's—are you sure that won't cost you too much?

We have been healing. Our strength is returning. They gestured to the stream, and an image flashed through Cleo's mind of the massive, thundering river it used to be. It had been reduced to a trickle, but it was going to come back. *We can do this for you. And then you must see that your people never try to deplete us again.*

You spooked everyone pretty bad when you took the crew. I think they'll listen. Cleo returned their smile.

Good.

Plus, our home has a lot of healing to do too.

The Other Place held out a hand. Cleo took it. *Gather all your friends.*

On it, Cleo said.

And when she blinked, she was back in the engine bay. The spark in the center of the engine was gone. Her friends were crowded around her, and they all cried out when she opened her eyes.

"We gotta gather the rest of the team," Cleo said. She took a second to savor her friends' hopeful faces, and the way Billie was looking at her like she was a sunbeam, shining suddenly through the parting clouds. "And then, Kal, you have to fold us back to the mountain."

✳

THE WIND AT THE summit was harsh enough to burn Cleo's exposed cheeks and whip up Billie's loose hair into a golden storm around her face. Billie didn't seem to notice, though. She was too busy looking down at the tiny urn in her gloved hands.

"I should probably say something," she said softly.

"Only if it feels right."

Billie took a breath and held it. "I don't know what feels right. I didn't even speak at Neil's funeral. I couldn't stop thinking about how perfect a eulogy he would have written himself."

The sunset glinted red and silver off the finely etched surface of Neil's urn. Cleo blinked a couple of tears out of her eyes and didn't wipe them away. She was getting better about that: letting the tears fall. "Do you want me to start?"

Billie nodded silently.

"Okay, picture this. A cartoon of an astronaut in a full space-suit lying on a couch in a therapist's office." Billie smiled, just a bit, and Cleo racked her brain for a worthy joke. "Oh, and the office is on another planet, like there's weird plants around or something, and the therapist is an alien. And the caption says, *I just don't know how much more space I can give her.*"

Billie laughed, sudden and bright, and clapped a hand over her smiling mouth. "That's so fucking bad."

"What, you don't think I'm gonna win *The New Yorker* caption contest in Neil's honor?"

"Absolutely not. *Way* too derivative." Billie giggled so hard she snorted. It was adorable. "God, I love you."

Cleo laughed too. As she took Billie's mittened hand, she looked up at the sky. To her left, the icy mountains extended out in darkness, toward the blackened, night-red sky dotted with stars and streaked with rainbows. To her right, Proxima Centauri sat on the horizon, setting this world on fire. Above her, there was nothing but color. And, beautiful as it all was, she couldn't wait to go home.

And in front of her was Billie. Cleo couldn't wait to go home with Billie.

Unbidden, the words she'd heard at that other funeral all those years ago returned to her:

Though my soul may set in darkness, it will rise in perfect light; I have loved the stars too fondly to be fearful of the night.

Billie had tears streaming down her cheeks and into her scarf. And, as Cleo watched, she held the urn up to her lips, whispered a few words, uncapped the lid, and threw the contents out into the sky. Cleo snaked an arm around her girlfriend's waist, and they watched as the ashes joined the snow, glittering and twinkling every color under the red-dark sun.

※

IT HAD BEEN A bit of a feat to gather all 203 members of the *Providence* crew in one place. Especially when they all had very strong reactions to the news that they were supposedly going back to Earth in just a few minutes, ranging from disbelief to frenzied joy to tearful hugs to "Wait, you have to let me gather some mosses, at least, for proper study back home."

Cleo zipped herself once again into her dad's old NASA jacket, for luck, and hovered unhelpfully as Billie corralled the last few crew members into the big cavern.

"Where do you think they'll drop us?"

"I don't know, Cleo. You're the one who talked to them."

"They didn't say. How great would it be if they dropped us all on Mr. Reid's doorstep? Or what if they're not even close and we end up in Tanzania or something?"

"Then at least you'll have me, the world-famous martyred starship captain, to explain the situation."

Cleo shoved Billie playfully in the shoulder. "You're right.

They won't be inclined to help out infamous interdimensional space criminal Cleo McQueary, so I'll need to have the Honorable Captain Lucas with me."

Billie laughed, full and unguarded and snorting like nobody's business, and kissed the top of Cleo's head. "I highly doubt you're *infamous*."

"Hey, we pulled off the heist of the century, probably—"

"By accident."

"Yes, but the news channels breathlessly recounting our exploits have no way of knowing that."

"Please. Your mug shot would be too adorable for anyone to take you for a hardened criminal."

Cleo stuck her tongue out at Billie, just to get that eye-crinkling smile out of her, then scrambled up a stumpy stalagmite so she could see out over the whole cavern.

"Hey!" she shouted. "Everybody listen up!"

All 203 of them looked at her, faces shining with the purple-green glow and also something like hope. And Kaleisha, Abe, and Ros too, making faces at her even as they gripped each other tightly. Elijah, diligently shushing the people around him. Billie, staring up at her with all that love.

"Get ready," Cleo said, her words echoing. "We're going home."

Cleo leapt down from the rock, and Billie folded her into her arms. Everyone else around them, it seemed, was also joining hands. Cleo closed her eyes, reaching for that river she'd just stood in. As she did, she felt it flowing between all of them, felt the dark matter web connecting her body to Billie's, connecting them both to every person in the cavern, connecting the core of Proxima B to its star to the vastness of space and everything in it, every galaxy, every star system, every planet, including—

Earth, she felt a voice say. Maybe it was her own, maybe not.

And then there was a blinding flash of light—Cleo buried her face in Billie's chest, squeezing her eyes shut against it, and felt Billie bury her own face in her hair—

And then there was darkness.

A dim, predawn light, actually.

Cleo opened her eyes, and saw the *Providence* compound. They were standing where *Providence I* had stood. And a recent rainfall must have washed the clouds clean because the sky above them was miraculously, beautifully blue.

A deafening cheer went up among the crew. There was crying, whooping, laughing, hugging, kissing, dancing, tangled multi-person embraces that seemed like they'd never end. Cleo was kissing Billie, kissing the tear tracks off her cheeks, and then she was clinging to Kaleisha, then Abe was spinning her around, then she and Ros were jumping up and down, then Billie and Elijah were screaming at each other ecstatically over the roar of the crowd, then Cleo was watching all the people she loved and thinking, *This, this is home—*

Then one person was running out of the mission control building, then another, then a whole flood of them. Cleo grabbed her friends and dragged them forward, toward the sleepy, rumpled NASA people flowing toward them. Ahead of the pack were two men, two men who were sprinting like their lives depended on it, who looked like they hadn't slept in months and they didn't care—

"*Dad!*" Kaleisha screamed, and launched herself at Mr. Reid. They hugged fiercely, both of them blubbering incoherently, and Cleo was so busy watching them that she didn't realize the other man was in front of her until he spoke.

"Cleo?" her father said.

And Cleo hugged him, even though she couldn't remember the last time she'd done that.

"Dad," she whispered. His shirt smelled like the detergent he'd been using all her life. "Sorry for scaring you, probably."

"I . . ." He hugged her tighter. "I'm just glad you came back." His hand landed on the logo of the NASA jacket. "Oh. You still have this."

Cleo nodded wetly into his shoulder. "Yup. Never go anywhere without it."

They stayed like that for who knew how long. Finally, Cleo pulled away, wiping her nose without even trying to hide it. She looked around for Billie, and smiled at the sight of her an arm span away, blatantly hovering, the rising sun glancing off her hair and *God*, Cleo didn't regret a thing, did she—

"Dad," Cleo said, taking Billie's hand and pulling her into her orbit, "this is Billie."

Billie smiled and stuck out her hand awkwardly. "Mr. Mc-Queary. You might know me as—"

"Captain Lucas." Cleo's dad shook Billie's hand and did a very passable impression of a man who had a clue what was going on.

"*Please* call me Billie."

"Cleo, would you mind telling me why Captain Wilhelmina Lucas is holding your hand—"

And Cleo laughed, because she was happy and she was home and her dad and her girlfriend were going to get along fucking *swimmingly*, and she propped an elbow on Billie's shoulder and said:

"Yeah, so. Funny story."

THE END

ACKNOWLEDGMENTS

I started writing this book when I was twenty-two years old; I handed it in to my editor when I was twenty-seven. There was a whole lifetime in those five years, and within that lifetime are so many people that I'll never be able to stop thanking.

First, my indomitable agent and friend Roma Panganiban, who is a better advocate for my work than I ever dared dream. I feel so lucky to have gone from overworked assistants together to (still overworked, but much happier about it) partners in crime (the crime being selling my debut novel, I guess). And my editor at Harper Voyager, Nate Lanman, who made it clear to me from the first words out of your mouth that you understood Cleo and Billie and the story I was trying to tell on an elemental level, and who never stopped—despite a strike and a pandemic and a lot of wedding planning—making me into a better writer.

Thank you as well to my brilliant UK team—my agent Ren Balcombe and my editor Brendan Durkin—for championing *The Stars Too Fondly* across the pond. I'll never forget the confidence you displayed in me, right off the bat; it means the absolute world.

A million thanks to my first writing teacher, Professor Andrea Hairston, who taught me how to tell whatever goddamn story I please and also how to take critique without dying inside. Speaking of, this book would absolutely not be what it is today without the kind and clever notes of my friends Mae Juniper Stokes, Kason Hudman, Niv Badrinarayanan, and Julie Evans, who read early drafts and answered all my unhinged questions. Same goes for my brother Colin, who was generous enough to become an actual engineer and to tolerate my many calls asking whether such-and-such contrivance at least *sounded* like science.

To the rest of my family—Braden, Ozzie, Benjamin, Dad, Zoë, Grandma, Grandpa, Brenda, Sherri—thank you forever, for your unflagging support and belief in me. You can skip the end of chapter 15. To my friends, whether new or old enough to remember my tweenage declarations that I was going to be an author when I grew up, I literally could not have done it without you.

This one goes out to the very vivid dream I had on July 11, 2018, that eventually became this story; to *Star Trek: Voyager*, the best and worst show in the world; to Mimi, who certainly did not help me write this book and possibly even hindered the process, but who is still the best puppy in the world.

And, finally, to Rachel: my egg, my bean, my love, and my girl. You're the one who's been by my side for the entire lifetime of this story, from being my best first date ever two months into the first draft to becoming my wife two months before I delivered the final manuscript. Thank you for being my forever first reader, thank you for taking Mimi to the dog park whenever I needed to pound out a couple thousand words, and thank you for inventing love with me so I could write about it.

CONTRIBUTORS

As a former publishing worker herself, Emily Hamilton knows exactly how many people it takes to bring a book into the world. She would like to thank everyone at HarperCollins whose hard work made *The Stars Too Fondly* possible.

Contracts: Katherine McKim

Copyeditor: Karen Richardson

Cover design: Owen Corrigan, with special thanks to Galen Dara

Editorial: Nate Lanman

Interior design: Alison Bloomer

Managing editorial: Jennifer Eck

Marketing: Lara Báez, DJ DeSmyter, Kaitlin Harri

Production: Andrew DiCecco, Greg Plonowski

Production editorial: Hope Breeman

Proofreader: Chloe Bollentin

Publicity: Lara Báez, Danielle Bartlett

Publishing office: Jennifer Hart, Clifford Haley

Sales: Andy LeCount

ABOUT THE AUTHOR

Emily Hamilton is a science fiction author who writes about women kissing in space. She is also an award-winning staff writer at the alt-weekly newspaper *Seven Days*. She lives in Burlington, Vermont, with her wife and their tiny dog, Mimi.